PRAISE FOR DARTS AND FLOWERS

Funny and LGBTQ+ affirming, Darts and Flowers is a story about teenagers who are desperate to be loved, validated, and part of a community.

FOREWORD REVIEWS

The book has a big heart and should please fans of both high-school comedy films and YA fiction.

KIRKUS REVIEWS

This is a well-written, laugh out loud (even during the painful scenes) epic that takes the best of high school, Twelfth Night-inspired dramedy and infuses it with current social sensibilities, wrapping it all in a warm, hopeful hug.

BOOKLIFE BY PUBLISHERS' WEEKLY

DARTS AND FLOWERS

DARTS
AND
FLOWERS

DEAN BACKUS

Torchflame Books
LARGE PRINT
Vista, CA

ISBN: 978-1-61153-651-5

Library of Congress Control Number: 2022914000

Darts and Flowers is published in 2025 by: Torchflame Books Large Print, an imprint of Top Reads Publishing, LLC, 1035 E. Vista Way, Suite 205, Vista, CA 92084, USA

www.torchflamebooks.com/large-print

The publisher is not responsible for websites or social media accounts (or their content) that are not owned by the publisher.

Cover and Interior Design: Jori Hanna

This Large Print Edition is set in 16-point Iowan Old Style type. This is a work of fiction. All characters, organizations, and events portrayed in this novel are either products of the author's imagination or are used fictitiously.

To my grandmothers Joyce and Frances,
who thought I should,
To my parents, Jim and Jo, and my mother-in-law Judi,
who hoped I would,
And to Jonathan,
who always knew I could.
God love you all.

These are kids that are very intelligent;
they just happen to be misdirected
—Harper Reed, on youth of the 1990s
(*Masters of Deception*)

PROLOGUE

Everyone knows how it ended: with the Honor Council meeting.

And all the revelations.

And the multiple clarifying questions, such as "*You* did that? But I thought ..." that followed afterward.

What people tended to fight about, later on, was *how* it all began.

Brian, blonde and handsome, said it was his fault since he tended to blame himself for most things. Red-haired, scrappy Zack now said it really wasn't *his* fault—though, of course, a lot of it was. The others chimed in until the crosstalk was deafening. Finally, Brian's sister, Jamie, yanked off her fencing mask, slammed the tip of her foil into the floor so hard it cracked and yelled that she was going to shish kabob the next person who revisited the subject since she never, ever wanted to discuss it again.

The one thing they all agreed on was that it started five years prior, on the day Josh moved away.

CHAPTER 1

"*Z*ack, it's pushing seven o'clock! Get your *butt* in *gear!*"

Zack Standish, all sixteen years and five feet six inches of him, was sitting on his bed on the first day of his junior year. He had his headphones on and was listening to some extremely loud and crunchy music by the Red Hot Chili Peppers on an ancient Sony Walkman while determinedly brushing his teeth; nonetheless, his mother's voice sliced right through the music, just as it would solid steel.

He reached under the bed, pulled out his ashtray, filled with half-smoked butts, and spat out his toothpaste, then immediately regretted it. "I'm coming, just a sec!"

He shoved the ashtray back under the bed and grabbed—*ick*—a crusty sock, threw it back underneath the bed out of sight, located a bandana, and tied it around his neck. Though Beth refused to buy him a skateboard—"You'll crack your skull open," she argued—the skater look spoke to Zack. He cultivated it carefully, especially since he had been attending the Watson Christian Academy on a scholarship from sixth through his current eleventh grade, and thus constantly felt like he was drowning in an endless sea of Abercrombie plaid and pastels. From one wall, a poster of Kurt Cobain stared down at him.

There was a knock at the door, then a *bang* as Alex vaulted into Zack's room; after all this time, Zack still hadn't gotten around to installing a lock on his door. Over the past five years, Alex had matured to a happy, good-natured little boy of almost seven, with brown hair like Beth's that seemed perpetually in his eyes. Frankly, Alex was *so* happy and so relentlessly cheerful and kind and loving that it kind of freaked Zack out.

"Hi, Zack! Good morning, I love you!" The

little boy threw himself at his older brother like a missile, giving Zack a huge hug.

Although he secretly liked the attention, Zack put on his long-suffering face and disentangled himself. "I love you, too. What do you want?"

"Are you going to drive us to school today?" Alex had a missing tooth, giving him a definite jack-o'-lantern appearance. He grinned even wider with anticipation.

"I did almost every day last year, didn't I?" Zack was madly combing the room for his shoes and a cap. Actually, he'd only driven Alex to kindergarten once or twice a week when Beth had the opening shift at the bookstore. Still, with Alex's happy chatter going nonstop for the ten blocks to his school, it had *felt* like an everyday occurrence.

"Except for after the accident," Alex reminded him helpfully.

"That was *not* my fault. There didn't use to be a pond in that part of the park." Zack tried on a hat, then discarded it, yanking a comb through the spikes in his hair until they were even spikier. If he stuck a fork in an electric socket, he wondered if it would help, hurt, or make any difference at all.

"Why were you even driving *in* the park?" Alex was a treasure trove of questions today.

"Slamming a six-pack of Mountain Dew probably had something to do with it," Zack muttered, checking his reflection. The magic combination had probably been the Mountain Dew *plus* the hit from the stoner dude hanging out behind the tenth-grade dance, but there was no point in corrupting Alex with every gory detail.

As Zack eyed a zit near his earlobe in the mirror, he suddenly noticed that Alex had something hanging from his left hand. Alarm bells started ringing inside Zack's head. "Please tell me that's not what I think it is."

Alex looked down and clutched the object to him, a shadow crossing his face. Zack groaned inwardly. "Alex ... please. Don't tell me you're taking that *thing* for Show and Tell."

"Mommy said I could." This was Alex's all-purpose defense response; unfortunately, she usually did.

Zack tried to keep his voice on an even keel, but it began to rise in frustration anyway. "Mommy believes in the Tooth Fairy and the Green Party. Alex, I'm telling you, you're going to be laughed at. Boys don't carry around dolls—especially ones with their faces half-melted off!" His voice ended in a shriek.

Alex scowled, dug in his heels, and Zack had the weird sensation of watching his little brother's face morph into his own. "No one laughed last year. I told them she was in an industrial accident." Describing this, Alex looked as pleased as a member of the Addams Family.

Zack knew he was beaten. As usual. "It's my fault for teaching you to read," he groused as Alex beamed at him yet again. More or less put-together, he shooed his little brother out of his room and down the stairs to the kitchen, racing him the last few feet into it.

In the kitchen, Beth was wearing one of her nicer tailored suits—the one from a downtown store, not the outlet mall—but her hair was as askew as her sons'. She scraped some light-brown scrambled eggs and hashed blacks (not browns; blacks) onto plates for them and then dumped both pans in the sink. A low groan emitted from her as she poured the oil-black coffee: "There is no way in hell I'm going to make it through today."

"You didn't *have* to stay up till two watching

the Keanu Reeves marathon, Mom," Zack said slyly, snagging the first poured cup. Zack had passed Beth's room on a bathroom run in the middle of the night and seen her deeply engrossed in her bedroom TV around one-thirty as her boyfriend, Mark, slept undisturbed next to her.

His mother shot him a death glare and poured a second cup. "That was *last* Sunday. This was Brad Pitt."

"Oh, silly me." Zack's gift for sarcasm had not diminished with age; if anything, it had only developed into a sharper point.

"Silly me, too," Alex chirped, bouncing in his chair. He loved mornings in the yellow kitchen, with the faded wallpaper, the ancient appliances that murmured as though they were having their own quiet conversation, and the sun waving at him through the window over the sink.

His mother and brother eyed this euphoria warily, but all Beth said was, "Youth … no appreciation for the arts."

Zack shoved a spoonful of the rubbery eggs and charred potatoes in his mouth and tried to will his gag reflex not to kick in; it was a battle. There was a reason that the Standish boys usually favored cold cereal in the mornings or pastries from the corner patisserie, which Mark would often fetch during his morning run.

Beth, however, was unaware of this subterfuge and said, "Alex, honey, eat some breakfast."

"That's okay, Mom, we're—" Alex nearly blew things higher than the Space Needle, but he intercepted Zack's warning glance. "Uh, okay, I'll have some toast." He snatched the only non-burned piece from the chipped plate in the middle of the table as Zack glared at him. They munched fixedly for a moment while Beth shook some instant cocoa into her coffee for extra flavor —the "poor man's mocha," she called it.

His plate rearranged to look like he'd eaten, Zack fumbled in his pocket for his car keys and finally extracted them, tossing them to Alex. "Go warm it up for me," he whispered, and Alex dutifully slid from his seat with one last mouthful, grabbing the grease-stained lunch bag from the countertop. Their mother was busy chiseling the burned mess off the pots and pans, but she gave Alex a quick kiss as he flew from the kitchen.

On the way out, Alex nearly collided with Mark Hendricks, Beth's friendly, rumpled boyfriend who'd moved into the Standish house three years prior. It now seemed as if he'd always been there. "Good day, all," Mark mumbled sleepily. He caught a hug on the fly from Alex, who grabbed his backpack from the hallway and disappeared, singing a collection of loud, off-key notes. "Hey, Zack."

"Hey, Mark." Zack felt the brief, warm pressure of Mark's hand on the back of his neck, and Zack looked at him as he padded through the kitchen. Mark's hair was a mess of brown waves and curls in the morning; he wore flannel boxers and a threadbare T-shirt. Out in public, most people would've just assumed that Mark was Zack and Alex's father or uncle, and the boys were happy to let that assumption ride. Mark was a freelance writer who did articles on this new thing called The World Wide Web for various trade journals and magazines while plugging away at a novel in his spare time; he probably wouldn't get showered and dressed today till about one p.m. But he'd also clean up the kitchen, do three loads of laundry, and make a home that Beth and the boys were happy to return to, so they didn't have anything to complain about.

Zack reminded himself yet again that his life

was in a good place. The hard knot that had briefly formed when he thought of his father eased a bit.

Mark surveyed the wreckage that was reputed to be breakfast, and leaned over to Zack, speaking *sotto voce,* so Beth didn't hear. "She tried to cook again, didn't she?"

"It means so much to her, we figure once a year ..." Zack feigned compassion for his mother's ineptitude in the kitchen. Anything that involved more than punching buttons on a microwave might as well have been Sanskrit to Beth.

Zack suddenly checked his watch; it was already 7:15 a.m. He grabbed his plates and threw them in the sink, hoping for a quick escape; unfortunately, his mother was too quick for him and grabbed his arm, planting a kiss—*ew*—on his temple. "Have a great day, sweetheart. What say we try to make a few more friends this year, along with that super GPA?" She took some quick swipes at his hair.

Zack quickly re-mussed it. "Real-world, mom. Not fiction. Real-world." For the past several years, his mother had been co-owner of Undercover, the fantasy and science fiction bookstore;

Zack was convinced that all the magical elements of her regular reading were beginning to affect her brain. They'd certainly affected the house, which was now awash in strange dragon, alien, and gargoyle statuary. On his grouchier days, Zack called it Discount Narnia.

"Is Alex already in the car?" Beth queried. This, unfortunately, was punctuated by the sound of Zack's motor revving in the driveway. Zack grinned frantically at Mark and Beth and fled before there could be recriminations.

In the driveway, Alex was sitting placidly in the passenger seat of the beat-up green 1974 Volkswagen Beetle that Mark had bought Zack for his birthday last year. His brother threw his backpack into the backseat and himself into the front, pausing just long enough to sniff a forgotten sandwich left on the dashboard. "Charged and ready, Captain?"

"Warp speed, Mr. Sulu," Alex rejoined serenely. They peeled out of the driveway and down the street.

A few miles away, in the luxurious Italian villa-style mansion that was home to the Esau family, Brian Esau lay on his bed chewing his fingernails to shreds. He was wearing a pair of boxers and a blue Calvin Klein T-shirt and staring fixedly at the ceiling while listening to a relaxation CD of waves and a woman's soothing voice: *"You are feeling very relaxed. You are cared for. You are secure. You have nothing to worry about ..."* His ragged cuticles, spotted with dots of blood, suggested otherwise.

Brian's life had begun to change when he was thirteen, and his father had installed a Bowflex machine in the basement recreation room. This machine, combined with the Esau genes favoring height, had turned the slender, bird-like boy into a six-foot-tall blond young man that, on the football field, resembled nothing so much as Hoover Dam on two giant, tree-trunk thick legs. In the privacy of his bedroom, however, it was another story. There, he still felt like a scrawny kid who wasn't big and strong at all; in fact, he felt as small and wet and frail as something newborn in a forest, something that could be devoured at any moment.

He rolled his eyes toward the picture on the side of his bed of the lovely teenage girl, small and delicate as a violet, and tried to will himself into a state of Zen. (Could you *will* Zen?) The effort was interrupted by a sharp rap on the door. "Brian? It's me."

"Come in, Jamie." She would whether he gave permission or not.

His sister slipped into the room, quiet and insinuating as a shadow, and Brian did a double-take. Jamie, now fifteen, had taken advantage of the lack of a dress code and chosen a first-day-of-school outfit guaranteed to make young men go barking mad, featuring a black miniskirt, a white dress shirt open just enough to show a glimpse of crimson bra, and a man's fedora. Her golden hair hung loosely over her shoulders. Anyone who had seen her five years ago would have scarcely recognized her; only the slightly amused look in her ice-blue eyes remained the same.

She posed indolently near the open doorway. "What do you think?"

"You look like a Vegas slot machine about to pay off."

Jamie lifted an eyebrow. "I see we took our Prozac this morning ..."

She moved into the room and smartly turned off the stereo. "You know, I think therapy is helping you identify your hostility, but not fix it, which is kind of like saying 'Ah, piranha fish! Aha!' the whole time you're losing both legs."

She was already at his bureau now, picking out socks and underwear. This done, she yanked open the closet doors as though they were naughty children in need of discipline.

"I already have one therapist, Jamie. I don't need two." Actually, Brian would've settled for one effective doctor that didn't make him feel like jumping out the window after his sessions, but he didn't want to get into that now.

"Ah, but we are the *privileged*." Jamie slid a variety of shirts from one side of the closet to the other with a critical eye; no, no, no. "Hell, we have four cars, two houses, assorted domestics —" Her voice trailed off for a moment in stupefaction. "—and some fifty-five identical blue dress shirts with complementary sweaters. Brian, *when* are you going to start taking some risks fashion-wise?"

"Jamie..." Brian paused so long that Jamie actually turned around and looked at him as though expecting him to have sprouted a second head. "I feel like I'm going to seriously go off the deep end sometime soon. Therapy, football practice, I can't be a different person every few hours depending on the situation and who I'm with. I don't think I can take much more of this."

Jamie was—momentarily—almost thrown, and she *hated* feeling thrown. He looked incredibly vulnerable, sitting there with his arms wrapped around his pillow as if it were some sort of fluffy shield. For a moment, the ghost of a skinny, frail kid flickered in his worried eyes, and Jamie came dangerously close to being touched.

She quickly recovered, however, and laid out his clothes with her customary briskness, Mary Poppins crossed with General Patton. "Oh please —Ken dolls don't get suicidal. Now get dressed and come eat some kiwi so Mother doesn't go nonlinear on us. We have to pick up what's-her-name in fifteen minutes, and I don't want to listen to her whining."

She moved to the door, then noticed that her brother hadn't moved but instead sat staring morosely at the clothes at the end of the bed. She went to him and quickly—very quickly—ruffled his hair. "Come on, bro—it'll be okay. Now, go turn into Superjock. Your public awaits."

Checking one last time to make sure that he was more or less focused, then frowning ferociously to herself, she left, closing the door behind her.

As the door clicked, Brian toppled back over onto his bed and stared out the window for a moment. Superjock. That's what the kids called him at school. Football star in the fall, basketball star in the winter, baseball star in the spring. He ran miles every day. He downed plates of lean protein. He pumped iron till his muscles ached. He had the prettiest girl in school next to him every day. He had decent grades, caring parents, tons of money, a *sports car* for Chrissake. What more could he want?

"Why do I always have to be Superman?" he wondered aloud. He wondered what it would be like, for once, to have someone else do the lifting, someone who'd scoop him up and fly him away to his Fortress of Solitude. Brian saw the dark hair, the penetrating eyes, the jawline you could cut your finger on, felt the strong arms holding him as they soared up, up, and away into the dazzling blue sky. He buried his face in the man's shoulder and pulled the red cape a little tighter around him.

God, he thought, I'm going to be a teen statistic on *Oprah* before I'm twenty.

ZACK AND ALEX pulled into the drive-through of Tastee-Freeze for breakfast, part two. Zack slid the Beetle alongside the order-speaker and, without waiting for a greeting, rattled off, "Two pancake breakfasts, one scrambled egg, six hash browns, four orange juice bottles, one coffee, sixteen napkins, and ten straws."

A hiss emanated from the speaker, followed by a female voice. "Oh, it's *you* again. Anything else?"

"Got any Maalox?" Zack chirped, pleased at being recognized. In the passenger seat, Alex was busy counting off buy-one-get-one-free coupons.

"No, sir."

"Some illicit substances?"

"Not for *you*."

"Nothing else," Zack muttered, defeated.

"Drive through, sir. Have a shitty day."

"Love you too, sweetheart," Zack called. A scratch of static was the only response. He gunned the motor more than was necessary and shot around the side of the building.

As Zack dug in his ashtray for change, Alex

suddenly said, "Why do I have to go to public school and you to a private one?"

"Because Mommy and Mark love you more than me," Zack said witheringly. Bags appeared at the window, courtesy of a dangerous-looking Goth girl. "Oh, can we get some sweet-and-sour sauce and mustard with this?" Zack said none-too-innocently as he handed her a couple of bills and a bunch of the discount coupons.

The packets were hurled into the car's interior, and the window banged shut. "Wench." Zack pulled away from the diner.

"Why don't you leave the school?" Alex was doing his best impression of a puppy worrying a bone to death; he wouldn't be satisfied until Zack gave him the answer he sought—which could be anytime between now and doomsday.

"I need good creds if I'm going to get into a kick-ass college and become rich and buy and sell the free world." Zack had no idea how exactly he was going to accomplish this—details were not his forte—but he'd heard that it was good to have a goal.

"Mommy says you don't have any friends at the Academy," Alex offered around a mouthful of pancake.

Zack processed this for a moment and then decided on a tactic unusual for him: complete and utter honesty. Slowly, he said, "I had a best friend until I was about twelve. Then he moved away, and ... I dunno, I just don't relate to those people."

He stared down the road at the trees whizzing past and thought about Josh. There had been emails, one every few days at first, then one every week or two, none of them really sounding like Josh and all filled with "happy talk": Los Angeles was warm and required lots of driving, the names were all in Spanish, he liked his new middle school, his dad wasn't wild about the new job after all, yadda yadda. There'd been a postcard from Disneyland and one from Mexico. They'd talked on the phone a couple of times, haltingly, as if afraid to say how much they really missed each other, and then that had stopped too.

Then, one day when Zack was fifteen, he'd suddenly realized that he hadn't heard from Josh in almost a year. Had their whole friendship been a mirage? He was just picturing Josh sitting atop a camel, the poor beast buckling under his weight next to a pond of blue water with one palm tree in a vast, empty desert when Alex's next words went through his brain like an ice pick: "Mommy says you should try to be friends with Brian Esau."

Zack went thermonuclear, and his voice was almost a screech. "NO, NO, NO! He is a zoid, he always was a zoid, and he will always *be* a zoid. Never." He thumped the steering wheel. *"Never."*

Alex was used to his brother's overreactions. Calmly, he said, "Mommy says you hate him because he drives a nice car and dates Melissa Hoff, and you want to."

The name *Melissa Hoff* caused a slight stirring in Zack—something that seemed to cause a stirring in his heart, his stomach, and other things— but he quickly rearranged his features. He also made a mental note for the future to yell at Beth for discussing anything personal with Mark within Alex's earshot, but for now, he simply growled, "Eat your damn hash browns, Alex," and accelerated. He barely even noticed his younger brother grinning at him.

A SHORT DISTANCE away in a brick English Tudor-style house, Melissa "Missy" Hoff was sitting at her breakfast table, munching cereal in a distracted way. She was a shy, pretty girl with flowing dark hair and large brown eyes that had most of her class silently dying with lust or envy, even though when *she* looked at her reflection, she still mentally saw the frizzies and braces from middle school. She could barely stand to look at the pictures of herself that her mother had insisted on getting done at the portrait studio last year—one of which now graced the table beside Brian's bed.

At the other end of the table, in a lavender bathrobe, Mrs. Hoff was sipping her coffee and looking over the day's headlines while her daughter pushed her multigrain yogurt-flavored Cheerios around in her bowl. "Is Brian picking you up for school?"

"Mmm-hmmm."

"He's such a nice boy. He shows such care with you ... you should always be kind to him." Mrs. Hoff had been kind to a boy in her high school who'd been president of the robotics club; now, he was an executive at a high-tech firm based in Southeast Asia, and she had a lovely home and a beautiful daughter.

"I do try, Mama," Missy said distantly, her

eyes fixed on the lace doily underneath the fruit bowl on the dining room table. For heaven's sake, who used doilies anymore? Who was this woman, her mother? And would Missy end up like her?

"It's not every day a girl moves to a new state and two weeks later lands the school's star athlete and heartthrob." Mrs. Hoff gave a little mewling sound at the end of this thought. Missy stared blankly into the hallway at an ancient picture of her father in high school, and his skinny, seventeen-year-old body, his flushed complexion, his downy hair that fluffed up like a baby chick's. She wondered—unkindly?—if her mother ever dated a boy like Brian Esau, the tanned, leanly muscled aquatic instructor at the local pool; would it even have entered her mother's mind to try?

"Mama, I know." Missy set down her spoon and struggled to collect the thoughts fluttering around in her mind like so many confused butterflies. "It's just … sometimes I'm not sure Brian's really happy with me. I know his sister isn't."

This last confession, almost blurted, made the color come to her cheeks, and she cast her eyes in her lap, much as her father used to.

"Jamie Esau is entirely too full of herself for my taste," her mother said, a noticeable coolness creeping into her tone as it always did when Jamie's name came up. "Men like someone who will listen to them, not argue their every little word. No, Jamie isn't going to be a very happy woman someday, so you just pay her no mind. You just concentrate on making Brian happy."

As if in answer to this, Brian's horn sounded in the driveway. Missy had already collected her school gear before the sound died away, and the kiss that she delivered into her mother's hair barely touched her head as she raced down the hall. Her mother's last words hung in her ear, however, and as she yanked the front door open she thought, *What about what makes* me *happy?*

The yellow Triumph was waiting, motor running. Brian was wearing his letterman jacket and looked the picture of James Dean's eternal cool. Jamie, entrenched in the front seat, smiled Cheshire Cat-like at Missy as she reached back and opened the rear door for her. It was only when Missy and Brian were alone that Missy ventured to ride in the front seat. She kissed Brian's temple, breathing in the lemon-sage smell of his conditioner, and buckled herself in.

IN ANOTHER HOUSE down the road, he opened the curtains and squinted out into the sun's morning glare. He turned, and walked out of the room, down the stairs, and into the kitchen. A note rested on the table propped up against a water glass:

Good luck at school today. I'm downtown handling moving details. See you tonight. Love, Dad.

He grabbed his car keys from their hook and pulled the door shut behind him.

He slid behind the wheel of a blue MG, hoping his designer jeans would make the right impression. The motor purred to life, his polished shoes pressed down on the gas, and the car eased down the driveway and onto the road. A cloud of dust followed in his wake as he accelerated.

CHAPTER 2

Outside of his school, Alex was trying to extricate himself from Zack's car. Once successful, he fist-bumped his brother. Mollified, Zack handed the smaller boy the dreaded doll, as well as two dollars for lunch—Beth's lunches tended to trigger diarrhea.

Zack watched Alex trot his way over to where his first-grade line was assembling next to teachers holding signs, envying his brother's enthusiastic greetings to friends from kindergarten. When had he, Zack, become so self-protective, so armored, so guarded?

Involuntarily, his stomach jumped again. He imagined walking into a school where he wasn't on scholarship, and everyone knew it; where he didn't drive a car that looked like it was made out of crushed felt; where his clothes weren't regularly scanned by kids whose weekly allowance was more than he spent on Christmas presents for his family every year; where someone would look at him as if he wasn't Zack Standish, outsider; where someone might even think he was— God forbid—attractive.

Someone like Missy Hoff.

Missy and Zack had made eye contact on the first day of tenth grade, passing each other in the hall. The girl's delicate face and dark eyes had speared him as quickly and cleanly as a lance through his heart, and he'd just been on the verge of saying something devastatingly witty to her (he was still wondering what that might have been) when the universe seemed to crack in two and slide into Bizarro World.

Out of the classroom next to them had strode a newly grown, newly buffed, tan, blond boy who'd spent the summer mornings working out in his basement, his summer afternoons working at the local pool, and his summer evenings practicing his breaststroke. He was some four inches taller than last spring and so tan and handsome that Zack would not have recognized him had the boy not given him a look of sheer hatred as he slid his arm around the girl's waist.

Zack stood, pinned like a dying insect to the middle of the hallway, as Brian Esau ushered away the girl of everyone's dreams, his hand tucked securely (oh so securely!) into the back pocket of her jeans. Neither of them looked back at him.

So now, a year later, Missy Hoff was still chained to the wrist of Brian Esau—Brian Esau, the 80-pound weakling turned 800-pound gorilla. Brian Esau, who now looked at Zack with the cool contempt of someone who knows he could squash you like a bug; he just doesn't want to get his hands dirty. Brian Esau, the big man on campus, the golden boy with a psychotic sister with a mean right hook. Zack rubbed his jaw at the memory of that afternoon, but he hadn't forgotten Jamie's warning: he'd left both of them alone in their own little galaxy as they drew more and more stars into their orbit. They were the top of the food chain; he should be grateful that he was just a lower-level invertebrate, like a coelenterate or a jellyfish, and not plankton or krill like the kids in Band or the Chess Club.

Why was he obsessed now with love and friends, which he so clearly didn't want or need?

A BMW cut in front of Zack, and as they approached the light it managed to just coast through the traffic signal while it was still yellow. Zack, stuck behind as the light of course turned red, glowered at the other car's exhaust as it vanished in the distance.

The problem is, he thought, that if my life were a movie, I wouldn't want to be the lead actor. I should be the comic relief. Or one half of a comedic duo. And when you're one half of a comedic duo without the *other* half to play off, it doesn't work very damn well.

The light changed again and Zack drove toward school, a cloud of freshly-fallen leaves spiraling in his wake. The radio blasted an old Queen song at him, and thinking about Freddie Mercury and seeing the just-turning-orange leaves hit Zack with a wave of melancholy. By the time "You're My Best Friend" had ended, Zack was parked and skulking grimly up the green lawn to the brick-and-ivy hulk surrounded by apple orchards that was his high school.

‿

BRIAN TOSSED questions behind him to Missy as he drove, eyes focused like lasers on the road. "So, who do you think you'll get for trig this year?"

"Oh, I think I'll get Sanders—he teaches all the upper-division stuff. Will you be in it with me?" Missy tried to keep the plaintive note out of her voice, worried she sounded a little whiny.

"Depends. If it doesn't interfere with football or my therapy," Brian countered, swinging the car around the corner. Between getting his psyche beaten up and his body beaten up, fall was just going to be a barrel of laughs.

"Maybe I should go out for cheerleading. Then we could see each other more," Missy said, ruffling the hair at the back of his head. She loved his hair, how thick and golden it was. He was like a movie star, the cut-out version of the perfect boyfriend. She saw him made out of foil and printed on the inside of a chocolate bar wrapper, all sparkles and bittersweet shavings, to be savored when alone in her room. If only his parents didn't insist on sending him to therapy, she thought. He just needed to relax.

Jamie Esau rolled her eyes behind her Jiminy Cricket-style glasses and immersed herself in

Frederick Nietzsche's *Beyond Good and Evil.* Perhaps Nietzsche could be as useful to her as Niccolò Machiavelli's *The Prince* had been. Jamie liked things that were useful.

Brian eased the car into a parking spot. Jamie inhaled deeply as she surveyed the hordes, her eyes glittering like a reptile's when the sun hit them. "Another year ... I feel like Katharine Hepburn."

Brian had no idea who Jamie was talking about, so he stared at her blankly in response. She gathered her things, purred, "Don't be too long, kidlets," and strode up the path to school as people scrambled to get out of her way. She entered the building smartly, never looking back.

"She hates me." Missy's voice broke into Brian's daze as he watched his sister vanish. It was not a statement of self-pity, just a fact.

"She doesn't hate you." This was a bald-faced lie, and Brian knew she knew it.

"Brian, when I left my sweater in your trunk, she threw a feral cat in after it," Missy said levelly. It'd been an ugly holiday sweater, one her mother had insisted on her wearing, and the cat had actually done her a favor—but the fact still stood.

"She just doesn't know you," Brian said, as if wishing would make it so.

"And doesn't want to. Listen, I don't want to talk about Jamie right now; I can't do anything about her. I want to talk about us. Are you happy lately?"

"As happy as I've ever been," Brian said honestly. He couldn't remember a time in his life where he'd ever been really, truly filled with absolute happiness, but much of the time he was with Missy he felt a certain calmness and sense of pleasure come over him, especially when people looked at them together in public. He felt like he belonged to someone at those moments, and the noise in his head quieted down to a surly mumble.

"Meaning what?" Missy cut through his self-protective membrane, and he felt momentarily exposed, like something in a lab with a scalpel hovering over it.

"Meaning … meaning sure I'm happy. Aren't you happy?"

"I guess so … if you are."

"Well, okay then."

There was a weird pause during which Missy scanned Brian's face, looking for clues to a puzzle she didn't realize she had been trying to solve. Her voice sounded almost hard when she spoke. "Your therapy sessions must be really something if you offer as much to him as you do to me."

"Why?"

The hardness vanished, and her words came in a rush of emotion. "Brian, you know I love you. But sometimes I feel insecure, and ... you're not the most open person to share your feelings. So ... if you are ever unhappy and want to break up with me ... just be honest, okay?"

She fidgeted with the silver ring he had given her last year for their six-month anniversary, turning it around and around her finger in such a way that she didn't seem to realize she was doing it.

Brian felt a rush of pity for her and moved to kiss her very gently, feeling the softness of her lips, the gentle brush of her hair against his face. "Hey ... nothing's going to break us up if I can help it."

"But can you help it?" Missy's face was impassive, but her eyes held a flicker of vulnerability.

There was a long pause as they stared at each other, before Brian finally mumbled, "We'd better go in."

AT SCHOOL, Zack had received his locker
combination from a frazzled-looking Filipino
woman holding court at a card table just outside
the office. This time, at least, his locker was more
or less in the center of the school. Being in one
wing or the other could prove problematic if you
subsequently had a class at the other end and
needed to stop off at your locker for books, paper,
etc.; more than once, he'd skated into class just
as the second bell rang—literally skated—until
the school specifically outlawed rollerblades.
They could take his wheels, but they couldn't
take his fashion. At least, they hadn't yet. Thank
goodness there was no dress code, or his scholarship status would stand out even more than it
already did.

He passed through a sea of faces, most familiar but none he knew well. There was Logan,
as morose as ever and working the Tim Burton
look, all black with spidery drawings on his
sweatshirt and jeans. There was Madison, who
was sporting several shades of lip gloss simultaneously; Zack wondered if her lips glowed in the
dark. There was Kat, who always seemed to be

channeling some sort of global-hippie thing and was also a scholarship student; they weren't friendly, but she nodded as she passed him. There was even an androgynous kid Zack didn't know flashing a "YEARBOOK" lanyard, already—already!—taking photos of the crowd.

And against the main staircase leaned Hank Gaston, the school's biggest asshole, tossing a football with his teammates and laughing about the summer vacation he'd taken with his family to a resort in Cape Town, South Africa. *Cape Town,* for God's sake! The closest Zack had made it to Africa this summer was babysitting Alex when his mother and Mark were both working and watching *The Lion King* and *Jem and the Holograms* ten thousand times. He shifted his gaze away from Hank to ensure there would be no eye contact—Hank would just call him a "buttwipe" or some other charming endearment.

Zack frowned at his printed schedule. First period was free, but there was an assembly in fifteen minutes; might as well go stake out turf now. He pushed his way through the seething mass of teenagers, all wandering in different directions and squealing or punching each other's shoulders as they re-found each other after the endless nine weeks apart. Movement, everywhere there was movement.

It was amazing how you could be surrounded by a thousand people and an ear-splitting level of noise and still feel lonely.

CHAPTER 3

Inside the main auditorium, the assembly was just about to begin. Since no one had been to class yet, kids were still hanging out with their friends, and there was a cacophony of schedule-comparing, summer vacation recapping, squealing (the girls), and fist-bumping/shoulder punching (the guys). Zack, leaning against a pillar in the far corner, surveyed the flotsam and jetsam of teenage humanity almost in an out-of-body way, David Bowie echoing through Zack's brain as he sang forlornly about poor Major Tom, lost somewhere out in space.

Zack saw Brian enter with Missy, and his heart skipped a beat momentarily. She looked damn good, but the moment was spoiled as they were immediately absorbed into an amoeba of athletes and upper-echelon girls. Brian made eye contact with Zack and his expression hardened into a glare. Zack glared right back and shifted his gaze away, only to find himself staring at the opposite corner and—was there no escape?—Jamie Esau. She was comparing schedules with friends, and he had to admit, she looked terrific: blond, confident, vivacious.

As if an inner radar went off in her, she looked up from her schedule right at him and smiled winningly. It seemed so warm and so genuine he almost smiled back; then he remembered who she was and he gave a snort of dismissal and inched his way around the pillar to focus on the kids near him, other "fringe elements" who didn't seem part of a crowd. Mutants and freaks, he thought; we all should've been at Professor Xavier's school for the X-Men, not here.

A cutting-edge boy next to Zack noticed that Jamie and Chantel were looking at them. "She's really something, isn't she?"

"She sure is," Zack said distantly, his eyes on Missy.

"No, not her, man. Jamie." The guy swiveled

Zack away from Missy and Brian, and back toward Jamie and Chantel; this time, Jamie threw in a little wave.

Zack put on a big show for the guy, whom he barely knew. "Pffft. She's whack, man. She emulates guys who are running third-world dictatorships. Now Missy ... there's an *un*complicated woman."

"But have you seen Jamie? I mean look at her!" the guy insisted.

Zack huffed. "Why anyone can tolerate Jamie Esau for more than two minutes is completely beyond me."

The other guy shrugged and shook his head.

MISSY FOLLOWED Brian's eyes and noticed the glare on his face—she'd seen that glare before: every time he encountered Zack Standish. She touched his arm. "Aren't you going to end it this year? Didn't you say it's been going on for five years now?"

Brian's arm felt like concrete under her fingertips, and his face might have been carved from the same material. "You didn't know him as a kid. He always hated me."

"I just think if you talked to him—"

"Hey, whose side are you on, anyway?" Brian snapped and instantly regretted it. A flush of crimson came to Missy's cheek.

"You don't have to be nasty." Missy's eyes welled with tears. It was so unlike Brian to be cruel, she wasn't sure how to handle it. Brian turned away, disgusted—at her for being so obtuse, and at himself for being such an ass.

"Just don't sound like a mother, okay?" Brian whispered, but it came out so sharp it was almost a snarl.

"I'm sorry, Jesus! Excuse *me* for caring."

"Keep your voice down," Brian hissed. "People are staring."

"Well, why shouldn't they? Do I always have to be on *display* with you?" This brought a look of shock and hurt from Brian that made her immediately regret her words.

IN HER CORNER, Jamie was talking with her best friend Chantel Robinson, a devastatingly beautiful Black girl who looked like Naomi Campbell, only better. Both of them eyed Zack as though they were on an ornithology day trip and he was some rare exotic bird, all crimson plumage and occasional screeching.

Chantel leaned in close. "You really think he hates you?"

"No, he enjoys the conflict too much," Jamie mused. "It's emotional Viagra."

"He really is kind of cute, don't you think?"

"And, God help us, he has a brain. Fortunately, he doesn't know it." Jamie had mastered the art of talking out of the side of her mouth while smiling; Miss America couldn't have done it better. Jamie directed her attention to her brother and scoffed. "What my brother sees in that stick girlfriend of his is beyond me."

THE SOUND of a microphone being tapped cut all conversations short. "Can I have your attention please?" Mentally, however, at least five people in the auditorium were barely listening to the principal.

When the new kid finally stepped into the auditorium several minutes later, the principal was still droning on about school policies involving the parking lots, litter, etc. He stood at the back close to the door, trying to be inconspicuous, next to an administrator-type woman. The principal was shifting gears:

"And now, on to more pleasant things: welcoming new students to Watson Christian Academy. When I call your name, please stand so we can welcome you. Freshmen, anyone sitting beside you can help you find your way. Returning students, please make our new students feel welcome and help them when needed. In the ninth grade, we have two new students, Alicia Harris and Zoe Greenwall."

The auditorium applauded, somewhat less than enthusiastically.

"In the sophomore class, we have Rie Tomonaga and Alvin Russell."

Applause scattered through the gym, more dutiful than enthused; yay, Rie and Alvin.

"And in the junior class, we have Joshua Bradshaw."

Zonk!

Zack whirled around so fast he almost got whiplash, in complete shock as he searched the sea of students for that one familiar face. Brian turned almost as fast, looking as if he had seen a ghost rising straight from an open grave. Missy, seeing his reaction, touched his arm, but he took no notice of her. Jamie craned her neck, intensely interested, but her emotions were hard to read. Chantel, trying to glean all the undercurrents to this bombshell, scanned Brian's, Missy's, and Zack's faces for clues as to what might be happening.

Josh stepped out of the shadows and grinned amidst the scattered applause, giving a little self-deprecating wave. He was taller, and his baby fat had largely melted away, though his face still had a pleasant roundness to it. His hair, longer but dark as ever, still hung in his eyes, as well as just past his ears. He wore a white dress shirt, a small necklace made of shells, fashionably worn blue jeans, and dark boots.

It took a lot to impress Jamie, but... He. Looked. *Terrific.*

As Josh looked around the auditorium, his eyes suddenly locked on Brian, and a question lit up his face; Brian, dumbstruck, nodded slowly. The grin on Josh's face grew wider.

His eyes slid further around the room and

suddenly found Zack, now out from behind his pillar, all former attitude and coolness completely jettisoned. Zack was waving like a flag in a high breeze, and Josh's smile became so wide, his face looked like it might split, like a Halloween pumpkin. His teeth looked as if they'd been newly polished.

Zack felt as if he'd been hit by a semi-truck load of happiness. His friend was different in some ways, but he was still *Josh*—unquestionably, irrevocably, inalterably *Josh*. A million questions shot through Zack's mind, like wild zigzags of electricity, but the hall was too crowded right now to get to Josh. A subsequent wave of longing crashed down on Zack, like the ocean surf over a lonely, beached starfish.

As if reading his mind, Josh moved his hands in a "you-me-together" gesture, and then moved his finger over his watch to indicate "later." Zack bobbed his head in understanding; the ocean wave receded, and the sun came out.

Jamie was watching the unfolding dynamics intently. Chantel touched her arm. "Do you know him?"

"I did." Jamie pursed her lips a bit, as she

sometimes did when thinking something over very hard.

"What's the 411?"

"I don't know ..." Jamie watched as Josh's eyes slid back to Brian, and she noted her brother's dumbstruck face. She had always prided herself on being two steps ahead in the chess game, and suddenly there was a new piece on the board she hadn't anticipated. "Remind me to take a meeting with him later today."

CHAPTER 4

SOME YEARS AGO

It had been the sort of warm August day in the Seattle suburbs that might make anyone think there wasn't a problem in the world, but for twelve-year-old Zack Standish and his best friend Josh Bradshaw, it was the worst day of their lives.

The movers had almost finished loading the moving vans and were in the last stages of swarming all over Josh's house and the vehicles. Soon, only the empty husk of the wedding-cake white house would be left, hosting a new family —one Zack knew he would hate with every fiber of his being. Hatred was good. Hatred gave him energy. If he stopped hating, if he relaxed for just a moment, the tears might come, and that would be the worst thing of all.

A spray of water from the neighbor's lawn sprinkler dropped a shower of tiny diamonds in the sunlight, but Zack's brain was already running, running through a dark, deadly green jungle that vibrated with every slow, deadly *boom* of a gigantic ape's footstep. *King Kong.* He'd been six years old, and he watched *King Kong* at Josh's for the first time during a sleepover. Afterward, Zack had slept on the floor in a sleeping bag next to Josh's bed, and he kept reaching up during the night to touch Josh's fingers, to make sure he was still there, in case *Something*—some nameless, creeping source of terror—came out of the dark to drag one of them away.

Now, today, *Something* was finally here.

Nicholas Bradshaw, Josh's father, came out with the movers and barely managed to cram a lamp into his overstuffed SUV. He tiredly ran his fingers through his dark wavy hair, flecked with a few strands of gray. Zack glanced over at Josh. His face was a closed book, his eyes downcast, black bangs covering his eyebrows. His fists were jammed in the pockets of his jeans, and with his stocky build, he looked like a dark star on the verge of imploding. Zack knew the feeling, and crossed his arms over his chest and the worn shirt he'd chosen specifically for today that read "KILL 'EM ALL" in humongous letters. Angry heat rose through his face and all the way up into his coppery hair, and he felt like he might burst into flame at any moment.

The boys hadn't said anything to each other for quite a while now, and when Zack spoke Josh jumped a little bit. "I think I'm going to have to kill your father for this."

This, Josh knew, was ridiculous. Zack didn't have a father—well, he did, but the man had decamped for Tucson two years ago—and Nicholas had been Zack's de facto father, as well as Josh's, since then. Josh decided to try humor: "Okay … you'll just have to come to California to do it."

There was a slightly ominous pause, in which Josh could almost hear Zack's mind going *click click click* as he considered this, a chamber being spun in search of a bullet to fire. He murmured, almost to himself, "I'll have to rent a car."

Josh eyed his friend with a mixture of apprehension and admiration. He could see it now: Zack borrowing his mother's credit card and striding—all four-foot something of him—into Avis. The clerk would laugh at him, and Zack would try to go for the guy's throat with a ball-point pen. Security would come running; it would all wind up on the news. The whole scenario was so typical of Zack that a faint smile tugged at the corner of Josh's mouth.

Zack didn't see the action movie playing through Josh's whirling mind; he was too busy glaring at Nicholas as he crossed the grass to them. Both raised their eyes but neither greeted him as he called, a little too loudly and heartily, "How're you guys doing? Okay?"

Zack wanted to shout, "No! This is *not okay!* You're taking away my best friend in the whole world and moving two states away and I'll probably never see him again!" But he knew Josh wouldn't appreciate it, and if Zack did that, the tears would once again threaten to erupt. Instead, they both nodded half-heartedly.

Nicholas was not fooled. He put one hand on Zack's shoulder, and with the other gently stroked the side of Josh's face and hair. He tried to make his voice gentle, so gentle. "I know this move isn't what you guys expected or wanted … actually, me neither. It's just how my job worked out. But it's gonna be all right with a little time, I promise."

Both boys were like iron under his touch, but Zack managed a little shrug and Josh a small nod. What else could they say? Adults ran the world— the whole stupid, messed-up world.

Nicholas didn't push it. He only said to his son, "We're about ready anytime you are, buddy." A final squeeze of the shoulder, and the man pulled away, striding to his car to get out some sodas for the just-finishing movers.

Zack's clenched fingers abruptly nudged something deep in his pocket. "Crap, I almost forgot. Here." Zack extracted a piece of plastic, which he thrust at Josh. "You gave this to me a few years ago, so now I'm giving it back to you. Keep it until we see each other again."

The collapsing kaleidoscope from Cocoa Blasters! It had fallen out of the cereal box into Josh's bowl the morning after a sleepover in third grade and Zack had immediately called "dibs." Leave it to Zack, Josh thought, gripping the toy tightly, to do the right thing at exactly the last possible moment. His eyes—at last—filled with tears. "Thanks, Zack."

"Okay, okay, enough of that shit. Here." Zack

thrust a grimy bandana—probably used when oiling his bike chain—at Josh, who found a some-what clean corner to swipe at his eyes. Zack tried his tough-guy voice. "Listen up, boy. We're al-ways gonna be best friends. You write me, or I'll come find you and kick your ass from here to Honolulu."

"Yeah, you and what army?" Josh handed Zack back the bandana, a little bit of bravado restored. Zack couldn't kick Josh's ass if he tried and they both knew it; for one thing, Josh was a head taller and some twenty pounds heavier. But Josh knew that Zack never would try, and Zack knew it, too.

There was a sudden *screech* of bike tires on gravel, and both turned. Behind them, a few feet away, a sweaty, frail-looking blonde boy had pulled up on a ten-speed bike, hesitating as if afraid to come any closer.

Zack exhaled in a hiss, and he barely managed to drop his voice to a strangled stage whisper. "Oh, Christ ... not Brian Esau. Not today."

"He came to say goodbye, cut him some slack." It galled Zack to no end the way Josh in-dulged Brian—the scrawniest, most pathetic little weasel in their class—with his kindness. One day in elementary school, when choosing sides for dodge ball, Josh had even chosen Brian for their team, just so he wouldn't have to be last picked. Zack could've sworn the P.E. teacher had already blown the whistle to end class when Brain launched the red rubber missile—*bam!*—right into Zack's head, the tiniest little smirk decorating Brian's stupid face as the ball bounced away. They were *on the same team!* Idiot.

Josh ambled over to Brian, who as usual looked as if he were about to burst into tears. Zack watched them through narrowed eyes, like some sort of comic book vigilante who only struck at night, as Josh led Brian away from Zack, and around the front of the van. Zack watched the two sets of legs stop, then move together in a quick fashion.

A wave of confusion crashed over Zack, followed by nausea. Had they just *hugged*? Zack and Josh almost never hugged, not when Zack's father had left, not even when Josh's mom had died. This was completely unlike Josh, the big rock, and Zack surmised that Brian must've hugged Josh, thrown himself at him like some goopy, emotional girl. What a tool.

Things suddenly seemed to speed up, like a film being projected much too fast. It seemed that the movers had thrown their soda cans into the trash; then Nicholas was locking the front door and slamming his car doors shut. As the two moving vans' motors started and a blast of exhaust filled the air, Hurricane Josh suddenly came right at Zack, grabbing his friend full force and squeezing him tight.

Zack waved his arms for a moment, helplessly caught like a bird in a snare; then just as he started to relax and felt Josh's hair brushing against the side of his face and his arms—much stronger arms than Zack had thought—around him, Josh abruptly pulled away and ran to the SUV. Then, much too suddenly, as goodbyes still floated in the air, the driveway was empty, the house abandoned, and a cloud of dust settled gently in the air between two pre-teenage boys.

There was the sun and the breeze and a Josh-sized hole in the world where once he'd been.

Zack shot Brian a look of pure, unbridled hatred. He took a step, pebbles crunching under his feet. Brian watched him in a state of paralyzed terror, a rabbit watching a gun's muzzle being aimed at its head.

Zack strode purposefully forward until he reached the boy standing behind his bike. Then he pulled his arm back, as far, far back as California, and like a freight train slammed it forward.

The fist connected squarely with Brian's face, and a spray of spittle with a trace of blood dotted the pavement and gravel, red on varying shades of gray. Zack thought it looked like some kind of modern art.

Brian fell, the bike atop him. Through the bent metal and spinning tires, he saw Zack's face settle back into something cool and expressionless, the Hulk once more Bruce Banner. Far away, a jay screeched in the trees.

"Thanks, Brian," Zack said, almost politely. "I feel much better." He turned, threw his leg over the frame of his bike, and started pedaling toward home, never looking back. In truth, his insides felt like a pumpkin scraped out for a jack-o'-lantern, but he wasn't going to let Brian see that.

No one would see.

A HALF-HOUR LATER, eleven-year-old Jamie Esau was watching the old movie *Hello, Dolly!* on cable in the family living room. She was sitting on the floor, back against the sofa, her butterscotch-colored braids hanging down her back, her round face and cool blue eyes locked on the TV screen. The heroine was singing her opening song about arranging relationships for profits and pleasure. Jamie's eyes widened; she liked profits as well as pleasure—who wouldn't? She was interested in seeing how it would unfold.

Alas, at this moment her bruised and bloodied older brother limped into the house and passed by the room. His eye was turning the color of an eggplant, his mouth and shirt were covered with blood, and he had an enormous gash on his leg, not to mention road rash.

This did not bode well.

Jamie's eyes narrowed. "Brian, are you okay?"

He shook his head.

"Did Zack do this again?" There'd been at least one previous scuffle a few months ago between Zack and Brian, the morning after the one time Brian had slept over at Josh's. That time, Zack had split Brian's lip.

A nod.

"Is Josh gone?"

Another nod, but Brian's face had already crumpled. Emitting a high, whining cry, he ran

upstairs, slamming the bedroom door behind him.

Jamie sighed, reached for the remote, and hit
record. (Would she *never* get caught up on her en-
tertainment?) As she set her jaw and marched
out of the house, she wore an expression remarkably similar to the one Zack had earlier.

A SHORT TIME LATER, Zack was draped over an
easy chair in the living room of his house,
throwing a rubber ball against the wall. The ball's
impact was beginning to make a dark spot, and
this brought him a glimmer of pleasure. Thump.
Thump. *Thump.*

He continued throwing the ball, even as his
mother came in with Zack's baby brother Alex
balanced on her hip. "Zack, honey, do you think
you could hold off on that for a bit until after the
baby's had his nap?"

Thump. Thump. Thump.

"Are you upset about Josh?" Out of the corner
of his eye, Zack could see his mom's concerned
face, and no matter what he said or did now,

she'd come in later that night when he was crying and rub his back until he fell asleep.

Thump. Thump. Thump.

"I'd like to buy a vowel, please?" Despite her empathy, a sharp note crept into Beth's voice.

"Oh, listen to the funny lady." Zack retreated to his favorite all-purpose weapon: sarcasm.

"Sweetie, I know it's not easy. It's never easy to say goodbye to someone you love very much." Beth reached over to smooth his spiky orange mop of hair. Alex grinned and drooled a huge glob of spit on his overalls as his mother and brother conducted this little U.N. parley.

"You and dad didn't seem to have any problems," Zack said, immediately wishing he hadn't. It was wrong of Zack to go to the bad place and mention *him*— who'd come home from work one night last year, announced "I don't think this is working out," and had promptly moved to Arizona with one of his co-workers, Sandi, who just *happened* to have bought a condo there recently. Who hadn't sent child support for three months until Beth got a lawyer involved. Who forgot Zack's birthday, and sent a $25 Red Lobster gift card a week later, forgetting that Zack hated seafood.

Zack winced as all this flashed through his head, and then winced again as he saw his mother's face.

Beth looked down at the floor for a moment, then up and away at a very interesting crack in the ceiling, a sure sign that she was trying to keep from losing her temper. Then she offered a too-sweet smile, like a mom in a TV commercial. "Dinner's at six. Beef stew and guilt. Try to show up."

Alex gave another cheerful screech. Beth gave Zack one more glare, the kind moms learn how to uncork the first time their kid does something rotten, and disappeared around the corner.

Zack sat, a thundercloud of remorse and hostility, wanting to throw the ball and yet valuing his life too much to do so. He was thinking he'd go outside and shoot some hoops—envisioning Brian Esau's face on the backboard—when the doorbell rang. With a sigh of a thousand martyrs, he roused himself from the chair and opened the door.

He saw the world from his front porch for a split second, with something in the middle of it. Then he saw a fistful of knuckles coming at him, and there was nothing he could do about it. Jamie

Esau's fist connected squarely with Zack's jaw, knocking him to the floor in a sprawled heap, like the basement laundry chute vomiting his dirty clothing from the ceiling.

The blow stunned him for a moment to the point where he couldn't feel anything; then he felt way too much. A relentless, throbbing pain seemed to envelop his entire head, not to mention the tailbone he'd bruised when he fell.

He looked up at Jamie; for an eleven-year-old, she seemed twenty feet high. Her words, when they came, might have been ice cubes clattering to the floor: "Lesson one, Zack: Don't screw with me. Lesson two: don't screw with my brother. Follow these rules, and we'll probably get along. Got it?"

As she spoke these last words, Jamie suddenly smiled—a bright, wintry smile that reflected light off the ice and the snowdrifts, but no warmth. She did not blink, did not say anything to Beth, who was suddenly behind Zack, but instead turned and walked deliberately and decisively down the steps.

As she receded into the distance, Zack looked up at his mother. Beth was looking after Jamie, then looking down at him, and Zack saw the same look Beth had worn when she saw his split knuckles after the first run-in with Brian. She'd bandaged up his fingers while giving him a serious ear-reaming, then made him call and apologize to Brian, but he'd actually called the KMEL radio listener line and faked the conversation with Brian. Karma, it seemed, was a harsh, ugly mistress.

Alex squealed happily again, as Beth bundled him off for a rock-a-bye and a nap. Zack remained where he was, miserably sitting in the entranceway, surveying the blue sky and the warm sun just outside beyond his reach and the wreckage of his life. Nothing, he knew, was ever going to be right again. For Zack Standish, this was The End.

But, of course, it was really only The Beginning.

JOSH REALLY THOUGHT it began at the sandpit, some eight years before this. Before preschool, even.

He'd been playing in the park with a red plastic truck, making it do laps in the sandpit and minding his own business, while his mother chatted up another young mother on a nearby bench. Then all of a sudden, a boy with hair the color of grated carrots appeared out of nowhere, a blue Volkswagen Beetle clutched in one hand, eyed Josh's toy, and declared, "I play now."

Josh was not a fan of being challenged. He held onto the precious truck like it was a talisman of some sort, as the other boy tried to pry it from his fingers, failed, then resorted to screaming and flinging himself on the sand. At this, Josh very calmly walked over and sat on him.

After a few minutes of dramatics—during which the boy's mother and Maureen Bradshaw sat there and laughed at them—the orange-haired boy finally gave up. Then they played together, sharing their toys (even the precious red truck), and had such a good afternoon their mothers made plans to see each other the next day. The other boy left his toy Volkswagen bobbing behind in the wading pool, where they would retrieve it the following day.

As his mother tucked Josh in that night, she asked him what he'd like to say for his nightly prayers. Josh was very meticulous about prayers before bed; they helped keep away nightmares.

"God bless Mommy, God bless Daddy, God

bless Hammy." Hammy was Josh's hamster, quietly running on his wheel perched on the dresser.

"Anyone else?" Maureen smiled at her son's sweet, grave face.

Josh looked confused for a moment. "Can I pray for my new friend?"

"Of course," his mother said gently.

"....and God bless Zack." With that and a kiss on his forehead, Maureen shut off the light.

Josh never told Zack he prayed for him; he just did it. Josh figured Zack could use the assistance.

IT HAPPENED like clockwork every spring: there would be a day when Seattle would throw itself on the floor like a giant two-year-old having a tantrum, complete with howling gusts of wind, teary storms, and a full-on weather meltdown. It was a perfect day to stay indoors with board games and a good book and watch the mayhem outside through a living room window.

But this year, unfortunately—which happened to be exactly six months before Josh left, in early March—it happened when Lego Con was scheduled at the Seattle Center Arena, and Beth's mother had volunteered to babysit Alex so Beth could take Zack and Josh to the show.

When Josh thought back on it later, the day had been a disaster pretty much from the get-go. Alex was fussy and cried when they left, Beth realized halfway downtown that she'd forgotten her wallet, and the entire Puget Sound population and their pre-adolescent children had apparently decided a day inside looking at plastic snap-to-gether models sounded just peachy. They'd driven around for half an hour looking for street parking, the admission prices made Beth clench her jaw and sigh as she paid them, the concrete floors were painful to walk on, and by four o'clock everyone's patience was subterranean.

"Can we at least get a churro?" Zack queried as Beth, exhausted beyond words, herded them out of the building and into the damp, gray twilight.

"No," Beth responded through gritted teeth. Josh wished at moments like this that he could just sink through the concrete and avoid the barely concealed mother-son hostility. "We're getting pizza tonight."

"But you said we could buy something, and

we didn't." Zack huffed. The new Lego kits on display were amazing—two hundred dollars (starting price) worth of amazing. Beth had said "No" to hot dogs, "No" to sodas, "No" to the grab bags of random Lego pieces— "You won't even know what sets they go with," she'd snapped, which even Zack couldn't argue with— and he was not feeling particularly amenable.

"I'll order you a dessert with the pizza," Beth said, closing her eyes for a split second in a God-give-me-strength way as they walked.

"That's not the same thing," Zack muttered. Josh kicked a rock as they hurried along, and looked at his feet. He wished Zack wouldn't argue with Beth; it made his heart hurt. But he couldn't say that out loud.

They were hustling up Broad Street toward the parking lot when they saw him about half a block ahead: an older man, somewhere in his forties or so, standing on the edge of the curb waiting for the light. He had two forearm crutches and was leaning on them in a somewhat weary way as his trench coat whipped about him in the wind, his hat pulled down over his face to shield himself a bit from the elements. He looked like a daddy-long-legs as he deliberately set one crutch down into the street with the changing light, then the other, slowly dragging his feet behind him. He looked tired—not in the way Beth or Josh or Zack were, but Old-Testament-prophet tired. Beaten-into-the dirt tired. Maybe that's why he was moving so, so slowly.

He was not even a quarter of the way across when the light changed. A hundred or so horns began to sound all at once. The man tried to wave, feebly, but that only made his balance more precarious. Josh's stomach collapsed like an elevator in a disaster movie.

Before any of them could say anything, Zack hollered "Be right back!" above the howling wind and rain. Then he was gone, racing ahead so fast the sound barrier almost cracked. By the time Beth and Josh reached the corner, Zack was already in the middle of the intersection.

And now the cacophony of horns was almost unbearable, and some people were actually flicking their lights at them. Josh watched, frozen in terror and clutching the slack-jawed Beth's arm, as his friend inched forward alongside the man, one step at a time.

But Zack didn't flinch.

In the rush of cars, Josh didn't see if Zack

reached for the man's arm, or if the man let go of his crutch for a split second to loop it through the boy's. But now they were linked, a unit; if a car—God!—if a car accelerated, they would both go down together in a heap.

Zack, fully in Cyrano de Bergerac mode now, held up his free hand against the tide of automobiles. Josh stood paralyzed watching his friend, Zack's red hair flaming like a campfire in the dusky storm, as he marched inexorably toward the opposite curb.

The light for the traffic turned red again, and a few obviously enraged drivers snuck around behind them through the intersection where they'd already trod. Zack was oblivious. He talking to the man now, and apparently said something funny, because the guy threw back his head and roared with laughter, even as the sound was swallowed by the cars and the wind.

They reached the other corner, and it was then that Josh finally snuck a look at Beth's face. She was completely windswept, and little drops of rain beat at her and ran down her cheeks and wet her hair. But she was looking across the street at her son waving goodbye to the man limping away into the darkness as if Zack had just oh-so-casually passed out five thousand loaves of bread and fishes to the masses of Seattle. Her eyes glistened, and she murmured almost to herself as if she'd forgotten Josh was there. "When he comes through, he really comes through."

At that moment, Josh felt a warm rush of love for both Beth and Zack—a rush so warm, that he hardly even noticed the storm anymore, or Zack running back across the street to join them and cheekily greeting them with "So, we get two desserts tonight, right?" For many years Josh told himself that Zack had done a kind and good thing, and that was what was important.

But Josh secretly knew—even if helping the man was his prime motivation, Zack's secondary motivation wasn't far behind: For a few minutes, Zack had managed to bend an entire city to his will.

CHAPTER 5

An eternal ten minutes later, assembly was over and students spilled out into the hallway to look for their classes. Zack burst through the door like a missile and saw his friend leaning against the wall, arms folded, smiling wildly. As he saw Zack, he stepped forward and opened his arms so wide they seemed to reach across the entire hallway.

Zack ran to him, then suddenly caught by years of conditioning, he put up a palm for Josh to slap. There was an awkward scuffle as they sort-of-collided, sort-of-hugged, then broke apart; both were laughing—Josh a low chuckle of plea-sure, Zack almost-hysterically. His words came in a splutter: "What the—what the hell—oh my *God*, you sonuvabitch!"

"We just moved back three days ago," Josh said happily. His voice had dropped a pitch; its rumbling timbre messed with Zack's head. "I wanted to surprise you. How are your mom and Alex?"

"Great, great, Mom's now part-owner at the bookstore. Oh, and Mark, her boyfriend, moved in—he's awesome."

"Can he cook?" Josh's face was so momentarily concerned, that they both dissolved into giggles again. "Yes. God, you remember my mom's cooking."

"Of course I do, it's seared into my brain and stomach. My dad was amazed I came home alive from dinner with you."

Nick! "Oh God, how is your dad? Did his company ever take off?"

"Yeah, he's a big-shot internet consultant now that everyone's on it. So since he's mostly either working from home or on the road, he bought the old house back."

Zack stared at him. *Internet consultant? Maybe he could help with Mark's writing.* That thought passed quickly. He could hardly believe his ears. "You're back at the *house?*"

Josh smiled. "Yeah. It reminds him of mom, so ..."

The sentence hung in the air just a moment too long, and Josh's face altered subtly as he looked past Zack's shoulder.

Brian had exploded out of the auditorium door, Missy right behind him, but now he stood frozen to the spot as if he'd bumped into some invisible force field that allowed him to approach no further.

Zack turned and tried to simultaneously sneer at Brian and smile at Missy, which didn't work very well; he looked as if he were having a stroke. Josh, however, seemed delighted. "Hey, Brian."

Brian's brain seemed to be defrosting. "Uhh ... hi."

"How's it hanging?" Josh spoke as casually as if they'd seen each other two days prior, instead of five years.

"Fine ... it's fine. I'm fine." Brian still seemed encased in ice. Josh now took a step forward and raised his hands, as if to embrace Brian, but Missy stepped forward and grabbed one of them. "Hi, I'm Melissa Hoff. I'm Brian's girlfriend."

"Nice to meet you. Josh." He shook her hand and smiled, but awkwardness still hung in the air.

There was a pause, then Missy said, a little too brightly, "So … you were all friends back before junior high?"

"Actually, Josh and I have been friends since preschool." Zack inserted himself into the middle of the conversation, and everyone's gaze shifted to him, including Missy's. He flushed a little bit. "We've only known Brian since *fourth* grade."

"Missy and I have been going out since last year," Brian said to Josh, draping one arm around her and trying to ignore Zack. She didn't seem appreciative but didn't make a scene.

"Uh-huh," Josh said noncommittally.

"We're very close," Brian continued doggedly.

"Ah-hah," Josh said, even more noncommittally. He and Brian seemed to be speaking in some sort of language Zack and Missy couldn't understand.

Zack's face darkened, and he was beginning to resemble a thundercloud. Lightning flashed in his eyes. He and Missy were just beginning to exchange questioning looks when the auditorium door *banged* open again and Jamie and Chantel were suddenly there, like Maleficent and her pet raven appearing from a bolt of green fire.

"Hail, *hail,* the gangs all here. Hey, bro'," Jamie caroled. She ignored Missy, of course. "Zack. And Josh … what a surprise. Last time we all heard from you, your departure had just caused Zack to beat the crap out of my brother."

Josh, seemingly caught off-guard for the first time, turned and gave Zack a look somewhere between questioning and scolding. Zack shrugged, not-quite-sheepishly.

Brian flushed red, then went white as his sister continued, smoothing her words out as though they were a satin bedsheet. "You always were an influential guy. We *must* do lunch some-time and catch up. Ciao."

She touched Josh's face for an instant, like an Italian movie star, smiled dazzlingly, and strolled away, Chantel behind her mouthing "Ohmy-GOD!" Another potentially ugly pause was saved by the ring of the bell.

"That's class, Bry—I think we have history together." Missy pulled at Brian's arm, trying to recapture his attention. He turned, blinking, looking at her for a moment as if he had never seen her before.

She continued, "Come on—you can talk to your friend later. It was nice meeting you ..." She piloted Brian down the hallway almost as if he were in a daze. Josh and Zack watched them go.

"You always have this effect on people?" Zack cracked, pleased to have an audience again for his wit besides his little brother.

"Do you have a first period?" Josh fixed Zack with a steady, probing look.

"Not that I couldn't skip for this." In truth, Zack had the period free, but he wanted Josh to think that he'd made an extra effort for him.

"Let's go talk."

THE GYM WAS EMPTY; the coach—already!—had the class outside running laps in the warm autumn air. Josh picked up a basketball and tossed it easily to Zack, who was in the middle of another monologue. "I really can't believe you're here! I was just talking about you to my mom and Alex this morning. This morning! Psycho-weirdness, huh?" He dribbled, took a shot, missed, passed it back to Josh.

"Is there anyone here I'd know from junior

high?" Josh asked casually. He also bounced the ball once, twice, and took the shot: *swish*. The ball sliced through the net like a dream.

Zack pretended not to notice, picking the ball up and dribbling it around Josh, showing off his moves. "A few changes... Jason and Karyl transferred, Teresa and Matt and Heather moved. Oh, and Tim." Bounce, bounce, throw; *boing*, he missed again. Instead of passing the ball back to Josh, he growled and dribbled forward again.

Josh's eyes snapped up to Zack's face. "What happened to Tim?"

"Attempted suicide. People found out he was gay." Zack went for the layup and aced the shot. He caught the ball and came back around, continuing: "Was messing around with another guy down in the science rooms one day and got caught. Tried to shoot himself with his dad's gun three days later."

It'd been quite the scandal for a week or two, especially since Tim had been a well-liked student and the eighth-grade vice-president; fortunately, the gun had jammed and Tim had only grazed his head, but he was out for the rest of the year and didn't come back the following year, supposedly being sent to a rehab facility. The other kid, some newbie, had transferred away a few weeks later. There'd been a school assembly where they'd shown pictures of Tim and talked about his "depression," since the principal didn't feel it was "appropriate" to go into the details. Zack barely knew Tim, didn't think it was appropriate to fake emotions he wasn't feeling, and had thus blown the assembly off, hiding in the library with a Game Boy borrowed from his cousin. He'd heard about it after the fact.

Zack pivoted, sending the ball to Josh, but Josh had turned away and was taking a seat on the bleachers. Zack chased after the ball, then noticed his friend's face. Josh wasn't one who set his emotions on display, but now his brown eyes were filled with sadness.

Concern gripped Zack like a vise. "Hey, you okay?"

"I should've known." Josh's voice was heavy.

Zack tried to be comforting. "Hey dude, no one knew he was queer. You're just lucky you weren't really good friends; he might've made a pass at you or something." He giggled at the thought of Tim trying to touch Josh's arm in an overly friendly manner and getting put into a chokehold for his efforts by his friend, the ox.

Josh didn't laugh.

As his own laughter awkwardly died away, Zack said, in a slightly accusing voice, "Hey, what's the matter? You used to laugh at this kind of shit."

Josh was staring into space, but now he turned and looked at Zack, and Zack had to really look deeply into Josh's eyes to find his friend in there. Josh's voice was flat, like all the air had been squished out of it.

"Zack, I used to be a lot of things—or think a lot of things—that haven't turned out like I thought. Now, I feel like I know who I am ... but that's not the same as what—who—I was. Get it?"

He was up again, and dribbling the ball; Zack just looked at him and mutely—if apologetically —shook his head no.

Josh exhaled sharply and passed to him again. "I just want you to know, whatever's happened, no matter what I've realized—I'm still Josh, and I'm still your friend."

Zack nodded, happily, and returned the ball. Josh bounced it a couple of times, looking at it the way God might examine the Earth from space.

He was still perusing the ball, not Zack's face, when he took a deep breath and passed the ball to his friend, almost as if sending it over on the exhaled words: "Aaaand … I'm gay."

The ball bounced off Zack's chest and rolled away. There was an ominous pause, during which the universe seemed to shiver and crack in two.

Zack suddenly erupted into a scream that made his earlier one that morning look like a whisper. Josh, used to this, rushed over and clamped his hand over his friend's mouth. "Are you calm?"

Zack nodded.

"Are you sure?"

Zack nodded again. Josh removed his hand, and Zack immediately began screaming again. Josh tried to replace the hand, only to have Zack try to bite it. Josh lightly slapped his face, Zack returned it, and for a moment they were both five years old again, fighting in the sand pile.

Sweaty, faces tingling, they both paused for breath, eyes locked on each other's faces.

Zack's brain had gone directly from the wash cycle to advanced spin and was now moving too fast for him to keep up. He flashed on a hundred memories of changing clothes in front of Josh, of talking about girls with Josh, of holding Josh's hand on a kindergarten field trip. He felt like the water in his brain was draining away now, swirling him down into a dark vortex where nothing made sense anymore. It was Bizarro World all over again, only worse.

Josh, however, was borderline seething. For almost five years, he'd stared at e-mails from Zack and had hit "Delete," had picked up the telephone receiver and stared at it for minutes at a time, unable to dial Zack's number. Now he'd finally admitted the truth—and shards of broken glass seemed to lie all around him.

Life wasn't fair.

"Didn't you listen to a thing I said?!"

"Do you like to wear women's clothes?" Zack shouted back. He knew he was borderline hysterical but didn't care.

"No!" Josh was incensed. Zack, actually, had been the one who went out in drag for Halloween when they were ten, so he could send his father the pictures and hopefully induce a coronary.

"Leather?!"

"*No!*"

"Quiche?"

"No." Josh was beginning to get a little impatient.

There was another pause as Zack searched his mind—aha! "TEA!"

Josh shifted uncomfortably. "Some ... *times* ..."

"AHA! Earl Grey?" Zack was triumphant.

Josh just looked at him like he'd sprouted a second head, Martian-style. "Starbucks chai."

Zack processed this for a moment. "I don't think you're gay."

"*What?*"

Zack was now trying to be helpful, which usually made things worse. "Seriously, I know. How can you not do any of those things and still be gay?"

Josh's face took on a slightly mischievous look. "I could *prove* it to you ..."

Zack jumped about ten feet.

Josh finally laughed, a hearty, reassuring sound. "I'm *kidding*, Zack. I could never be attracted to you. You're my friend."

"Oh, okay, I get it. Fine. Thanks a bunch." Zack stalked after the basketball.

"What?"

Zack got right up in his face: "I'm not good-looking enough, am I?"

Josh couldn't help it; he burst into giggles.

Zack, undeterred, went into one of his favorite poses, The Eternal Martyr. "Oh, fine. Go ahead, laugh. No, it's not enough girls turn me down right and left, my best friend turns up and tells me he's gay but doesn't find me attractive either. Where did I go wrong? Is it me?" He sniffed his armpit and winced.

"Zack ..."

"So, how long have you ... known?" Zack suddenly dropped all trace of self-involvement and fixed Josh with one of his most intense, probing looks, the one where he let you know that he was there, really *there*. Josh felt a warm rush of gratitude.

"I've had an idea since I was eleven or so, I guess. It's just one of those curveballs God pitches you, like left-handedness, or photographic memory." He eyed Zack's spiky locks significantly. "Or red hair. Something that makes you a little bit different."

"Does your dad know?" Zack tried to imagine telling his mother something like this and couldn't do it. Beth probably would've burst out laughing.

Josh nodded. "I told him a couple of years ago.

I was going to a gay youth group in L.A. and didn't want to have to hide where I was going or who my friends were. It wasn't serious—I mean, I didn't really date anyone. But I didn't want to lie to him."

"And he was okay with it?" Of course he was, he was Nick. Duh.

Josh nodded again. "He was a little thrown, but he recovered pretty quickly. He just hopes I make him a grandpa someday."

"But how do you ..." Zack stopped, thought about it, tried again. "I mean, how do you know ... have you ever been in love?"

"Only once, and it never went very far. You?"

"Guess some things are the same on both sides," Zack mused, laughing a little at the situation as both of them relaxed. "I haven't had much luck either."

Josh grinned. "Yeah ... well. You haven't been crazy for *anyone* the past few years?"

"Keep it on the D.L.?"

Josh nodded.

"Missy Hoff. Brian's girlfriend. I don't know, she's just ... so ... I don't know." Zack's desire sapped his ability to articulate. "You know?"

Josh smiled; he knew.

Zack continued, "I guess it'd be kind of how you'd feel about...?"

"Paul Rudd."

"*Really?*" At least Josh had taste. "Okay, tell me this much: if you could've had anyone we both know, who would you have picked?"

"Remember I told you I've only been in love once?" Josh wiggled his eyebrows.

"Yeah?"

"It was Brian."

Five years of details suddenly clicked in Zack's brain. He was on his feet, almost shouting with happiness: "Of *course*! Jesus, how could I have missed it. God, all this time ... I never knew why I was jealous of him, I just knew you liked him—I mean, of course you *liked* him, but this—wow. It all makes sense!"

Josh was really laughing now. "Standish, you crack me up. After all this time, I come back and tell you I was in love with a guy you hated, and you're excited about it. Why?"

A thought suddenly sparked in Zack's brain, like a fresh-struck match. "Josh ... how did Brian feel about you?"

A shadow of wistfulness crossed Josh's face. "I think he loved me too, once—if he knew what it was. Now, I dunno. What are you thinking?"

Zack was on his feet, pacing furiously. The words tumbled from his mouth so quickly, that it was almost as if they had to escape his skull. "What if ... what if he still does? What if he's not in love with Missy at all? Or maybe he is, but that was before you came back. Think how he was looking at you, it might be true."

"What good does it do for Brian as long as he's with Missy?"

"What good does it do *me* to want *Missy* as long as she's with *Brian*?" Zack's face lit up like a carnival midway in Hell. "Don't you get it? The two of us combining forces can get them un-involved."

"You want us to break them up for our own devices?!" Josh leaped to his feet as Zack nodded. "Why, for God's sake?"

"For sex, of course! Why else?" Zack snorted impatiently.

"That's unethical," Josh said slowly, trying to resist the uncoiling figure in his mind that resembled a hungry serpent.

"True."

"And unscrupulous."

"Agreed."

"And dangerous."

"Uh-huh." Zack's eyes were positively sparkling.

"And mean." Josh threw this down defiantly.

Zack blew like a little volcano. "Oh, for Chrissake. *Mean?* That is pathetic. This isn't mean. This is about right and wrong!"

"Right!" Josh countered triumphantly.

"*Wrong!*" Zack was ensnared in his word choice; Josh regarded him blankly. "I didn't mean that! I mean, the right people—for us—are paired with the wrong people: each other. We have a moral obligation to realign the cosmos and set things straight." Then, as Josh glared at him: "No pun intended."

Josh shook his head. "Standish, you've gone totally non-linear on me. How would we go about pulling this off *if* we were serious? What plan of attack would we use?"

Zack was thinking again, his eyes glazing over as his mind worked like a giant role-playing game considering various strategies. "I don't know ... I've never broken up two people before. I need a foolproof strategy. And I need your help, *Mr.* Bradshaw. I can't do this alone; it's a heaven-sent opportunity—for *both* of us."

Josh let this proposal marinate for a moment, eyeing Zack as Eve might have eyed a serpent with a fresh apple pie. "Are you doing this for you, for me, or so you can humiliate Brian?"

Zack smiled, his face betraying nothing.

Josh continued, "We were best friends for eight years—we practically lived inside each other's heads. I don't want anything to mess that up now. Can I trust you?"

Zack raised his hand in a pledge. "As much as I trust myself."

"This isn't going to turn out like the motorized hide-a-bed, is it?" Josh asked grimly. He was thinking of eight years prior, on a warm spring Saturday. There had been a garage sale, a dilapidated lawnmower, a sofa bed with wheels, and a hill involved, all sparked by Zack's casual comment, "You know, we *could* ..." It had all wound up in the local newspaper, and both boys had lost Game Boy privileges for a month.

"One foul-up. Just one. There didn't use to be a pond there, I swear." Zack draped an arm around his bud and gave him a little squeeze. It was surprising how broad-shouldered Josh was now, but he was still Josh. "This'll work. I know it."

Josh still seemed unconvinced.

Zack leaned in close, remembering the radio from this morning on the way to school a million years ago, and an ancient LP of his mother's that he and Josh used to play. "Don't make me sing "You're My Best Friend.""

"I know I am," Josh said, pretending to be smug about it, and ducking as Zack tried to punch his arm.

Laughing, the two friends exited the gym, arms slung around each other's shoulders. The door slammed behind them, and there was only silence in the gym.

Then there was a sound of a match being struck.

In the corner, behind the bleachers, there was the inhale of smoke, then an exhaled breath.

Jamie Esau leaned against the wall and stared thoughtfully at the ceiling, a very, very pleased expression on her face.

CHAPTER 6

The Wednesday just before Easter, the year Josh's mother died, the church was filled with lilies. They were placed all over the area in front of the altar, bursts of white in green-foiled pots. Maureen Bradshaw had looked beautiful laid out in her casket, her hair dark like her son's, looking like Sleeping Beauty awaiting a magic, awakening kiss that would never come. They'd done such a good job on her makeup and clothes that no one would've known how thoroughly cancer had decimated her body, how scarred her arms were from the IVs and the needles.

The service had progressed smoothly thus far, with ten-year-old Josh sitting close to his father,

Nick's arm draped comfortingly around him, and assorted cousins and grandparents in attendance. Josh had been so numb for the past several days he'd barely been able to register who had come to the service until he heard a "Pssst" right behind him, and Zack was there, touching his shoulder gently. Beth must have combed Zack's hair that morning so it lay in place like strands of soggy redwood. He wore the only dress shirt he owned, which was deep purple, and a red tie. Beth was there as well, hugely pregnant with Alex; swathed in black, she resembled a sniffling Hawaiian volcano.

It happened when the priest was busy prepping the wine for communion, pouring it into the chalice as the thurifer waved the incense and the bells rang in the distance, and the church was quiet except for the occasional stifled sob from an elderly woman. As the acolyte poured the dark stream of reddish-purple liquid into the chalice, Josh was staring dumbly at the eaves of the church and wondering how life was going to go on without his ever being able to see his mom again. Zack leaned forward just enough so that Josh was able to feel his breath tickle the hair on the back of his neck, and murmured, in a voice filled with anticipation, "Ooh ... Welch's."

Josh let out a whoop of laughter and immediately tried to disguise it as a cough; however, behind him he heard the crisp sound of Beth's hand swiftly connecting with the side of her son's head, followed by Zack's wailed protest of, "Ouch, Jesus!" This had set Josh's father, who'd been silent most of the service, into a paroxysm of laughter, and, as the bewildered priest stood paused at the altar, Beth dragged her protesting son up the church aisle and waddled out the door with a *bang*. Then Josh was laughing along with his father, and then they were both crying while laughing and holding each other, and the smell of the lilies was overpowering, and the only thing Josh knew for sure was that, for good or ill, at that moment he loved Zack so much that he thought he might burst.

SHORTLY AFTER THE man Zack only referred to as "Him" had moved to Arizona, Nick had taken Josh and Zack to a movie at the local single-screen movie theater. It was one of those prototypical "family" pictures starring some faded sitcom dad with lots of people falling through ceilings and floors, dogs eating Thanksgiving turkeys, and the occasional fart joke.

Josh had laughed his way through most of the picture, Nick had chuckled a few times, but Zack had been quiet—indeed, he'd hardly said anything for a couple of weeks, aside from monosyllables. Then a scene came in the movie where the father had had a talk on a park bench with his young son, at the end of which they embraced. And suddenly, Zack shot out of his seat and bolted up the aisle.

Nick, seated on Josh's left and rummaging in his popcorn bag, didn't seem to notice Zack's disappearance. Josh quickly murmured "Be right back" to his father and ran up the aisle.

Zack wasn't in the lobby. Josh's worried eyes scanned the outside of the theater just beyond the windows; no sign of him. He ambled to the restroom, which had clearly seen better days; no one was visible. There were two stalls, however, one of which had a door hanging open. The other one was shut.

Josh moved slowly to it and pushed, but it refused to move. Then, from inside, Josh heard a sound more horrifying than anything he'd experienced since the last days before his mother died: Zack was crying.

In the stall, sitting on the toilet lid, Zack sat shaking, gut-heaving sobs punching their way out of him. He heard the door to the restroom open and tried to control himself, but he couldn't. His body couldn't get air; he felt like a scuba diver trying to surface too quickly, as if his lungs were collapsing.

He watched a pair of sneakers approach the stall and stand facing him. Josh's shoes. Josh wore green high-tops; no one else Zack knew did. The shoes stood facing the stall for a long moment, and then there was a tentative *tap-tap-tap*.

"Go away." Zack tried to sound assertive, but it came out choked. The scarred-up stall door with the jean pant legs and green high-top shoes stared blankly back at him.

"Go away!"

The shoes didn't move. The door wore scratches and jagged, unintelligible writing Zack could relate to. He felt just like that battered, beaten, messed up door, and he hated it, hated it with every fiber of his existence. He also hated

Josh, hated his father, hated all fathers, hated the whole screwed-up world.

The shoes still didn't move.

"GO AWAY!" He knew he was completely hysterical now, but he didn't care. The sobs were ripping his body in half. He was covered in tears and snot, and he knew his freckled complexion was probably making him look like a slimy strawberry. He cried even harder as he thought about the note his father had left on his dresser in the middle of the night, and his mother smoking in the kitchen in the gray light of early morning, her eyes red and exhausted. He hated that Alex would never even know what a father was.

Most of all, Zack hated himself for driving Him away.

The shoes moved back a step, and more of Josh's legs came into view. He sat in front of the door, and the latch jiggled in the lock as he pressed his body's full weight against it. He just sat there, as close as he could get yet still separated, waiting.

"Go away." This time his voice was a scratchy whisper, his tears evident. His throat burned, and his face was hot.

His friend didn't move. The bathroom floor

was dark-green and sticky and gross; still, Josh sat, not saying anything. Just waiting.

After another minute or so, Zack drew a sleeve across his snuffling nose and wet cheeks, composed his breath, rose, and very slowly opened the door, pulling it inward. Josh still sat where he'd been propped against the door. He looked up at Zack, his expression placid, but his dark eyes filled with grief.

Zack washed his face as Josh stood and joined him at the sinks, looking at their reflections. There was a warp in the mirror that distorted the image, making it hard to see the space between them. Josh waited silently as Zack dried his face with a paper towel, as he took one last shuddering breath, and tried futilely to smooth his red cowlicks down.

There was silence as they stared at each other, their eyes saying a thousand things that could not be said out loud, could never be said at all.

They walked silently back to the theater auditorium. They could see Nick halfway down, laughing his head off at something onscreen. They slowly descended the aisle into the darkness, and it was only then that Zack reached out and put his hand on Josh's shoulder, letting his friend carefully guide him back to the safety of their seats.

JAMIE NOTICED IT FIRST.

Brian, everyone said, was the "sensitive" one. "Oh," relatives clucked, "what a sensitive boy. He seems to feel things so deeply." Brian was always the one to cry at Disney films; he was the one who tried to package up all the change from his piggy bank in an envelope and mail it off to the starving orphans in Africa. He was the one about whom teachers commented: "What a kind boy," or "What a sensitive young man." True, he could barely make a decision without almost splitting his brain in half, and although he was wiry and fast on the playground, he lacked strength and coordination. And his grades were no more than serviceable, compared to Jamie's roster of A's. (Jamie's most memorable comment was "Works hard.") Still, people said, "What a nice boy. What a good guy."

Yet sensitive, loving, delicate Brian, lost in his own little world of fantasy books and role-playing games, of zoning out in the pool with his headphones on, never seemed to notice what was going on with their mother.

At first, she just started sleeping in more and more. She still came down and had breakfast with them, but more and more she would rely on the housekeeper to have something prepared when Brian and Jamie entered the kitchen on school mornings. Eventually, they exclusively ate toaster strudels and frozen waffles and cold cereal. "Things you like," their mother said absently, but Jamie liked her mother's soft scrambled eggs, and potatoes, and pancakes, and her mother wearing her fuzzy blue bathrobe, laughing as she shook her dishwater blonde hair back out of her eyes while the bacon sizzled and the *Today* show played on the kitchen TV.

Then she started coming into the kitchen right before they left for school, looking bleary-eyed and confused, hair flyaway, robe askew, no makeup. She kissed them in a vague sort of way, as if reminding herself who these strange people under four feet tall were, and sent them out the door for carpool. She had driven them at least a couple of times a week for the first year or two, and then she'd stopped.

Then she stopped coming down for breakfast at all.

Jamie peeked in on her one morning in the third grade, after she'd woken, dressed herself, done her own hair, readied her backpack, checked the morning paper—comics, of course, but also the financial page since her father had bought her shares of Microsoft, Disney, and Starbucks—started toasting some frozen waffles and microwaving sausages, and knocked on Brian's door.

She hesitated for just a moment outside her parents' bedroom door, trying to push down a vague feeling of unease that she couldn't put her finger on. Her father, she knew, had already departed for his morning workout and the office before dawn, as he always did; her mother would be alone.

The door made a soft murmuring sound as it drew over the plush navy-blue carpeting. The shades were down, and her mother was in bed with her sleep mask on. She murmured in her sleep in an agitated way, like Brian did. There was a large glass on her nightstand, and the smell from it curled into Jamie's nostrils like something strong and noxious.

She stood there for several moments, her pigtails gently swinging against her shoulders, watching her mother sleep. Her mother's head shifted on the pillow, and she suddenly emitted a long moan, a terrible, lonely sound. She looked, Jamie thought, like a watercolor painting that'd been left out in the rain and was beginning to blur.

Silent as a ninja, she picked up the glass and sniffed it. Definitely something not kid-friendly. How much of this did her mother drink? Was it every night? Why? And how did her mother manage to put herself together before they got home in the afternoon?

Her mother stirred suddenly, and before Jamie had time to think, her mother had pushed the mask back and was staring at her with bleary, accusatory eyes.

There was a pause during which time seemed to slow down, stop.

Jamie felt her insides turn to a mass of wriggling insects, but she managed to keep her voice even. "Want me to take this down for you, Mom?"

"No." Her mother's voice was cracked, weary. "Leave it. I'll take care of it." She sighed after saying this, as though it had been a tremendous effort.

"Okay." Jamie backed away slowly, not taking her eyes off the misshapen pile of bedding, the stack of tabloid magazines on the nightstand, the smell in the room that seemed to creep under her fingernails and skin. Something unnervingly close to fear seemed to grip her brain; for the first time since she could remember she was unsure what to do, think, or feel, and this unfamiliarity was more frightening to her than her mother's condition or the mysterious glass.

She had just made it to the door when her mother croaked out, "Honey ... I really need to sleep in the mornings. Just get breakfast and get off to school. 'Kay?"

"'Kay." Jamie's hand was on the knob. Escape was imminent.

"Make sure Brian's up and all right," her mother murmured, her voice fading away like a distant radio signal. She sank back into sleep, saying something like "Mumble mumble worry mumble."

Jamie closed the door behind her and stood at the top of the stairs, listening to the house tick.

Far away downstairs the toaster popped, and she jumped a little.

I could scream like a banshee and, probably, no one would notice. She could mount a broomstick and fly around the house, and her mother would continue to slumber on, her father would burrow deeper into Investors Business Daily, and her brother would only put his headphones on and continue slaying trolls and minotaurs on his computer.

Something glistening above her in the corner caught her eye. A silver thread danced in the light, and at the end of the thread, perched next to the ceiling, was a tiny spider the housekeeper had missed. It didn't move; it just sat there, waiting. Waiting. It had all it needed to catch prey, to take care of itself, to survive. Jamie admired the creature.

She was eight years old and completely alone.

It was a terrifying emotion.

And yet … a strangely intoxicating one.

CHAPTER 7

In the second-period English classroom, Ms. Sullivan was wandering the aisles. She was one of those arty-type English teachers, the kind who wore multi-hued scarves tied just so at her throat, kept her hair in a frizzy cloud, and favored funky earrings and necklaces from Sri Lanka and New Mexico. Jamie, Chantel, Brian, Missy, Josh, and Zack were scattered around the room in their usual pairings of choice, along with some twenty other kids oblivious to the drama unfolding about them. They were, instead, focused on Ms. Sullivan's choice of drama: *Twelfth Night*.

"Now," Ms. Sullivan exulted, giving a big toothy smile as she twirled about the room,

"*Twelfth Night*. Shakespeare's timeless, ageless comedy about how people fall in love, often as not with the wrong people, but for the right reasons."

Zack was writing Josh a note: *What if we kidnapped them?*

"In Shakespeare's day, the women's roles were played by young boys, yet in this play, we have a girl disguised as a boy, and another falling for her to add to the confusion ..."

Missy slipped Brian a note: *Please don't be angry —I love u.*

"In *Twelfth Night*, deception ... trickery ... foolishness ... all help or hinder the characters on their quest for true love."

Chantel slipped Jamie a note: *Is he taken, do you think?*

"Those who believe themselves to be wise are revealed as fools, and those who at first may seem to be foolish are actually quite intelligent ..."

Brian returned the note to Missy: *I love u 2— sorry just thinking.*

"And woven throughout the action is the poignant, eternal quest for love, often at any cost."

Josh wrote back: *Get real. U might as well drug their food.*

Zack considered this for a moment.

"For these characters, to love another person and to love life are inseparable."

Jamie wrote back: *I wouldn't get my hopes up, hun.*

Josh, his upper lip tickled by a stray hair, suddenly sneezed. All five of the others said "Bless you" simultaneously.

THE MORNING SPED by giving way to lunchtime. The Academy wasn't large enough to break down into all the social subdivisions usually found at your average public school, but there were still definite pockets of cliques, and people who were less than welcoming when a strange tray hit their table. There were unspoken rules about these things, and everyone knew them, as if by osmosis. Those who didn't know learned very quickly. The cheerleaders avoided the anime/manga devotees, the Emo boys avoided the Juicy girls, the jocks avoided anyone who wasn't a jock, the stoners tended to eat on

the steps outside, the bulimics ate near the bathroom, non-white kids only sat with white kids if
their parents made more than six figures, and
everyone pretended it was all perfectly normal.

Today the entire room seemed abuzz with one
topic of conversation: who was the new junior
boy, and what was he doing palling around with
Zack Standish, rebel without a clue? Zack had
been coming to the Academy since he was in seventh grade, when he was a loud, scrappy, spazzy
kid who always seemed to want to belong somewhere, but never put out any sort of friendly ges-
tures that encouraged it. He did soccer for a year
or two, then quit; he'd done a year in a small
vocal ensemble, then quit. He was a stream constantly moving and reshaping itself. At lunch, he
usually put on his headphones with his Walkman
and found an empty hallway. Would he be joining
the crowd today? Especially with that new dark-
haired boy sitting down with a tray, looking
around him expectantly?

In the farthest corner, Jamie finished writing a
note, folded it crisply, then passed it to Chantel,
who backhanded it neatly onto a passing tray. It
was then carried to another table and picked up
by a spy-like guy in a trench coat, sunglasses, and

headphones. He strolled backward and passed it to a girl fixing her eyes in her compact; she didn't look up as she snapped it up in the compact and passed it over; it was next speared by a large boy in a flannel shirt, using his salad fork, and passed on to a mousy-looking girl's tray. She carried it for several seats, then oh-so-casually handed it down to a hand reaching up from underneath one of the tables. The hand disappeared and reappeared in front of Josh, dropping the note on his tray. He did a double-take, looked around him cautiously, and opened it:

Meet me in the theater after school—must talk. A friend(?)

Josh set the note back on the tray and looked up to see Zack carrying a tray of his own. Josh waved; as he did so, the hand reappeared, snatched the note, and replaced it with another one. Josh did a double-take, looking around him apprehensively, then quickly opened the next note:

P.S.—Don't mention this to Zack.

JOSH DIDN'T HAVE time to look around him as Zack walked up to the table and set his tray down. Josh unobtrusively dropped the note in his pocket as a rat-like kid scuttled out from under the far end of the table.

"God, what a morning," Zack exhaled. "Free for a Big Gulp after three o'clock?"

"I gotta do some stuff—new kid paperwork," Josh said hastily. "I'll connect with you later?" Hopefully, the stranger wouldn't want him for very long.

"'Kay," Zack said happily, his mouth full of food. He couldn't remember the last time cafeteria food had tasted this good; for that matter, he couldn't remember his last time sitting in the cafeteria for lunch. Had the walls always been that color? He'd eaten alone for so long that the place looked almost as unfamiliar to him as it must to Josh.

Abruptly, a shadow fell across his mind as he remembered their conversation that morning. Was Josh planning on coming out to *everyone* in school, besides Brian? Would the whole school thus think that Zack was gay as well for hanging out with Josh? He'd always felt like an outsider at the Academy anyway; now he was faced with the possibility of being even more of an outcast. The Scarlet Letter, he thought; but instead of "A" for Adulteress, it would be a "G" for Gay. Or "Q" for Queer.

Well, Zack had always been the first in the fight—any fight. Now, he might actually have a reason to fight. Josh was worth it, Zack thought. Anyone who was willing to go to the mat for him —and to help him land Missy—was worth it.

He almost grinned at Josh, like a complete goon, to make up for thinking his cowardly thoughts earlier, but thought better of it. For now, he was just happy to be eating a wilted green salad, a warmed-over burrito, and an apple turnover with his friend.

In the cafeteria line, Brian Esau watched Zack and Josh sitting together, and felt his insides stick together, like letters on an old keyboard. Then, with a rush of gratitude, he noticed Missy's wave and joined a table filled with football players and their girlfriends in the opposite direction behind a pillar. Some days, it was almost a relief to be invisible again.

CHAPTER 8

The clock on the wall read three-thirty as Josh entered the plush darkness of the theater. He strolled down to the front row, then ascended the stairs and walked on stage, looking around him at the empty space. He felt a slight flutter in his chest, but no overwhelming sense of foreboding. Probably just a prank, he thought. New kid hazing. No big deal.

There was a distant *ka-chunk* noise, and lights very abruptly flooded the stage. Then a female voice echoed throughout the auditorium:

Love is a smoke made with the fume of sighs, Being purg'd, a fire sparkling in lovers' eyes, Being vex'd, a sea nourish'd with loving tears.

What is it else? a madness most discreet A
choking gall, and a preserving sweet.

Josh grinned. He'd read this play at his high
school in California the previous year and had
enjoyed it so much that he'd wound up memorizing several of the speeches. He squinted out
into the blackness and the one glaring white light
and said:

O, speak again, bright angel, for thou art As
glorious to this night, being o'er my head, As is a
winged messenger of heaven.

As he finished this speech, there was a step
to his right. Jamie ascended the stage, her hat off
and her hair pulled back. A tiny smile played on
her lips, but her eyes showed no trace of
warmth. "Romeo, Romeo … wherefore art thou
Romeo."

"Lady Macbeth, I presume," Josh returned,
unruffled.

Jamie looked unaccountably pleased with this.
She took out a cigarette and lit it, drawing closer
to him but still standing slightly away. "Ahh,
you're a smart one, all right. I figured you
couldn't be as dumb or obtuse as Zack can be,
and you've been gracious enough to prove it
to me."

"I'm glad I could help," Josh said neutrally. A safe response.

"You've only begun. As you may have guessed, I am more than a little "up" on the situation between you, Zack, my brother, and his vanilla-yogurt girlfriend."

"Are you." A small icicle of fear pierced Josh's stomach. He wasn't even a hundred percent sure when he'd woken up that morning if he was going to come out to anyone at the Academy, and then Zack had caught him off-guard and made him spill the beans; thank God it'd gotten resolved. Now, he suddenly realized, more than one other person knew about him, and he knew little or nothing about this person in return.

What *else* did she know?

"And I think I can help you." Jamie exhaled smoothly, the smoke wafting up into the darkness like a cool gray thread. She had the same look blackjack dealers in Vegas often have: avid, yet polite. They know they have all the time, and all the cards, in the world.

"Uh-huh," Josh returned, waiting.

"*If* you help me." There it was.

There was a long pause, so pregnant its water was nearly breaking. Josh cracked first. "How?"

Magnanimous in victory, Jamie let the words pour forth like a stream of warm pancake syrup. "You want my brother. Zack wants Missy. Now, I have nothing against you going after my brother … oh, you're surprised? I know Brian better than he knows himself. I know the barbed wire he laces around his mind. If you can get past the barricade, more power to you. *But—*" Suddenly, she was there, right there, in his face; a Cheshire cat materializing out of thin air with claws and teeth bared, "—I told Zack once, I'll tell you once: don't screw with me or my brother in-dis-criminately. Got it?"

Josh nodded; he got it, all right. He was also becoming seriously unnerved.

Jamie was pacing around him now, getting closer and closer, like a shark responding to blood. "Now, I can influence Brian subtly to be open to your attention; that's a snap. But the second part, Zack wanting Missy … a toughie. No one seems to ask what Missy wants, and who cares? But some attention will have to be paid to what *I* want if we're all going to be happy campers and for things to go smoothly."

Josh was almost afraid to ask, but the pause she left hanging—like a ready noose—indicated that he was supposed to do so. He swallowed, and said, more casually than he felt, "What do you want?"

Jamie's back was to him. She pivoted around like a music-box ballerina and eyed him as a tiny smile twitched her lips. It was a smile that said she'd already won. "Eventually, I want Zack."

"Zack?! ... Why?"

"He amuses me ... and he has the potential to be a decent human being. Which, in case you didn't notice today, is a rather precious attribute at this school. He's original, he's driven, and he's very cute." A brief shadow crossed her face, and she added, in a burst of complete honesty, "Besides, you're out of the running."

"In other words," Josh tried to make his voice cold, "you're asking me to double-cross and betray my best friend." He only sounded shaky on the word *friend*.

"Metaphorically screw a friend now, literally screw a lover later," Jamie countered. Her smile had no amusement.

"Give me one good reason why I should say yes." His brain was beginning to defrost a little bit, and he now saw that she was relying on his acquiescence a little too heavily. Maybe if he pushed back, he could reclaim some high ground.

Jamie looked at him for a long, long moment, sizing up his challenge. Then she once more began moving toward him—slowly, ever so slowly, as a spider does when it knows its prey is trapped. Her voice was devoid of all inflection; she might have been reading a list of vocabulary words in a foreign language, all of them describing advanced weaponry.

"I can give you a bunch of reasons. One: you'd be making me happy, and that's not without its benefits. Two: it's better for Zack, since Missy can't begin to match what I can give him. Three: it shouldn't interfere with you and Brian at all if you're careful. Four: if you don't see the devastatingly brilliant logic of points one, two, *and* three, I will blow this whole thing sky-high and the whole school will be infested with the completely false—but very potent—rumor that you and Zack are lovers, causing legendary homophobe Hank Gaston to marshal his thugs and turn you two into road pizzas."

Josh had a brief memory of Hank: big, ugly, mean. This tracked.

She was right in front of Josh now, and her

eyes mesmerized him. Her brother's eyes that morning were bright, worried pools of deep cerulean; Jamie's, in contrast, were the color of blue only seen in the deepest ice crevices at the top of the world—a place without a flicker of heat or life.

Josh knew he was sweating, and his throat had gone dry. She turned rather suddenly and started to walk away, as if she had already gotten the answer she wanted. He was galled at her arrogance, and his voice came out harsher than he'd expected. "I don't suppose you've stopped to consider we're *all* getting in way over our heads?"

Jamie had almost reached the stairs, but she turned and looked back at him with an expression of mild amusement. Her voice took on a slightly reproachful tone, as if he were an obstinate child wasting her time. "Josh, if you're going to one-up the sharks, you've got to think like a piranha. Swim in my end of the pool or get ready for blood. I'll look forward to hearing from you. Don't keep me waiting. I have a few more lives to manipulate by the Back-to-School Costume Dance, and there are only so many hours during the day."

She smiled at the thought of this, a Great

Lady now pulling on her gloves after lunch on her way to a matinee of Light Beheadings. Jamie walked through the theater door and became a silhouette in a burst of sunshine. The door closed behind her, and simultaneously the stage lights abruptly and mysteriously shut off.

Josh looked and felt like he'd been hit with a two-by-four. He walked slowly offstage and down the stairs, feeling as though he were descending into something dark and sticky and threatening. And for the moment, he couldn't think of any way out of it.

It was like walking into an alternate universe when Josh stepped out into the sunshine. He walked to his car, his thoughts a jumbled box of non-connecting puzzle pieces. He felt simultaneous relief and a pang of dismay when he saw Zack sitting on the hood of his car, smoking and leafing through a comic book. "Hey, schmuck," he said.

Zack jumped up, alert and bright-eyed as a cartoon squirrel. "Hey, you. Going home?"

"Yeah ... gotta unpack my room some more." This was true; Josh and his dad had only been back in the house for a few days, and his room looked like several aisles at Target had exploded simultaneously.

"Want help? I'm a great designer," Zack offered.

Josh almost smiled, but Jamie had left him feeling like a small country invaded by the Marines. "Thanks, but I can do it myself. Really. I mean … I do want to hang with you. But today's been a little overwhelming, and I gotta put my head in order. I'll call you later, I promise."

Zack's face fell, but he quickly propped it back up; his words came as though he were fumbling for them in the dark. "I guess … guess we're not twelve years old anymore."

"Guess not." Josh said it as gently as possible, but with enough finality to make sure the conversation didn't continue to limp forward.

There was an awkward moment where they weren't sure if they should slap hands, embrace, or punch each other; they wound up doing a sort of collide-and-spin-away maneuver, just enough to convey affection, before sliding behind their respective steering wheels.

CHAPTER 9

Beth was in the driveway maneuvering an ax into a log with a *thunk* when her son pulled in. Zack turned off the motor and leaned out of his car window to yell at his mother. "Hey, crazy lady, what're you doing in our driveway?"

"Waiting for my obnoxious teenage son to come home and flick me crap, of course."

He took a seat on the rockery a safe distance away. Beth gave the stump another *thunk*, and it split in two. "Okay, banality 101. How was your first day?"

"Josh is back," Zack said, as full of portent as if he'd announced the Martians had landed.

Beth was surprised, but fortunately not in

mid-swing with the ax. "Really? Oh, honey, how wonderful. He and his dad moved back?"

"Yeah, and he goes to the Academy. Wild, huh?"

"Nick Bradshaw—" Beth smiled a little. "That man never could make a decision for very long. I'll have to call him and give him some severe shit." The last word slipped out of her unnoticed.

Zack was fiddling with his shoelace. "Mom … Josh is … different."

"Well, it's been almost six years. By now, I assume he has shoulders."

"He's got more than that." Fiddle, fiddle. "He says … he's gay."

Beth paused again, digesting this, studying her son carefully. Zack was determinedly avoiding her expression, then looked up, then promptly looked down again. His mother only said, "Hmm," as if thinking aloud.

"Yeah. Hmm," her son rejoined.

"How do you feel about him?" Beth asked, no bull.

"It kinda freaked me out for a while. It's weird," Zack said honestly. It felt good to be able to be completely candid with someone about the whole thing, especially since Alex was at his friend's house like usual and wouldn't be there to interrupt. Though Zack hated to admit it, sometimes he needed his mom's full attention.

"Not 'it.' *Him.* How do you feel about him?" his mother asked. She was looking at him as though his answer was very important. Zack caught on.

"He's still Josh. Still the best friend I've ever had."

"Good. Don't break him down into parts and say 'it.' Love all of him, or at least accept him as he is. He's a courageous boy to confront something like this so young—lots of people never do. And he must trust you a great deal." Beth smiled a little, but her tone was more serious than Zack could recall in recent memory.

"Oh, I did. No problem." Beth gave him a slightly suspicious eye; it was unlike her son to give in so easily. Zack tried to smile innocently. "Well … I'm gonna go wash for dinner and look at *Playboy* for a while."

As he exited, Beth rolled her eyes skyward in exasperation and brought the ax down with an extra-vigorous chop. "Men …"

OUTSIDE OF THE BRADSHAW HOUSE, Josh pulled into his driveway. He got out of his car and was headed for the front door when he was distracted by the sound of shrubbery rustling. He paused, examined the innocent-looking green leaves, shook his head, and went inside.

As the front door shut, a young Japanese man in a trench coat popped out of the bushes, looked at the address, and skulked off down the driveway, taking out his cell phone and dialing as he went.

He listened to the ringing and listened through her voicemail message: "Hi, this is Jamie. I'm busy with my stockbroker, plans for world conquest, and in general being a force of nature. Leave a message at the tone, and depending on who you are and what it is, I might get back to you. Speak!"

The young man did so. "Jamie, this is Yoshi. Josh has moved back to his old house. 6469 Westview. Father arrived home earlier, no one else on premises. Note from maid saying she'll be in tomorrow. That's it. I take personal checks or PayPal, by the way."

Yoshi clicked the phone shut and hurried

down the road, disappearing behind a grove of innocent-looking evergreen trees.

BRIAN EASED his car to a stop outside of Missy's house. He was bruised from football practice and in a foul mood. From the back seat, Missy stroked the back of his neck and shoulders, wishing there was something else she could do for him. Jamie was in the front seat, still reading, and doing her best to ignore the intimacy between them.

There was an awkward pause before Brian said tentatively, "I … uh … shall I call you later?"

"You can if you want to." Missy tried not to apply any pressure to the statement. Instead, it came out cavalier.

"Do you want me to?" Brian asked, a little uncertain.

Jamie gave an ever-so-slight *harrumph*.

"Sure," Missy returned.

"Okay, I'll call," Brian finished decisively.

Jamie lost all patience. She slammed her book shut and bellowed off-key, "AFTER YOU'VE GONE…AND LEFT ME CRYING…AFTER YOU'VE GOOOOOONNNNEEE…." Mrs. Hoff appeared in the window with a look of consternation as Missy grabbed her school things and fled inside.

Brian turned on his sister like Wolverine. "Why do you always have to torment her? Why does it bother you that the two of us are happy, huh?"

Jamie's voice was lightly dismissive. "Brian, I don't want to, you know that. It's just that I know you could do so much better." She draped her arm lovingly around his neck. Her next words were weighted ever-so-slightly: "I'm just ... joshing you."

Brian walked into the trap and looked at her a little too quickly; she fluttered her lashes at him. With a muffled curse, he threw his car into reverse and backed out of the drive.

CHAPTER 10

As dusk fell, Josh snorkeled his way through a plateful of his father's linguine alfredo. Nick carried the pot from the kitchen into the dining room for refills. "More, son?"

"God, yes. Please," Josh said, tearing into another slice of bread. His mother had been Irish, and Nick was mostly Spanish; nonetheless, there must've been some Italian in the bloodstream somewhere for him to love a pasta dinner as much as he did. His father even let him have a tiny glass of red wine to accompany the meal.

"Good to see you with an appetite again— you've hardly been eating anything the past week." Nick set the pot down on the wooden disc

Josh had painted in kindergarten with trees and flowers for Mother's Day. Seeing it on the table made Josh feel simultaneously reassured and a little sad, like the soft glow from the vintage jukebox in the main hallway that his mother had given his father as a thirtieth birthday present.

"Nerves, I guess. Was kind of shaky about today."

"But it worked out, didn't it? Zack was glad to see you, Brian was glad to see you ..." Nick let the observation hang in the air, awaiting Josh's affirmation.

"We can hope." Josh decided to push the envelope a little bit, and went for a refill of wine, grabbing his father's glass along the way.

"Your talk with Zack went all right, you've got good classes ... sounds like a great day." Nick smiled at Josh as though he were a dad on a 1950's sitcom, with everything solved via a pipe and a firm-but-kind demeanor.

Josh felt a rush of love and some sympathy for his father. Nick was getting a few more flecks of grey at his temples, and the lines around his eyes were more pronounced. Josh didn't like to think about this for very long.

"I know, I'm just not sure what happens tomorrow. I got through the first day talking to Brian without passing out and in general making a total spectacle, but tomorrow I might have to *really* talk to him."

He returned to the table and made a big show of setting his father's wine glass down, like a *maître d'* in a fine restaurant, then unobtrusively setting his own glass back by his food.

"I thought that's what you wanted." Nick sipped his wine carefully.

"I thought so too, but ... Jamie Esau wasn't exactly what I expected either." Josh almost spilled the beans about the meeting in the theater, but going into it would only make his father worry, so he stopped himself from elaborating.

"People rarely are. That's what makes life interesting." Nick's eyes were distant for a second, and then they seemed to snap into focus. Damn, he'd noticed Josh's wine refill. "Son, I know it's hypocritical to set double standards, but ... I wish you wouldn't drink like that."

"Fine, I'll have an IV put in."

"You are a funny boy." Nick retrieved Josh's wine glass and set it on the other side of his dinner next to his own glass. "How're you going to do your homework half-drunk?"

"Trig and Current Events? Polynomials and the Clinton-Lewinsky scandal? I *need* to be drunk." He smiled, and Nick smiled back; good, Josh wasn't really in trouble. *Phew*.

His father reached over and rubbed his hair—a habit Josh used to hate, but about which he'd stopped complaining after Mom had died. A momentary rush filled Josh's heart. "I love you, Dad."

"I love you, too. I just wish I could've given you an easier life."

"Dad, God made me gay. Not you or Mom or alcohol." Was this going to be one of *those* conversations? Josh hated talking about it with his dad, even though Nick was completely supportive. In fact, he was *so* supportive and well-intentioned, that Josh always wound up feeling kind of weirdly tense and embarrassed afterward.

"I didn't mean that. I just meant more stability."

"That's probably why I like Brian—he just seems like a perfect fantasy boyfriend." This probably fell under the Too Much Information column. Still, it was true; nothing ever seemed to happen to the Esau family—they'd always lived in the same house, their parents were still together and alive. Josh wondered what that was like.

"They're a very strange family. Never cared much for the parents; Zack's mom was much more my speed." Nick laughed. "Did I ever tell you about—"

"—the strip Trivial Pursuit game. Yes. Many times." Josh finished his father's sentence. It had involved a weekend trip to a cabin, and many vodka shots had been consumed by the adults; Beth won, but she'd worn her sunglasses all the next day.

"Smartass." Nick smiled. "My point is, sometimes it's a very fine line between friends and romantic partners."

"I dunno, Dad. It's all kinda weird." Josh didn't know what else to say.

"Kinda," his father nodded.

AT THE STANDISH HOUSE, Zack was determinedly scraping the last of the sauce from the plate so vigorously Beth was afraid he'd take the pattern off as well. "Great casserole, Mark."

"Yeah, great," Alex parroted, emulating his brother's example.

"Not as good as what your mom was making before I sent her out to chop wood. I'm sorry I burned it, hon." Mark's eyes looked sincere; Beth, however, merely took a sip of her wine and smiled wickedly at him.

"C'mon, Alex, help me clear the table." Zack and Alex grabbed the leftovers and headed out to the back porch to the garbage cans. They scraped the plates in and then peered inside.

"What is it?" Alex finally asked.

"I have no idea," Zack murmured, staring into the can with horror.

"Is that what Mommy cooked?"

"Looks like."

"I think it's trying to get out."

"We'll tear-gas it later." Zack slammed the lid shut and backed away quickly. They both raced back inside, each trying to get in first, Zack whooping and Alex screaming happily. The phone rang, and Beth mumbled with muted happiness before she yelled, "Zack! It's for you."

Zack picked up the receiver: "Yo."

"It's me," Josh said. "Just said hi to your mom."

"Hey, you. I got a plan."

"What's up?"

"Word was hot around school today that the Dynamic Duo is having problems." Zack had overheard this from a girl who was telling her friend she'd heard it from a guy who'd heard it from another guy, who'd overheard an argument in the hall between Missy and Brian after lunch. "We'll target their insecurities about how wrong they are for each other—and everyone knows it. Gain their trust."

"Lie, you mean."

"Utilitarian fabrication." Zack was proud that his vocabulary came in handy when he wanted to rationalize something.

"Are we going to hell? I'm getting a very warm feeling. I wasn't meant to play God." Zack could hear the guilt edging into Josh's voice.

"Don't freak on me now. Meet me in the parking lot tomorrow morning to finalize details."

"Aye-aye, cap'n."

"Gotta bail. Later."

There was a *click* before Josh could think to say anything else.

GEORGE ESAU, a handsome forty-something blond man in a sweater, sat at one end of the dining table with his wife Phyllis at the other, both rigidly polite. Their decidedly different off-spring were between them, munching fixedly. No one had said anything for at least two minutes.

Jamie finally set down her fork. "Mother ... Father ... I've decided I'm dropping out of school. I'm joining a lesbian commune in Santa Cruz and am going to weave baskets for all my days."

Jamie's father glanced at her and decided not to acknowledge this.

Jamie's mom smiled painfully. "Jamie, dear, please don't use that kind of language at the dinner table."

Brian stared at his plate.

Jamie looked from one of her parents to the other. "Oh, I'm sorry. BASSS-ket, BASSS-ket, BASSS-ket. Was that the word? Or was it ... Santa Cruz?"

"Stop annoying your mother, Punkin," her dad said, eyes on his brisket.

"I am sixteen years old; I am not a 'punkin.'

Nor am I a squash, a tomato, or even a zucchini. I am a young woman. A woman who would like to have a dinner where words are exchanged between people!" Jamie knew her voice was bordering on shrillness, but she couldn't help herself. How was she always able to keep such control of herself at school, yet being at home with these people sent her completely off the deep end?

"Jamie ..." Her mother dropped her fork and put her head in one hand.

"Can't you just let us eat in peace? Just *once?*" Brian snarled. Jamie tried at least once a week to get some sort of reaction out of her parents by announcing a strange new hobby or a bizarre political philosophy that had caught her attention, but it was as fruitless as holding a lit match under a glacier.

Jamie threw down her napkin. "If it gets any more peaceful in this house we might as well open a funeral home. 'Esau morgue and take-out. You stab 'em, we slab 'em.'" She pushed her chair away.

"Young lady, finish your dinner," her mother insisted, taking a sip from her highball glass.

"I've lost my appetite!" Jamie flung back, stomping from the room.

There was a pause after she left, as though a dish had broken. Then George sighed heavily, his eyes flicking from Brian to his wife, and he said, "Well … at least we still have one kid who doesn't rock the boat."

Brian said nothing, but his face was a morass of emotions.

Shortly thereafter, walking down the hallway heading for his room, Brian stopped as he heard Yoshi's message playing back on Jamie's phone. His sister was sitting on the bed listening, her back to the door, beneath the various French reproductions on the walls, surrounded by her assortment of medieval weapons and the poster declaring "God grant me the serenity to accept the things I cannot change, courage to change the things I can, and the automatic weaponry to make the difference." Brian thought about saying something, then turned away slowly and wandered down the hall to his room. He thought about calling Missy and decided against it. He didn't have it in him tonight.

CHAPTER 11

That night, Zack dreamed that he was a secret agent, and Missy was captured by a nefarious supervillain in a warehouse intent on world domination (of course), tied up, and left for dead. He eluded the laser death-rays, the moat of crocodiles, the walls that shot darts, and fought off a phalanx of guards, all of whom had Brian's face. At last, he reached the interior of the warehouse where she was being held, and in one swift movement stripped off his wetsuit to reveal the handsome tuxedo underneath. He saw Missy tied to a pillar, her hair covering her eyes, her body trembling under the blue satin sheath. But when he reached her and cupped her chin in his hand and tilted her head back to gaze into her eyes and take the hungry kiss that waited for him, he discovered to his horror that it wasn't Missy, but Jamie. She smiled at him wolfishly and took the kiss anyway, as he struggled to free himself from her iron embrace.

JOSH HAD one of his Jesus dreams, where he was in church kneeling and praying before a life-sized sculpture of Christ. When he looked up, however, he saw it was Brian tied to the cross, clad only in a loincloth, the crown of thorns causing a scratch on his forehead that dripped blood onto Josh's spotless white shirt. He looked down at Josh sorrowfully, his blue eyes filled with love and helplessness. Josh said the first thing that came into his head: "I didn't know you had blue eyes."

"No one really looks at them," Brian/Jesus responded. In the choir loft, Mary J. Blige, Destiny's Child and Madonna were leading a gospel ensemble in "Like a Prayer," as Josh leaned over and kissed Brian's feet.

JAMIE DREAMT she was Alice in Wonderland again, and the Hatter and March Hare had just told her there was no room at the tea party. She stomped her way down the garden path, her blue pinafore rustling over her striped stockings, looking for the White Rabbit (who, for some reason, had a shock of spiky red hair). She found herself leaning on a giant mushroom talking with the Caterpillar, who seemed in a weird way to resemble Chantel, and who informed her that her size was all wrong. "Take a bite of the mushroom," she advised while exhaling a cool stream of lavender smoke from her hookah, "and you can find what size will best help you fit in." Jamie broke off a tiny piece and did so and proceeded to grow twenty stories tall; from far below, the Chantelpillar was heard yelling, "No, no! You're too big now! You have to come back down here to be with us!"

But when Jamie took a bite of the other side of the mushroom, she proceeded to shrink right down past the mushroom until she was barely the size of a blade of grass. "No, no, no! You don't listen at all!" the Chantelpillar yelled, far above her head. "You're hopeless. Goodbye!" Suddenly she was a beautiful black and crimson butterfly ascending into the dazzling blue sky, and Jamie was lost in a garden of oversized flowers that eyed her with barely veiled hostility. A dahlia snubbed her; a tiger lily growled.

In the distance, Jamie heard her mother's voice yelling, "Off with her head!" Trying to fight off her rising sense of panic, she searched frantically for the door out of Wonderland—a door for which she was much too small to reach—and was still searching when she awoke.

MISSY HAD the naked dream she'd had too many times before. She was at school, and everyone there was naked, even the teachers and the principal. When she looked down at herself, however, she saw that she was wearing her usual sweater, skirt, and knee socks. People in the hallways laughed at how ridiculous she looked, but every time she tried to peel off her sweater or take off her socks, they remained firmly attached to her. Then Brian was at her side, wearing a giant fig leaf, like Adam. "I'm sorry I don't look right," Missy apologized.

Brian looked sad. "You have way too many leaves," he said, pulling at the arm of her sweater. "My therapist says that people shouldn't worry about leaves so much."

"But how are you going to play football?" Missy asked, worried that he would be injured without any protection.

"Oh," Brian said, "it's all virtual now. Don't worry." As he said this, the entire football team walked by, all playing a mass-synced electronic game, and took him away with them. Missy opened her mouth to cry out, but someone touched her arm and she turned. It was Josh, wrapped in layers of fabric Indian style, complete with a turban.

He looked in her eyes and said, "I understand we understand each other."

BRIAN DREAMED he was in a swivel chair, being spun around and down a chutes-and-ladders style ramp. He was wearing boxer shorts splotched with hearts all over them. He spun past Chantel,

Jamie, and Gwen Stefani, all singing "Sweet Talkin' Guy" like a '60s girl group, complete with beehive hairdos. The seat hit some sort of bump and ejected him; he flew through space, toward a giant, crimson heart-shaped pillow, on which Missy and Josh were reclining. Both looked at him interestedly as he fell toward them, covering his eyes, wondering whom he was going to crush first.

CHANTEL DIDN'T DREAM at all.

CHAPTER 12

The following morning, Josh met Zack in the parking lot outside the Academy. Zack spoke in low, urgent undertones, as though he were in a crime thriller. "Okay, so we know what we're doing, right?"

"I'm targeting Missy, you're going after Brian," Josh confirmed.

"Right."

"We ask, don't demand. We imply, don't state. We are subtle people working cautiously toward our goal." Josh wore a look of studious concentration.

"We are horny people. Don't over-romanticize it."

They walked to the front door of the school together, nodded at each other, and headed off in separate directions. Above them, unnoticed, Jamie Esau was leaning out the window, smiling and watching them as one might a marionette show. Then she, too, disappeared.

TUESDAYS, Josh had math class first. He was pleased to find Missy sitting there as well, wearing glasses on a chain to help her see the whiteboard. He rather brazenly slipped into the seat next to her, nodding in a casual but definite way.

She took him in—the wavy dark hair, the open-necked tuxedo shirt, the jeans, the boots— and nodded back, a little hesitantly. He mouthed "Hi" at her silently as the moth-like teacher, Mr. Pearson, began a droning spiel about polynomials. Josh took a piece of paper and wrote her a note:

Are you in love with Brian?

He passed it to her when the teacher's back was turned; she opened it, looked at him with confusion, dashed off a quick few words underneath his, then returned it to him.

Yes—why?

Josh considered tactics for a moment, then wrote another sentence and passed the note back. Mr. Pearson continued his drone. Missy opened the paper:

Just wondering—you've been dating 4 awhile. Ever consider anyone else?

Missy was visibly shocked. The note she returned to Josh had a certain rigidity to the penmanship, as though she were pressing a little too hard while writing:

Why would I do that?

Josh shrugged a tiny bit, no more than an inch-high lift of the shoulder. He wrote again. Missy practically grabbed it out of his hands as he lifted it to pass it to her.

I dunno—2 see what someone else is like?

Missy stared at him, almost offended; then, seeing he was trying to be honest, she wrote back, no expression on her face.

Not that it's your business, but we haven't had sex yet. We're waiting till the time is right.

Josh registered this news in happy disbelief, leaning back, a glimmer of triumph on his face.

For the rest of the period he took notes on trigonometry, grinning silently to himself. He didn't even notice the way that Missy kept staring at him, as a fly might stare at a Venus flytrap before it snaps shut around it.

DOWN ON THE ATHLETIC FIELD, Brian was doing morning warm-ups in a pair of sweats and a tank top. Zack approached him slowly, thinking to himself how much he was going to hate this, but trying to plaster a friendly look on his face. *I must look insane.* He approached the Golden Boy.

Brian was startled at Zack's approach. Surely, Zack wasn't walking toward *him*? Why in God's name? But no, Zack said "Hey," and raised his hand in a casual greeting, as though they spoke regularly.

Brian's eyes flicked to the right, then to the left; he checked behind himself as well in case there was someone else there to whom Zack might be speaking. No one was there. Feeling like a complete tool, he pointed at himself incredulously.

"Yeah, you. How's it?"

What the hell? Zack came to a stop in front of Brian and looked down at him expectantly.

Brian felt as though he'd gone into a parallel universe. His voice came out more hostile than he'd intended. "What?"

"Now, is that how we talk to our friends?" Zack's tone sounded as though he'd said, Do you think it might rain?

"You're not my friend," Brian returned. Harsh, but true.

Zack's eyes widened, and he acted as though he'd been stabbed with an invisible dagger. He staggered about, gasping for breath, making gurgling noises. "Ooh … ooh … somebody, remove this knife in my heart, please! Such language from a former Boy Scout."

"I never was a Boy Scout, I quit the Cub Scouts when I was twelve," Brian informed him coldly. He'd gone to camp, and his entire suitcase of clothes had been dumped in the lake on the second day. He didn't even have to push the issue; his mother had called the Scoutmaster, and that was that. The navy-blue shirt still hung at the back of his closet, metal badges gleaming dully.

"Really?! I wasn't either." Zack had lasted two

meetings at the Scouts before he told them they were junior fascists-in-training and that he hated their uniforms. His father was, unsurprisingly, not thrilled. "And you thought we had nothing in common. Imagine that! It's too bad, you know? I mean," Zack groped for words, "you'd look really good in shorts. Objectively speaking, of course."

"Of course." Brian was practiced at being non-committal.

There was a pause, during which both boys were aware of the sprinklers clacking and the distant buzz of an airplane.

Zack began again, fumblingly, as though wrestling the words to the ground. "Of course—one should not—limit oneself. Like, I mean . . . the new experience can be very ... rewarding. For instance ... would you like to take a shower with me?"

"Sure," Brian said, losing himself momentarily in the dream. He leaned forward, inhaling the smell of soap on Zack's neck, seeing the tiny stubble of orange on his lip, realizing with a shock that he'd subconsciously wondered for some time what it would feel like, Zack's lips and Zack's teeth and Zack's tongue and . . .

And then he was himself again, shaking his

head, letting the dream pop like a soap bubble, but his chest was tight with fear. Zack was still babbling.

"Like, you know, some people like ketchup on their hamburgers, some like mustard. But sometimes you don't have to choose, you can have both. You could even have pickles, or onions."

He leaned toward Brian; even though no one was around, his voice dropped to a stage whisper. "You don't even have to have burgers. You can have … hot dogs."

Brian just stared at him for a moment, then rose, dazed, and walked away as though he were a little drunk. Zack yelled after him, "But you don't have to! I mean, I can't tell you what to do. Or eat! … Good talk!"

Then, to himself: "Shit."

BETWEEN CLASSES, Chantel and Jamie fought their way into the girl's restroom. A line had formed, and gossip hung thick in the air like hairspray.

Chantel grabbed Jamie's arm. "Did you hear

Josh tried to make a pass at Missy this morning?"
Her coffee-colored eyes were wide with shock.

"Did he?" Jamie's voice sounded as far away
as Siberia.

"*Ten* notes. What else could it be?"

"You'd be surprised," Jamie murmured, entering a stall. As she did so, her eye caught Cassie
Newton, a sloe-eyed brunette at the mirrors,
who'd made Mr. Braeburn cry in class earlier by
deliberately asking about his Alzheimer's-
stricken mom. Jamie was planning on doing this
herself one day when she wanted to get the class
off-topic, and Cassie's presumptuousness annoyed her. She made a mental note to have a very
sincere conversation with the Dean of Students
about Cassie's insensitivity toward Mr. Braeburn.

Chantel continued her conversation through
the stall door. "I mean, Brian and Missy have
been going together for almost a year now.
Doesn't that mean anything? Men are such
pricks. They treat women like we're a jockstrap or
something, you know, lend it back and forth."

There was a *flush* and Jamie emerged, still
looking slightly annoyed. "Chantel, men do not
loan jockstraps back and forth. What guy is going
to admit that the jock he just borrowed is too big

for him?" Jamie arched an eyebrow at her friend, then turned toward the mirrors. Damn, she'd forgotten to cover the scar from fencing on her upper right temple. She pulled a strand of hair over it.

"Mmmm," Chantel commented, struck by Jamie's logic.

"Besides," Jamie continued crisply, fluffing her hair, "there's an eleventh commandment, according to men: Thou Shalt Not Wear Anything That Has Touched Another's Genitals. It's the same reason they can't touch tampons."

"Why?" Chantel had no brothers.

Jamie leaned in a bit, conspiratorially. "They're afraid of sticky things. Body fluids, and the like."

"Wow." Chantel seemed impressed.

"Notice how they always have to have a sock by the bed?"

AT LUNCH, over chicken strips and Caesar salads, Josh and Zack compared notes. Josh went first. "I found out they haven't had sex."

Zack dropped his fork. "I sent him running for

the hills just talking about picnic meats. How'd you swing that?"

"*She* told *me*." Josh grinned, not too self-effacingly.

Zack leaned back in his chair, genuinely impressed at his friend's chutzpah.

Josh continued, "It's scary, you know? I think this might actually work. Maybe she's really getting tired of him."

"Maybe ..." Zack pondered his salad dressing packet for a moment, then looked up at Josh. "Let's tighten the screws."

JAMIE, looking miffed as she checked her watch, stood amidst the teeming masses outside the lunchroom, Chantel beside her. Yoshi scampered up, still wearing his trench coat. They exchanged no greeting. He gave Jamie three of Josh's notes to Missy and showed her a picture of Brian and Zack talking outside. Jamie reached into her blouse and extracted a couple of bills, which she surreptitiously handed to him. "*Merci, cheri*. More of the same tomorrow." The picture was actually a little blurry, but it would work for now; maybe

Chantel could ask Robin, the Yearbook Kid she sometimes hung around with, to get some additional shots.

"Useful boy," Chantel commented as Yoshi nodded and scampered away.

"He's using me as a reference when he sends in his application for the CIA," Jamie murmured, examining the notes. Jamie's parents had taken away her flip phone months ago after her morning-long conversation with her broker had sent the stock market into a tailspin. "Looks like the Messrs. Bradshaw and Standish have attempted to put their plan into action. Guess I'd better throw some gas on the fire."

"How? Are you going to help break up Missy and Brian, too?" Chantel's face glowed with the drama of it all.

"Chantel, I do that every day. I just need to be ready to chase the ambulance before the body grows cold."

"Girrrl, I love it when you're nasty," Chantel trilled, tossing her braids back. She dissolved into giggles, and Jamie allowed herself to lose her composure for a moment and join her. It hit her with a momentary pang that she'd been working her enigmatic half-smile for so long, it'd possibly been years since she'd really, truly laughed.

MID-AFTERNOON, Josh pursued Missy down the hallway. She pulled her books to her chest and quickened her steps, but his long legs strode right with her. "Why not?"

"*Why?*"

"Why not?" Josh repeated, like a child asking for more ice cream.

"You're very presumptuous! Why are you so interested in what I do or who I see?"

"'Cause maybe you don't really love him." Josh applied no pressure, no weight, to the words.

"But I do!"

"Then maybe he doesn't really love you."

Missy stopped so abruptly that Josh almost bowled into the guy walking behind him. She looked mad, genuinely mad. "What makes you say a thing like that?"

"Well, it's possible, isn't it?"

"Possible. But you make it sound probable. Or positive."

There was a pause where Josh didn't know what to say, and his conscience gnawed at his insides like a hungry ferret. She looked like she might cry at any moment, and the thought that he was potentially causing her to do so made him feel creepy. In complete honesty, he said, "I just … don't want to see you get hurt. Okay?"

Missy looked at him as though he were one of those toads you're not supposed to lick, unsure whether he was dangerous or just disgusting.

Josh backed away slowly, still keeping eye contact, then turned and strode off. Missy was left standing in the hallway, wooden as a pier, as teenage flotsam and jetsam drifted around her. Someone cried "Smile!" followed by a sudden bright flash. She turned to see a skinny, somewhat androgynous teenager in a college sweatshirt and Greek fisherman's cap, grinning like an idiot. "Yearbook!" they caroled.

Missy fought memories of an old commercial. *This is* so *not a Kodak moment*.

CHAPTER 13

After school, Josh and Zack sat in the bleachers, sprawled over several seats, eyeing the huddle as football practice began. Brian was easy to pick out; he was gesturing to his teammates somewhat agitatedly. His face was flushed peppermint pink and a few strands of sweaty hair stuck to his brow.

"I'm still not sure this is ethical." Josh couldn't help remembering Missy's face as he'd walked away. With an effort, he re-focused on Brian as the huddle broke and Brian jogged to position. The football pants emphasized all the right places, and Josh forced himself not to stare for too long.

"I never said it was." Zack's voice listed across the air to Josh. The sun was warm, and for the moment things seemed right with the world.

Brian fired a spectacular pass down the field, and the receiver sprinted for the end zone. Josh whooped in approval almost automatically; Zack looked over at him, amused. "Guess it's not *too* unethical, huh?"

"What about Missy?" Josh surveyed Zack's face.

"What about her?"

"*You* gotta do something tomorrow. I can only tear apart her cosmic security so much. Start putting the moves on her."

Zack gave the impression of being completely unfazed by this task. "Fine. What are you gonna do about Brian? How're you gonna keep him busy while I play kissy with Missy?" He began rapping: "But Brian can't get *pissy* cause he's too much of a *sissy*, and—"

"I don't *know*."

Josh said it with such vehemence that Zack once again removed his eyes from the field and looked at him.

"This is really scary for me, Zack. I haven't dealt with him for six years except for a couple of postcards; I don't know where to begin. What if we're wrong? What if that was a one-time thing and now he's changed? What if he punches me out?"

Zack was losing patience with Josh's obsessing; lightning flashed in his eyes. *"What if, what if, what if.* My God, you sound like a lawn sprinkler. What if cows could sing? Stop worrying about things that aren't, or didn't, and can't be … and from what we know about Brian, his being with Missy falls into any of these categories." Zack gave his friend a cocky smile.

Josh didn't notice. He was too busy staring moodily at the sky, and Brian was so busy staring at Zack and Josh, that none of them saw several players rush at Brian. *Crunch!*

AFTER PRACTICE, Brian drove Missy home. By the time they reached her house, a sizable chunk of Brian's face was swollen and the color of an eggplant. Neither of them said anything as she exited the car, letting the grim mood hang in the air between them. She turned back at the front door as if to say something, only to have Brian squeal away. She growled in frustration and stomped into the house.

Missy rummaged through the cupboards until she found a large bag of tortilla chips, a package of chocolate cookies, a leftover cheesecake, and—as an afterthought, instead of regular—Diet Cola. She carried her bounty into the living room and collapsed in front of the TV. The old show *The Love Boat* was rerunning on cable; how *exciting* and *new*. She'd just stuffed a mouthful in when the phone rang. "Hello? … Oh, hi. … Right, right … yeah. Tomorrow? … Three-thirty. The Blue Room … okay. Okay, thank you. I'll be there. Goodbye." Missy hung up the phone just as the show began, looking listlessly at all the happy, happy passengers about to embark on their voyages of love—with presumably no icebergs ahead of them.

CHAPTER 14

The Sweet Shoppe specialized in jaw-dropping, gut-busting ice cream sundaes. The booth table groaned under the weight of a banana split the size of a torpedo, a half-finished extra-thick chocolate milkshake, and the remains of a double cheeseburger.

Jamie, crisp as a new dollar bill, was sitting on one side of the table, spectacles balanced on her nose, scribbling in a notebook. "What else do you know?"

Across the table from her, beyond the food, Alex Standish stared at her levelly, knowing full well he needed to be careful with his words. "He doesn't like you very much. He likes Missy. He likes Josh. He doesn't like you or Brian."

"Why does he like Missy so much?" Jamie's pen hovered above the paper. *Maybe Zack had confided in the little twerp.*

"He says she's pretty and doesn't think too much." Alex contemplated a French fry. Jamie was pretty, but Alex could tell she thought about things *way* too much.

Jamie threw down the pen in irritation. "I know that! I can't help it that I'm brilliant and cute instead of dumb and beautiful. People just don't understand that John Locke actually meant something once! There's more to life than the Spice Girls and *SpongeBob SquarePants!*"

"I watch *SpongeBob SquarePants,*" Alex offered helpfully around a mouthful of ice cream. Jamie gave him her best steel-melting glare, but Alex was unimpressed by her theatrics, living as he did with Zack as his brother. "Maybe Zack needs to spend some time with Missy. Then if he finds out she's boring, he'd be with you."

Jamie's eyes narrowed to tiny slits, making her look like something that might crawl out from under his bed at night. Her voice, when she spoke, was very far away. "Hmm. I need an arena

... someplace I can watch it all happen, and then ...”

She began to gather her things together, and her voice was light and breezy once again. "Thank you, Alex, you've been very helpful."

She pulled on her jacket as if trying to convey something, but Alex didn't move.

"What time do you have to be home?"

"I told my mom that Jacob and I were playing *NBA Jam* until six. Can I have another shake?"

"That wasn't part of the deal, kid," Jamie said in what she hoped was a very Barbara Stanwyck way. From the booth behind Alex, Chantel turned, eyeing Jamie with cool amusement over her sunglasses.

"You said you'd pay for information. You haven't paid for me to keep quiet yet," Alex chirped, capping it with a loving smile. He knew he was cute when he smiled. He also knew that he was right.

Jamie was—momentarily—thunderstruck. She surveyed him with something very close to admiration as she re-opened her purse. "Oh ... I like how you think, little man."

CHANTEL DROVE ALEX HOME, dropping him in front of his neighbor's house. He squeezed out of the back seat from behind her, then came around to Jamie's front side window. She leaned out and smiled. "Our secret?"

"Our secret," Alex agreed, extending his hand for the coded handshake Chantel had taught him.

Jamie smiled again, coming dangerously close to meaning it. "Someday you're going to make some lucky girl very happy.

Alex shook his head. "I'm going to live with my friend Jacob when we grow up." He gave a little wave at the two girls, then tore down the block and across the lawn to his house. He dug out his key, and the front door slammed behind him.

Jamie spoke to the air. "They say the best ones are always married or gay."

Chantel finished the thought: "Or under ten years old."

ALEX WANDERED down the hall to the kitchen, where Mark was preparing a casserole for dinner. "Hi, Mark."

"Hi, bud. Back from Jacob's early?" Mark smiled at him, and Alex felt a rush of gratitude for this nice man who didn't try to sneak an extra can of veggies into the casserole when no one was looking, as their mother sometimes did.

"Yeah ..." Alex paused, surveying the cut-up pieces of lamb, the cheese, the leftover mashed potatoes. "Mark, is it worse to tell somebody the truth, even if it causes bad stuff, or to lie and protect somebody?"

Mark smiled at Alex's grave little face. "It's up to the individual, kiddo—sometimes another person doesn't have to be involved; you can lie to protect yourself or tell the truth and take whatever comes with it."

"Oh." Alex turned this over in his mind for a minute. "What would a smaller person do?"

"I think that if a smaller person was protecting a bigger person, that's a really brave small person. I also think that if they have any questions they should ask for advice." Mark raised his eyebrows significantly at Alex, but he said nothing. "But at your age, there's not much bad stuff you can do that you couldn't be forgiven for somehow, so don't sweat it." Mark dabbed a bit of potato on Alex's nose.

Alex wrapped his arms around Mark's torso and rubbed the potato onto his shirt, pausing just a few seconds longer than necessary to soak in the hug. "Thanks, Mark."

"Anytime, sport. That's what I'm here for."

A car door slammed outside, and they heard Beth utter a primal scream of relief at being home for the day. Mark and Alex looked at each other, and Mark said "Operation C." By the time Beth made it into the house, kicked off her shoes, and padded into the kitchen, her youngest son was holding a bouquet of garden-picked flowers, and her boyfriend was holding slippers and a tumbler full of something on the rocks. She laughed and laughed, and Alex knew it was because there was something so nice about people knowing you so well and loving you anyway.

CONSUELLA, the Esaus's housekeeper, was applying an ice pack to Brian's swollen face when Jamie walked in. She relieved Consuella so she could return to prepping dinner and inspected her brother's face carefully. She adjusted the ice pack and said, "One of your nastier ones, bro."

"You seen one worse?" Brian tried not to sound too surly, but he couldn't help it.

"Yeah, on Mom after the Nordstrom's sale." Jamie didn't smile as she said this, but her tone was ironic enough to cause the corners of Brian's mouth to curl slightly upward.

He regarded her cool blue eyes for a moment. "What do you know about Zack?"

"Other than that he's cute and brain-damaged?" Jamie's voice was even lighter; she sounded like she might float away like a balloon bouquet at any moment.

"He was talking to me today and … I had the weirdest feeling he was coming on to me." Brian felt incredibly exposed saying this aloud, but it also brought on a sense of relief. The avid, hungry expression on Zack's face and his gregariousness on the field had gnawed at Brian for hours. Now, saying the words out loud, he felt as though some sort of puzzle piece had just clicked into place.

"Maybe he was," Jamie said casually.

Brian almost fell off his stool. "Why me?"

"Why not? You're not visually offensive." This was Jamie's version of a compliment.

"We've hated each other for years. What's the deal?"

"Maybe he's just being friendly. It's your junior year, maybe he wants to offer peace. 'Make love, not war' and all that nice shit." Jamie was being evasive now, Brian could tell. But what she was hiding, and why, he couldn't fathom.

"Why do I have the feeling you know something?" Brian narrowed his eyes.

"Because you're a paranoid head case," his sister said. Then she smiled, the kind of smile that made Brian feel as though something cold and wriggly was crawling up the back of his neck. Almost as an afterthought, she added, "And because maybe I do." She kissed his bruise gently—whether to make it better or to apply just enough pressure to make it hurt, he couldn't tell—and exited the kitchen.

"That girl is too smart for her own good," Consuella muttered as she peeled the vegetables.

"Or anyone else's," Brian added glumly. All he could think about was his bedroom, his headphones, and a few hours of peace in the dark.

AFTER WATCHING football practice Josh and Zack went back to the Standish household. Josh smiled at the same tile floor, the same house blessing cross-stitch hanging on the wall, the same ugly vase that Zack had made for Beth in third grade. "Not much has changed."

"Still Middle America, in all its vomitizing normality," Zack said. He wasn't usually a snob, but he wasn't blind to the fact that entering his house was considerably different than entering Josh's.

"That why you're still always rebelling against it?"

"Drop dead."

Josh might have returned the insult, but a piercing scream sounded from the end of the hall and Beth came running toward them to sweep Josh into a tremendous hug that made his heart ache in a good way.

Dinner was superb; if Josh hadn't liked Mark almost instantly, the food would've clinched the deal. Mark, for his part, hadn't met Josh before, and Alex didn't remember him except as numerous pictures in the family photo album. Much of dinner was spent reminiscing, and by the time eight o'clock rolled around Beth had almost laughed herself sick.

Josh recalled a certain ill-fated vacation on

which he'd accompanied the Standishes: "And then there was the camping trip Beth and Zack took me on, and I almost drank the kerosene for the stove because she'd put it in a thermos."

Tears rolled down Beth's cheeks as she struggled to catch her breath. "And his *expression*! 'Beth, this Kool-Aid smells funny ...'"

"Giving new meaning to the term 'having gas,'" Zack added, which set his mother off again. She covered her face with her napkin, she was laughing so hard, and this sent Alex into a giggle fit, too. Mark looked from one to the other with a bemused grin; it was a nuthouse, but his affection was clear on his face.

"After that, I was afraid to go anywhere with her, even to the mall," Josh finished.

"Ecchhh." Beth wiped her eyes and fought to recover her composure. "You wouldn't want to—they've redone it, so now of course it's even worse. I ran into Phyllis Esau there last week, and she stole my parking place."

"Her adorable children, the Manson family, in tow, no doubt," Zack jabbed. He and his mother were both getting into a rant that made Josh somewhat uncomfortable, but when he flicked his eyes across the table, he found that he was being observed.

Alex was watching Josh with a very thoughtful expression, and the look in his eyes made Josh uncomfortably remember his talk with Jamie yesterday afternoon. There was a pause as Zack and Beth caught their breath, and Mark diplomatically said, "Who's ready for some dessert?"

After goodbye hugs from Mark, kisses and promises to call Nick soon from Beth, and a viewing of Alex's bedroom and toys, Zack walked Josh to his car.

"Okay, we've survived the first day, dinner with my family ... we're invulnerable. Now we know what to do for tomorrow?"

"Big guns—I target Brian, you go after Missy," Josh said promptly.

"Kee-rect."

"What should I do to, like, connect with him?" Josh twisted his shell necklace around one finger so hard it almost broke.

Zack tried not to sound irritated, and failed. "Kiss his whole face, I don't know! I spoke to the man today for the first time in years; you still probably know him better than I do. Just don't go overboard—the whole school was buzzing about you zapping Missy. Be subtle." Zack's eyes glowed in the porch light.

"How?" Josh looked like a kid again, and Zack felt a twinge of sympathy.

"Do something to remind him how he felt when you guys were twelve."

CHAPTER 15

When Zack was seven years old, he was invited to a birthday party. Everyone in his class was invited, so in a sense, it wasn't that big of a deal; on the other hand, it was for Trent Kowalski, whom everyone knew was the richest kid in school. Second grade was the only time Zack and Josh were in different classes, so Josh wasn't invited. Zack had to go alone.

His father dropped him off outside the house. It was a lovely spring day, and the vast lawn seemed like a green slope rising into eternity. Zack clutched the gift bag to his body as he rang the bell. Inside the bag, a cyborg action figure lay suffocating in magenta tissue paper.

The door opened, and a woman with a black dress and a white apron peered down at him. "Hello Mrs Kowalski, thank you for inviting me to Trent's party," Zack exhaled in one breath. Beth had drilled him on this for half an hour, and he was determined to succeed at it.

"Oh, honey," the woman laughed, "I'm Angela, Mrs. Kowalski's housekeeper. Bless you, you thought I was the missus!" The woman laughed and laughed, her fillings catching the light. She had something stuck in her teeth.

Zack flushed crimson, and he was too aware of his sweaty dress shirt sticking to his body. In the hallway, two kids who'd witnessed the proceedings burst into giggles, and ran into the living room, yelling "You guys! Guess what Zack just did!" He felt Angela's beefy hand guiding him into the room filled with twenty-two screaming kids playing party games, but all he could think about was how stupid he felt.

Things went steadily downhill. Trent opened his gifts, and someone else had given him the same action figure Zack had; of course, Trent opened Zack's gift second. A know-it-all girl in a princess dress turned to Zack and said "Ha, ha!" and Zack, furious, gave her a shove. She fell over and bumped her head, and her wailing brought adults scurrying in. Zack claimed it was an accident, but he felt the questioning eyes, saw one lady shake her head at him, and again he felt hot and embarrassed.

And then came the piñata.

Zack was the eighth kid to have a turn whacking the giant paper-mâché football strung up in the doorway between the dining room and the living room. The piñata was developing a serious crack along one side, and one or two more serious whacks would take it out. He could hear the excited babble of the other kids as an adult tied the bandana around his eyes. His trembling fingers clutched the baseball bat as a lifeline. He stepped forward and swung; whiff, nothing. He swung again and connected with the tip of the piñata, felt it ricochet off the bat and swing away from him. The noise from the kids increased with excitement.

Zack stood perfectly still for a moment and felt a light breeze rush past him; yes, the piñata had just swung back. Now it was swinging away once more. Now ...

Thwack! Zack swung the bat with every ounce of power in his wiry frame. There was a gorgeous *crack*, and then a cacophony of sounds. He'd done it! He'd beaten the piñata! Every voice in the room seemed to cry out at once.

"Oh, look!"

"Oh, my God!"

"Oh, oh!"

He ripped the blindfold from his eyes, and blinked, trying to focus his vision. Yes, there it was! The piñata was on the floor and had indeed burst open. A crowd had gathered around it. Zack threw himself on the shattered husk and grabbed handfuls of hard candy, stuffing his pockets.

Suddenly, he realized no one else was getting candy. Everyone was staring at him. The cries he'd heard weren't excited or happy cries; they were cries of horror and distress. All the kids and the adults were looking at him with accusatory stares, or glares of pure hatred, or simple in-credulity. And there, on the floor, in a heap of crumbs and icing, was Trent's birthday cake—the beautiful multitiered layer cake that had been waiting on the dining table on a series of stands.

Zack looked at the piñata once more and saw one whole side of it was covered with icing and cake crumbs. With a rising sense of panic, Zack suddenly realized what the final whack on the piñata had done, and what the crashing sound really was.

It was a moment beyond terror. Zack stood there, paralyzed, his hands still full of candy from the piñata, as some thirty pairs of eyes pinned him in place like a tiny, wiggling worm to a bulletin board. Then some five pairs of kids—Trent being one of them—burst into tears. A hand grabbed Zack's wrist and pulled him up and away; a blur of faces spun past him, and then he was sitting in a dark room. The door slammed, and the voices were muffled and far away.

Zack stayed in the room for what seemed like an eternity, trying not to cry as his vision blurred over and over. When the door opened, his father was looming over him. He clutched him by the back of the neck, and they were moving again.

Back to the front hallway, his father saying things like "So terribly sorry … don't worry, we'll take care of it … always like this, don't know what to do with him …" His father had parked halfway down the block, and his grip didn't loosen all the way to the car. No one in the house saw when his father slammed him up against the driver's side of their car and gave him five stinging, open-handed slaps on his exposed butt before driving him home in stony silence.

His father made him write a letter of apology to the Kowalskis and sent him to bed without supper, though Beth snuck a sandwich to him later that night. Zack was in bed with his face to the wall, but he heard the *clink* of the china plate as she set it on his dresser, smelled the peanut butter, and felt his mother's gentle touch as she ran her fingers through his hair.

Beth had only gotten an abbreviated version of this story from Zack's father, and for many years later she referred to it as "Zack's introduction to high society," and would laugh whenever she told it to people—*it's in the past, it's just a funny story now, no big deal.* Zack would sit uncharacteristically silent as people laughed and laughed and laughed. She didn't know about the spanking, and Zack never told her.

CHAPTER 16

When Brian was six years old, his aunt asked him to be in her wedding. He would be the ring bearer, and Jamie would be the flower girl. No one asked Jamie if she *wanted* to be the flower girl; they just assumed. Brian, however, they asked, and he responded very gravely, "What would I have to do?"

His Aunt Jan, her husband-to-be, and his mom and dad all looked at each other and laughed. "Why, just what it sounds like!" Aunt Jan threw her head back, eyes sparkling. Brian thought she was the prettiest lady he had ever seen, even prettier than his mother. Aunt Jan looked like Cameron Diaz, and her boyfriend Tad looked like one of those big, handsome men you saw in Sports Illustrated in a football uniform.

Tad ruffled Brian's hair. "It's no big deal, little man. We'll just have rings for your Aunt Jan and me, and before the wedding starts you walk up the aisle carrying them on a little pillow. You stand there until we ask for them. That's pretty much it. Can you handle that?"

"Sure," Brian said. That didn't sound too hard. He was often afraid to try things that he wasn't good at lest he embarrass himself, like jumping off the high dive, but he could handle this.

"And you'll get to wear a nice suit." Aunt Jan smiled at him. "And Jamie will look adorable! Now, Phyl, what do you think about the flowers?"

Brian wasn't interested in the flowers, so he left the adults chattering in the living room and went to find Jamie. She was watching TV and brushing a toy pony's mane. "Guess what! Aunt Jan wants us to be in her wedding!"

Jamie's eyes flicked to him, then back to the screen. Onscreen, Daffy Duck was trying to avoid handling a bomb, which was about to go off in his face. "I don't want to."

"But we get to wear nice clothes," Brian said.

"And you get to be a flower girl, and I'm going to be a ring bearer. It'll be fun."

Jamie's face didn't move. "I don't think so." Her voice was distant, and Brian could tell her mind was somewhere else. There was no point in talking to her when she was like this, so he went off to play in his room.

The next several months went by uneventfully, and the rehearsal went off without a hitch. Their mother must have said something to Jamie, because even though she didn't seem terribly excited about being in the wedding, she wasn't resisting it.

On the wedding day they were all in the back of the church and the string quartet was playing something classical and boring. Tad and his groomsmen were standing at the front of the church and Aunt Jan looked like she was wearing a dress made of white cotton candy. She nudged Jamie gently forward with her little basket of flower petals, and Jamie declared, "I don't want to."

Brian turned around with a mounting sense of terror. He'd heard this tone creep into Jamie's voice on previous occasions, and when it did, there was nothing—not God himself—that could compel her to move. He stood there, in his tiny black jacket and purple bow tie and shorts, awkwardly holding the pillow with the gleaming rings, as various lilac-garbed bridesmaids knelt before Jamie. She was wearing an ivory dress with tiny lavender flowers, but she'd pulled her hairpiece out and now her hair was entangled. Her eyes were a frightening shade of blue that looked like they might fire lightning bolts at any moment.

Lynda, Jan's maid of honor, looked up at Jan with an expression of dismay. "Should I get her mom?"

"No! Honey ..." Aunt Jan bent over and tried to lift Jamie's chin, which was welded to her chest. "Don't you want to take some flowers down the aisle and show everyone your pretty dress?"

"No," Jamie said—so flatly the words might have been two-dimensional.

"But why not?" A plaintive note was creeping into Aunt Jan's voice. At the front of the church, Tad craned his neck and gave them an expectant look.

"I don't want to," Jamie said. "I don't want people looking at me."

"But sweetie—" Aunt Jan looked on the verge of tears. Behind her, the bridesmaids fluttered and cooed like worried doves. She looked at Brian in desperation. "Brian, can you get her to go?"

"No." Brian's voice shook. Jamie's eyes locked on his, and a flicker of something—respect? gratitude?—darted through them and was gone. He looked at Aunt Jan. "If she doesn't want to, she won't. That's it."

"But—" Lynda looked completely bewildered, as if they were all speaking a foreign language.

Something suddenly seized hold of Brian's mind, and he spoke up before he was fully aware that he was speaking. "I can do both, Aunt Jan. It's no big deal." Some bridesmaids were still trying to sweet talk Jamie and getting nowhere; everyone else stared at Brian. He reached over and grabbed the basket of flower petals from Jamie, gripping it in the space between his palm and the pillow of his right hand. It was a little awkward, but not bad; the pillow was light. He dipped his left hand into the basket and sprinkled a few petals, demonstrating. "See? I can hold both of 'em."

"Well—" Lynda was frowning, looking as though something wasn't quite right. But Aunt

Jan, tears glistening in her eyes, bent and kissed the top of his head. "Yes, sweetie, you sure can." She straightened up, dabbing at her eyes and laughing lightly. "You are such a sweet boy!"

Brian glowed. He turned, tall and straight as a toy soldier, and marched through the door and down the aisle of the church toward Tad. He kept the pillow perfectly steady with his right hand, and with his left he scattered a trail of flower petals. As Brian approached, Tad's eyes widened, and then a gigantic grin crossed his face. A ripple of conversation flowed through the guests, but Brian didn't look at anyone else; he kept his eyes in front of him, on the altar and the priest and Tad. Then he was standing right up front, and Tad's hand put gentle pressure on his shoulder, and Tad's warm breath was in Brian's ear. "Nice job, kiddo. Way to go."

Brian flushed with pleasure. He turned and looked behind him, along with the other grooms-men. The bridesmaids were coming down the aisle, smiling at him. Brian's scanning eyes found his parents. They were in the middle of a pew surrounded by people and couldn't get out. His father looked grim, and his mother looked ready to cry. Brian felt a pinprick of fear stab at him.

Had he done something wrong? His mother turned and gestured threateningly toward the back. Jamie was in for it. He, Brian, had done something good. Things were okay.

Then why was his father still frowning at him?

Aunt Jan came down the aisle, and a few hundred cameras went off at once. She looked beautiful, and she was all smiles. Tad stepped down and took her arm, guiding her up to the priest, and it was only then, before Brian turned toward the front with everyone else, that he saw the tiny figure in white at the back of the church. She had closed the door and was leaning against it, watching the proceedings through the glass. She looked very far away, very alone, and—though no one except Brian could tell—very, very angry.

CHAPTER 17

When Josh was eight years old, he was cast as the prince in the school's production of Snow White. He'd mostly been cast because he was one of the few boys who was as tall as Vonnie Bucher, who was cast as Snow, and they would thus contrast satisfactorily with the seven smaller kids playing the dwarfs. It was one of the easiest gigs in the show; show up at the beginning and exchange small talk with Snow at her wishing well, declare his love, then disappear off-stage for an hour until showing up at the finale for the kiss and the awakening.

It was this part that had Josh worried, and he told Zack so. "Why do I have to kiss her?"

"It's how the story goes," Zack said matter-of-factly. He had been cast as Sneezy the dwarf and had been practicing various loud and theatrical sneezes over the past several days, as well as blowing his nose like a French horn. "We saw the movie, remember? He has to kiss her so she can wake up."

"I don't want to kiss her," Josh muttered. "Especially in front of a whole bunch of people. Can't I just blow her a kiss?"

"No, that's moronic. Here, this is what you do." Zack stopped in the middle of the sidewalk where they were walking home from school and gave a quick look in both directions; no one was about. Before Josh knew what was happening, Zack planted his hands on both his shoulders, leaned in, and brushed his lips 1/1000 of an inch in front of Josh's—so close, Josh could smell the peanut butter on Zack's breath.

"There, see? Easy. You don't really have to kiss her, just make it *look* like you did. If you kneel with your back to the audience before you lean over, no one will be able to tell."

Josh was still trying to unlock the gears of his brain from his best friend almost kissing him, but Zack yelled, "Race you home!" and took off running in a blur of red hair, yellow T-shirt, and blue jeans. Josh chased after him, heart pumping as he ran, unsure why he suddenly felt lightheaded. Maybe it was all the running.

On the night of the show, Josh was standing backstage when he suddenly had an attack of nerves, and while Vonnie was singing her opening song, Josh ran to the closest restroom and threw up. Fortunately, he hadn't eaten much dinner, so he was able to recover quickly and get back inside the auditorium for his cue. The audience made an audible "Awww" sound as he proclaimed his love for Snow, and he grinned. He saw the flash as his father took his picture, and his mom, frail from the chemo, was beaming with pride. Backstage, Zack gave him a thumbs-up and a big grin. The audience rustled with excitement when Josh returned at the end of the play and, overcome with grief at losing his beloved, knelt to kiss her.

Unfortunately, Josh had approached the bed from the upstage side, and Zack's plan to have him somewhat obscured from the audience was now shot to hell. Josh looked at Zack, who was kneeling facing him, dwarf cap in hand; Zack's face wore an expression of helpless resignation.

Josh mentally cursed Mrs. Engle, the drama teacher, for even casting him in the stupid play, leaned forward, and very lightly planted an air kiss just below Snow's mouth. However, Josh hadn't rinsed out his mouth from vomiting earlier, and even more unfortunately, Vonnie Bucher had eaten very greasy Chinese food from Panda Express for dinner. The combination of the two sent her into a fit of heaves to rival Josh's earlier that night.

"She's alive!" Zack improvised as he whipped his cap under Vonnie/Snow's mouth and planted his body in front of her so that she was blocked from the audience. "The poison is leaving her body! True love's kiss has saved her! Hip hip hooray!"

"HOORAY! HOORAY!" yelled all the dwarfs, their rejoicing and the audience's applause effectively drowning out Vonnie's upchucking. By the time Vonnie had recovered herself enough for Josh to help her rise from her bed, Zack had tied his extremely moist and smelly hat in a knot and thrown it offstage, where, by some divine injustice, it managed to hit Mrs. Engle. That, of course, is what everyone talked about the next day, and poor Vonnie was called "Vonnie Puker" for the rest of elementary school. No one blamed Josh; his role in things was forgotten, compared to Zack and Vonnie's transgressions.

Josh, however, thought about that moment on the sidewalk with Zack for quite a while, and he wasn't sure why. All he knew was the smell of peanut butter made his heart ache in some weird way.

CHAPTER 18

W hen Missy was eleven years old, she was finally invited to sit with the cool girls in her class at lunch. Why they asked her Missy had no idea; generally, the other girls in her class had only whispered about her, occasionally casting glances at her figure. This was the equivalent of being summoned to the palace.

"Join us this Friday," Raquel, the strawberry blond, said to her, eyes narrowed. "You have to wear something pink, because that's what all the girls in the Groovy Girlz Group, the G.G.G., do. And don't blow us off." Raquel and three of her friends smiled at Missy and walked away.

When Thursday night came, Missy heard

something unexpected downstairs: her father had come home early from his trip to Australia. She almost broke the sound barrier running down the stairs and into his arms, nearly knocking him over as he laughed. Her mother smiled from the dining room doorway. "Hey, be gentle with the old guy!"

"Not a chance," Missy said, her arms around him, inhaling the scent of airline seats. "I thought you weren't coming home till Sunday."

"I wasn't," her father said, stroking her hair. "But I had the chance to move my flight up, and do you know what I want to do tomorrow?" Mr. Hoff wasn't the sort of man one would describe as jovial, but at that moment he looked like he was lit from within by fireflies.

"No," Missy said. Whatever he wanted, she'd give it to him unquestioningly.

"I want to spend the day with my girls," Mr. Hoff said, squeezing her shoulder. "I think I'll make us a huge breakfast, with chocolate chip pancakes. Then I thought we'd drive to the water-front and have lunch somewhere outside. Then a funny afternoon movie, and a barbecued steak for dinner. What do you say?"

"But I have school," Missy said. Anxiety niggled at the back of her mind about Friday, but she couldn't remember what was so important about that day.

"Joe, really," Mrs. Hoff said. "Taking her out on a school day? And I've got ten million things to do tomorrow."

"Cancel 'em," Mr. Hoff said airily. "I have to work all weekend for a presentation on Monday, then I have another trip to Malaysia on Tuesday. I want tomorrow to be all about us as a family. You can get someone from your women's group to take over your duties for the day, and I'll write Missy a note for school. We'll throw in a trip to the aquarium to make it educational."

"Well ..." Mrs. Hoff still looked somewhat perturbed, but when she saw Missy's glowing face she sighed. "I guess I can call Meg and have her take over some of the phone calls and plans for the lunch next week."

"That's the spirit." Mr. Hoff gave Missy another squeeze and a kiss on the top of her head, and took his bag upstairs, whistling.

The day had been wonderful, the best Missy had had since she could remember. Her father had told funny stories over breakfast and done weird impressions that made her laugh and

laugh, and even her mother seemed to relax a little. The weather had been cool and gorgeous, and
they'd walked all over the waterfront, seen the
fish at the aquarium, and everything had unfolded just as her father had hoped. It wasn't
until they were halfway through the movie that
Missy remembered her invitation to have lunch
with the G.G.G.s. *Oh well, it was too late now*. She'd
explain on Monday what had happened.

The glow from the day with her family lasted
until Missy walked in the door of the classroom
on Monday morning before school started and
saw the eight pairs of eyes turn and lock on her.
They rose as one and crowded around her desk
while the teacher was busy writing on the board,
speaking in low, menacing tones, pink and white
lollipops dipped in cyanide.

"Where were you on Friday?"

"I had—a thing to do with my family," Missy
stammered. "I mean, we had a day together. We
went to the aquarium."

"The aquarium?" Raquel's lip curled in disgust. "You chose a day with your parents over
lunch with the coolest girls in school?"

"Well—" Missy fumbled. "My dad came home
early, and we don't see him that often, and—"

"I don't know," Hannah chimed in. "She wants to hang with her parents? Doesn't sound very G.G.G. to me."

"Or maybe," Kara, said frostily, "she was just scared. Scared to be with us. Maybe she's just a big baby. You think she's a big baby?" She looked at Missy as though she'd found her in the wastebasket. "Just a big, fat baby." Her eyes were reptilian.

Missy was immobilized in her chair. Her vision blurred with tears, and she wanted to cry out for the teacher, but it was like one of those nightmares where your voice is gone. The girls all took up Kara's phrase and began to chant it softly, as if casting a spell. "Missy's a baby, just a big fat baby. Oh, look at the baby tears! Oh, we'd better call Mommy and Daddy ..." Their voices were high and thin, like sweet, poisonous gas.

The bell rang, and the girls pulled back, except Raquel, who leaned over and breathed in Missy's ear, all in a rush: "You're a fat, stupid, bitch whore is what you are, and no one in this school likes you. We were just asking you to have lunch to see if you were stupid enough to accept, so we could all laugh at you." Raquel shot a quick look at the teacher to see if she was looking; her back was still turned. Raquel grabbed Missy's left breast and titty-twisted it so hard Missy would've cried out, except that she was weeping, and she couldn't catch her breath.

Raquel moved swiftly away as other students poured into the room; no one seemed to notice Missy. She took a shuddering breath and wiped her face with her arm and did not look up from her desk for the rest of the morning. At lunch, she was the first one out the door to hide in the library; the afternoon was the same as the morning. She said little or nothing the next day, nor the next day, nor the next.

In her closet, Missy had a little bag that she'd bought on the waterfront, filled with souvenirs of the family's day together. There were ticket stubs and stickers and some photos, and she'd bought some cool scrapbooking borders and supplies at the local craft store that weekend to do a wonderful series of pages so that she'd always remember that day. The little bag filled with souvenirs and craft supplies stayed in the back of her closet for a couple of years. When they moved, she threw it out.

CHAPTER 19

When Chantel applied to enter the Watson Academy in seventh grade, she'd just come off a bad sixth-grade experience. She'd worked on a report about bees, and her teacher had accused her of plagiarizing it. "It's too good," the man said, his eyes hard little marbles. "You must've had help, or copied it."

"I didn't." Chantel's eyes widened in shock and horror at the accusation. She'd worked for days on that report. She'd gone to the library for books and watched documentaries on PBS. Anything there was to know about bees, she knew. "Really, Mr. Trainor, I did it all by myself."

"Uh-huh," Mr. Trainor said. His words burned

like acid. "Sure you did. I've had kids like you come through my classes before, and none of them were worth a damn academically. And you just expect me to believe that you're not only smarter than all those other kids I've had, you're also smarter than every other kid in this class? You expect me to believe that?"

"You can believe what you want, but it's the truth," Chantel said, trying to keep her voice strong but wavering a little at the end. She'd never had a conversation like this in her life. "I know what I did, and … I … I know the grade I deserve." A flush of perspiration raced across her forehead, but her mouth was dry.

"Oh, what you deserve," Mr. Trainor said, rolling the word around in his mouth like something he wanted to spit out. "You'll get what you deserve someday, little miss." And he picked up a red pen and wrote "F" on her beautiful report with such force he almost tore the paper.

Two days after Chantel aced the entrance exam at the Watson Christian Academy, she and her parents came back for an orientation meeting. Afterward, a skinny, older white lady stopped her and her parents as they were about to leave. "Mr. and Mrs. Robinson, would you hold on for a moment please? Mr. Falcon, our principal, would like to speak to you."

"Is there a problem?" Mr. Robinson asked, an ever-so-slight edge coming into his voice. Chantel felt her mother's hand tighten on her shoulder.

"No problem at all." The lady smiled at the Robinsons a little too warmly. "We've seen Chantel's scores from her previous school, and we have little doubt that she's definitely Academy material. We were actually wondering if we could speak to you about her modeling for us."

"Modeling?" Mr. Robinson sounded bewildered. Chantel looked at her father; he looked downright confused.

"For our publicity materials," the lady trilled. "Chantel is pretty as well as smart, and we feel that she'd photograph beautifully. She's the epitome of what we want Watson students to embody. Do you have a moment?" She ushered Chantel's parents into an office, simultaneously gesturing to Chantel to have a seat in the lobby. The door closed behind them.

Chantel took a seat on the black vinyl sofa, somewhat dazed. At her last school, they'd underestimated her. Here, she was treated like a visiting dignitary. What was going on?

"They want you for the catalog cover," a voice said next to her. Chantel turned and saw a blond girl sitting on an adjacent couch, sorting student ID cards by surname "Don't worry, it's a good thing."

"Why?" Chantel asked.

The girl didn't look up as she sorted her various piles. "The numbers boost a percentage point or two for every minority kid they enroll. They'll trot you out for the catalog, for videos, for the website, for anything you'll agree to. The good news is you'll probably get to have first crack at the best classes."

"Thank you, but I don't need anyone helping me," Chantel countered. This white girl's know-it-all attitude was off-putting, but almost against her will, Chantel was interested.

"They're not going to help you. You have to be smart enough to get in here on your own." The girl finally looked up, her cool blue eyes revealing nothing. "They're just going to try to make things as nice as possible for you to want to stay. By senior year, you'll be running the show."

"You seem to know a lot about how the system works around here," Chantel said. A glimmer of something sparkled in a corner of her mind that seemed somehow familiar. "I'm Chantel." She offered a handshake.

The girl accepted, and the hand that slipped into hers was small but had a firm, lingering hold, delicate as a spider's web yet just as strong. "I'm Jamie."

CHAPTER 20

The following morning, after dropping Alex off at school, Zack's car squealed into the Academy parking lot with a grinding sound—*damn,* he was in the wrong gear again. As he exited the car and slammed the door, he caught a glimpse of his reflection in the car window and lit a cigarette, striking a male model pose. He hated to admit it, but he really did look good. Knowing that he'd be talking to Missy today, Zack had worn his best dress shirt (purple and black stripes) and slacks. At breakfast, when she saw him, Beth had almost choked on her coffee. Zack had thought fast and said it was for Leadership class; he didn't actually know what the Leadership class was or anyone in it, but considering his mother had actually made an "Ooh" sound and clutched a napkin to her mouth, her eyes filling with happy tears, he figured he'd made a good choice. That, or she'd be calling the FBI shortly, asking them who this stranger was they'd brought in the night to replace her son.

Out of the corner of his eye, Zack saw Josh's car, and his mind exploded like a fireworks factory with a match tossed into it. Josh was sitting on the hood of his car waiting for him, looking completely ill-at-ease, as well he should have: Josh was wearing a formerly oversized *Star Wars* T-shirt from his pre-middle-school days that now encased him tightly, like shrink-wrap. A backward baseball cap completed the look.

Zack threw down his cigarette in disgust. "Jesus, Mary, and Joseph, what goes on in your head?"

Josh looked wounded. "You said to remind him of how he felt when he was twelve. I drew a blank. This was all I could think of."

"A *blank*?! You drew a vacuum! Are you intentionally trying to throw this whole thing down the drain?"

Josh glowered at him. "You're wearing torn

sneakers with your outfit, who the hell are you, Calvin Klein?"

"Okay, truce. Truce!" Zack ripped the cap from Josh's head, a microscopic improvement, but an improvement.

They began to walk toward the Academy's front doors; Brian and Missy were nowhere to be seen, but in the distance, Josh noticed Jamie watch their approach, wince as if in pain, then put on dark glasses and skulk into school.

Zack and Josh walked a little faster.

Chantel, sitting on a bench and applying makeup, watched them pass; all three nodded at each other but exchanged no words.

The boys walked faster still.

Yoshi leaned out of a car and adjusted his sunglasses, and the boys strode even faster.

Suddenly the Yearbook kid popped out of nowhere and took their picture. Zack and Josh broke into a full-fledged run and dashed inside opposite doors of the Academy.

As Josh reached the top of the stairwell, he startled in terror: Jamie was sitting on a ledge, waiting for him like a shapely blonde gargoyle. Her voice pealed like a church bell on Christmas morning: "She sees you when

you're sleeping, she knows when you're awake
…"

She hopped down and hooked her arm
through his as they walked. "How goes?"

"I'm supposed to talk to your brother today,"
Josh muttered.

"Use simple words and short sentences."

"I don't even know what to say," Josh con-
fessed. "Even if I didn't have this plan, I still have
no idea how to approach him."

"Well, you've got one thing in your corner."
Jamie smirked at Josh, sent a death glare at
Cassie Newton while they passed, and just as
quickly returned to her calm, composed smile.
"He already thinks Zack was coming on to him
yesterday. He's so rattled, if you're even slightly
subtle he'll walk right into your hands."

"Aha," Josh said, not feeling "Aha" in the
slightest. "Seduce somebody without actually seducing them."

"Just be yourself, my dear." Jamie dropped
Josh off at Chemistry. "Fate and I will arrange the
rest." She favored him with another of her movie-
star cheek-pats and moved off, students scattering as she passed.

Fate. Yeah, right. The Greeks believed in fate, and

look how that *always turned out.* Josh muttered a curse and entered class.

ZACK SCANNED the Computer Science classroom until he saw Missy. He decisively slid into the seat next to her before she could reserve a spot for Brian. Missy was wearing a strawberry-colored shirt today and had pulled her hair back with a sparkling metal clip. Zack contemplated her earlobes for a moment, wondering what it would be like to nibble on one of them.

Missy's eyes slid toward him, and she nodded ever-so-slightly. She was wearing Christina Aguilera's perfume, and the scent uncoiled itself into Zack's nostrils. He shifted in his chair.

When Brian entered, moments before class began, Missy shot him an apologetic glance. Zack smirked as the very confused Brian made his way to the back, where he sat at a diagonal, eyes locked on the front row.

The teacher, one of those sloppy, sweaty Jabba-the-Hutt types, began to drone on about the syllabus while drawing on the whiteboard, and Zack went for the kill. He leaned over just close enough so that Missy could hear him, and whispered, "Heard it's over."

Missy looked at him in shock. Her voice came out in a whispered screech. *"What?"*

"Heard it's over, you guys are calling it quits. Everyone knows it."

Missy was apoplectic. "Everyone does *not* know it! I don't know it! Who are these phantom people out there who know so much more about my life than I do?"

Zack heard Brian extract a pencil from his notebook, inserted it in his portable sharpener, and began to methodically twist it in circles. Zack giddily wondered if Brian was imagining it was Zack's head.

Zack was smoothly unperturbed by Missy's muffled rage. *"You* told Josh you guys weren't hooking up yet after a year; that's interesting in itself. Then there's the fighting all the time, he treats you badly, he's tense and distracted."

Missy opened her mouth to respond to this, then shut it. What could she say? Zack was right.

Zack continued, "I, on the other hand, am sensitive, attentive, and can give you the best time of your life."

Missy's expression turned to one of outright horror. Zack grinned and blew her a little kiss.

In the back row, Brian broke the pencil in half.

The teacher chose this moment to finally turn from the board, point to a programming question, and wheeze, "How would you solve this, Melissa?"

As if headed for the electric chair, Missy rose, stammered a bit, stopped, looked at Zack. He fluttered his eyelashes at her. She giggled shortly, then suddenly burst into tears and dashed for the door. "Excuse me, I have to—I have—*excuse me* ..."

Zack beamed in victory. Round One, and he didn't even break a sweat.

MISSY DIDN'T RETURN to class. Zack shot out the door when the bell rang, inches ahead of Brian's reach. Jamie appeared out of nowhere and linked her arm through Brian's, quick as light. She shepherded him into the hallway commotion. "Heard Missy went waterworks this morning."

"I don't want to talk about it," Brian muttered.

"I think she's becoming more unstable, Bry. Even you have to admit you two are having big-time problems."

"Meaning what?"

Jamie kept smiling at various people, even though it never reached her eyes. "Meaning it's important that you guys dig in your hooks and show everyone once and for all that you are two united as one, that clean-cut heterosexuality marches on, that you two are *still* the once and future social rulers of the Academy."

"How are we going to do that?" Brian pushed, waiting for the other shoe to drop. With Jamie, there was *always* another shoe. A closetful of shoes.

"I'm going to help you. When Mom and Dad go on their weekend anniversary trip, *we* are going to throw a party." She stroked her brother's face and sailed off, leaving him—as usual—completely nonplussed and agitated.

CHAPTER 21

"*A party?!*"

Josh said it so loudly that some of the stoners at the next table actually snapped to attention and stared at them. They'd chosen a corner table in the cafeteria so as not to be too obvious, but now Josh was on the verge of spilling the beans anyway.

Across the table from him, Jamie nodded carefully, like a trial lawyer hearing expert testimony, but keeping an eye on the clock. The note she'd sent to Zack from the office to discuss his immunizations was only going to buy them so much time.

Josh continued, "What's the point?"

"It's the perfect environment for everyone to be in the same place at the same time, and for you and me to manipulate things the way we want them to go."

"Manipulate people, you mean," Josh corrected.

"If you want to get technical."

"I think we should, based on how much we trust each other."

There was a mutual flash of teeth, as though both were posing for paparazzi, then they returned to their wary expressions.

Jamie re-commandeered the conversation. "*Ahem.* Anyway. I shall exert my considerable powers of persuasion over my brother and Melissa, and this Saturday night—no wait, that's the back-to-school masquerade ball. *Drat.* Oh, well, Friday. My parents leave for a twentieth wedding anniversary trip tomorrow night, not to return till Sunday evening, and I'm sure Consuella won't mind. It's just a matter of getting Missy drunk and vulnerable, then together with Zack, thus making Brian insanely drunk and melancholy. Then you make your move, and I and a bit of over-the-counter pharmaceuticals make ours."

"What are you talking about?" Josh was al-most afraid to ask.

"A little extra incentive to make sure Mr. Stan-dish never finishes carrying out his plan. Missy will wake up many hours later down on the couch, Zack will wake up with me. Easy. You— it's your ball game."

Strike three, I'm out. Out. He'd walked into the Academy determined to be "out" if anyone ever asked about his love life, and look where that had gotten him. First Zack, then Jamie, and now here he was being offered Brian on a silver platter, like the beheaded John the Baptist. All he had to do was go along with the plan.

The burrito he'd half-eaten churned in his stomach. Even though he knew it could backfire, Josh had to know. "Just out of curiosity—you don't have a single shred of decency, integrity, or compassion in your body, do you?"

Jamie's expression was as smooth and unruffled as a frozen pond at daybreak. "What's your point?"

As Josh stared at her, a plastic tray loaded with food *banged* itself down next to them. Both turned and met Brian's suspicious gaze. Jamie excused herself a little too brightly, gathered the remnants of her lunch, and retreated—presumably, Josh thought, to Mt. Doom to plot her recapture of the Ring.

There was a silence—not an uncomfortable one, just empty—as Brian went to town on his salad. Josh watched him. A strange ritual of look-then-look away followed, as neither seemed quite willing to make extensive eye contact.

Finally, Brian's blue eyes locked onto his gaze. "What?"

"Nothing ..." Josh swallowed. "Just remembering."

"Remembering what?" Brian was also remembering things, but he wasn't sure what Josh was referring to.

"Stuff." Another pause. "I've wanted to talk to you for three days."

"Why didn't you?"

"I didn't know what to say." No point in hedging.

"Do you now?" Brian's eyes were unlike Jamie's, Josh noticed, remembering that first day in the theater. Her cool blue made it difficult to read her emotions; Brian's were a deeper shade of cerulean that seemed to intensify what he was thinking or feeling. Right now, they looked like they might bore right through Josh.

Josh shrugged a little, then grinned, embarrassed. "No … but I don't mind if you don't."

Brian shook his head no.

There was another uncomfortable pause.

Josh grinned a little wider. "I saw you play the other day."

Brian laughed; his teeth, Josh noticed, were still perfect, no fillings. Brian's laugh was also a little embarrassed. "Yeah … well. You mean the one where I got sacked?"

"No, the great one. Well, *and* where you got sacked." Josh laughed.

And then he was talking too freely, he didn't notice how quickly the words were tumbling out of his mouth as he deliberately kept his gaze just past Brian's ear on the windows and the blue, blue sky beyond them. "Remember that time you spent the night at my house in sixth grade, and we laid in our sleeping bags and stayed up 'till four in the morning, talking about movies and what we wanted to be when we grew up? I wanted to be a lawyer, and if you didn't become a football star, you'd be a pilot …"

They'd been talking and talking and then not

talking not saying anything just staring and staring and then reaching out slowly oh so slowly and touching Brian's skinny shoulder and his neck and the little strip of skin right under his hair and not knowing what he wanted and suddenly thinking he did know what he wanted and blue eyes met brown, blue eyes filled with fear and shame and Brian rolled over and said Goodnight, but Josh knew he wasn't asleep.

"When we were kids, I knew exactly what I wanted, it was really clear. Now I'm supposed to be thinking about college and a career and everything, and all I know is I want to be happy. That's so simple, but … it's all there is. The rest of it is all bullshit if you don't know who you are and what you want … and what makes you happy."

Josh looked right at Brian, looked deep in his eyes, let the cerulean blue fill his heart like a gigantic Hawaiian wave, and said, "Do you know what I mean?"

Brian's face was a mask of barely controlled despair. He wadded up his napkin and said, very carefully, "I think … I'm just going to be a pilot. It's easier than trying to be happy—and to be honest, I'm not sure I know how."

Brian rose, took his tray, and headed toward

the exit. In the distance, Zack stood with a tray of food; he watched Brian go, then looked at his friend with an expression of sympathy. He might not ever understand parts of Josh's sex life, but Zack knew all too well what it was like to feel alone and shut out.

Bruised hearts were universal.

CHAPTER 22

God, Jamie hated gym. Mental exertion was quite enough for her; sweating with other people was unthinkable. Fortunately, Chantel was in her class as well, so they could at least keep each other company in their misery. As the coach was blowing his whistle in some warped idea of an incentive, Jamie and Chantel were jogging around the track. Jamie was giving Chantel the latest updates. "So that's where we're at. Spread the word about the party? Tell Robin to bring the camera and lots of film."

"What am I, a P.A. system?" Chantel complained, swiping at the perspiration on her forehead.

"I thought that's why your name was Chan*tel*; you run around and blab everything to everyone," Jamie huffed. They jogged off the track, Jamie intercepting a handful of notes and pictures from Yoshi as they headed toward the locker room.

Chantel was an insatiable gossip, it was true, but she didn't tell everyone everything. She just let Jamie think she did.

CHAPTER 23

Zack wandered among the stacks in the library, wondering which of the newly featured novels on display might have some racy scenes to peruse. Without warning, a hand reached out, grabbed his collar, and hurled him against the wall.

Zack fumbled for words as his head slammed into the wall, just under the oversized poster proclaiming READ in large colorful letters. "Brian, I can explain—"

Missy interrupted him with a clenched-teeth growl. "Shut *up*!"

A dull, aching throb reared in the base of his skull. Missy's cheeks were hot pink, her hair was moist with perspiration, and her eyes were blazing with anger. She looked like she might clock him good and hard. Zack was simultaneously in pain, somewhat afraid, and more than a little turned on.

Missy's words came in a torrent. "I have *never* been so humiliated as I was this morning. Now I want to know what the hell you and Josh are up to and why you keep harassing me! Brian and I are going through a difficult time right now, and outside pressure is very difficult for him to handle. Now please—if you seriously know something, *please* let me know. *Now*."

Could it be so simple? Zack saw his future handed to him on a silver platter, complete with a peeled-radish rosebud. He managed to suppress a smile, kept his eyes on Missy as he fixed an expression of care and concern on his face, and let a note of deep sincerity slide into his voice.

"Well, it's just that, you know, I hear from a lot of different sources. And the general report from the field is that Brian is getting tired and bored. It's stale. He didn't even eat with you today, did he? It's nothing you've done. Any relationship that's been going on this long without …

something happening ... is going to dry up eventually."

Missy chewed on her lip for a moment, letting her eyes drift to a large copy of *The History of Comic Books in America* off to his left. Her eyes filled with doubt, and when she spoke it was as though she were trying to translate her thoughts.

"I was so nervous about STDs and everything ... You think I *should* have sex with him?"

Red alert! Zack's tongue body-slammed his brain while he tried to calm the internal hurricane. "No, no, no. I mean—uh—it's wrong to force things with people. You gotta let it be natural, with someone who can treat you like you should be treated. You seem like ... a really good person." Well, that at least was true.

Missy gradually released her hold on him. Zack gently reached out and placed his hand on her arm and offered the capper. "I just—I want to make sure you're happy."

It could've been something from a Nicholas Sparks novel. He let the words sink in, let her gaze drift back to his, before he slid his hand down her arm, her wrist, her hand carefully—oh so carefully—and held her gaze, smoldering at her for a moment.

Missy drew a long, shuddering breath, and Zack felt as though he'd been given some sort of unspoken, invisible test. For possibly the first time in his life, it was one he'd aced.

AT THREE O'CLOCK Chantel bopped among the tide of teenagers, extolling the party this Friday night at Jamie and Brian's. She moved easily from group to group, her face ablaze with excitement; no cheerleader could've conveyed more enthusiasm. Chantel started with the most popular clique in school, which would set the bar nice and high; moved on to the artsy types and the jocks, then stoners, the Goths, even the geeks and nerds. It was like watching a gorgeous pinball ricocheting off different bumpers.

In a quiet alcove, just near enough to hear but far enough away to be inconspicuous, Jamie sat reading *Les Liasons Dangereuses* and monitoring the situation.

Brian was walking down an upstairs hallway when a guy he barely knew raced by, yelling, "Hey, heard y'all are throwing a bash this Friday, dude. Way to go!" By the time Brian had reached the stairs, three other people had passed him, discussing this unknown event.

Understanding came slowly to him, defrosting in his mind like the alien in *The Thing*. He grumbled, "Jamie!"

As his stride picked up speed and purpose, he almost ran into his girlfriend, exiting flushed and confused from another hallway. "What's all this about you guys having a party this Friday?"

"I don't want to talk about it," Brian growled, grabbing Missy's arm and trying to pull her close.

"Oh, *God*!" Missy yanked her arm back and stormed away, leaving several kids staring after her and Brian with open mouths. He turned crimson, then purple, then white, then strode away toward his car.

IN A SIDE HALLWAY, Logan raced past Zack and Josh, and paused long enough to punch Zack on the arm. "Dudes! Party at Jamie and Brian's this Friday after the game! Get ready to rage!" He continued on in a streak of black.

"Notice how it's never 'Brian and Jamie?'" Josh asked rhetorically. Like that would happen in their lifetimes. Jamie would sooner swallow cyanide than put someone else first or admit error, even if Brian was a football star. Billing was everything.

Zack wasn't listening. He was still processing Logan's announcement and applying it to his recent conversation with Missy. "It's perfect. A social environment with lots of distractions."

"You actually think this is a good idea?" Josh was unnerved. Having Jamie and Zack on the same page gave him serious pause. *Could Jamie be right? Was Zack actually a good match for her?*

"If we work it just right. The trick is, hopefully Brian will finally break it off with Missy, then she'll come running to me for support. I need you to apply as much pressure as possible, Josh."

"Now, wait a—"

"Once she's mine, word'll spread. He'll turn to you for support, then … perfect!" Zack punctuated this with a weird, gleeful little laugh, like the Penguin facing Batman.

"Déjà vu," Josh said, almost wearily. This was all unfolding like some sort of potential bad dream, but he felt powerless to stop it.

"You know, I never knew how susceptible

people are before. If I could've come up with this plan ages ago, who knows what might've happened." Zack did a little end-zone dance, his eyes glittering. With his red hair and his short stature, he bore an uncomfortable resemblance to Rumpelstiltskin. "*And* no one suspects us, my brotha. We're the only ones who know!" He punched Josh's arm; it was going to bruise at this rate.

"Sure, Zack," Josh sighed. He remembered once again the portable hide-a-bed incident and wondered for the millionth time why he could never say no to his supposed best friend.

A teacher walked past with her arms full of notes and entered a sky-blue conference room. "Shall we get started?" She pulled the door shut behind her, and Josh barely noticed the sign marked "Private" decorating the door. Her voice was muffled as she continued her speech, and soon her voice had drifted too far to hear at all.

CHAPTER 24

Brian hated his shrink's office. He hated the oh-so-modest African violets in the little hand-painted pots, he hated the big wooden desk that looked antique but was probably from Costco, and he hated the windows with the gray blinds always closed. Most of all, he hated feeling like he did when the doctor would talk to him in that musing, contemplative way that made Brian want to stand up and scream, rip his shirt off, leap for the windows and shatter the glass that lay hidden behind the blinds. Would he then fall, plummet down seven stories to earth and splatter himself all over the sidewalk, like raspberry jam?

Or would he catch an updraft and soar away into the clouds?

These were, ironically, not the sort of thoughts he liked to discuss with his therapist.

The man had been writing for a little bit now, the *skritch skritch* of the pen the only sound in the silence. He stopped and looked at Brian, tried to smile a little. "Why a pilot?"

"Because they're always in control." Brian studied his chewed-up fingertips, the pattern in the carpet, the desk set. Anywhere but the man's face. "Because they fly high up above it all ... because they're respected."

"In what way?"

"They take care of people. They're responsible for people, y'know? They've got everyone's lives in their hands ... and they're okay with that. That's who they are. That's what they do."

In an alternate reality, Brian imagined joining the Air Force. He saw himself at cadet graduation, ramrod straight in his uniform, medals glistening in the sun. He saw his father and mother smiling and waving at him, his father turning to the man next to him and saying, "That's my boy down there!" He did not see Jamie anywhere; she was probably being tried for war crimes in The Hague.

"Do you see yourself as taking care of people? Taking responsibility for them?"

God, this guy never shut up. Brian tried desperately to remain polite, to be a Nice Boy. "I think so. I'd like to think so. I want to, at least." A weird flash of Aunt Jan's wedding shot through Brian's mind and was gone.

"Do you think you do that so you don't have to worry about taking care of yourself?"

How the holy hell would Brian know? "I dunno. Maybe … by taking care of other people, I could take care of myself." He sounded like a poster boy for Codependents R Us.

"Or do you just wish you could fly away from all your problems?" The light hit the man's glasses, so Brian couldn't see his eyes.

A rising sense of panic began to grow in Brian's chest. "I didn't mean to—I was just thinking about … I don't know."

"Are you still having anxiety attacks?" The man was trying to come off as compassionate, but he came across as overly solicitous and nosy.

"I think I'm about to have one right now,"

Brian said, fighting to keep his voice from quavering. In the midst of all the garbage in his head, at least he knew one real and true thing.

CHAPTER 25

Long after school ended, Zack was in his room slogging through *Twelfth Night*. It wasn't a bad play, just a simplistic one; if someone was going to play *him* like Toby, Maria, and Andrew played Malvolio, Zack was sure he would have figured it out in the early stages. He was complimenting himself on his ingenuity when the phone rang. "Speak!" he ordered.

"Arf, arf. Wanna biscuit," Josh deadpanned.

"Hey, Fido. What's going down?"

"How about me, on George Clooney?" Josh had had a couple of sips of wine with dinner, and the giddiness made him bold.

"Don't mess with my mind, Josh." Despite his

professed blasé-ness about Josh's sexuality, certain details and images still freaked Zack out.

"You wouldn't want me to mess with anything else," Josh said, almost sulkily. There was a brief pause where both boys reoriented themselves, then he continued: "What's the game plan for tomorrow, mastermind?"

The slight dig was lost on Zack. "Take a step back and cool it—they'll get overly suspicious if we push. I suggest we grill Jamie and find out more about this party she's throwing. Other than that, no pressure. Laying low will only confuse them more."

"Aye-aye, Captain."

"Zack out."

Zack hung up the phone and rolled over, returning to his homework and immersing himself in Illyria. In his kitchen, Josh gently banged his head against the cupboard a couple of times; Nick, entering with the dinner dishes, shot him a strange look.

IN HIS ROOM, Brian was leafing through yet another self-help book, this one called *You! Find-*

ing, Fixing, and Forgiving the Person Inside. His shrink had recommended it, and Brian figured if he could pull a couple of good quotes out of it, he'd skate through a couple of therapy sessions. A pile of homework he really needed to be doing lay at his feet, and he looked at it dolefully. The phone rang, and he reached for it. "H'lo …"

"I just wanted to see how you were." Missy's voice was soft and distant, almost hesitant.

"Okay …" Brian gripped the phone as though it were a ship's lifeline in the middle of a storm at sea. His knuckles turned white. "How was your afternoon?"

"Okay." Pause. "Listen, Bry, I'm going to have my father drop me off at school tomorrow on his way to work, so you don't have to pick me up."

There was a long pause, and Brian wondered if they'd been disconnected. He spoke again, his voice soft and vaguely defeated. "Okay."

"Okay." They were saying "okay" too much; it wasn't okay. "Well. I guess I'll see you around to-morrow." Her voice sounded as cool and remote as Pluto.

"Yeah. See you."

Click. Dial tone. Brian rolled over and, with another final click, turned off the light.

CHAPTER 26

When Josh and his dad had lived in Los Angeles, Josh took the bus to the Gay and Lesbian Center once a week to attend the youth group. His own school didn't have a Gay-Straight Alliance, and he wasn't courageous enough to start one on his own. Nonetheless, he'd already come out to his dad at fourteen; Nick said "Oh," misted up for about five minutes, then deftly regained his balance. Nick even helped him look online for gay youth resources in L.A. County and drove him to one or two till Josh figured out which one was most accessible by bus.

It was an interesting mix of kids, with girls outnumbering boys two to one (no surprise there), and a lot of kids who were non-white, poor, and even homeless. Josh felt somewhat out of place sitting on the folding chairs in the meeting room, as the various baby dykes, lipstick lesbians, and too-sensitive Goth and Emo boys with too much eye makeup chattered among themselves. He mostly listened, eyes scanning the various faces, feeling vaguely guilty for having a comfortable home and an accepting dad. Some of these kids had been disowned by their parents or had run away from home rather than come out to them. Darryl, a sharp-tongued African-American boy who was probably 115 pounds soaking wet even though he was sixteen, had been beaten up by his dad and brothers and dropped along the highway outside of Phoenix.

Josh listened to it all and took mental notes. He knew he wasn't "enough" of anything to stand out in this bunch; he was just Josh, himself. Frankly, after some seven years of playing Straight Man in The Zack Standish Show, it was enough.

And then one Thursday afternoon, the most beautiful young man Josh had ever seen had walked into the meeting. He'd worn a black leather jacket, and his hair was chestnut-brown and wavy. He'd looked around the room at the different kids, and then looked very deliberately at Josh, sauntered over, and sat on the metal chair next to him, even though there were at least three or four other empty chairs open around the circle. Josh felt his mouth go dry and his heart rate speed up. He looked out of the corner of his eye at the boy, who was surveying him with jade-green eyes, and a big, slow grin spreading across his face.

The group talked about queer rights vs. other social justice issues for an hour, and as usual Josh mostly listened, occasionally speaking up when he agreed with a good point. When the meeting ended, the boy leaned over to Josh and murmured, "You got a phone?"

"No," Josh said, flushing bright red. He knew he was a freak in Los Angeles; every single person had a phone, even kids in kindergarten. But he didn't have any friends at his school significant enough to want to call them at any moment of the day.

"Too bad," the stranger said languidly. He

smiled again, and Josh's stomach skipped. "I was going to give you my digits and program you into mine. Got a home number?"

Josh did, as well as a piece of paper. The boy's name was Garrett, he was sixteen and a model, and he usually attended a group at another location, but he didn't care for them. "No one there's as cute as you," Garrett said matter-of-factly, as if Josh was used to hearing this on a daily basis. He asked Josh for a date for the following Friday to see the newly-Oscared "Braveheart," and Josh blushingly, fumblingly assented.

Come Friday night, Garrett was forty-five minutes late meeting him at the theater, so they missed the movie. He showed up in a silver Lexus, phone at his ear, and his first words to Josh were, "Sorry I'm late, but I hear this movie sucks anyway. Wanna go to a party? Some friends of mine who live in Topanga Canyon are throwing one."

Josh was apprehensive. He'd told his father he was going to the movies and would be home by eleven o'clock; he knew Nick would be sitting alone at the kitchen table, working on his laptop, waiting for him.

"Could you get me back to Westlake in time?"

"Oh sure," Garrett said, eyes never leaving the road, phone still at his temple. "No problem."

The night sped by them in a blur of neon and heat.

The party was filled with the most beautiful teenagers on the planet; not even the kids at Josh's high school in Sherman Oaks looked like this crowd. *Hollywood inbreeding.* Most of the lights were off, except for those in the pool and various flickering torches, and the music—some sort of reggae—was deafening.

Garrett had ushered Josh in, grabbed a Bacardi Ice for him, steered him to a couch the size of Cleopatra's barge, and said, "I'll be right back."

For the next hour, Josh sat staring at the flickering waves of blue from the pool lapping against the reflections of the light, as laughter and breaking glass went on all around him. People sat down next to him, realized they didn't know him, ignored him, and left. Garrett finally reappeared with some shirtless kid even skinnier than Darryl, and even more gorgeous than Garrett. Garrett's pupils looked like overripe plums. "This is Jakob. He's up for a three-way with us. You game?"

"I haven't even had a two-way," Josh said,

trying not to yell it too loudly but also trying to be heard over the music. "*We* haven't even had a two-way. I don't think this is my scene."

"Your scene?" Garret's eyes blinked once or twice; his speech was thick. "Hey, no offense, I mean, you're cute and everything, but let's face it, you could lose twenty or thirty pounds. Jakob's modeled for Abercrombie. I just didn't want to completely drop you for the evening, so I thought maybe you'd like to join us."

"Nope." Josh stood. "I'm good. Thank you." To Jakob, Josh said, "Enjoy your … way. However many of you there are." Josh would've said a few more things, but Garrett's tongue was already patrolling the roof of Jakob's mouth. Without looking at Josh, Garrett handed him a fifty-dollar bill, mumbled "Cab fare" around Jakob's tongue, and dragged the two of them away.

Josh pushed his way through the mass of people to the kitchen where he found a phone, called a cab, and waited for them at the bottom of the driveway. He arrived home at 11:15 p.m., apologized to Nick, said the movie had been delayed due to technical problems and was terrible anyway, wished his father goodnight, went to his room, got into bed, cried for a few minutes, then fell restlessly asleep.

The following week, Josh entered his school's lip-sync contest. He wore a gray T-shirt and gray slacks, and, upon entering the blinding white spotlight onstage, proceeded to curl himself into a ball. Then the song "I am a Rock" by Simon and Garfunkel, a favorite of his mother's, started.

He didn't move, didn't look up. The entire school rocked with laughter. No one had noticed this kid for two years; where had he found the brains to come up with something like this? The roar at the end of the song washed into his ears like the tide, followed by stamps and whistles that shook the entire gym. For possibly the first time in his life, Josh felt almost triumphant.

They'd had to disqualify him, unfortunately, since Josh hadn't actually moved his lips to the words; the entire student body booed the decision, and Josh was subsequently given a special "Judge's Award," a fifty-dollar gift card to Claim Jumper.

Josh didn't go back to the youth group, and he didn't ever see Garrett again. For the next year and a half, people he barely knew would pass him in the hall and punch him on the arm appreciatively, exclaiming, "'I am a rock!' Dude, you are too funny." They'd laugh and laugh with appreciation, and after a while Josh almost thought in retrospect that it was funny too, the whole experience that inspired him was funny, that his heart wasn't really a cold, hard lump of granite.

CHAPTER 27

Wayne Ratzinger was going to be bad news. Everyone affiliated with Mrs. Jacobs' fourth-grade class sensed it: the kids, the teacher, the custodian, the school secretary, the crossing guard, the principal. Even the paper bag puppets the kids had made earlier in the year seemed to feel it, looking down at the weaselly, smelly, mean-eyed kid in the snot-stained T-shirt with fear in their Magic Marker eyes.

Wayne had shown up in the second week of January, stalking to his seat with barely a glance at anyone, his boots clattering on the floor. He threw himself down in his chair, and almost immediately hocked a surreptitious loogie into the hair of the kid sitting in front of him: Josh Bradshaw.

Josh turned slowly, very slowly, wiping the back of his head with his sleeve, but keeping his face carefully impassive. One aisle over, however, Zack Standish had no such self-restraint and immediately socked Wayne in the arm. Mrs. Jacobs only saw this part, of course, and promptly hauled Zack off to the principal. Josh spent the next two hours listening to the dark whispers coming from behind him, whispers from a kid who had never seen him before yet somehow seemed to sense his every secret thought—and hated him for it.

At recess, Josh met Zack behind the portable classrooms on the far end of the school grounds.

"We've got to get him," Zack growled, eyeing the kid through the gap in the buildings. In the distance, Wayne stood on a chunk of concrete, doing faux-Ninja moves with a set of nunchucks as the other kids kept their distance. Zack had been given fifty sentences ("I will not hit other kids in class"), but at least the principal hadn't denied him this tiny scrap of liberty.

"I dunno," Josh said heavily. He was bigger and stronger than Wayne—and Zack for that matter—but sometimes he seemed afraid of his own bulk, and hesitant to use force. "Maybe he's just new and trying to act all tough."

"Maybe," Zack said, trying to keep his voice even. "The back of your hair is all stuck together with dried spit."

"It is?"

"Yeah." Pause. "What happened while I was in the office?"

"Nothing. He just called me some names."

"What kind of names?"

Josh shifted. "Just insults and stuff."

Zack began pacing, a sure sign that he was plotting something. "Here's the deal. I'll talk to him later today, apologize, and say that I'm sorry we got off on the wrong foot. I'll ask him if he knows about the trail through the woods by Penn's Creek, and if he wants me to show him a shortcut home."

"Where does he live?"

"The Townsend trailer park. His paperwork was on the secretary's desk, so I checked it when she and the principal were talking in his office before he called me in."

"Jeez." Josh contemplated this for a moment. "Then what do we do?"

"You'll have already left school and hightailed it to the creek. I'll take him the long way to allow you plenty of time to get there ahead of us and make sure most of the kids have cleared out. When we get up near you, jump out and we'll work him over."

Josh was stunned, then glad for a fleeting second that he didn't have Zack for an enemy. "Sounds like a plan, man."

ZACK APPROACHED Wayne in front of a whole bunch of kids as they came back inside, apologizing grandly to make sure his generous gesture was noted by multiple witnesses *and* Mrs. Jacobs. Wayne, still shifty-eyed, shook Zack's hand and mumbled, "'S okay. I just couldn't see around that big dumbshit in front of me, so I went hair-trigger on his ass. He a friend of yours?"

"Naw," Zack said, dying inside, as Josh listened inconspicuously while inspecting the garter snake's tank. He made his voice as ugly and tough as Wayne's. "I don't know him. I just don't like kids beating each other up for no reason. Cool?"

"Cool." Wayne nodded and slid into his seat. An uneasy truce held for the afternoon, but Zack noticed that every time Wayne had to accept a piece of paper being passed back from Josh, he received it with murmured invective like "Hope this doesn't give me any of your gay germs, fat boy." Zack clenched his fists so hard the nails drew blood on the inside of his palms.

At three o'clock the school emptied, and sure enough, Wayne was planning on walking home. Josh, with a brief meaningful look back, disappeared out the door, and Zack, swaggering over, asked Wayne if he wanted him to show him the shortcut home: "I'll help you avoid all the spazzes and losers and shit." It made Zack a little uneasy how quickly these words rolled off his tongue, how easy it was to stride a little faster, talk a little louder, swear a little more. In the hallway, for effect, Zack even shoved some geeky little blond kid named Brian, who always seemed scared of his shadow, and he and Wayne shared a heartless laugh at the boy as he dropped his binder and nearly burst into tears.

The woods were gray and cool, with gnarled black tree branches reaching like claws toward the empty sky. Wayne talked to Zack, telling him about his old man not being able to hold a job, and how mean he'd get after a couple of shots of liquor, and how his mom had to work two jobs to support them, and how Wayne's cat No Name was his only real friend. Zack was just beginning to get a nauseous feeling in his gut when the clouds obscured the sickly, pale sun and Josh stepped into the path ahead of them. He looked like a silhouette, and his face was in shadow.

Wayne started, and his face, which had begun to relax into something almost friendly during their walk, resumed its sneer. He looked at Zack for reassurance, then at Josh. His words came, jagged and wounding, like a broken bottle's edge: "What do you want, you big fat turd?"

Josh took a step. He was looking right at them, but his face was a blank; only his eyes conveyed the depths of hurt and anger. Wayne turned to Zack, a nasty smile beginning to creep across his face, but it died when he saw Zack's expression. He looked like a guy who's just realized that he's outnumbered, and the only person he thought was an ally was about to screw him.

Wayne turned to run, but he wasn't fast enough. Zack got him by the shirt and tripped him, and in a few quick strides Josh joined the fray. There was punching and shouting from Zack, swearing and kicking from Wayne, panting and grunting from Josh, and a cloud of dust. A few moments later, Zack sat on Wayne's chest and arms and beat him about the face, while Josh sat on his lower legs, holding them still so they wouldn't thrash. Wayne was unloading every profanity known to man, and some Zack and Josh had never heard before. Far above the fray, a bird screeched in what sounded like mocking laughter.

Zack growled, "Keep holding him down." Josh, facing Wayne's feet, did his best, though the kid still thrashed around. Zack seemed to be sitting on Wayne's arms, his back against Josh's. Behind him, Josh heard a *zzzzzzziippppp* and then screaming. Wayne had gone from cussing and hollering to a sound that gave Josh chills. The screaming stopped, muffled for a few moments, and then resumed, and transformed into choking and gasping. Finally, with one final spasm, the body convulsed and threw Josh off.

Josh rolled over in the dust and felt a quick kick in his legs as someone stumbled over them. Then there was a wailing sound, a high, sobbing cry that sounded like a wounded animal running off to die, and Wayne disappeared, running blindly down the trail into the distance. Hiccupping, choking sobs and the sound of someone spitting floated back to them on a soft, cold breeze.

Josh looked over at Zack, who was sporting several cuts and scrapes on his face and arms, and his clothes were filthy. Zack was looking after Wayne with an expression of eerie calm, and though his breathing came heavy and fast, he seemed curiously unruffled.

They stood that way for a while, staring after Wayne in silence, until Josh finally said, "What happened?"

"Peed on his face," Zack said, very coolly, as though it was a completely normal thing. "Got him real good. Think I even sprayed in his mouth."

Josh was so stunned at the awfulness of this that he could barely register it. He somehow got to his feet and looked once more down the path where Wayne had fled, then back at his friend, his friend who had done this terrible thing for him. He didn't know whether to thank him or to run himself.

Finally, he mumbled, "Guess he won't bother us anymore."

"Guess not," Zack said agreeably, zipping his fly shut. He knew Wayne wouldn't talk; what kid would admit such a thing had happened to them? True, Zack'd have to explain his face and the condition of his clothes to Beth, but maybe she'd still be at work and he'd have time to change. It was worth it to teach the little bastard a lesson. *No one messes with my friend. No one.*

Why was Josh looking at him like that?

They didn't say anything else as they walked out of the woods, until they reached the corner where they separated for home. Zack said, "See you."

Josh said, "Yeah, later."

That was all.

Wayne stayed at school for another two months. He never said anything, never looked at anyone, just acted as if he'd gone catatonic. After spring break, he never came back. With two exceptions, no one else in the class ever thought about him again.

CHAPTER 28

Ms. Jonas' fifth-grade class was a problem, and by the second week of September it was cresting. The kids didn't seem to get along and were constantly forming themselves into little cliques. Group A wouldn't sit with Group B, Group C pouted if they were broken apart, Group D copied all their homework answers from each other. Thirty-four kids and almost all of them turned on each other daily like rabid ferrets. "It's the age," Mrs. Frankenheimer muttered consolingly to Ms. Jonas after she came into the teacher's lounge at three-thirty, in tears yet again. "Just let it go, Monica."

"But they're so mean," Ms. Jonas sniffled into her handkerchief. She was in her first year of teaching. Mrs. Frankenheimer wondered if she had grown up in Austria with the Von Trapps.

"Don't you have any kid who isn't part of the problem?" Mrs. Frankenheimer probed.

"No, no one," Ms. Jonas said. "Well, except for this one girl—an adorable girl with blond braids who is polite as can be, and always turns her homework in on time and in perfect condition." It didn't matter where Ms. Jonas sat her, she melded into the group as if she were a small cell being devoured by a larger host. She was the only kid so far who hadn't been rebuked, hadn't spoken out of turn, hadn't been drawn into any number of turf battles going on. True, she seemed to keep to herself somewhat, preferring to eat lunch outside the library and then spending the rest of the time flipping through old copies of The New Yorker. And at recess, she wandered the perimeter, seemingly lost in thought, but not in a dizzy, confused way. Purposeful. Yes, that was the word for the girl. Purposeful. Her name was Janie … no, that wasn't it. Jamie. Yes.

"Maybe you can utilize her," Mrs. Frankenheimer suggested. "If she's that pliable and good-natured, praise her in public. Show her as a role model. Offer covert suggestions to her about how to make friends. Maybe she can be a good class leader."

"You think?" Ms. Jonas' tearful eyes brightened.

As if by magic, something wonderful happened the next day. Ms. Jonas swore that the teacher's lounge had been empty during her conversation, yet Jamie had come in that morning and stood at her desk oh-so-adorably playing with a braid, and had asked her in a soft, beseeching voice before class, "Ms. Jonas? I have a special class project in mind I'd like to do, but it's secret. Can I get your permission to come in fifteen minutes early tomorrow?"

"Why certainly, dear," Ms. Jonas had said, smiling warmly. "Is it something you can tell me about then?"

"Oh, you'll see," Jamie said, smiling winningly, the modern embodiment of Rebecca of Sunnybrook Farm. "You'll see when everyone else does."

And Ms. Jonas was so charmed by her guilelessness and her enthusiasm that she agreed. Maybe Jamie was going to demonstrate leadership to the class without even being asked. She giggled a little to herself at such a silly, if lovely, thought.

The next morning, when Ms. Jonas arrived, Jamie was already sitting at her desk, head down, working quietly and unobtrusively in her workbook seconds before students started filing in.

But the classroom! If Mary Poppins herself had landed, she couldn't have worked such magic. Each and every desk had a festoon of ribbons and a balloon attached to it. Each desk had a dusting of glitter. Each had a small treat, perfectly matched to the kid. (A banana Laffy Taffy for Jazmine, a rope of red licorice for Naveah, a full-sized Butterfinger for Karl, etc.) Each kid had a small toy or favor. Even Ms. Jonas had a single red rose and a box of truffles on her chair. Murmurs of surprise and exclamations of "Oh!" rippled through the room. Ms. Jonas saw a lovely pink flush come to Jamie's downcast cheeks.

The bliss lasted for about two minutes, then Arnella decided that Lydia's new hair comb should be hers instead of Lydia's and snatched it.

Connor decided it was more fun to throw his bite-sized Baby Ruths at Greg, and did so, and a candy war broke out. Pete began chasing various girls with his new "Robin Hood" style bow-and-arrow set. The noise began to increase, and Ms. Jonas felt a rising tide of panic as the class slowly slid more out of control than she'd ever seen it. She stood in the middle of the chaos, first pleading and finally almost shouting, "Class, please! Please! PLEASE!"

The chaos was really peaking by the time Mrs. Frankenheimer waddled in, looked around the room with a death stare, and silenced the crowd. The kids meekly slid into their seats as Mrs. Frankenheimer went on a rant about how awful they were, after Ms. Jonas had prepared such a nice surprise for them! What was wrong with them? There would be consequences for such misbehavior, she could tell them that! Throughout this verbal harangue Ms. Jonas stood, paralyzed and useless, at the front of the room, trying not to look at Jamie. Her face had no expression on it whatsoever, but her eyes were the most frightening things Ms. Jonas had ever seen since she'd started teaching. She would have to speak with the girl later.

As it turned out, she didn't have to; Jamie approached her during silent reading and politely asked if she could please go to the office and call her mother to pick her up, as she didn't feel well. Numbly, the teacher nodded her assent. Jamie went to her desk, collected her things, and quietly left the room.

The next morning, Ms. Jonas entered her classroom and found the door unlocked. Today, however, every child was in his or her seat, hands folded, silently waiting for her. Ms. Jonas felt her pocket; no, she had her keys, she'd gotten them back yesterday. She stared at the forty-eight pairs of eyes, and they stared at her. Finally, she broke the silence: "Who unlocked the door?"

No answer.

"Did someone let you all in?"

No answer.

Ms. Jonas walked slowly to her desk and dropped her purse and jacket on her seat. She scanned the room. The day before, the class had left bits of ribbon and smashed candies and broken toys everywhere at the end of the day; her entreaties and threats had been for naught, and she'd personally been on her hands and knees for an hour after school trying vainly to clean up some of the mess before the custodians arrived. She'd seriously considered calling in for a sub and taking a mental health day. But here she was, and here was her class, seemingly overtaken by the Pod People. And the room was eerily, spotlessly, perfectly immaculate. What was going on?

Then she noticed something even odder than everything else in the room. All of the kids had scooted their desks out approximately a foot closer to the edges of the room, and there was now a good five-foot barrier of empty space completely surrounding the desk at the front of the room. And at that desk, her hair pulled back so tightly it looked like it was painted on, dressed perfectly in black, was Jamie Esau. Unlike the other students, her face did not indicate fear; indeed, she looked perfectly unruffled and calm. Her voice, when she spoke, was as dry as smoke. "Good morning, Ms. Jonas."

"Good morning, Jamie," the teacher returned, trying to sound strong but quavering on the name. "What—?"

"It's all taken care of," Jamie said pleasantly. She was smiling exactly as she had not forty-eight hours previously, yet now there was something in her eyes that was—what? Remote. She was there, and yet not there, as much or more so as she had ever been. Yet her presence, her energy, seemed to have uncoiled itself and wrapped around every child in the room so thoroughly and so artfully, they didn't have time to cry out. "There won't be any more trouble."

And there wasn't, not for the rest of the year. No one changed seats, no one was late, no one acted out, no one set so much as a hair out of place. In June, Ms. Jonas was given an award at the school assembly for "Most Well-Behaved Class."

Once, just once, in February, she'd tried. As everyone left the class—quietly, as usual—as Jamie picked up her books, Ms. Jonas gathered her courage and said, "Jamie, I've been thinking —perhaps I should call your mother. I'd like to talk to her about—"

"I don't think you need to do that," Jamie returned, in a These-Aren't-the-Droids-You're-Looking-For way. "My mother's very busy."

"Ye-es," Ms. Jonas said, falteringly. "Well. Maybe we could find some time—"

"No," the answer came, very softly. Just no. Then, almost apologetically: "I don't think so."

And then, for possibly the first time since that

morning in September, the eyes had looked right into hers, and the universe had shuddered. Before she could recover, Jamie had left the room, and Monica Jonas was alone in the classroom, with only a lone fly buzzing forlornly against the window.

CHAPTER 29

When Brian was eleven, his grandfather went into a nursing home. Once a month the entire family would make the sojourn to the Happy Acres Assisted Living Center to spend an afternoon sniffling into handkerchiefs (his mother), pacing the floor and asking meaningless questions about the facilities (his father), or robbing Grandpa blind via gin rummy (Jamie). Brian mostly sat in a corner and tried not to stare at the banana pudding-colored walls with desperately happy posters splattered on them—"If you REST you RUST!"—and tried to ignore the stale smell of urine, medication, and death.

His grandfather barely noticed him, which was bad; when he did, it was worse.

"Brian," the old man wheezed, giving him a rheumy stare. "So, how're things with you?"

"Fine," Brian said automatically. He always said "fine." Weasels could have been devouring his guts, and Brian would still maintain a placid expression, still murmur "fine." No trouble, no bother.

"School going okay for you?" Grandpa looked at Brian with an expression that mixed mild affection and raging contempt. He always thought his grandson looked like a milksop; he needed to be out in the fresh air, running around more. Better yet, he should be shooting things.

"School's fine," Brian said. "I got an A on my last report card."

"Must not be that tough a school," his grandfather groused, scanning his cards.

"Dad," Mrs. Esau pleaded.

"I'm just teasing the boy," Grandpa snapped irritably. "Why is everyone so goddamn sensitive all the time?"

"He knows you're teasing, Al," his father said, one ear glued to his cell phone. "Right, Brian? Grandpa just likes to tease you guys."

"He doesn't tease me," Jamie said matter-of-factly, not lifting her eyes from her cards. She was in the process of taking her grandfather to the cleaners. Grandpa paid five cents for every card she put down, and Jamie was determined to win enough to buy an ice cream bar from the snack shop in the lobby. Two would be better.

"Tell Grandpa about pee-wee football," Brian's mother wheedled. "Dad, did you know Brian's going to play football?"

"Football?" Grandpa scowled, pronouncing the word as though a bug had flown in his mouth. His eyes peered from his wrinkled visage, examining Brian with a mixture of contempt and disbelief. "You? You want to play football, boy?"

Actually, no, he didn't; Brian had signed up to make his parents happy. He wasn't as strong as most of his teammates, nor as skilled at handling the ball; he could, however, run like the wind, and that combined with getting in people's way seemed to be enough most of the time. Strangely, this also seemed like a metaphor for his life. Brian opened his mouth to answer, but his father interrupted.

"Oh, he's wiry," Mr. Esau said, glancing appraisingly at his son, "but he's fast. He'll bulk out in adolescence if he follows our family pattern, and we'll just keep him training until then."

Brian's throat felt dry. All the adults were staring at him, and he didn't know what to say. He nodded, croaked out "Yeah," and let it be. From the bed, Jamie gave him a penetrating look before laying down her cards with élan: "Gin."

"Sonuvvabitch!" Grandpa barked, throwing his cards in a heap. Brian's mother interjected with some sort of moist cry, possibly because of her father's cursing, possibly because of her daughter's refusal to indulge him by losing. In the ensuing commotion—"He said he'd pay! He *said*!" Jamie seethed—Brian shot from his chair, muttered to his father, "I need the bathroom," and headed for the door.

"Why don't you use Grandpa's bathroom?" his father queried, looking annoyed.

Brian would rather have chewed on broken glass. "I ... like the one in the lobby."

His father shrugged, in that "whatever" way he had. Brian fled.

He didn't really need to use the bathroom; sometimes, he just needed air. Brian wandered out to the lobby area, avoiding the huge Samoan aides who were laughing and teasing each other as they wheeled elderly patients from place to place. Their booming voices and massive bodies —one of them had a chest the size of a small refrigerator—paralyzed him with terror, especially when one caught his eye and boomed "How you doin', man?"

Words failed him, as they so often did, and he stood there in mute terror for a moment before offering a whispery "Fine" while the man grinned and kept walking, a large white rag hanging from his rear pocket. Brian stared at the way the rag swayed past the man's meaty, uniform-encased butt, then, somehow embarrassed for reasons he didn't understand, he shifted his gaze to the wall. A poster of a shirtless boxer in his seventies barked "OLD AGE AIN'T FOR SISSIES" at him.

"Oh, boy?" came a quavering voice.

Brian turned. An old woman was in front of him, parked in a wheelchair and wearing a yellow bathrobe. Her hair was long and hung about her in a gray, tangled mane. The light caught her glasses so her eyes weren't visible; he saw only her pink and gray gaping mouth, minus teeth.

Normally, Brian felt a jolt of terror when strangers spoke to him; he always instinctively wondered how long it would be before he said something wrong or needed to start running. However, for some reason, he didn't feel anything like that right now. He felt his feet move, and he took a step forward. "Yes?"

"Oh, help me," the woman moaned. Her voice was a strange sort of quiet wail, a keen that didn't have enough breath to achieve full power. She shut her eyes as if in extreme pain and reached her hand forward. Instinctively, he reached out and took it, and she pulled him closer to him. "Help me."

"How can I help you?" Brian asked. She looked like a storybook grandma, not like Brian's who was still alive, who wore designer golf outfits and had her hair and nails done every week.

"Help me," the woman almost sobbed. "Please help me." Her grip on his hand unexpectedly grew tighter, like a baby's when it grabs your finger.

A rush of pity filled him, and Brian felt completely unlike himself. He reached out and touched the woman's hair, smoothing it back; despite its tangles, it was soft and clean and felt like silk threads under his touch. "I'll help you, I promise. Let me go tell my dad."

"Please come back?" the woman cried. "Please come back and help me."

"I promise." He slid his hand down the woman's arm and extricated himself from her clutching fingers.

He ran back to the room, bursting in with such a clatter that everyone actually stared at him. Unused to the attention, he flushed. "Dad, I need to talk to you."

"Right now?" His father was in the middle of another call and was even more annoyed at the interruption. His mother was still dabbing her eyes, and Jamie—a wave of gratitude filled him— had Grandpa's full concentration. Several dollar bills and loose change piled at her side indicated that the gin rummy game was still going on.

"There's a lady," Brian exhaled breathlessly, sweat tickling his forehead. "She says she needs help. She asked me to help her. We need to find someone."

His father looked at him for a moment, muttered, "Ben, I'll call you back in a sec," then shut the phone. He guided Brian out of the room, hand on his shoulder, and stared with him back toward the reception area. "What lady?"

Brian pointed. "The lady in the yellow

bathrobe." He could see her, even all the way down the hall, gesturing futilely to passers-by; if the facility had been perfectly still, he might have been able to make out her words, instead of just her high, mournful tone. No one seemed to be listening to her.

Mr. Esau looked, then sighed, briefly gripping Brian's shoulder. "That's just an old lady, son. She probably has dementia. That's why the aides are here, to help people like that."

"But she needs my help," Brian said doggedly. "She asked me to help her, and I said I would. Isn't there something I—we—can do?"

"No," his father said very gently, "Not really. That's why she's here. Let's just let the staff take care of her, okay? That's what they're supposed to do."

Numbly, Brian let himself be guided back into the room. He stared at the sickly beige walls for another hour, listening to his grandfather complain about any number of things, while every few minutes Jamie would utter "Gin!" His mother occasionally interjected a feeble question or two about how grandpa liked the center—he didn't— and his father talked on the phone and chimed in now and then about how the Mariners were doing in the playoffs.

As they left the center, Brian tried to keep his eyes trained on the floor, but as they walked out through the reception area, his gaze was dragged upward by an invisible magnet. The woman in the yellow bathrobe wasn't yelling or crying anymore; she looked like she'd been given some pills of some sort, because she was staring vacantly into space, a tiny bit of spittle in one corner of her mouth, her lips moving slowly but no sound left her. Her eyes caught Brian's for a split second, and an emotion he couldn't read—sorrow? anger? accusation?—flashed through them, then was gone, swallowed up in the clouds. Brian felt his eyes fill with tears, and it was a relief when Jamie, who'd been watching his face, inexplicably tripped over some invisible piece of fluff on the floor, caught Brian's hand for support, and held it all the way out to the car.

That night, Brian dreamed he was back in the care center, pushing a whole army of old people's wheelchairs toward the main door. He zoomed from chair to chair like a hummingbird among flowers, helping the old people get momentum so that they could take over pushing themselves. He knew they had to get through the double doors to be outside in the sunshine, and he ran and ran, pushing them all, giving special aid to the woman in the yellow bathrobe. The doors opened, and the laughing crowd of senior citizens pushed themselves outside into a blinding blaze of sun, but Brian was busy making sure everyone had made it through. By the time he turned back from checking the hallway, the door had slammed shut and locked, trapping him inside. He beat on it and screamed and cried, but no one heard him. Then, when he turned around once more, he saw the big orderlies coming toward him, no longer smiling, no longer friendly, but as huge and implacable as a solar eclipse. Brian threw up his arms in front of his face as giant hands grabbed him and shook him and shook him, and it wasn't until he awoke with his face on the damp pillow that he knew it was over, and that he had failed.

CHAPTER 30

One day in the mid-90's, it occurred to Chantel that there were no black Disney princesses.

Sure, *The Lion King* was set in Africa, but there were no humans in it. There was an Indian girl at the end of *The Jungle Book* who did little more than giggle and carry a jug of water. The two closest to Chantel's heart were Princess Jasmine and Pocahontas—and even they looked more like white girls with really good tans.

She asked her mother about this.

"Those are the stories the Disney people chose to animate, honey." Her mother sighed, frowning at the pile of documents she was sifting through as part of the brief she was filing. "A lot of the stories they filmed were from Europe, and there didn't use to be a lot of people like us there. So I guess it didn't occur to them to fix that when they made the movies."

"But what about Jasmine, and Pocahontas, and the Indian girl? Why is the only role model from Africa a lioness named Nala?"

"I don't know," her mother said. "Maybe the people who decided to make those movies didn't know enough about African history and stories for children."

"Are there some good African stories?" Chantel twirled her braid in her hand. "Something with a pretty black girl or lady?"

"Let's find out," her mother said, closing the tome in front of her with a *bang*. It was a nice day, good for a walk to the library down the street.

So down they went, and the librarian, a stunning woman with deep brown skin, a thousand bracelets, and a necklace seemingly made of precious gems, listened to their request. Then she showed them to the Children's section, where they checked out an animated story based on an African folktale: "Kirikou and the Sorceress." Chantel's mother set her up with the DVD player in the living room, gave her a bowl of air-popped popcorn, and returned to her case.

For the next hour and a half, Chantel watched the story of brave Kirikou, a West African baby who demands to be born while still inside his mother. She watched him battle the beautiful yet frightening sorceress, Karaba, who had captured all of the men from the village. Karaba was like a Black version of Maleficent from Sleeping Beauty, but with wild pointy hair and exposed breasts. Chantel watched the little boy outwit the evil witch-woman at every turn, saving his friends from disaster and the sorceress's traps. Then, at the climax, she watched Kirikou remove the poisonous thorn from Karaba's spine, unleashing a terrifying scream but freeing her from her torment and also removing all of her evil powers. Kirikou then received a magic kiss from the former sorceress, grew into an adult man, and married her after they returned to the village.

Chantel had screaming nightmares for a week.

Her mother almost lost her case because she'd overlooked a key detail from the sleep deprivation.

Her father wrote a nasty letter to the library.

The librarian told her supervisor that it wasn't

her fault if modern families couldn't understand a beautiful African folk tale. After all, it wasn't like she'd recommended the original version of the story, where Kirikou killed Karaba. And besides, didn't white people still read The Brothers Grimm to their kids, with stepsisters' eyes being pecked out and stepmothers dancing to death in red-hot shoes? Ultimately, the librarian was transferred to another branch.

Chantel's mother bought her a black Barbie and introduced her to *A Different World*.

Chantel filed all of this away in the back of her mind.

CHAPTER 31

The following morning, Jamie and Chantel were stationed on a bench in front of school, wearing sunglasses and trying to resemble movie stars at Cannes—Jamie was even wearing a Prada raincoat, which she thought was very Heidi Klum. They were unprepared for reality to intrude as abruptly as it did when Zack and Josh, without warning, strode up to the bench and sat down on either side of the girls.

Jamie lifted her eyebrows in surprise, or an approximation thereof. "Well, gentlemen ... to what do we owe the pleasure?"

"You're having a party tomorrow night," Zack said tersely. It was not a question.

"Yes." Jamie was as forthcoming as the Sphinx.

"Why?"

"My brother wanted to show people that he and Missy are still a functioning unit," Jamie said blandly—so blandly, it might even have been true.

"And *you* agreed to it?" Zack's voice indicated that this was as likely as dinner with Santa Claus. Chantel and Josh simply sat and watched as if it were a subtitled movie.

"You're *so* smart. Isn't Zack smart, Chantel?" Jamie turned and looked at them over her glasses, a Sun Goddess whose rays could scorch the Earth to a cinder. "We might actually have you peeing *over* the waistband in a week or so."

"Just give me the time and tell me if I need to bring my own stuff." Zack sounded like a bar fight about to break out.

"Eight o'clock, we provide everything. You *do* know how to use silverware, not eat with your hands, right?" Jamie said. She intended this to come off as snappy repartee, but harshness marred the effect.

"Don't worry." Zack shot to his feet. "Coming, Josh?" He was striding away even as Josh offered a mumbled apology—the only thing he'd said—and chased after his friend.

Chantel peered at Jamie as she watched them go, noting the color rise to her friend's cheek, her eyes glittering like pale blue stones. Jamie's words hissed in the air like a slow-burning fuse. "Chantel, I swear, that boy is going to drive me to the drink. Why is he so annoying, but just so freaking *cute?*"

Thankfully, the bell rang before Chantel had to formulate an answer. She put an arm around her friend and murmured, "Let's go to class."

"Why not, since they were nice enough to have one." Jamie gathered herself, resetting her features much as Eleanor Rigby did via the face in the jar by the door. "And where's Yoshi? I've hardly seen him at all this morning." All her minions were disappointing her; the floggings would have to be reimplemented.

As they walked past the plastic garbage can, neither of them noticed the lid rotate and open, just a crack. *Flash.*

IN THE UPPER hallway of the academy, Missy reviewed her first-period notes before entering class. She was so engrossed in French verbs that it wasn't until Brian said "Hi" that she looked up, noticed his presence, his unwashed scent.

He looked terrible, disheveled and red-eyed, like he'd been up all night, and was wearing a flannel shirt and jeans. Then again, Missy had pulled her hair back in a ponytail this morning rather than styled it, and had her glasses instead of her contacts.

He took a seat next to her, and his words came in a rush, as if he had to get them out before something was too late. "Listen, I know ... this week has been rough on us. So ... all I'm asking is that we try to get through the party tomorrow, just to be civil to each other. After that, I don't know what'll happen, but let's try one more time to enjoy each other's company."

He looked absolutely miserable; his eyes scanned the lockers, the floor, the drinking fountains, anywhere but her face. A shimmer of liquid appeared in his eyes, brushed his lashes. "I mean ... even strangers are least polite to each other."

Missy had no idea what to say. She looked at this boy, this stranger, whom she had loved for over a year, and it was as if she were peering through the wrong end of a telescope. How did he get so far away from her, how did he become so foreign and so tiny? Why did it now feel as though they were orbiting completely different galaxies?

She took his hand, and he searched her face; finally, at last, a tear fell, streaking its way down his cheek like a falling star. His hand felt warm and familiar, yet it was attached to the arm and body of a stranger.

He muttered thickly, "I guess ... I guess I'm not much of a boyfriend, huh?"

There were no words left. She just sat there, numb, holding his hand, as he wept silently. In the empty hallway, the late bell sounded

Neither moved.

CHAPTER 32

Mid-morning, Miss Sullivan was enjoying a cup of tea in the teacher's lounge during her free period with Mrs. Nystrom, the calculus teacher.

"God, what a morning," Mrs. Nystrom sighed, easing off a shoe to rub an instep across her calf. "And this is only the first week. The gum, the phones, the excuses for not having their home-work done, the gossip. The school seems to be a-buzz with Brian Esau and Missy Hoff's impending breakup."

"I know," Miss Sullivan sighed. It had been *the* hot topic in second period.

"Seems a shame—he's such a nice boy, she's

so sweet. They seemed perfect for each other."
Mrs. Nystrom liked to see students she approved
of paired off, Noah's ark style, to eventually prop-
agate the human race.

"Sometimes nice people don't hold up that
well under pressure," Miss Sullivan said thoughtfully, stirring a packet of Splenda into her Con-
stant Comment tea. "Only my personal
experience, of course. I've always thought people
who are scrappier—the ones who have something
to fight for, the ones with something truly at
stake—they're the ones who fly higher and far-
ther." She chuckled a little. "If they ever get off
the ground."

"You think Brian has it in him to be something like that?" Mrs. Nystrom looked at her
skeptically. "Missy, perhaps, but Brian?"

"*Especially* Brian," Miss Sullivan emphasized it
firmly.

"Why?" Mrs. Nystrom looked a little
confused.

Miss Sullivan smiled. "Because no one believes he can."

CHAPTER 33

During lunch, Jamie enjoyed a bagel and lox sandwich—extra red onion—with Chantel when she felt her spider-sense tingling. She looked up over her shoulder into the leering red face of Hank Gaston, the biggest asshole in school. His bloodshot eyes bored into her like a drill with a dull bit.

Hank flicked his tongue out and licked his lips, as though he were some sort of giant sun-burned lizard squatting on a rock in Death Valley. "Hey, sweets ... heard you're throwing a big party tomorrow night."

Jamie hated people outside her circle using nicknames on her. "What of it, Hank?" she returned, as cold and bored as an ice salesman in Antarctica.

"So ... am I invited?" Hank leaned in closer, as if his letterman jacket and canned-beer breath would somehow make her swoon.

"Have you discovered humor? Of course not," Jamie snapped, crisp as an ironed sheet unfolded with a whip-crack.

"What if I decide I want to show up anyway?" Hank leaned toward her ear and lowered his voice to a husky purr. "Get a look at you in your best dress ... or out of it."

"Go directly to Hell, do not pass Go, do not collect two hundred dollars." Jamie punctuated this by very deliberately spearing a cherry tomato in her salad, eliciting a spray of crimson juice. Her jaw was clenched a little too tightly. Chantel unobtrusively put down her yogurt container and pulled a glass of ice water a little closer, to be hurled at Hank in the event of an emergency.

Hank didn't flinch. "Maybe I'll drop by for a bit anyway and shoot the shit with your dickhead brother." The word *brother* snapped off his lips like a riding crop.

For a split second, Jamie forgot who she was, where she was, all her plans, everything, and a flash of pure, white-hot rage engulfed her. She shot to her feet, right arm coming around in a punch, but Chantel and another girl grabbed her and restrained her. An adjacent table of kids paused with sandwiches and chili fries halfway to their mouths.

Jamie would've spat at him, but Hank took a quick jump back, a little smirk on his lips. He blew her a kiss and waggled his tongue at her, then moved on, a couple of his troglodyte friends chortling *Heh-heh-heh* and high-fiving each other.

The girl holding Jamie's arm—Kat something, the hippie chick—spoke first. "Wasn't he thrown off the football team for doing drugs?" Her eye caught Jamie's; she wore an expression of *can-you-believe-that-idiot?* Jamie felt slightly mollified.

"Couldn't prove it—he cleaned out his locker before they got to it." Chantel was proud, as usual, to fill in the gaps of information.

Jamie had almost regained her composure, but her voice, far from channeling a Dark Lord, sounded shaky and girlish, and even—horrors—borderline teary. "I don't want him in my house." Then, almost as an afterthought: "And I don't want him near Brian." She could take care of herself in a pinch, she thought, but she would have to emotionally protect Brian from the thugs of the world. She would always take care of her brother, even if she had to ruin his life in order to fix it. Wasn't this how troops operated in Vietnam? *We had to destroy the village in order to save it.* Hey, she *had* learned something in World Studies last year.

ZACK AND JOSH were balanced on the ropes course up in the woods behind the school, as part of today's P.E. activities. The course involved giant steel cables strung taught between giant cedar trees in various pretzel-like configurations designed to teach the students balance, teamwork, etc. At this moment, Josh and Zack were on parallel cables, pressing into each other, gripping hands, trying to avoid leaning backward or too far in either direction lest they lose their toehold and fall the big four feet to the earth.

"I dozed through the movie in fifth." Zack panted, his white-knuckled hands nearly cutting off the circulation in Josh's fingers. "What's the good word?"

"Brian and Missy are going to keep things

going through tomorrow night, and after that who knows." Josh raised an eyebrow at Zack, which was all the extra movement he could handle at the moment. Beads of sweat coursed down his face and soaked his gym shirt. "This is what I got from a girl who got it from another girl who was in the john and heard them. *More* interesting: some scary-looking guy named Hank-something plans to crash tomorrow and raise some hell."

"Hank Gaston?!" Zack jerked so abruptly that they both nearly toppled off the cable; Josh glared at him as they re-oriented themselves. "Yikes. Why was he harassing Jamie?"

"Her party, her world," Josh countered flippantly. Hank seemed like the type who always had to have an audience of a couple of dunderheads around to laugh at everything he did and cheer him on, be it "spilling" food on underclassmen, knocking others over in the halls, or just yelling insults from passing cars. Classic bully behavior. A lightning-quick memory of the scuffle with Wayne flashed through Josh's mind, and he felt a brief shudder of shame.

"She'll ease him right into the hospital," Zack grinned. "Hmmmm."

"What 'hmmmm'?"

"Nothing," Zack said, a little too quickly.

"Still mad at her for this morning?" Josh asked casually. They continued to move their feet together along the coil, slowly, slowly, toward the platform and safety.

"Oh shit, I wasn't mad," Zack huffed. "She's fun to argue with. Thinks she's so smart."

"She *is*." Only Josh knew how much.

"I know, I just wish *she* didn't know it."

They fell off just before reaching the platform. Zack later claimed that Josh jumped; Josh claimed that Zack pushed him.

CHAPTER 34

After school, Brian was in the locker room getting ready for practice. His head hurt, his heart hurt, and he was not in the mood for crap.

Unfortunately, his teammates hadn't received the memo.

"So, Esau," Antonio bellowed, slipping on his shoulder pads, "give. What's going down between you and Missy?"

"Yeah," Tom Deacon said, stuffing his gym bag in his locker. "This is like Matt Drudge material. Everyone wants to know."

"I don't feel like discussing this with anyone, okay?" Brian snarled, yanking his jersey on. All day long, he'd felt people looking at him with something akin to pity, and it reminded him of his grade school days when he'd been a punching bag for bigger, meaner kids. He didn't like remembering those days, didn't like feeling like he was cresting some sort of strange roller coaster, with God-knows-what waiting for him at the bottom dip.

"But you *are* breaking up, right?" Callan would not let it go. Brian hated this asshole, a lean muscle machine with glittering, rat-like eyes and a brush of ginger hair. Callan was the type who would be on Missy's doorstep as soon as he was sure Brian wouldn't cream him for it.

"We'll be together tomorrow at the party. That's all I know right now. Now *lay off!*" Brian slammed the locker for emphasis, his cheeks burning. A small crowd had gathered during this exchange, as the boys exchanged worried glances.

"Bry, we know you're a private guy." Antonio looked genuinely worried, which made Brian feel better; maybe someone really did give a shit about him, Brian, not Brian Esau, football star and romantic washout. "We're just concerned. I mean, no sane man would dump a woman like that. People aren't that crazy."

"Unless," Callan drawled, "they're retarded. Or going queer."

Brian was an animal unleashed. He threw himself on Callan, letting his fists speak for him, letting himself morph into something raw and wild and ugly, something that wanted to hurt. He slammed his fists into Callan's face, feeling the flesh give way, hearing the *smack* of impact. The whole world was red, then purple, then black; all he knew was bodies and noise and hands grabbing helplessly at him, and the cool, hard floor beneath their bodies as they slammed down again and again. It wasn't until the coach's whistle sounded, cutting through the din like a scream, that he finally went limp.

COACH REYNOLDS SAT in his office, grimly surveying the bruised and scratched young man before him. "Mister, you've punched about every button I've got this week. You come late to practice, your playing is for shit, you have mood swings like the San Andreas fault." He glared at the boy. "Is it Missy? Is that what's causing this?"

Brian said nothing. Missy was just the tip of

the iceberg, but if the coach was willing to make excuses for him, what more was there to say?

The coach sighed, looked at the ceiling for a moment, then back at Brian. "I'll discipline Callan for starting this thing, but … you realize you're looking at indefinite suspension from the team at this point, don't you son?"

Brian nodded. Nodding was all his throbbing head could handle.

"Is that what you want?" The coach picked up a pencil and bopped the eraser against the desk a couple of times as he waited for his answer. *Bump, bump, bump.*

Was that what he wanted? Brian had no idea. It was as if God was a waiter, looking at him with a giant pad in hand, offering him a variety of life's daily specials. Football? Academics? Girlfriend? Just a friend? It was all too much. Brian felt a desperate longing to be in a Communist country, with only one kind of coffee, one kind of cheese, one brand of TV, no choices, no decisions. Choosing meant risk, risk meant failure. He was so tired of failing.

He said the truest words that he'd probably ever spoken in his life, without anger, without bitterness—just pure, simple truth. "I don't know what the hell I want."

Coach looked weary. "You're out of tomorrow's game, then. We'll talk again next week if you want to stay on." He picked up a playbook and began to flip through it, as if Brian had simply vanished.

After a long moment, during which he tried very hard not to cry, Brian did exactly that, leaving the coach alone in the empty office.

CHAPTER 35

Josh was driving home at 3:45 p.m. when he saw the figure up ahead, walking alone by the side of the road. He did a double-take, then slammed on the brakes so abruptly his tires squealed a little bit in protest.

He bumped to a stop right in front of Missy. "Um ... would you like a ride?"

Missy shifted her bag in her hands. She squinted into the sun, then back at Josh. Her expression was hard to read, but her voice was firm if soft: "On one condition: We don't discuss Brian or me."

Josh nodded assent, a little hesitantly. Just as hesitantly, Missy placed her books in the back seat of the blue MG. She hopped in the front seat, ponytail bobbing in the wind, but she didn't turn her head to look at him. He pulled back onto the road, silence thick between them.

Finally, Missy spoke.

"I mean, if I don't want to discuss someone or something, I shouldn't have to."

"Right," Josh chose a safely neutral response.

"I don't see why my life is on such display. Today I talked to over fifteen people, all wanting to know what's going on. It's not fair." Missy's voice wobbled a bit, but she kept her eyes straight ahead.

"No," Josh said quietly, in complete agreement.

"This school is just too small." A cemetery whizzed by, where a white balloon danced forlornly, tied to a potted miniature rose bush placed next to a grave. "I can't handle the way everyone knows everyone else's business."

Missy was staring very fixedly in the distance, but now she turned her head a bit to look at Josh sideways. "We're in the process of breaking up, by the way."

"Are you." Josh sounded regretful. In a way, he was.

Missy began talking faster and faster. "I mean, almost-seventeen is just too young for me to think that my life is over, and to go live in the hills or something ... But still, you know, you invest a year of your life in a relationship, it's kind of hard to just take it off and throw it in the corner like an old sweatshirt ..."

She would have gone on, but sobs overtook her, and she buried her face in her hands. Her face was blotchy with tears, and she breathed raggedly, as though something in her chest was broken.

Josh eased the car to a stop by the side of the road. He didn't have a handkerchief, and he felt awkward and stupid and hated himself. His hands gripped the steering wheel tightly. After an awful pause, he turned to her and exhaled, in a rush: "I'm sorry ... I'm so sorry."

Missy took a quick swipe at her eyes and looked at Josh, suddenly remembering that he was like she was a year or so ago, a stranger to the school. It wasn't his fault that he was suddenly in the middle of all this drama. She looked into his brown eyes, at his handsome face, and a sense of peace began to come over her. He looks kind, she thought. Not just handsome, but kind. Maybe he really does understand.

She finished drying her tears with the back of her hand and took a shaky breath. Her words were halting, fragile, like newborn fawns in their vulnerability. "Do you ... do you think I'm pretty?"

Josh didn't move—face, body, anything. Only his lips parted as he mumbled, "Yes."

"Does—does Zack?"

A muscle twitched in Josh's stony countenance. His voice was rougher than the first time, rougher, yet somehow gentler, too. "Yes. Very."

Missy smiled a bit. Someone still noticed her. Someone still thought she was pretty, desirable, special. Before she could help herself, she leaned over and gave Josh a quick kiss on the cheek.

They spoke no other words till Josh dropped Missy in front of her house.

"Bye." Pause. "Thank you."

"Bye."

Encyclopedias could not hold all that passed between them in those four words.

CHAPTER 36

On his lawn, Zack was busy playing Pickle with Alex and Mark as the sun set. Beth, sitting on the porch, laughed and laughed as her sons tag-teamed the older man, brought him down giggling uncontrollably onto the expanse of lawn. There would be grass stains in all their clothes, she thought. No matter. With enough time and effort, most things were fixable.

Zack felt almost as euphoric as he had on Monday, when he first saw Josh again. They'd had pizza for dinner, and he had no homework to do tonight. It was a warm evening, and he felt strong and invincible. His and Josh's plan was proceeding smoothly, and tomorrow night would be the deciding factor, when he'd finally pair off with the girl of his and everyone's dream. Everyone would finally see how he belonged, how he wasn't the outsider kid anymore. Everything he wanted was within reach.

Alex didn't have a thought in his head; he just laughed and laughed and laughed, especially when he dove onto the base and knocked Mark over.

AT THE BRADSHAW HOUSEHOLD, Josh was clearing plates off the dining room table and bussing them out to the kitchen. His father was rattling off details of his business trip. "So, I'll fly out early Friday morning, close the deal that afternoon, do the meet-and-greet thing on Saturday, and should be back Sunday morning sometime. Think you can handle things by yourself till then?"

"I'll cope somehow, Dad," Josh said absently. Nick looked at him curiously, then decided Josh was just preoccupied with being a teenager. He felt a slight pang as he watched his son, almost a grown man, rinse his dishes in the sink, the overhead light catching his eyes and cheekbones just the way it used to catch Maureen's.

How odd it was, when past and present collided and overlapped.

AS THESE THINGS went down outside her window, Jamie sat in her room, homework spread out before her, simultaneously studying and watching Lauren Bacall slink her way through *To Have and Have Not*. How, she wondered, could one *have not?* Then again, Jamie had to admit, she was used to having things—and if she didn't have them, she got them. That was that.

Brian walked by the room, paused, opened his mouth, closed it, kept walking.

AT THE AIRPORT, Brian helped his parents unload their bags for curbside check-in. There was a moist hug from his mother, and a handshake and shoulder grip from his father, reminders to keep the house in order and watch out for Jamie. (Funny his parents used that expression: *Watch out for your sister.* He knew they meant "take care of her," but that wasn't the first thought that sprang to mind.)

He stood waving after them as they trundled through the revolving door and disappeared into the crowd, looking at his reflection going around and around in circles. A sad hulk, he thought. I look like a sad hulk of something. He felt like the Tin Woodman of Oz, a hollow metal shell, nothing ticking or beating inside at all.

MISSY LAY IN BED, swathed in her nightgown, turning over the day's events in her mind. Was she definitely single, or not? That seemed to be question number one. Brian had made it seem like they were definitely going to break up, but when? And was there anything she could do about it? *Should* she do anything about it? What on earth would her mother say? And why should Missy care what she said?

She let her mind drift back to the first time she'd seen Brian. How tan and gorgeous he'd been in that green swimsuit! He'd emerged from the locker room at the pool in a dark green

Speedo when all the other boys were wearing long jams and trunks. All the girls at the pool were in lust with him, yet he never seemed to make eye contact with anyone, except her.

But it wasn't his body that she'd noticed most of all. It was the way he moved—cautiously, deliberately. And his eyes didn't seem to match up with the rest of him—they were the eyes of a small boy, or a childhood toy. That was it: a toy. Brian was like a teddy bear somehow transported into the body of a Greek god, and he moved as if the bear were piloting him from inside. Had he seen how fragile she was inside, as well? Did they think that they could somehow protect each other, encase themselves in some kind of Bubble Wrap of love, against the knocks and dings of life?

Well, here they were, a pair of cracked objects seconds away from collapsing into a pile of shards. What sort of cosmic super glue could hold them together? How could she know for certain if he still cared for her?

And why, if she cared so much about Brian, were Josh and Zack running through her mind? Josh, with his floppy brown hair, his dark eyes, his broad shoulders—not a gymmed body, like

Brian's—and his cool sense of style, and the probing way he looked at her. And Zack, cocky, obnoxious Zack, with his flame-red hair, his blazing eyes, his crackle-and-pop personality that made her feel ... well, different. With Brian she felt protected. With Josh, she felt understood. But with Zack, she felt ... excitement. Energy. Like anything could happen, and just might. Was it wrong to feel like this?

Missy rolled over and hugged her pillow tightly to her, pressed it across her stomach. She felt as if it were the only real thing she had to hold onto.

CHAPTER 37

When Jamie was ten years old, her mother sat her down and explained the facts of life to her. She did this in her most caring way, emphasizing the wonders and miracles of human love and reproduction, as well as the responsibilities involved. She ended her speech—which, according to the kitchen clock, had been proceeding as a monologue for almost fifteen minutes—and looked beseechingly at her stone-faced daughter.

After a few moments of silence, in a voice that sounded as if something sticky was lodged in her throat, Jamie said, "So ... I am going to be bleeding and in pain and nauseous for roughly three to five days a month for the next thirty to forty years of my life?!"

She stormed from the kitchen, and Mrs. Esau didn't see her for the next two days until Jamie had mined the Internet for enough data to assuage her initial reaction. Her mother left the box of tampons—and the exposed instructions—in Jamie's bathroom. Nothing more was said.

WHEN BRIAN WAS eleven years old, his father took him for a drive and they got milkshakes at a local fast food place. While sitting at an outdoor table at a comfortable distance away from other customers, Mr. Esau suddenly said, apropos of nothing, "So Brian ... you know how the penis works, right?"

Brian was so shocked that he blew into the milkshake cup instead of sucking, and a giant bubble of chocolate—like something out of the La Brea tar pits—exploded out of the cup, across the table, and into his father's lap.

His dad jumped up, swearing a blue streak, and proceeded to knock his own soda over on himself. There was much yelling, even more napkins, and his father drove them home so he could change his clothes. During the drive, Brian asked to listen to the sports news, and the broadcaster's unctuous recap of last night's Seahawks game was the only discussion in the car.

Several weeks later, Brian had a long talk with Uncle Tad when they were alone together, fishing on a lake during a summer family vacation.

CHANTEL WAS STILL REELING from Kirikou when she asked her mother about all the details of reproduction. Her mother took her back to the library and asked the new librarian for a good book covering the subject. And this time, the librarian came through: she loaned Chantel a book called *The Wonderful Story of How You Were Born*, and her mother read it with her. It answered most of her questions for the time being.

However, a couple of years later, Chantel had a few extra questions, so she returned to the library and mimicked the librarian's actions on how to look up books via the card catalog so her parents didn't see her using the encyclopedias at home. With another librarian's help she found the 300s section of the Dewey Decimal System, and within a short period of time had researched quite a few interesting topics she thought might come in handy someday—things she would occasionally think about during church, and smile quietly and beatifically to herself, usually during the communal prayers.

Missy's mother asked her first. "Sweetie, do you have any questions about where babies come from?"

Missy didn't. She'd already heard in Sunday school that babies were gifts from God, sent down as magic diamonds that grew in mothers' tummies. Everyone in her second-grade class was very impressed by this, except for Narissa Oglethorpe, whose mother was a nurse, and who loudly announced, "That's not how it happens!" She was taken outside by the teacher and given a talking-to and spent the rest of the morning sucking on a chocolate-flavored lollipop and glowering at everyone in the room.

So no, Missy had no questions.

"That's good," her mother smiled. At age eleven, she gave Missy a copy of *Baby and Child-care: From Birth to the Teen Years*. Missy never asked her or her father any questions, just re-

read certain passages of the book over and over until her eyes felt like they would burn holes in the pages.

The book said very little about what to do when your boyfriend seems to be drifting away from you, and you feel helpless to stop it—aside from prayer.

WHEN ZACK WAS in fifth grade, his mother brought home the Judy Blume trinity from the '70s: *Are You There God? It's Me, Margaret*; *Then Again, Maybe I Won't*; and *Forever*. Two copies of each.

"What's this stuff?" Zack asked suspiciously. His taste ran more toward comic books, choose-your-own-adventure novels, and other daring tales of magic, escape, and adventure. This looked suspiciously like reading that was good for you.

"Book club," Beth said cheerfully.

"Whose book club?"

"Ours," his mother said briskly. "We're both going to read these books, one at a time. Each day we'll do a chapter, and each night we'll discuss it."

"These books look lame," Zack muttered, scanning the covers. "What are they about?"

"Relationships," his mother said. "Boys and girls. Stuff like that."

"Why are we reading them together?" There had to be a trap or something built in here somewhere.

"Because," Beth said, hands on hips, giving her son a look of death, "you're getting to an age where you might have questions about some of the issues in these books. So I thought it would be good for us to go through them as a team."

"Uh-huh," Zack said unwillingly. Well, at least one of them had a boy as the main character, if the cover was to be believed. "I don't suppose there's a reward at the end of this?"

Beth sighed. Everything with her oldest son was a negotiation. "Two movie passes?"

"Six," Zack said quickly, jumping at the offer. "Two for each one."

"Deal," his mother said, grabbing the victory. They shook hands. From the bouncy chair in the corner, Alex emitted a happy squeal.

They read all three books, one chapter a night, and talked about each chapter for ten minutes as measured by the kitchen timer. At first Zack felt strange discussing some of the personal topics in the books with his mother, but he had to admit, she did such a good job of putting him at ease, asking casual yet specific questions, and making little jokes, that the six weeks went by quickly.

When they were done with *Forever*—the book Zack tended to read when he was alone in his room—Zack had to ask. "Mom? Why did you do this with me?"

"Why?" Beth asked, arching an eyebrow. "Was it embarrassing?"

"Kinda," Zack said heavily. 'Kinda' was an understatement. Being grilled by his mother about what he felt about the sex scenes in a teen novel had now become his number one item on the list of Ten Thousand Things Never Do Again in This Lifetime. But his dad hadn't been home for dinner for the past couple of weeks due to business commitments, so Beth was the best resource he had for the moment unless he wanted to talk to Nick.

"Well," Beth said. She paused a moment, looked at her hands, played with her wedding ring, stared into the distance while she gathered her thoughts, then spoke very slowly. "Here's the thing, kiddo. My parents never discussed any of this stuff with me, and most of my friends' parents didn't discuss it with them, either. And there was a lot of misinformation back in my day. Some girls got pregnant and had to drop out of school to raise the baby; others had abortions and never even told their parents. And some girls wound up dating guys who treated them very badly. And some people got diseases you can't even imagine."

Zack was stunned for a moment. He knew his mom had been a teenager once—that is, he grasped the concept in the abstract. He'd seen the pictures of her in the photo album: the hopelessly outdated hairdo, the ancient rock concert T-shirt, the bright smile that seemed familiar yet also mysterious and unknowable.

"Anyway." His mom gestured into the air, waved her hand, as if she were brushing away cobwebs or cigarette smoke. "Anyway. I just wanted to try to give you a little more info than I had. Maybe you'll find it useful, maybe not." She gave him a crooked grin. "Don't say I didn't try, though."

Zack was genuinely touched. He relaxed just long enough to put his arms around his mother for a moment, let her hold him, smelled the trace of Chanel perfume. She always smelled the same; it comforted him. "Thanks, Mom."

"No prob," his mother said, kissing the side of his head. "What movie are you going to see?"

"Something R-rated, hopefully?" Zack smiled wickedly. His mother swatted his arm.

He kept his promise; Zack would not make his mother's mistakes. He would make entirely new ones.

A WEEK after Josh's mom died and her memorial service was over, he was seated at the desk in his room one evening doing his homework—not that there was much to do, his teachers were bending over backward to be nice to him right now. He needed a ruler for his math homework involving number lines and opened the center desk drawer.

Without warning, his heart, which had been badly bruised for the past couple of weeks, jumped in his chest and spasmed. There, in the center drawer, was an envelope, and on the envelope was written his name, in his mother's handwriting.

Josh felt as if something wild and desperate

was fluttering inside of him. He picked up the envelope with trembling hands, ran his hands over it, traced the swooping lines of his mother's signature. With a burst of something like frenzy, he tore the envelope open.

Inside was a single piece of pale lavender stationary, and, in fragile, neat handwriting, the following message:

> *My boy:*
>
> *I know I don't have much time left, so I want to make sure that I use what time I have the best way I know how.*
>
> *The greatest joys of my life have been having your father as my husband and having you as my son. One of the greatest sorrows I have is that I won't be able to be with you on your wedding day.*
>
> *All I can say is, when you fall in love, I hope it's really and truly love, and that it's reciprocated. Sex is going to be an important part of your life someday, but sex without love is only a shadow of all that it can be.*
>
> *Please ask your father if you have any questions along the way about this subject, and I've also asked Beth if she'll "stand in" for me if you have a question your father can't answer.*

Know that I would give all I have to watch you become the fine young man I know you will be some-day. If I can do anything to help send along someone special for you, I'll try my best. Don't wait for me, though—go try to find love yourself. It's too important to wait for. And when you find it, don't let it go.

All my love,
Mama

Josh's eyes blurred with tears. He folded the letter up, slipped it back in its envelope, and put it back in the drawer. He thought of it many, many times in the years to come, but there were other times when he wondered if, in fact, he would ever find the kind of love his mother was talking about. And his mother had been right: sex was something anyone could do by themselves—but love was a thing that required a partner.

CHAPTER 38

Friday morning, Zack was seated at the kitchen table, head in his arms. He'd been so giddy last night thinking about Jamie's party and everything coming together that he hadn't gone to sleep till almost one-thirty in the morning. When the alarm went off, he'd somehow managed to get out of bed, dress himself in the past week's discards, brush his teeth, and stumble downstairs, but now the mists of dreamland were beckoning him home again. There was a skateboard tournament going on, and Zack was starring in it while Missy clapped and cheered from the judge's box. A sleepy grin crossed his face at the image.

There was a nudge at his elbow. Alex prodded him with the ancient Graceland coffee mug that no one knew where it had come from, and Zack, unthinkingly, grabbed it and swallowed the brown liquid in one gulp. He immediately shot from his seat, unleashing a stream of obscenities, and stuck his whole mouth under the kitchen faucet until whatever-it-was was more or less rinsed out.

He turned, breathing fire, on his younger brother. "What the *hell* was that?!"

"We're out of coffee," Alex explained helpfully, "so I took some of Mark's chocolate-covered espresso beans and cappuccino Jelly Bellies and some soy milk, put it in the blender, then put it in the mug and microwaved it. Are you awake now?"

"*Oh* yeah." Zack couldn't have been more awake if he'd been struck with a hammer. He ushered his brother—who was midway through a long description of *his* dreams from the night before, which seemed to involve various anime cartoons he wasn't supposed to have seen—out of the kitchen and toward the car.

JOSH MADE a cheese omelet with leftover potatoes done home-fry style for breakfast. It was unlike him to indulge himself in this way on a weekday—he'd managed to peel off some twenty-five pounds over a year by sticking with cereal or yogurt smoothies in the mornings five days a week—but he was feeling jittery, and the ritual of prepping and cooking food relaxed him. Besides, being in the kitchen and working amidst the cool stainless-steel appliances reminded him of his mother preparing food and helped reassure him.

He cracked the eggs into the ancient robin's-egg-blue bowl and beat them until they were a sunshine-yellow froth, then added some grated parmesan and mozzarella, along with basil, garlic, and oregano. He set the eggs aside and began to slice the leftover potatoes into cubes, throwing them into the pan with a handful of spices. The eggs would cook in the leftover oil from the pota-toes. It was a ritual he'd performed many times since his mother had died, and he'd grown sick of Pop-Tarts in the morning.

As Josh methodically prepared his meal, his mind drifted back to his dream from the night be-fore. He and Zack had been lost in a cave, he remembered, and neither of them could find their way out of the dark passage. At one point he thought he saw a glimpse of daylight up and off to the side, but Zack said, "No, we ought to go on," and Josh had followed him further into the blackness, their torches growing fainter and fainter. Then Zack had turned a corner, and Josh was suddenly alone, his torch almost out, and nothing but darkness reaching out to embrace him. He was just opening his mouth to holler for help and see if someone heard him when he woke up.

Josh slid the potatoes onto his plate and poured the egg mixture into the pan, frowning at the golden goo. He didn't have to be Sigmund Freud to figure out that he was worried about tonight—was that what the passage was? Was Jamie's party a dead end, or the beginning of something? Was Zack leading them in the right direction? Why was he such a mess of nerves, when he was—potentially—on the verge of getting everything he wanted?

Josh folded the omelet, slid it next to the potatoes, and pulled out the O.J. carton so he could swig from it while eating. He hopped up on the counter and stuck his fork into the warm food, inserted it into his mouth. It tasted delicious, all he could've hoped for.

Then he turned and promptly vomited into the sink.

JAMIE DECIDED on her power tie for the day: purple with peppermint-pink stripes. She'd read an old article once about "power ties," and immediately decided that she needed some, courtesy of the Macy's men's department. She still wasn't exactly sure what a "power tie" *was,* but this one had jumped out at her, and looked sensational with her white blouse, black skirt, and a hat with a lavender band.

It was a good thing Chantel was picking her up this morning because it was pushing eight o'clock and Brian had yet to make an appearance. Jamie frowned at the front hallway clock, frowned again as she heard the horn in the driveway, then took one step up the stairs, the better to project her voice to the upper level. "Brian, it's almost eight! School is rumored to start this century!"

A loud *thud*—the sound of her brother presumably throwing himself out of bed—greeted her ears, followed by the yanking-open of his bedroom door. She added, for good measure, "I'm going with Chantel, see you there!" and vamoosed out the front door. What *would* that boy do without her running his life?

Chantel was wearing black and white with green accents. Jamie approved. They complemented each other: The Mistress and The Apprentice.

BRIAN WAS SO frazzled he could barely think coherently. He ran around his room, a towel clutched haphazardly about his waist, dripping water from his shower all over the carpet. He grabbed underwear, socks, a clean shirt, and jeans and threw them in a pile on the bed, madly grabbing each item as he needed it. It was the second night in a row that he'd gotten crappy sleep, and his brain felt like a giant soggy cotton ball. Dressed, he vaulted his way down the stairs and into the kitchen, stuffing a bagel in his mouth for the road. He'd be late to pick up—

No, he wouldn't.

After ten minutes of racing like a madman, he

suddenly came to a screeching halt in the middle of the kitchen. The hum of the refrigerator and the slight *plop plop plop* of the faucet was all he heard. That, and his thoughts, so loud that his football coach might as well have been in front of him, shouting the words in Brian's face.

He didn't have to pick up Missy. It was very possible that after tonight, he'd never pick up Missy again.

He felt so overcome with this realization that he had to sit for a moment on a kitchen chair, staring dully at his mother's shelf of African violets. He'd basically told her they were over, hadn't he? After tonight, he was a free man.

Free to do what?

Free to *want* what?

An abrupt memory of being in a Baskin-Robbins with his grandmother when he was younger, maybe nine or ten, forced its way into his mind. It had been blistering hot outside, and standing in the cool, air-conditioned store, he'd been suddenly paralyzed with indecision. Thirty-one flavors? Where to begin? What if he chose wrong?

"Pick something, Brian," his grandmother had sighed impatiently, tapping her lacquered nails on the countertop. "Don't keep the boy waiting."

"That's okay," the kid had said, shrugging and smiling down at Brian. He had shoulder-length brown hair and looked sort of like an actor on a teen soap opera. Brian blushed, panicking, not wanting to make a decision, not wanting to leave this cool, pink world with the smiling boy. His grandmother had sighed and leaned closer to the young man. "He just can't commit to anything. Never could."

Brian's head was on the verge of exploding from the pressure. He gasped a little, and said, too loudly, too emphatically, "Vanilla."

"Vanilla?" His grandmother's voice rose in disbelief. "Is that really what you want?"

No. "Yes." No.

"Wanna make it at least French vanilla?" the kid asked, giving Brian another smile as he tossed the hair back from his face. Brian had a sudden flash of a boy in his class, Josh Bradshaw, who also had dark brown bangs and dark eyes.

"Sure."

The French vanilla was better than regular vanilla, deep yellow in color and rich in flavor. It still wasn't really what Brian had wanted, but it was good enough. He kept licking at his cone the whole time his grandmother drove them home in her silver Escalade, muttering to herself, "Can't believe we went to Baskin-Robbins—thirty-one flavors!—and he gets vanilla. Doesn't that beat all." When they got home, he had given the rest of the cone to Jamie, who had eaten it in two bites flat.

The next time his grandmother took him to Baskin-Robbins, the boy wasn't there, and a bored-looking Asian girl with too-shiny lip gloss had served them. His grandmother spent the first two minutes recapping the whole vanilla experience for the girl, who looked like she couldn't have cared less. A wave of anger had gripped him, and he'd felt an unusual hatred toward his grandmother. Without waiting for her to finish the story, he ordered a double-scoop cone of Rainbow Sherbet and Peanut Butter and Chocolate. It was so disgusting that he only ate half of it, then pretended to trip so he could drop the cone. His grandmother didn't take him for ice cream again after that.

"Is that what you really *want?"*

"He just can't commit *to anything."*

He tried. He had tried. When he tried, he embarrassed himself. When he tried, he chose wrong. When he tried, he cared too much. He wanted to stop caring. He wanted—oh! He wanted—so much. Yet, what he wanted most of all was to not want anything.

Brian stared at the little honeybee saltshaker on the counter, embracing the hive pepper shaker. His eyes blurred.

CHAPTER 39

Mrs. Hoff drove Missy to school, fretting the whole way about Missy's not talking to Brian the night before, not to mention not getting a ride from him. "I just think you need to be careful, honey. Make sure that you haven't made any rash decisions."

"I haven't, Mama." Missy laid her head back on the headrest, stared at the visor, at a to-go menu for a local Chinese restaurant that they'd never gotten around to ordering from. How long had it been tucked there, forlornly advertising honey-walnut prawns and Happy Family and fried rice, as yet untried and untasted?

"Don't be dismissive, Melissa," her mother

said, a bleating tone creeping into her voice, like the persistent lamb pursuing Mary. "You may think you have all this figured out, but it's hard to go back once you've closed a door behind you. I'm just concerned, that's all." Her mother looked like she was regretting her church group supper scheduled for that evening.

"Mama, I'll see Brian tonight." Missy tried to suppress her irritation. "I told you, he's having a few friends over, and we're going to see each other then. We'll talk *then*. If I have any other news flashes between now and tomorrow, I'll let you know."

"I hope you know, Melissa," her mother spoke slowly, letting her words defrost syllable by syllable, "that I wouldn't let you spend the night at just anyone's house after a party. It's only because I know the Esaus are a nice family that I'm comfortable with this. Any *other* boy, from any *other* family ..."

Like Zack Standish, perhaps? "Well," Missy rejoined, trying to keep her voice from acquiring an edge, "you don't need to worry. I'm sure no one else would want me to come over—or want to come to our house."

"Oh, honey," her mother said, and suddenly

her eyes filled with tears. Melissa hated it when her mother cried, as it automatically made her want to burst into tears herself. Fortunately, they pulled up in front of school right then. Missy ejected herself from the car as if catapulted, then stopped, turned, and bent to look in the window. Her mother was wiping her eyes. Missy felt lower than pond scum.

"Mom, you don't have to worry. I'll make good decisions. If I don't see you this afternoon, I'll see you tomorrow morning. And if anything gets weird, I'll call you. I promise." She said all this in a rush, around the lump growing in her throat.

Mrs. Hoff wiped her eyes once more. "I just wish your father was around right now. I think we need him at home."

"Maybe *you* do," Missy said, her voice jagged like broken glass. "I'll be okay. I'm always your good girl, remember?" She didn't want her father home, didn't need him. He and his damn business trips for days or weeks at a time, and the travel itinerary accidentally emailed home from the company's travel bureau for him and his administrative assistant, Cheri, detailing five days in

Hong Kong with one hotel room. She'd deleted it before her mother saw it.

She slammed the car door and stalked toward school, not looking back.

CHAPTER 40

The day crawled by.

Clocks ticked. Flies buzzed against windowpanes. Kids swarmed the halls between classes, vanished into rooms when bells rang; fifty-five minutes later, they emerged again.

Brian made up a quiz in Math. Jamie nearly blew up something in Chemistry. In Social Studies, Chantel tried to explain white privilege to a roomful of kids who didn't get it. Zack read the part of Malvolio aloud in English class. Missy had another meeting in the Blue Room with Ms. Sullivan and several other kids during lunch. Josh conjugated French verbs.

At three o'clock, kids burst out the doors of

the school like a pipe had exploded. By three-thirty, the parking lot was completely empty except for Ms. Sullivan's car. She was grading the *Twelfth Night* quiz.

At four o'clock, Jamie, Chantel, and Consuella were running around in all directions in the Esau kitchen, opening the fridge and various cupboards. Brian took one look and fled to his room in search of something violent to play on his computer.

At five o'clock, Yoshi was sharpening pencils and laying them out meticulously on the desk next to his notebook. He also had his phone charged and ready. Simultaneously, across town, the Yearbook Kid was testing various lenses on a brand-new camera.

CHAPTER 41

At six o'clock, Zack was standing in front of his closet, holding up one appalling outfit after another in front of Alex, while Green Day blasted from his stereo. Alex just kept shaking his head no—no to the tuxedo T-shirt, no to the retro "He-Man" T-shirt, no to the "Shuck Me Suck Me Eat Me Raw: Brady's Oysters" T-shirt. No, no, no.

"Which one do *you* like, little Mr. Tom Ford?" Zack finally growled in frustration.

Alex calmly pulled out a cream-colored dress shirt with a faint fleur-de-lis pattern in it, a pair of black jeans, and a dark tie. He raised one eyebrow Mr. Spock-style at Zack, something he'd been practicing lately in the bathroom mirror.

"I'll look like a missionary," Zack moaned.

"You'll look nice," Alex said firmly. "And remember, don't wear sneakers."

"Oh yeah?" his brother snarled. "Well—just you remember, I can turn you upside down."

"You *wouldn't*," Alex breathed, mixing mock horror with delicious anticipation.

"Oh, no?" Zack dove and grabbed him by the ankles, and in one smooth move jerked him topsy-turvy so that Alex's hair brushed the floor. He then proceeded to swing his brother back and forth like a giant pendulum.

"Stop!" Alex shrieked, giggling uncontrollably. "Stop, stop!"

"What's this?" Zack intoned ominously, Indiana Jones sighting a new discovery. "This looks like someone's exposed tummy! Maybe we should ... *tickle it!*"

Alex's hysterical giggles and shrieks eventually attracted their mother, who firmly retrieved her younger son from the Tickle Monster, and Zack suited up. Finally, he stood regarding himself in the mirror. *Maybe it is better to dress up.* Missy was used to Brian, so she clearly liked guys who made the effort to look nice.

He skulked to his mom's bathroom and

checked; yep, Mark still had some Perry Ellis shaving lotion in the cabinet—kind of old school, but it would do in a pinch. Zack put a few little dots on his neck, where his lightning-quick shower shave had left a couple of minor scratches; no big deal, the collar of the dress shirt would cover them. *Damn, Alex really does know best.*

Zack eyed his reflection critically for a moment. There was still the red hair, a fact of life he couldn't do anything about, but the sun had given it more of a strawberry-blonde tint. The freckles were another thing over which he had no control, unlike most students' tanned, glowing complexions. Still, he didn't think he looked too bad. He almost looked like he could pass—as if he were a regular kid at the Academy, a kid with money and a sports car instead of an ancient VW bug. A kid who was popular, with a whole bunch of friends. A kid whose parents never divorced. A kid who belonged. A kid who deserved a girl like Missy Hoff.

Zack stared at the mirror, and his eyes widened as a thought suddenly appeared in his mind, like a tiny little weed freshly sprouted. Did he really want Missy? Or did he just want what she *represented?*

Did he want a girlfriend, or did he want a ticket into first class?

Oh, this was stupid. Of course he wanted Missy! She was beautiful, wasn't she? Didn't he lie in bed at night, and wonder what it would be like to kiss her, to hold her, to slide his hands down to the small of her back, then further? Wasn't he just thinking of her fifteen minutes ago in the shower? Wasn't she everything he could want, anything any guy could want? Well, any guy except Josh.

Josh. Zack's eyes widened further. Did Josh really think about Brian the way he thought about Missy? Did Josh want to do things to Brian that Zack wanted to do to Missy, or did Josh want Brian to do them to him? While Zack was on task to land the girl he'd obsessed about for months, years, would Josh be with Brian? Would he, Zack, have to *watch* Josh with Brian? The thought made him feel skeevy. And what would happen when people found out about Josh? Would they assume things about Zack as well? Would all of his plans hit the wall at eighty miles an hour?

He couldn't ditch Josh. Josh was his friend. But maybe ... maybe Josh wouldn't go through with the Brian angle. Maybe Zack could talk him out of it or distract him or something. Maybe Josh could keep his sexual orientation on the "D.L.," as they said on the talk shows. Or just wait until Zack and Missy were a proper couple, so no one would jump to the wrong conclusions.

And what about the Esau spawn? Zack hadn't been to their house in years. When his mother was dropping off some classroom materials for Brian and Jamie's mother, he'd sat in the car while she ran up to the door. It had been raining, and he'd sat in the front seat feeling like a freak when he noticed Jamie staring at him curiously from the rain-streaked living room window. He'd never seen a porch that six people could stand on before, much less a private driveway. What would the inside of the house be like? Fear ran a cold, narrow finger down his neck as he remembered the piñata disaster of his youth.

But this wasn't a party like that; this was just a bunch of kids getting together, no pressure. He didn't have to impress anyone, except Missy. There wouldn't be any drama, nothing would get broken or damaged. This wouldn't be like other instances in the Zack Standish Hall of Infamy. He would be coolly aloof to Jamie and Brian. He would make a great impression. He would show himself to be the perfect boyfriend. Missy deserved nothing less.

He needed help with his stupid tie; he never could tie them himself. He went and found Alex, who stood on a chair and did a Windsor knot for him.

MISSY ENTERED HER ROOM QUIETLY, stared down at the beautiful white dress lying on her bed, looking like a deflated wedding cake. Attached to it was a note.

Have a wonderful time—love you so much—
Mom.

It was a little Audrey Hepburn-esque, and not as form-fitting or colorful as one Missy would've picked herself. Still, she knew this was her mother's way of papering over the stresses from the morning. She undressed quickly and slipped the dress on, contorting her body to get the back zipped up. She pushed her hair back over her shoulders, then pulled it forward again. Yes. That was the look. She pulled one of her favorite necklaces from her jewelry box, one Brian had given her on their year anniversary, a gold heart with her birthstone in the middle of it, a sapphire chip.

She would drive her father's car tonight since he was out of town—the cloud-gray Mercedes. How odd it was that she never thought to drive most of the time, getting rides from her mother, or Brian. Maybe it was high time she drove herself someplace.

JOSH TOOK one last look at himself in the mirror, pawing at his hair. He had to get out of the house now if he was going to pick up Zack on time, but he couldn't help yanking off the dark green shirt he was wearing in favor of a deep crimson one. He'd go with the bolo tie and wear his cowboy boots; might as well embrace the Southwest look full-on. Dr. Seuss's words floated through his head. *Why fit in when you were born to stand out?* Josh loved that.

He was acutely aware of the silence in the house with his father gone on his business trip. Could his mom see him? It had been almost five years, yet there were still moments where he felt like her presence was nearby—when lying in bed, he could almost swear that he felt someone gently touching his forehead. Would she have liked this shirt? What would she have to say about this whole thing with Zack, and the party, and Brian? Would he have made her proud of him?

His stomach gurgled again, but he'd eaten nothing for hours. The clock chimed. He splashed some cold water on his face, letting the droplets run down and drip off the dark spikes above his forehead.

"All right," he said to no one in particular, "let's do this."

CHAPTER 42

It was approaching eight o'clock by the time Josh and Zack pulled up outside the Esau house. Lights spilled from every window, and loud dance music was already amping up. The driveway was lined with luxury sports cars and "hand-me-down" Beamers that bored, forty-something housewives and moms bequeathed to their children while trading up to newer, better models (of cars, usually, but also occasionally husbands). For a brief, guilty flash, Zack was glad Josh had driven them; he didn't need any extra reminders tonight about how much he didn't really belong here.

Josh slid his eyes over to his friend, and for a moment thought he saw Zack's jaw tighten. His own guts felt like they were on a ride at Knott's Berry Farm, but he was determined to see this through—for himself, for his friend, for the sheer masochism of it all. At least this time he had Zack with him, unlike The Garret Incident.

"Come on," he said, a little too loudly and gruffly. Zack squinted at him a little suspiciously, but followed Josh up the driveway, slamming the car door too emphatically behind him.

They walked through the slightly open front door into a sea of faces and a roar of noise; it seemed as if a healthy chunk of the Academy's population was here, based on the seething mass of Old Navy, Sean John, and Juicy Couture surrounding them. Zack took a moment to scan the digs: the tiled foyer, the expensive art—well, Thomas Kincaid—the draperies in the living room, where approximately fifty kids were draped over the Laura Ashley furniture, noshing on snacks and drinking out of plastic wine stemware. (That was definitely a Jamie touch; no paper or red solo cups were in sight.) Josh was less impressed with the surroundings, as they weren't that different from his own home; however, he did notice that there seemed to be a preponderance of expensive furnishings and designer pieces meant to impress visitors, as if most of the room had been ordered verbatim from a catalog. There was even a pile of polished stones in the hallway powder room sink, for reasons no one could quite fathom.

I would feel like a guest even if I lived here, Josh thought. *A guest in my own home. A guest in my own life. Is that how Brian feels?*

There was a stir in the crowd, a murmuring ripple that coursed through the room, and heads turned to look just behind them. Zack and Josh turned to see what was attracting everyone's attention.

Jamie was making her entrance. She paused on the landing, surveying the crowd of kids like Madonna in that Eva Peron movie, lifting her arm just enough in greeting. She was wearing a strapless, backless black dress that looked like it had been spray-painted on her and dangling silver earrings. Her heels were sky-high, and black and silver as well. A faint, sly smile played across her lips, not enough to show teeth. Zack was about to comment on how she looked like a shark, like in the old Bobby Darin song, but Josh was busy staring at Jamie as if he had never seen her before —indeed, he looked as if he had been turned into a block of wood.

Then she was standing right in front of them, ignoring the chorus of girls oohing and ahhing, blind and deaf to the boys looking at her the way starving hounds might look at a chicken dinner. She extended her hand to Josh as if meaning for it to be kissed, then in one smooth move yanked it away from him as he took it; then she did the same for Zack.

Her voice, like her earrings, was silvery. "Well darlings, welcome, welcome. I assume it's been quite some time for one or both of you, yes? Let's go in."

They couldn't resist her if they tried; her arms were already linked with theirs like chains, and she moved in between them, ushering them along as smoothly as if they were human bookends to her novella.

Then they were in what seemed to be another living room, also filled with kids. This one had ceramic plates propped on a picture rail around the ceiling, with different flower patterns etched on them, and a dangling chandelier that looked like an icy relic from the Fortress of Solitude. Chantel, wearing a purple top, blue jeans, and boots, was circling the room collecting keys from kids into a fedora—Jamie's, Josh presumed.

Josh's heart suddenly hiccupped; Brian was slumped in a corner in an armchair, wearing something designer that Jamie had probably picked out for him; the deep blue shirt matched his eyes. He looked out of place and miserable and was staring at a table loaded with snacks as though guacamole was the most depressing thing in the world.

Zack reached around Jamie and nudged Josh in the ribs; he'd noticed Brian too. They tried to exchange significant looks, but it was difficult with Jamie turning from one to the other, chatting blithely about the refreshments, the drinks, "Oh please drop your keys with Chantel, *so* glad you're here." Quite a change from yesterday morning.

There was a commotion behind them, and Hank, goons in tow, banged into the foyer extra loudly to demand attention. He was yelling something undecipherable above the din, puncturing it with raucous laughter. His friends, Moe and Curly, joined him.

Jamie's smile tightened. "Excuse me, I don't remember inviting any bad fairies to this christening. I'm going to have to go sharpen my spinning wheel." She was so busy smiling at Josh as she purred this that she was nearly decapitated by Kat bringing out another huge tray loaded with food, this time miniature pizzas.

"Did you do all this by yourself?" Zack asked, surveying the groaning table.

"Consuella helped," Jamie said dismissively. "She's in the kitchen; she'll surface if there's trouble."

"Oh, I doubt there'll be trouble," Josh said, trying to sound reassuring, though that was far from how he was feeling.

Zack and Jamie regarded him with, ironically, near-identical smirks; however, they were too busy looking at Josh to notice each other.

There was yet another commotion behind them, as several girls all rushed to the front door squealing simultaneously; everyone turned to look. Missy had entered in her knock-your-socks-off white dress, Cinderella at the ball. Girls crowded around her all talking in half-finished interjections.

"Oh, miGOD!"

"I *love* that!"

"You look so—"

"Where did you—"

Jamie, completely upstaged, uttered a snort of disgust and bit into a loaded cracker, promptly dusting the front of her dress with crumbs. Zack, oblivious to her distress, absently began to step forward toward Missy; Josh gently but firmly restrained him as Brian pushed his way through the crowd to Missy's side. He leaned in and kissed her cheek—a little hesitantly, if you were looking for it, but with enough honest affection to provoke a chorus of hoots and catcalls from some semi-blitzed guys. Brian guided her into the room as people applauded and wolf-whistled, the once and future Homecoming King and Queen.

Zack was so narrow-eyed by this point that he was nearly blind; similarly, Jamie's mental wheels were spinning like mad. Josh and Chantel, unlikely allies to the unfolding drama, looked at each other with matching expressions of concern, brown eyes both flashing *can you believe this?*

Jamie reached into the bosom of her dress and

extracted the world's smallest bottle, the kind Alice would've found lying around in Wonderland with a *Drink Me* message tied to its neck. The entire room was dancing, drinking, or fussing over Brian and Missy, and there were several glasses of champagne already poured with little wine charm baubles snapped around the stems. She needed less than ten seconds.

In a smooth movement, she pulled several of the glasses to the front of the table, surreptitiously pouring drops of liquid into the two front drinks and stirring it up with her finger. Zack, focused on Missy and her vaguely troubled smile, was oblivious.

Two people in the room, however, were watching her every move: Josh and Chantel.

Jamie turned, in her best party-at-the-Macbeth's style, and held up the champagne glasses, smiling as dazzlingly as Las Vegas at night. "Chantel ... why don't you take a drink over to Missy? Zack ... drink?"

Chantel took the glass with a significant look, smiled, and melted into the crowd.

Josh shot Jamie a panicked glare; he was going to spill the gourmet cannellini beans soon if she didn't calm him down. He looked like he was breaking into a cold sweat, but Zack had his eyes locked on Missy and didn't notice.

Jamie leaned in close enough to Josh that he could smell the gardenia perfume trace on her neck, and her voice caressed him like silken thread: "Not a roofie—not dangerous, just ground-up sleeping pills. Just to make sure it all goes smoothly."

Josh, not reassured, opened his mouth to speak, but Zack was already swigging from the glass she'd offered him. He downed at least half of it in one gulp, making a face at Josh. "Ugh. Champagne—piss with an attitude. Isn't there any beer around here?" He grabbed Josh's arm and pulled him away from Jamie, dropping his voice to a hoarse whisper amidst the din. "You grab Chantel and go talk to Brian. I'll hit Missy. Got it?"

Josh felt like he was on his way to the death chamber, but he nodded, swallowed, and said, "Right." It was too late to stop the wheels from turning now; anything he did to try to get Zack out of the party and away would only cause a scene.

But Zack was suddenly outflanked by Chantel, offering a glass to Missy while simultaneously easing Brian away from her and in another direction. Frustrated, Zack stepped back into the foyer, still swigging from his glass.

As Chantel pulled Brian away, Jamie glided to Missy's side, complimenting her on her dress and clinking her glass in a toast. A look of confusion and disbelief crossed Missy's face, followed by a look of wonder and shy gratitude. Was Jamie expressing sympathy to her for Missy and Brian's troubles? She smiled tentatively, but did not raise the glass to her lips, even as Jamie sipped from her own. Josh's stomach did another flip-flop.

A fast dance song came on the stereo, something from the '90s New Jack Swing renaissance. Chantel had an arm around Brian and was trying to get him to dance with her; Brian's eyes were fixed on the floor, despite Chantel's attempts to engage him. A group of kids moved aside to give them room, and as Chantel stepped up her efforts, Brian actually began to move his hips and grin a little bit. He looked close to enjoying himself. Chantel grabbed his hand, twirled herself away from him, then twirled back in, bursting into a loud, throaty laugh as they bumped into each other and eliciting a chuckle from Brian. Intrigued, Jamie and Missy set their glasses on the edge of the table and moved to the growing edge of the circle to watch the dancers.

Suddenly, Josh realized that this was the moment if he was going to do something bold. He looked to his left: Jamie and Missy had their backs away from him, and to his right, Zack was still in the foyer talking—egad!—with Hank, who seemed to be having a few problems standing upright. Brian and Chantel were dancing, and no one else was at the food table.

He skulked around behind the platters of food, reaching innocently for a chip. Jamie's glass, with a little snap-on charm of turquoise beads, was right next to a cut-glass punch bowl, Missy's glass, with the same charm design only bedecked in peach and orange beads, was over closer to the veggie tray.

No one seemed to be noticing him. *Now*.

In one almost-smooth movement, Josh grabbed both glasses, popped the charms loose, and switched them, a little bit of Missy's slopping over onto his hand. Flustered, he set them both down too hard, watched the liquid sloshing and spinning in the glass as he did so. He grabbed a napkin and was drying off his hand when he realized people were applauding.

He looked up again; the dance was over, and Brian and Chantel had stepped apart. Brian, abashed, was looking at the floor and very shyly at Missy, but Chantel—*was looking right at Josh.*

Josh didn't move; he was struck stock-still with terror. Jamie and Missy's backs were still toward him; they were also applauding, and they hadn't turned. Maybe Chantel was looking at Jamie?

But then Chantel's lips slowly curved into one of her trademark Mona Lisa smiles, and Josh's stomach elevator crashed to the ground floor.

He looked at her with desperate pleading in his eyes, hoping against hope. *What did she see? What does she know?* Would she tell Jamie immediately, or let him sweat for a while?

What had he just done?

Jamie and Missy were back, standing in front of him, Missy commenting, "I didn't know that Brian could dance like that."

"There's a lot of things you don't know about Brian," Jamie said, trying not to sound too cryptic. "Here, try the smoked herring, it's good." She proffered an appetizer cracker to Missy with a bit of seafood and some sort of cream cheese spread on it. "Oh, but you'll probably need to drink after this, they're *very* salty." Jamie's eyes slid over to Josh, and though her face remained coolly composed, Josh saw for the first time that night a flicker of hunger in her eyes.

She thinks she's won. His throat closed up, as though he'd swallowed lye.

"Oh, my," Missy said, her mouth full of appetizer. She picked up the glass—the safe glass—and took a sip from it, then a larger gulp. "You're right, it *is* salty!" She laughed a little bit, nervously. "What do you call this again?"

"Cold fish," Jamie answered, pleasantly at first, but by the second word her voice had regained its machete edge. Task accomplished, she turned abruptly on her heel and walked away with the other glass, leaving Missy standing alone by the buffet, a look of hurt bewilderment on her face.

Josh opened his mouth to say something to her, but Jamie was already making eye contact with him from across the room. He had to get her somewhere before the drink kicked in, or make sure Chantel was with her when it did.

Missy turned to face him and he thought he'd be trapped, just as Zack came up behind her and gave Josh his best watch-and-learn look. "Didn't think you were going to avoid me all evening, did you?"

"I didn't have time earlier to say hello ... Hello," Missy said, turning and smiling at Zack. She took another tentative sip of her drink. Zack gave Josh a quick jerk of his head: go now. Well, at least Missy would be with him, Josh thought. One less thing to keep track of.

Josh eased himself around the buffet and headed toward Jamie. As he left, he looked back at them; Missy had spilled a little on herself, and Zack was assisting her with a fistful of napkins. On the far side of the room, Brian was sitting in his chair again, drinking another glass of something that did not look like fruit punch. His sad eyes were locked on Missy and Zack, and he looked like nothing so much as an old teddy bear that a child had abandoned in a forgotten corner in favor of a new plaything. Chantel knelt beside him and whispered something in his ear, gently guiding his head and gaze away from the couple.

Josh slid casually up behind Jamie, who was monitoring the room while more or less lurking behind a giant potted plant. What was she now, an extra in an old spy movie?

"It's working," Jamie breathed. "In a little

while Zack will squire Missy upstairs for their night of passion, only to have both of them pass out in each other's arms. Missy wakes up in the laundry room, and Zack wakes up with me. Perfect."

"Yeah ... perfect," Josh said, not very convincingly. His head hurt.

"So," Jamie smirked, "Mr. Bradshaw. My brother is over there, getting slowly but surely bombed out of his mind. In about twenty minutes, he'll be all yours."

"He's not that drunk, is he?" Josh frowned. Brian definitely looked as if he were starting to plod down the road toward Sleepytown, but it wasn't even nine o'clock yet. How long and how much had he been drinking?

"I decided to help speed things along." Jamie looked as pleased as if she'd hand-planted the deadly poppy field outside of Munchkinland. "Chantel took him some special champagne earlier as well; he'll be ready for beddy-bye real soon." A nudge in Josh's direction seemed like exactly what her brother needed but was afraid to act on; Jamie—of course—knew what was best for him.

"I didn't want that!" A bolt of anger shot

through Josh, maybe even something akin to rage. A couple of kids looked at them strangely and moved away.

"I just handed you your dream on a silver platter, and you're complaining?" Jamie's eyebrows were raised almost to her hairline.

"Maybe I don't want to be handed a dream." Josh's voice was shaking, but he felt strong, stronger than he had for quite some time, as though his words were channeling some sort of life force that inspired him. "Maybe I don't want to just manipulate my way into seducing someone, like you do. Maybe I want someone to really love me for who I am, someone who'll talk to me because they want to, not because drugs are making them." He lowered his voice, Clint Eastwood-style, and almost spat the last words at her smug face. "And *maybe* I want nothing else to do with you tonight." He took a step back from her, ready to use this as an exit line.

Jamie's face didn't move, but a flush of pink came to her cheeks. Her voice, however, remained cool and calm. "The night, Mr. Bradshaw, is young. Much is yet to transpire." Her words were as cold and hard as cemetery marble.

"Wait half an hour," Josh said, almost exulting

as he stepped away. He was dangerously close to being cocky or confrontational, but he couldn't help it. "You don't know how much."

CHANTEL OPENED the door for Zack and Missy to step out onto the patio. Though the day had been warm, it was starting to become overcast, and the moon was covered with clouds. Neither of them felt cold, however, and the fact that they were alone outside gave both of them a warm glow.

Zack spoke first. "How're you feeling?"

"Fine ... I'm fine." Missy let the pause hang in the air for a moment between them, then added, almost as an afterthought, "Brian looks nice, doesn't he."

"I guess so," Zack responded tentatively. Discussing how Brian looked wasn't quite his idea of romantic foreplay.

"Josh says you think I'm pretty ... do you?" Missy had been staring across the lawn at the floodlights when she offered the remark about Brian, but now she'd turned sharply and was facing Zack.

Zack felt his heart slam into overdrive like he'd just had a triple-shot espresso. He decided to try an approach unusual for him: complete honesty. "No … I think you're beautiful." He swallowed as he said the last word, so it came out sort of choked, but Missy didn't seem to care. She was looking at him as if she'd never seen him before, as though he were someone and something entirely unlike himself. Zack felt a rush of courage. "I can't be near you; I can't even think about you without getting so turned on I go crazy."

After the last words he felt as though he might have said too much; however, Missy didn't seem to notice. She fixed him with a steady gaze, as though he were a particularly vexing math problem she was trying to solve in her head.

Her voice when she finally spoke was uninflected. "What do you want from me?"

"It's more about what I can *give* you." He figured if he made it seem like a generous gift on his part, she might be more receptive to his intentions.

Missy seemed not to hear this last sentence. She had turned back toward the house and was looking in the windows at the room full of teenagers enjoying themselves, all save one. Brian was still sitting in his chair, his eyes once again focused on nothing in particular, his face as desolate as the Black Hole of Calcutta.

She spoke absently, as though narrating a faraway bedtime story to a distracted child. "I used to think I loved him so much ... and that he loved me too."

Zack felt a surge of panic; his momentum was in danger of flagging. He took a step forward, daring to touch her arm, willing her to drag her eyes away from the window and look into his own. "Take it out on me. Let me do what he wouldn't. Let me ... be him. Only better."

Had he gone too far? He left his hand on her arm, felt the warmth of her exposed skin, then a ridge of goosebumps. He let his fingertips caress them for a moment, watched himself do it, then looked at her again. Her eyes looked lifeless, as though the spark had been drained out of them. Yet he could feel his own body crackling with energy, as though a hum of electricity was almost audibly emanating from him.

As he slid his hand down her arm, she slid her hand into his own and clutched it tightly. Her jaw was set resolutely, as though she were ready to lead a battalion. She whirled around, as if startled by her own decisiveness, and yanked him after her, back up the steps and into the house.

Missy pulled Zack through the party with grim determination, never pausing or losing stride. Zack, his face contorted in crazy glee, managed to give a hurried "thumbs up" signal to a gobsmacked Josh as he was dragged through the crowd of kids, several of whom shot them bewildered looks as the unlikely couple flashed by.

Josh watched Missy and Zack disappear up the stairs, then shifted his gaze to Jamie, who was standing against a wall watching them disappear and looking cruelly amused. Brian had finally been roused from his chair once again to dance with Chantel, but as Zack and Missy hurried by, he slugged the rest of his drink, devastation writ large across his features. Jamie and Josh almost collided as they simultaneously hurried to Chantel and Brian's side.

"Brian, why don't you and Josh go up to your room and look at pictures of when you were kids for a while, huh? It'll take your mind off things," Jamie almost cooed, straightening his shirt out a bit. Josh rarely got to see Jamie's maternal, caring side, and it frightened him almost as much as a full-on Bates Motel bloodbath would.

Yet her brother seemed to take it in stride, as though he were used to people telling him what to do. He slung an arm around Josh, and the full weight of Brian's body suddenly seemed to press on him.

Josh desperately tried to make his voice sound light and cheery. "C'mon Bry, let's ... go relive some old times." A possibly dangerous choice of words on his part, he thought, but Brian nodded assent in a sleepy, drunken way. Josh somehow managed to get Brian's legs to work and they lurched forward, like some sort of demented team in a three-legged race, weaving and bobbing their way out of the room and toward the stairs. Unlike earlier, when Missy had pulled Zack through the crowd, Josh and Brian didn't cause much of a re-action; the latter was obviously done for the night, and the new kid was just taking him upstairs.

Jamie watched them go, turned, and gave Chantel the same "thumbs up" gesture that Zack had given Josh a few minutes earlier. Jamie was grinning like a mad thing, and found it amusing that Chantel was grinning, too—very widely. *Too widely.*

Chantel reached for a sofa pillow, as Jamie's eyes rolled around once in her head, and she proceeded to pass out—*thunk*—very neatly and precisely on the floor. Chantel slipped the pillow under Jamie's head and, with as much dignity as she could muster, dragged her from the room. Only a few kids noticed that Jamie was out cold; even fewer cared.

CHAPTER 43

Moonlight streamed into Mr. and Mrs. Esau's room, highlighting the bed and leaving the rest of the room shrouded in shadows. Missy had only been in here once, to fetch a blanket while she and Brian were watching TV, and it seemed colder and more impersonal than she remembered. She stood like a statue in the middle of the room, looking balefully at the zigzag pattern on the duvet cover, at the neatly piled pillows. (What would they do with the pillows? Setting them on the floor seemed rude.)

She wondered why Brian had made no move to stop her as they'd passed him; was she subconsciously trying to *test* him? Did she want him to stand up, to fight, to turn Zack around and say, "Not with my girl, buddy," and deck him? If so, then why was she in here with Zack, about to do something that she'd wondered about, fantasized about, for so long with someone else?

Zack shut the bedroom door, locked it, and came forward, removing his jacket as she stepped out of her shoes neatly next to the bed. He felt like he was moving on the bottom of the ocean floor, like Pinocchio dreamily marching into the darkness to seek the whale. (Or wait, was it more like *Moby Dick?*) Why was he suddenly thinking about whales right now? He was alone with the perfect girl, in a beautiful bedroom, and he had everything he could hope for.

Didn't he?

He approached Missy from behind, moved in gently, let his hands run down her shoulders, let them ease the straps down. He leaned in and nuzzled her neck, inhaled the fresh, clean scent. She didn't smell like Jamie; Jamie smelled of sophisticated perfume. Missy smelled like floral soap and lotion. Zack let his nose and lips caress the hairs on the back of her neck and felt her tremble a bit at his touch as he lowered her zipper. She was like something found in a forest, a delicate blossom—

—who turned suddenly and gripped his arm and shoulder like a pro wrestler, and said, in a cold, flat, businesslike voice that sounded as if it were coming from another body, "Zack, this is my first time doing this. Treat me right, or I'll cut your liver out."

Zack, in shock, nodded mutely. Missy had stiffened as she turned, but she relaxed a bit as her eyes searched his face. Carefully, she reached behind her and finished the zipper, then reached out and tremblingly undid his shirt buttons. She took a step back, and the dress slid to the floor, causing Zack to involuntarily gasp a little. Missy was definitely *not* a minister's daughter; this, as far as he was concerned, was a very good thing.

Missy was unsure how to take his reaction, though the moonlight on his face seemed to be illuminating an expression of admiration. Hesitantly, she asked, "Is it ... am I ... all right?"

Zack smiled at her in sheer bliss. Then, like Jamie, he too passed out, falling like a cut tree: *thud.*

~

JOSH DRAGGED Brian up the stairs, trying not to bump into the family photos—Jamie in a grade-school graduation gown, Brian reading the Torah at his bar mitzvah, Mr. and Mrs. Esau on their wedding day a million years ago, smiling blindly and happily at their imagined, perfect future. He then piloted Brian into his bedroom, barely able to hold the football player's body upright.

Once inside, Brian lurched about the room like a dancing bear, banging into the furniture and mumbling to himself. Josh quickly closed the door before everyone came running to see what was going on. Brian finished his drink and, turning, accidentally let it fly against a wall. He regarded it with a drunken bemusement, oblivious to Josh's wince. "Crash, boom ... we all fall down."

He staggered forward, as if about to fall; Josh caught him in his arms, trying to keep them both from going down. The side of Brian's face grazed Josh's as he pulled himself up, so close that Josh felt a bit of stubble against his cheek.

There was a long, tension-filled moment as they looked into each other's eyes, then Brian pulled away and began undressing, flinging his

clothes in various directions as if he were shop-
ping via a discount bin. Josh stood awkwardly,
afraid to touch his exposed skin, but finally
stepped in to help when the shirt got caught for a
moment in the back of Brian's jeans.

Then Brian was down to his boxer briefs, and
suddenly Josh was fiercely aware of Brian's chest,
the fuzzy down of blond hair dusting his nipples;
his broad, exposed shoulders; his biceps the size
of oranges. He had an appendectomy scar, a thin,
ghost-like line of white against his tan stomach.

Josh backed away and started to leave, but
Brian caught his arm. His voice was slurred, yet
urgent. "Stay with me … until I'm asleep? I don't
want to be alone."

His fingers clutched at Josh's forearm, the grip
strong and unyielding. Brian pulled back his
sheets and slipped between them, yet somehow
his grip on Josh continued. Josh found himself
sitting on the bed as Brian heaved pillows in various directions, fumbling for the right combination of support. Then his body fell onto them as
though he were a marionette whose strings had
just been cut. Yet the hand still clutched for
Josh's sleeve, his wrist.

Brian now sounded as though he were at the

bottom of a well. "Just … stay with me a little longer. Please don't go yet."

As if in a trance, Josh moved his hand up Brian's arm. Daring more than he ever could've imagined, he stroked Brian's shoulder. Brian's eyes flickered shut, and a sigh breathed from his lips, the sigh of a sad, lost boy.

Without even stopping to think about whether he should or not, Josh smoothed the hair off Brian's forehead, letting its fine, cornsilk softness play under his fingertips. His voice, when he finally spoke, was the gentlest imaginable: "Okay, Bry."

If Brian had had his eyes open even a little, he might have seen the wetness glistening on Josh's cheek. But Brian was already fast asleep.

A WHILE LATER, Chantel made the rounds yet again, collecting a few more sets of keys to be put into the Esaus' wall safe; no one with any liquor on their breath was leaving the property. Consuella had been sent home, with a confirmation that she would be back in the morning to help clean up. Jamie was laid out on one of the sofas, her hands clasped neatly at her waist, looking as if she were waiting for the coroner to arrive. A few kids were asleep on various sofas and loveseats, but with two of the bedrooms unavailable, most of the party had dissipated. Using Jamie's room for anything was clearly not an option, lest the couple be disappeared to Guantanamo Bay come morning.

Chantel flopped down on the end of Jamie's sofa, exhausted, nursing a cold-cut sandwich and a ginger ale, and put her feet up on an ottoman. Hank chose exactly this moment to plant himself right in front of her. "Hey, choco-lat. What'd I hear about Zack Standish taking Missy upstairs? Ol' Bry will love that."

"I don't know, Hank," Chantel returned coolly, unflappable as Queen Elizabeth. "I think some things should be kept private."

"Funny, that's not what the football team says about you."

Hank didn't think that Chantel could volley into a standing position in one movement, but she did, quite impressively, and landed a stinging slap across his face to boot. He didn't flinch, even as his face turned various shades of dark red; he just smiled very slowly and dangerously. "Hostess with the mostess." He moved to the front door to meet his scum outside for a smoke, leaving Chantel regally fixed where he'd just been standing. Her gaze could've left a small, singed hole in the floor.

IN THE ESAU MASTER BEDROOM, Missy was engaged in the one-woman battle to get Zack up onto the bed. This was complicated by her efforts to keep the sheet wrapped around herself; oh, who cared, he was passed out cold. She threw modesty to the wind and let the sheet slip, though now her breasts were being rubbed in uncomfortable ways as she dragged Zack's limp body halfway up onto the mattress

She rotated his feet and managed to get them on top of the duvet, then went back and rolled his torso onto the bed. Each time she tried to put one of his legs up, it would immediately slip back and dangle over the side of the bed; oh well, hopefully, he wouldn't fall.

She re-wrapped herself in the sheet and, exhausted, threw herself down next to Zack, listening to him snore.

It was *not* exactly how she'd thought the night might end.

Should she go check on Brian, possibly slip into his room, ask forgiveness? No, she'd wait until early morning, less chance of someone walking through the hall then. She couldn't believe she'd thrown herself at this ... this *boy*, so inadequate in so many ways. Still, in the moonlight, she had to admit he was hellaciously cute. And it gave her a thrill, lying here with only a sheet wrapped around her, and his warm body pressed up against hers. Would Brian's body have felt like this? Would Brian have made love to her if she'd asked—demanded—that he do so? She was still wondering this when she finally dozed off, after getting used to Zack's gentle snore.

DOWNSTAIRS, at two-thirty in the morning Robin, the Yearbook Kid, was wandering around the house turning off the last of the lights and draping blankets raided from the linen closet over various sleeping kids. Robin paused long enough to take a bite of pizza and a swig of beer and turned to see Chantel's eyes glowing in the dark, where she was stretched out at the other end of Jamie's sofa. Through a mouthful of pizza: "The party of the year."

"Wait until the morning," Chantel murmured in response, her voice barely more than a whisper. "It ain't over."

And it wasn't.

CHAPTER 44

When Brian opened his eyes the following morning, he became aware of several things in short order. One, it was raining outside, and the room was gray and dim. Two, it was 8:17 a.m., according to the digital clock on his nightstand. And three, Josh Bradshaw was sitting in Brian's desk chair shirtless, his feet propped up on the end of the bed and his body turned toward Brian. Josh's face, however, was facing out the window as he watched the daylight breaking. He looked as though he'd been turned to stone.

Brian swallowed, but Josh didn't move. He marshaled his vocal cords, and managed somehow to croak out, "Josh ...?"

Josh turned to look at him. His eyes were swollen and bloodshot and his face was streaked. The room was cool, and his arms were going to gooseflesh, yet Josh made no movement to grab his shirt. He just sat there, staring at Brian, his eyes looking like burned-out buildings from a Holocaust documentary.

Brian finally broke the silence again. "What happened?"

"I discovered a few things last night," Josh said. He sounded like he'd barely slept, yet the pillows and indentation in the bed next to Brian indicated that Josh had at some point at least tried to lie down for a while.

Brian scooted forward in bed a bit. He felt strangely calm; of course Josh was in his room. Of course Josh was shirtless. Of course they'd shared a bed. It was as if no time had passed in the interim five-plus years, and they'd simply had a sleepover. Yet Josh didn't look unperturbed or calm, far from it. "Like what?"

"Like I don't respect myself very much ... and that my best friend is a putz."

"Why?" Brian had to agree with the latter part, but he was curious why Josh had just realized this.

Josh swung his legs to the floor, rose, and began to pace, as though he were trying to follow his thoughts on the carpeting. "Because he taught me so much. He taught me that trust is not essential to happiness, that manipulation brings great reward, and that human feelings don't really mean jack." He paced faster, and he almost spat the last part.

Brian was genuinely confused, and it must have shown on his face, because Josh stopped mid-pace, looked right at Brian, and let the words come in a rush. "We made a deal ... the two of us would try to break you and Missy up so that you'd both be in positions where we could sleep with you."

The shock of this hit Brian like a pitcher of ice water dumped over his head. This whole week ... then that meant—

No.

Yes.

Josh mistook the grinding of Brian's mental gears and his dumbstruck expression for anger. "I know, it's horrible. Your sister, the She-Devil, is mixed up in it too—manipulation, drugs, the works. I managed to stop her last night before things got any worse—but I can't justify the rest of my behavior. It was just wrong." He grabbed his shoes and socks and began jabbing his feet into them, unable to meet Brian's stupefied gaze.

DOWN THE HALL, Zack woke with a throbbing headache in an unfamiliar bedroom. He sat up and shook his head to clear the cobwebs, then started as he noticed Missy lying next to him, her face turned away toward the window. She didn't seem to be wearing any clothing but was wrapped, as if mummified, in a sheet.

He fumblingly tried to piece together the events of the previous night. Had something happened? No, aside from his shirt being unbuttoned, he seemed to be dressed. He remembered being downstairs on the patio and talking with Missy, then the blur of faces as she led him up the stairs. Everything else was a blank.

Zack felt a rush of embarrassment and fury at his ineptitude; couldn't he do *anything* right? Here he'd been thinking of last night for over a year, had planned for it all this week—and when the moment had come, he'd choked. What the hell? Wasn't this what he'd dreamed of? Why couldn't he think about anything other than getting out of the room as fast as possible, so he could hopefully find Josh and reconstruct the evening's events? He also, he realized, needed to pee like crazy.

He took one last, furtive look at Missy's exposed back and shoulders as he eased himself off the bed, trying not to wake her lest he have to explain why he didn't "close the deal." God, his head was throbbing. He tiptoed to the door and eased himself out into the hallway—and proceeded to bump smack into Hank Gaston.

Hank had slept on the hallway floor and wasn't in the best mood himself. He looked down at that pipsqueak Zack Standish, the Mouth That Roared, always trying to grab attention, and an angry flush purpled his features.

He jabbed one sausage-sized finger into Zack's bare chest: "Hey blemish, what're you doing in my corner of the world?"

Anger gripped Zack like a red-hot fist. He was already embarrassed and confused and felt like crap; Hank's smirk was a gallon of gas dumped on the fire. The words burst out of him in a defensive rush as he straightened up his shoulders in a pathetic attempt to be six inches taller. "It just so *happens* that I just spent the night with Missy Hoff." He was speaking too loudly, but he wanted to make sure the cocky asshole really heard him.

In the bedroom, Missy was just coming out of a dream where she'd been kidnapped by pirates, all of whom looked like Josh and Zack, and had been forced to walk a plank. She craned her neck as she heard the boys' voices, including Zack's defensive bravado. A sinking feeling filled her, as though she had in fact toppled off the plank and into the cold, black sea. The voices continued:

"Bullshit."

"Bull nothing. She was great. I was great. We were great. *It* was great!" Zack became redundant in his stridency.

"Lemme see."

Quickly, Missy threw herself back down on the pillow. She heard the door creak, heard the boys poking their heads in to view her, said a silent prayer of thanks that she still had her sheet tucked around her. Any pride she'd once had in her body was now obliterated at her being examined as though she were a prize cow at a county fair.

The door almost—but not quite—closed, and

Missy could hear the boys' voices again. Hank sounded almost admiring. "Holy shit, you *did* do it! How'd you swing it?"

"I'll tell you after I take a leak." The footsteps moved away from the door, and in the distance, Missy heard another door close.

Apparently, Hank had followed Zack into a bathroom to get an in-depth report on—what? Zack's fantasy of what had taken place? Could he be such a—a *jerk?* With a sinking heart, she realized: yes, he probably could—faced with Hank Gaston's withering contempt and Zack's craven need for attention and respect, he definitely could. She had been used—and she didn't even get the pleasure of enjoying it.

Missy sat bolt upright and wrapped the sheet tightly around her body. She needed to talk to Brian, to apologize to him, to make him understand how sorry she was. Maybe he would forgive her. Maybe it wasn't too late! She had to get to him before Zack returned to the room. Brian would probably be in his room. She hobbled toward the bedroom door and opened it into the hall.

DOWNSTAIRS, Jamie awakened suddenly, a shock of panic knifing through her. She processed instantaneously where she was; what had happened just before this? Why was she here? She grabbed her shoes from their resting place next to the sofa, vaguely registering Chantel asleep at the other end of the sofa, and ran from the room, searching, searching.

There were a handful of kids still asleep in various contortions throughout the downstairs, but none that she cared about. In a flash she realized her quarry must be upstairs—yes! They *had* gone upstairs, she recalled. Trying to run on wobbly legs, her head feeling like a split melon, Jamie tottered out of the room and began climbing the stairs. She wasn't sure why, but in her stomach she felt a kernel of something she hadn't felt for a very long time: fear—absolute, complete, and utter terror. She wasn't in control anymore.

JOSH HAD his shoes and socks on. Brian hadn't said anything for the past several seconds, but now he finally spoke, his thoughts coming slowly, as if they'd traveled a great distance. "So you … were trying to seduce me. And Zack and my sister were in on it too … why'd you stop?"

Josh was fumbling, trying to find his shirt; it had fallen partially off the bed and was caught in the baseboard. He gave it a desperate yank. "I couldn't go through with it—it wasn't right, it wasn't what you needed."

He'd wanted to—oh! How he'd wanted to. He'd tried to nuzzle Brian's neck, to pull him close, to run his hands over the exposed flesh, to inhale his scent, to be The Guy—the one that Garrett might have respected and wanted.

But Brian had whimpered in his sleep, almost in fear, and Josh had stopped, had pulled away, had rolled back over so he didn't have to face Brian, just as Brian had years earlier during their sleepover. Josh was still just a follower, still just an appendage of Zack, who'd probably banged Missy six ways till Sunday before the cocktail had kicked in. And Josh couldn't even dare something as simple as a kiss.

Now Brian's voice finally had an edge to it, and it sliced into Josh like a shiv. "You know, it's really funny the way people always think they know what you need, but they never ask you, they just *assume*. All this dancing tap-dancing around about *happiness* and *football,* and you just wanted to get me drunk, and ..." He stopped, and the words hung in the air like a waiting noose.

Josh finally managed to extricate his shirt. "Can we please forget this?"

Forget it all, forget everything that had happened this week, over the past six years, during his life. He'd rent a boat and sail off toward the South Pacific, never to be heard from again, never to feel again. He was a rock; the song he'd lip-synced to said so.

Brian leaped out of bed, and Josh had a flash from the previous night as he once again beheld the football player in his boxer briefs. He was in front of Josh, then right in his face, Brian's features twisted in something akin to rage. Years of long-suppressed anger made his voice shake. "No, we can't, dammit. I want some say in my life. Now you tell me *why. Why!?*"

He had his hands on Josh's shoulders, grabbing him, almost shaking him. Their faces were inches apart, and Josh's entire vision, his entire world, was Brian. Only Brian.

But Brian went on yelling at Josh, face contorted with fury. "*Why*?! Why did you do this?

Lying, manipulating, double-crossing—why to me? *Why?!*"

"*Because I'm in love with you, you idiot!*" Josh yelled, louder than he ever remembered yelling in his life, yelling because he had nothing left but the absolute truth.

He loved Brian. He always had. And he'd already fucked it up.

Missy, still wrapped in her sheet, opened the door midway through saying "Brian, I made a mistake—" and saw the two of them together, Josh's words still echoing in the air, him shirtless and Brian in his underwear, Brian clutching him, both of them even more emotionally exposed than they were physically exposed.

And she knew, in a lightning flash, that what she was seeing—how could she not have seen it before?—was the absolute truth.

"Oh my God." The words choked out of her, like stillborn infants.

Neither Josh nor Brian moved, frozen as they were like statues. Behind Missy, there was a *crash*, and Jamie barged past her into the room. Three heads swiveled, looked at her, and Jamie had a brief flash of what it must have been like to be on the ground in Hiroshima or Nagasaki, as the entire world turned into a bright white light of death.

She tried to access words, but all that came out of her was a rusty sound of "Errk." It sounded like the gate on a mausoleum.

Brian let go of Josh, but they still stood together, gazing at Jamie with loathing. Missy stared at her dumbly, trying to figure out where Jamie fit into what she was seeing. Jamie tried, too late, to recompose her features, to have a pleasantly bland expression—which immediately cracked as Zack, saying "Hey Missy, where—" and Hank pushed into the room.

There was another horrified pause, broken by, of all people, Hank, as he said just one word:

"*Whoa.*"

Then everyone was talking—or yelling—at once.

"Gaston, I'm warning you—" Jamie began through gritted teeth.

"Don't—" Missy collapsed into Brian's chair. "Please don't."

"What are you doing in a *sheet?*" Brian's voice jumped almost an octave in shock. This, from the girl who'd wanted to wait until "the time was right?"

"What are *you* doing with Josh, Brian?" Hank smirked as he recalled Callen's bruised face and stream of invective, cursing Brian as "that stupid cocksucker."

"What are you doing on my planet?" Jamie was trying to regain the high ground threatening Hank, but her credibility was decimated, and she knew it, everyone knew it. The world as she knew it could never be the same.

"Some plan, *buddy*," Josh hissed. He focused his fury on Zack like a laser, wanting to slap the freckles off his damn face. He'd never in his life thought he could hate Zack, not even during their worst predicaments, but at that moment Josh wanted to throttle him cross-eyed.

"Josh, I'm sorry—" Zack at least had the decency to look truly miserable. This was not how he'd envisioned last night and this morning going.

"Sorry? *You're* sorry?!" Brian turned on Zack like a lion about to pounce. "You just porked my ex-girlfriend. Why are you *sorry?*" Nine years' worth of hatred was bursting out of him, like a lanced blister.

"You did it, didn't you?" Jamie took a step toward Josh, her face dead white with rage. "The champagne. I'll have you *disemboweled* for this. I have to deal with all this with a *hangover!*"

She almost screamed the last words, and it was a horrifying sound. None of them had ever heard her raise her voice like that before.

"Jamie, what the hell have you done?" Brian's voice was deadly. He was looking at his sister like an executioner might a guilty prisoner.

Jamie exploded like the Hindenburg. "Tried to help you, you *big ... dumb ... ox!* Count on *men* to screw things up every time!" She'd already been borderline hysterical; her fury now pushed her over the edge, like a hurricane smashing into a coastal town and leaving nothing but splinters and wreckage in its wake. Her insides felt broken, like a crate of smashed china.

"You slime," Brian hissed at Zack, eyes cold and dead.

"You asshole," Missy whispered to Josh, tears finally beginning to flow. She rose, clutched her sheet tightly around her, and dashed from the room, pushing the vastly amused Hank into the hallway as she raced by. The master bedroom door slammed.

"I'm sorry ... everyone, I'm sorry," Josh mumbled. He felt so low, he was subterranean. He couldn't look at any of them, just lowered his head and fled after Missy, buttoning his shirt as he went.

The remaining four people in the room looked at each other for a long moment. Then Jamie said very flatly, "I'm going back to bed. I'll deal with this when I'm awake and sober." She took a step toward the door and proceeded to walk smack into the just-arriving Chantel.

"What'd I miss?"

Jamie dragged her out by her ear. Hank followed.

Brian and Zack stood facing each other, as they had just a few days—a few lifetimes—before. Zack was still speechless, and Brian's face looked as if it had been chiseled from granite.

Zack's mouth was as dry as Death Valley, but he managed to almost whisper, "Brian, I'm—"

"No." Brian held up his hand, stopping Zack's words in their tracks. His voice was quiet, but forceful, like God always sounds in the movies. "Just leave, Zack."

There was nothing Zack could say. He went, gently shutting the door behind him.

The front entryway of the Esau house saw a parade of people leaving it, more or less in a straight line: Josh, then Missy, then Hank, then Chantel. The door shut, and then Zack came flying down the stairs and yanked it open, racing out to the driveway.

He ran to the car Missy had driven and beat frantically on her window, but she refused to look at him. Her hair fell across her face, obscuring her expression as she pulled away.

Zack next dashed to Josh's car, virtually throwing himself across the hood in his desperation; Josh slammed the MG in reverse, shaking Zack loose, and peeled out of the driveway without looking back.

Chantel slid behind the wheel of her car, surveying the scene one last time with an unreadable expression, and then was gone.

Hank and Zack stood in the driveway regarding each other, but there was nothing to say. They were two strangers who happened to witness the same accident, the same fatalities, the same bloodbath. With barely a nod, they walked off in opposite directions into the gray, wet morning. The trees were beginning to lose their leaves, and they loomed against the empty sky, beseechingly reaching for a lost, green past that would never be the same again.

CHAPTER 45

The tears started on the drive home, and by the time Josh pulled into the driveway, his shirt collar was damp. He raced through the house, ripping off his clothes and flinging them in the upstairs hallway and about his room. He turned the shower as hot as he could stand it, letting the billowing steam obscure his naked body and his blotchy, tear-streaked face. When he was finally entombed in the glass shower stall with the warm water running over him, the final shards of ice in him cracked and melted, and he started really crying, crying loudly enough that it echoed off the tile, huge gasping sobs that punched their way out of his chest. He leaned his head against the tile wall, then banged it almost hard enough to bruise. He thought about Garrett and cried. He thought about Brian and cried. He thought about his mom and cried. And then he thought about Zack, and Zack's face as they left the Esau's, and how things had changed since Monday, and how things had changed since they were first best friends, a lifetime ago. He thought about everything he'd lost. And he sobbed as though his heart would never stop breaking into a thousand pieces, over and over again. He cried until the hot water, if not his tears, ran out.

MISSY WAS WRAPPED in a blanket on her back porch swing, staring grimly out at the softly falling rain. Her mother, thankfully, had taken one look at her, enfolded Missy in her arms, kissed the top of her head, and gently said, "You look like you need a mug of something warm." Oh, how did moms know these sorts of things? Missy had gone upstairs, left her dress on the floor of her closet, changed into her favorite flannel pajamas, and returned downstairs. Her mother was at the end of the table, working on a sewing project; she indicated the warm cocoa with a slight nod of her head. Missy took the mug, grabbed the blanket from the back of the living room sofa, and padded outside, bundling the soft wool cocoon around her and surveying the drippy, gray world.

The enormity of it all was still sinking in. Brian … had Brian ever loved her? Was she just a —a *prop*, a shield behind which he'd been hiding? Or had he really loved her—or at least thought he did—until Josh Bradshaw ambled back into their lives?

She reconstructed the image from the morning with an almost scientific precision: Brian in his boxer briefs, Josh shirtless, the two of them so close their faces almost touched. They could've kissed each other; for all she knew, they had.

The emotional betrayal of this nauseated her, even as a strange reaction she didn't expect snaked through her mind: curiosity. What would it be like to watch them kiss? What did it feel like when strong lips met strong lips, when stubble grazed stubble? What would they look like together, the blond, built athlete and the handsome, dark-haired boy? Their emotional intimacy threatened her, their physical intimacy ... well, it *intrigued* her.

Missy was so shocked at herself that she almost dropped her mug. Who was she, thinking these thoughts? Had her mother spiked the cocoa? Or had the past twenty-four hours just given her a chance to be further outside of her comfort zone than she'd ever thought she could be? She felt naked, exposed, as if she were standing on a cliff in Ireland, completely vulnerable to the elements and anyone who might see her. She felt like some sort of ancient goddess from before the birth of Christ, a deity of love and wrath the world would not, could never, comprehend.

She should have felt beaten down and broken; yet strangely, having lost what was most important to her, she now felt almost ... strong. People would be watching her tonight at the dance; it would only be what everyone expected if she didn't attend. She would have hundreds of pairs of eyes studying her, looking for the soft, vulnerable places where she'd been wounded, the scars from Cupid's misfired arrows. She would never let anyone see them. Brian, she realized, had been hiding feelings from her for months in a carefully choreographed play; now it was her turn to be in the spotlight, but similarly, no one would know what roiled beneath her placid surface. Zack had intended to use her and toss her aside, but he'd failed; now she was immune to his pathetic, fumbling machinations and sweet talk.

She was done wearing her emotions on her sleeve, done apologizing, done being vulnerable. She just didn't give enough of a flying...*fig* about these people to let them see what she was really thinking and feeling.

Missy laughed to herself. She'd never even dared to *think* this way before.

Back upstairs, Missy took a seat at her vanity and began pinning her hair up. A peculiar sense of calm held her close, whispered to her, helped her with her makeup. On her bed lay her mother's graduation gown, re-sewn and reworked into something new.

Her eye spotted the bedroom door behind her with the past week's school clothes still hanging on the back; she'd inadvertently left it slightly ajar. Doors, she thought slowly. Doors opening and closing. Doors unlocking, and then slamming shut behind you. Portals to another galaxy, and wormholes to another time. Doors.

She'd gone through a door in the past 24

hours that she hadn't even known existed last Monday, and now she almost audibly heard a key turning in the lock in her mind. Strangely, she was the one who turned it. Now she was on the other side of the door in a strange new world, and she had no idea whether the landscape would be familiar or threatening, comforting or alien.

All she knew was she was no longer Missy Hoff, Brian's showpiece girlfriend. She was not her parents' little churchgoing girl. She wasn't the girl who shrank in terror when Jamie turned the death glare on her or made cutting remarks that used to slice at Missy's soul. She wasn't someone to bend and buckle whenever a cute boy dropped a crumb of attention her way.

Vengeance. That's what she felt. The sharp, subzero blade of vengeance, and she was now wielding the scythe in a designer black hood and cape, complete with stiletto heels. Her chance would come. Eventually. She wasn't her mother. She didn't need Brian to be the person she was meant to be. She didn't need any of them. Not Brian, not Zack, not Josh, not Jamie.

She felt anticipation for tonight, but no apprehension—not like last night. She was like a ship at sea, turning directly into the path of the oncoming storm, as the waves crashed about her and beat at her hull. Despite it all, her bow remained pointed, and she sailed forward. For the first time, despite the waves and the wind, she felt an eerie sense of calm—almost relief. She didn't have to be anyone she wasn't. Though she didn't know who she was yet, she was certain she would figure it out eventually. It would take more —much more—than this tumult to swamp and sink Missy Hoff.

AT ONE IN THE AFTERNOON, Jamie was still lying in bed staring grimly at the clock on her nightstand. Her stomach growled, but she couldn't imagine any food that she'd want to eat. Consuella had tried to tempt her with some chicken broth with an egg stirred into it, but Jamie had wordlessly shaken her head. That was almost four hours ago.

After the revelations in Brian's room, she'd stalked through the house like some sort of robo-zombie, tossing the remaining handful of kids their coats and car keys as Consuella stood in the foyer, watching the surly stragglers leave. Then the front door had closed, and Jamie was left standing in the empty hallway with a middle-aged woman, about whom she knew next to nothing, staring at her with something like pity.

She'd come perilously close to tears then, to howling like the Furies, to collapsing on the stairs like Scarlet O'Hara after Rhett left her. Instead, she had numbly wended her way up the stairs, deaf to Consuella's queries and solicitations, and gone straight to her room. She thought she could go back to sleep, but instead she flopped down on her bed and stared at the pattern on her duvet cover until it became fixed in her vision even when she tried to shut her eyes.

I've lost. This was the big one, and I lost.

For years, Jamie had moved the people and events of her life around like chess pieces, always trying to think two steps ahead of everyone else to see what would provide maximum benefits to her. Some criticized her for this; others flat-out hated and feared her. She didn't care. She did what she had to, to provide some structure, some consistency to her life. The reason so much of the human plankton out there didn't—couldn't—understand her is that they didn't see how easily the chaos could descend, how quickly things could unravel, unless you were constantly, *constantly* vigilant.

Yet here she was, after all of her careful planning, her life reduced to a pile of dust and rubble. Why, why, *why* couldn't people do what you wanted them to, even when you knew it would be better for them? (Well, better for her too, but that was beside the point.) She'd had every one of them—Brian, Zack, Josh, Missy—choreographed in a perfect dance, and then all of a sudden everyone had had an attack of chorea. What had gone wrong?

Josh Bradshaw, for starters. Jamie ground her teeth so hard that her jaw almost locked. What the hell was he *thinking*? Everything had been set up perfectly, and then he'd sabotaged the whole plan—for what? An attack of conscience? Nerves? He'd wanted Brian; she'd seen the longing etched on his face so plainly over the past several days—especially the past twenty-four hours—that it was as obvious to her as the sun shining. Yet, in the clinch, he hadn't been able to go through with things—why?

It had to have been Josh who'd given her the spiked drink; no one else knew about it except the ever-loyal Chantel. But why had he decided to take her down with him? What did it benefit him to tear apart their carefully constructed web, enmeshing them all in sticky, inescapable snares? What did this mean for her and Zack's future, or for his and Brian's?

Brian! Jamie groaned and threw a pillow over her face to muffle her brief shriek of frustration. She'd been so busy thinking about Brian as part of The Plan and its disastrous fallout that she'd completely forgotten he existed as a separate entity, as her brother. Brian now knew Jamie had tried to set him up with Josh. He now knew she'd been engineering everything, alongside Zack and Josh. What was she going to say to make it up to him? Had she permanently damaged their relationship beyond repair? Surface evidence to the contrary, Jamie did love her brother; she often felt like he was the only person in the world who really *saw* her, faults and all, and still somehow blindly, stupidly loved her in return. She'd wanted Missy gone because then, maybe, Brian would be able to face up to who he really was, and what he really wanted—well, okay, if she hadn't detested Missy so much, she might have been willing to leave Brian in the dark a little longer. She'd honestly thought that being with

Josh might turn on the light bulbs in Brian's brain so that he'd finally realize it.

Instead, this morning seemed to have completely blown every internal fuse he had. The last she'd seen him, his face had looked like a marquee gone dark.

Jamie curled herself into a ball, clutching her stomach, trying to turn off the carousel endlessly revolving in her mind. She would have to attend the dance tonight—there was no question that she'd be missed if she wasn't there, and it would be better for damage control if she was able to confront her firing squad face to face. She would need to talk to Zack, to Chantel, to Josh—well, she wanted to kill Josh, but she'd probably need to talk to him first, preferably in a dark room with bamboo inserted under his fingernails. (Tying him down nude and covering him with honey over a fire ant nest appealed to her, too.)

Most of all, she needed to talk to Brian, to do something nice for him. As far as she knew, he'd had no plans to attend the dance, but maybe with the right incentive he could be persuaded—no! No, she'd just get Consuella to take her out for an hour and get a costume for him, and then she'd let *him* steer the conversation and make the final decision. She wondered, briefly, if Brian was capable of making a decision without her assistance, but she resolutely decided that he'd just have to—he had to grow up sometime. Maybe picking out his wardrobe for him all these years was a mistake? Oh well, she'd do it one last time. She didn't think about Missy—there was just no point, it would have been like contemplating a vestigial organ, like your appendix. Once it was gone, it was gone.

Jamie eased herself out of bed and slouched toward the bathroom like a heretic climbing stairs to a cathedral. She wondered briefly, sadly, what those vintage dames in the 1940s movies she loved would do in a situation like this. Barbara Stanwyck would've skipped town in a blond wig and sunglasses, driving a convertible. Bette Davis or Lauren Bacall would've just lit up cigarettes and smirked at anyone who dared to cross them. Rosalind Russell would've simply talked so fast that everyone's head would explode. Katharine Hepburn would've acknowledged that she was "a mess of a girl," but she still would've wound up at the altar with Cary Grant. Zack was hardly Cary Grant—Mickey Rooney was more like it— but Jamie still wanted him. She felt like music with a perpetual skip, but there was no escaping it: she was nuts about the boy. And she'd let her life and everyone else's get turned topsy-turvy because of it.

Jamie sighed as she turned the water on and stepped into the tub. The trouble with life was that there was no orchestral rise and end credits; things just got increasingly dark and yucky and screwed-up, and then stopped.

IN THE BASEMENT of the Esau house, Brian was lifting weights on his Bowflex machine, his body bathed in a river of sweat. The rhythmic flow gave him comfort and emptied his mind: lift, hold, release, *clank*. Lift, hold, release, *clank*.

Then, at odd moments between sets, in the silence, the words came into his head, so quiet they could've been whispered in Whoville, yet so powerful they seemed to shake the entire galaxy.

He loves me.

It was as if he'd spent his entire life listening to another language he'd never realized wasn't his own, and suddenly could understand what was being said. It was like Helen Keller at the well, spelling w-a-t-e-r. It was the boy Arthur pulling on a sword in a churchyard, and suddenly realizing that he was king. It was hang-gliding out over the Grand Canyon, where your amazement at being one with the sky is tempered only by looking down and wondering if you'll survive the landing.

Everything was the same, and everything was different.

Brian did his biceps, his triceps, and lat pulldowns. He worked his quadriceps, hamstrings, and calves. He benched two hundred and twenty pounds. He did fifty sit-ups. His body responded to every request he made of it, as automatic as machinery. Only his brain rebelled.

He *loves me. He* loves *me. He loves* me.

He didn't think about Missy. He didn't think about Zack, or his sister, or anything else. He just let those three words keep echoing in his mind, like a mantra. Slowly, ever so slowly, a shy, almost wondering smile pulled at the corners of his mouth.

∼

ZACK SAT in the easy chair almost exactly as he had some five years earlier to the day. He splayed his limbs as if he were a squashed daddy-long-legs, let his head lean against the chair's back. The TV was on, but he was processing nothing; the infomercial unfolding before his vacant eyes might as well have been happening on Mars.

He had seriously, *seriously* screwed up this time.

Zack dully ran through some of the greatest hits of his life thus far. The school play with the vomit cap; that was a prize-winner. The infamous piñata disaster. The time he and Josh had tried to be circus magicians and had almost succeeded in chainsawing eight-year-old Anastasia Popov in half before the plug popped out of the wall from too much tension, and his mother caught them. (Another inch, and Anastasia probably would've stopped screaming—permanently.) The "body fluid pie" contest; that one had gotten him banned from several kids' houses for a month. The lawn darts—relics of the '70s, purchased at a garage sale—blithely tossed at various elementary school classmates in an attempt to create a pattern of holes in the grass around their bodies. (That had gotten Zack banned from most classmates' houses for good.) The motorized hide-a-bed, which had caused a three-car fender bender at the bottom of the hill and gotten them on the news. The time when he was fourteen and Zack had let Alex wander away at the zoo, only to find him ten minutes later paddling merrily in the outdoor seal tank; Beth had grounded Zack for weeks, despite Zack's pointing out that *he* was the one who'd first taught Alex how to swim. Anything and everything from his childhood which might have contributed to his father's disappearance, despite Beth's protestations to the contrary. His life seemed at this moment to be one horror movie after another.

This, however, was the big enchilada. Zack had hit rock bottom in Hell, and not satisfied, had started digging.

The expression on Josh's face was what killed him. Zack had thrown himself across the front of Josh's car with the absolute intention of riding home via the hood if necessary. But Josh had looked right through him like he was … invisible. As if Zack had been erased from Josh's consciousness, from his memory banks. Zack had called every fifteen minutes for the past four hours, but Josh never answered the phone. Zack could drive over, but there was no guarantee that Josh would answer the door, either.

Zack ran a mental inventory with a masochistic kind of relish. Josh, his best friend—the one non-related person in the world whom Zack trusted, whom he knew he could count on—had given up on him. Well, why wouldn't he? Hadn't Zack masterminded this whole deal? Hadn't Zack dragged Josh into it, ignored his reservations, run roughshod over his qualms? Hadn't he jumped at the chance to score with Melissa Hoff, even if he was willing to pimp out his best friend to do it? Didn't he let Josh and Brian head into a collision course with each other, just so Zack could be with Missy? And then, unable to seal the deal, hadn't he bragged to Hank Gaston—*Hank Gaston,* a guy whom Zack detested, yet still couldn't resist trying to impress?

The one person Zack couldn't quite figure out in the whole mess was Jamie. Clearly, something had gone on between her and Josh—what? Something she hadn't been expecting. Had she been blackmailing him? Had Jamie also wanted Josh to get with Brian? But why then the champagne? Was *she* the reason he'd passed out? Did she want him that much? If so, he had to admit, it was a brilliant if fiendish move on her part—even with all of his planning, Zack hadn't thought to take things to that level of nefariousness. *Damn, that girl was good.*

Amidst the miasma clouding his mind, Zack felt a strange twinge of admiration for Jamie; it was like a British spy movie, where the two rivals meet at the end and shake hands, saying "Well played, old chap" as an airplane explodes to bits behind them. Well, they'd definitely done a good job in that respect—there was so much debris and destruction scattered around, Zack hardly knew where to begin, even if he'd had a whisk broom.

He was paddling so deeply in Lake Zack that he hardly noticed when Alex tiptoed into the room, surveyed his brother, then surveyed the infomercial. Alex did the Spock eyebrow thing. "Whatcha watching?"

"TV," Zack answered tonelessly.

"What's on?"

"I dunno."

There was a pause. Alex then asked, very gently, "Are you okay?"

For the first time, Zack's emotions flooded to the surface, and his eyes came dangerously close to filling. His voice was wobbly and scratchy. "No … I fucked up."

"Why?" Alex didn't even seem to register the swear, which would've normally cost Zack a dollar for Beth's "swear jar." But today, his focus seemed to be exclusively on his big brother's well-being. He moved right next to the chair.

Zack sighed, as though a huge weight was settled on his chest. "I made someone kind of fall in love with me when I didn't love them, and hurt someone else who cared about them. I also hurt my best friend—" his voice almost broke"—very much." Funny how simplifying the situation for a six-year-old stripped away a lot of the clutter in his head and allowed him to own up to his failings.

Alex nodded gravely. "You fucked up," he said. As Zack registered his use of the dreaded *f-word*, Alex added, "I still love you, though."

He leaned over the chair and put his arms around his brother, laying his little head against Zack's shoulder. Zack seriously thought he might break down and bawl. What did he ever do to deserve a kid like this in his life—someone who always seemed to love him, no matter what?

Normally it made him borderline nauseated; right now, it was a lifeline.

Zack put an arm around his little brother and pulled him in close, just for a moment or two. He smelled Alex's clean, soft hair, and a small, shuddering sigh escaped him.

Alex pulled back first and looked at Zack, his face comically serious. "Are you still going to the costume dance?"

"You think I should?" Zack wasn't used to asking Alex for advice, aside from clothing, but considering the wreckage he'd made of things thinking for himself, why not?

Alex nodded. "I think you should try and make your friends happy again."

Zack almost smiled in spite of himself. The kid may not have been the most sophisticated thinker, but sometimes, he was almost Zen in his wisdom.

THE LATE AFTERNOON light slowly began to dwindle. Brian was in the living room listening to the stereo via headphones. Bono was wailing

"Stay" and Brian was listening to the lyrics more carefully than he ever had before.

He was facing the doorway; otherwise, he would've jumped when Jamie entered the room, treading as deliberately as if the floor were strewn with land mines. "What time are you going to the dance?" She nearly yelled in order to make sure he heard her.

Brian lifted one headphone. "I'm not speaking to you until I'm not mad anymore."

"When will that be?"

"Has hell frozen over yet?" Brian's voice was as hard and cutting as a diamond.

Jamie's eyes narrowed. "Your costume's on your bed, if you want it. Otherwise, don't wait up." Her voice had regained some of its usual crispness, and Brian felt strangely reassured. Jamie might be bowed or bent, but she would never break. She left him, her heels tapping down the hallway.

Brian stared straight ahead at the empty room, listening to the wailing voice describing fallen angels and yearnings that could never be entirely fulfilled. Who needed Chinese fortune cookies when you had U2 for spiritual guidance?

ZACK WAS MODELING his costume in his living room, thrown together from some odds and ends —a union suit, a fake mustache, some handcuffs, and *voila!* Harry Houdini, master escape artist. Mark took his picture as Beth laughed and fussed over him. Neither of them had been around during the day to see his black mood, Beth had been held up at a backlog at the store; for all they knew, he was just having another great night after Jamie's party the night before. Zack felt a rush of pity for them; how little adults know. It's all right there in front of them, everything their kids are going through, and they don't even *notice*.

He let Alex walk him to the door and make sure Zack was sufficiently costumed one last time. Alex gave him a toothy grin and whispered, "Good luck."

Zack's heart filled and overflowed, and he did something uncharacteristically tender. He bent down, let his lips almost brush Alex's cheek, and whispered in his ear. "Alex, someday when I grow up, I hope I'm just like you."

His brother glowed. Zack went, jingling his

keys. No carpools with Josh tonight. Maybe, just maybe, if he apologized enough, he could fix that for the future.

CHAPTER 46

The night was warm, almost muggy from the rain that had blown through. The Academy parking lot was filled with cars; things were considerably more amped than the previous night at Jamie and Brian's since tonight the whole school was involved. Lights poured from every window; loud hip-hop music was blaring. Zack ambled into the Commons area, surveying several hundred kids in costumes. He nearly collided with Logan dressed as a video game orc. Yoshi was dressed as an old-time photographer and had tricked out his camera with an enormous fake flashbulb; similarly, the Yearbook Kid seemed to be working the abstract artist look via a black turtleneck splattered with paint and a beret, *tres* 1961. Some freshman chick was working the hot vampire look in some sort of Victorian teddy and thigh-high boots; Zack had to admit, it got his attention. Giant purple and yellow spotlights twirled about, illuminating strange shadows and pods of kids combining and recombining like cells in a petri dish.

But then the river of kids seemed to part, and Chantel, dressed as Cleopatra, barged up to him. She was festooned with gold, including a spectacular headdress, and carried two glasses—yikes—filled with punch. She gave Zack the benevolent smile of a queen, and extended her arm decorated with all sorts of bling to hand him a glass. "Hi, Zack."

Zack was momentarily stunned by her graciousness. "You one of the few still speaking to me?"

"We never had a hatchet to bury, sweetie," Chantel cooed, ignoring the small crowd gaping at them. She looked freaking fantastic, and she carried herself like she knew it. Zack had to grin a bit; he'd always kind of liked Chantel and felt bad that he never really got to know her since she'd always been a satellite to Jamie. He felt a brief pang as he wondered—for the first time possibly in his life—if that's how Josh used to feel in relation to him.

Chantel continued, a little too eagerly: "So don't worry about it. Want the scoop?"

"Talk to me; what's happening?" If anyone would know, it would be Chantel.

"Jamie and Brian aren't speaking—he's ready to have her drawn and quartered. He hasn't called Missy either though." Chantel looked ready to burst from sitting on this much dirt for hours; she was almost breathless. "Jamie can't get a hold of Josh, and Yoshi turned up no results."

Zack nodded; he hadn't been able to get a hold of Josh either. So far, details seemed to be locking into place, but he needed some clarification on a couple of points. "So, Jamie tried to get Josh to double-cross me so I wouldn't get together with Missy—but he then double-crossed her with the champagne, right?"

"You got it—everyone broke even." Chantel grinned. "You didn't get Missy, but Jamie didn't get you. No one was molested. Long live peace."

"A-fricking-men," Zack exhaled, clinking his punch glass against hers.

As they laughed, Zack suddenly saw Jamie slink into the dance—not in the obvious way she'd entered her party last night, more like someone who didn't care if she was noticed or not. Still, it was hard not to: Jamie was wearing a tailored suit a la Lauren Bacall circa 1944, complete with a hat the size of a flying saucer. No smoking was allowed in the Commons, but she still created the illusion of an invisible cloud of smoke coiling around her as she pulled off her gloves.

She broke into a disarmingly bright smile as she approached Zack and Chantel, flaring her nostrils in a supposedly sultry fashion. Her voice was a husky purr. "Hey Cleo, hey Steve. Someone whistle for me?"

Zack figured this was an arcane reference he was supposed to get, but didn't; still, he had to admit, she looked even better than she had Friday night. "No, but in that outfit someone might. Where's your brother?"

"Why do you want to know?" Jamie's voice was cool and even, but not confrontational; she sounded genuinely interested.

"I want to apologize."

Jamie lifted an eyebrow. "He's in the men's

room, getting dressed. Don't you think you should apologize to Missy?" Apologizing to Missy herself, of course, was out of the question.

"I'm going to," Zack said, surprising himself with how strong his voice sounded. He seemed to be channeling George Clooney in one of his don't-mess-with-me-doll roles. Jamie's other eyebrow joined the first one under the hat brim, and she smiled again, as if she were pleased with something. Zack added, a little too quickly, "Even if nothing actually *happened* ..."

"You're not *really* mad about that, are you?" Jamie asked carefully, daring to pout a little while keeping the hint of the smile. Chantel, amazed at Jamie's complete lack of embarrassment, blinked a couple of times.

"Who, me?" Zack shrugged, got a little bit of a grin going himself. "How many women try to knock out the man they're after, rather than let him be with another woman? It's perversely flattering to be wanted so much." He flushed a little bit, letting the warm glow overtake him. "I just went so hormonally crazy that I didn't think about other people's feelings ... I owe a lot of apologies."

Jamie wore an expression of complete sincerity as she touched his arm. "That's all right, Zack. I forgive you."

Chantel choked on her punch.

Jamie continued, a little too casually, "What about Missy? Do you … still want to be with her?" Nothing in her face seemed to indicate more than light interest, yet her eyes gleamed a little too brightly.

Zack sighed. He'd been thinking about this speech for a while, intending to say it to Missy's face; however, this seemed like a good opportunity for a dry run. "I don't think she deserves a schmuck like me … I'll tell her I made a mistake, and I'm sorry. I hope she does better next time."

How weird it felt, being utterly, completely honest. No defenses. Zack couldn't remember the last time he'd had no defenses. He almost chuckled as he added, "I think I need a girl who can hold me down to earth, keep me in line."

"That shouldn't be too hard," Jamie returned, almost—could it be?—flirtatiously. They were openly smiling at each other now; the sour undertone that lay beneath their banter two days ago forgotten. Chantel looked from one to the other in amazement, then saw something across the room and nudged the other two. They turned to look.

Missy had entered the room. She was dressed as a judge, complete with a long black robe and a gavel. Her upswept hair made her face seem unusually delicate yet severe, and her mouth was little more than a thin line. She made eye contact with the three of them, but as on the previous night she was immediately surrounded by a crowd of girls, all squealing over her outfit, who swept her away into the sea of students.

The three looked at each other; what was *that* all about?

"There goes the judge," Jamie commented. She'd been upstaged again, but tonight, for some reason, she didn't seem to care. Things were going so well thus far that she wasn't going to ask the universe for more. Yet.

"Here comes the brother," Chantel indicated with a nod. All turned again, and this time Chantel and Zack emitted small gasps of shock.

Brian had emerged from the men's room in full prince regalia—boots, tights, tunic, cape. Clearly, he'd finally made it upstairs to his bedroom, read Jamie's note, and decided to make an appearance. He looked like he'd just leaped off

the screen from a classic Disney animated fea-
ture; even Zack had to admit that he'd never seen
Brian look so dashing. He almost understood
what Josh saw in him.

Brian looked at all of them, his eyes hard little
stones; then his eyes slid over to the bunch of
girls and found Missy. Missy looked at him for a
split second, then broke the contact, turning back
to her squealing group.

Brian's eyes slid back to the others. The three
moved forward, Zack striding, the girls a little
more cautiously.

Zack extended his hand to him. "I'm sorry,
Brian."

Brian looked at Zack's hand for a long moment without looking up at Zack's face; then he
raised his eyes and looked at Jamie, who from behind Zack's shoulder mouthed, "Me, too."

Finally, his eyes met Zack's, and he took
Zack's hand, shaking it slowly and deliberately.
When he spoke at last, his voice was gravelly.
"This doesn't mean it's over, you know."

"I know." Zack swallowed noisily, his throat
having suddenly closed up. "I . . . I haven't had a
chance to talk to Missy yet."

Brian looked over the sea of heads at his

former girlfriend, as a wrinkle of pain creased his forehead. Then he looked at the three again, confusion on his face. "Where's Josh?"

Everyone looked at each other. They'd been so caught up in the unfolding drama of the past few minutes, they'd almost forgotten about him. "We haven't seen him yet," Zack offered, keeping his voice carefully neutral.

"Maybe he won't come?" Chantel added helpfully.

"He'll be here," Jamie said. "No one misses a hanging." The past few moments had almost lulled her into forgetting her vendetta against Josh, but now her anger flared again, raw and scorching. She had a few choice words to exchange with him, Brian or no Brian.

Brian was once again scanning the crowd, looking at Missy. Gentle regret filled his eyes, and Zack felt a pinprick of conscience.

Daringly, he touched Brian's arm, met his eyes, and they both looked at the girl who'd symbolized so much to both of them. "She's quality people, Bry. I just ... didn't realize how much ..." Shame enveloped him anew as he remembered Missy's face in Brian's room, and her devastation at Zack's betrayal. His face burned.

Brian, however, was still looking at Missy, determinedly sipping her punch and laughing carelessly with a group of kids he barely knew. He spoke absently, as though he and Zack were alone, as though there weren't a mob of kids in bizarre outfits surrounding them. "It's weird how in so little time ... someone can become like a complete stranger to you." He did not know this girl, this young woman, with the swept-up hair and the steely resolve in her manner. His time with her seemed to be drifting away from his memory, like a child's balloon caught in the breeze.

"Life can be very strange sometimes," Chantel murmured—to whom, it was unclear.

"I just want to go back to age thirteen, when I thought I knew everything," Zack blurted, unable to stop confessing all of his inadequacies now that he'd started.

"Not me. I want to go on to college, when I'll *really* know everything," Jamie said. West Point was high on her list; she liked the white gloves. Then she stiffened like a pointer catching a scent, as her eye caught the figure in the doorway. "Josh alert, folks."

Josh moved into the room slowly, as if he was

walking on the moon. He wore a spiffy dark business suit with spectacles, as if he were an executive or businessman of some sort; his black hair was combed back with a little too much gel, and slightly visible from one pocket was a small, silver flask. The flask explained his slow, deliberate walk; he was trying very hard to navigate the room without weaving. He glanced around the crowd, searching for—who? All of them, presumably, as his eyes locked on them and he began to inch his way forward.

His face was contorted into a sort of glower as he reached them, a bizarre replay of how they'd all stood the past Monday morning. "Hey ... the fab four. How goes?"

Zack's stomach lurched with nerves. He reached out tentatively to touch his friend's arm, as he had Brian's, but Josh jerked away as though Zack had given him an electric shock. He gave Zack a look that could have frozen water, and Zack, unnerved, took a step back. This was going to be the hard one.

"I always wondered what an AA costume would look like," Jamie murmured *sotto voce* to Chantel.

"Alcoholics Anonymous?" Chantel's eyes were the size of dinner plates.

"Absolute asshole," Jamie muttered.

"Aren't you someone I used to know?" Josh growled to Brian, right in his face. Zack prayed that Josh hadn't driven in this condition, lest the MG be wrapped like a pretzel around a lamppost out front.

Brian, however, seemed completely unfazed, or at least his expression didn't change. "Aren't you someone who shouldn't be drinking?" He spoke mildly, crossing his arms as if they were discussing the day's sports news. The glint of his small, gold crown reflected in his hair.

Zack reached for the flask again, and the unthinkable happened: Josh swung at him. Off-balance, Josh almost toppled over, but righted himself and, with a furious glare, turned and bolted for the door.

There was an instantaneous pause as Jamie, Chantel, Brian, and Zack all exchanged looks, and then raced after him as a group. Chantel hiked up the hem of her dress to move more quickly. Missy craned her neck as she watched them exit the Commons, a probing look on her face, but didn't follow.

They caught up with Josh by the stairs up to the library. This part of the hallway was dark, except for reflected light from the Commons and moonlight shining through the windows. Josh had taken two steps up the stairs, and Zack again reached up and grabbed his arm; Josh turned and swung once more, roaring, "Leave me the hell *alone!*"

Knocked off-balance, Zack fell back three steps, into Brian's arms. Chantel and Jamie helped get him to his feet. They all stared up the stairs in shock and disbelief, as though an exorcism was occurring in front of them.

Thirteen years of pent-up bile and fury was, at last, exploding out of Josh, all of it directed at Zack. His voice was ragged with fury. "You don't quit. You don't *ever* quit! You've screwed up my life and two other people's, and you *still … don't … quit!*"

He was almost screaming now, and the others felt pinned by his wrath, as though it were a giant mallet smashing down on them.

Josh went on yelling. "There is no *pond* here, Zack; try to explain your way out of it! You were my best friend. I trusted you. And I let you ruin *everything!* Just stay away from me."

This seemed to be the end of his anger. It had flamed out like a comet, leaving only cinders behind. He turned to mount the stairs, and Zack, undaunted, started behind him.

With the swiftness of an assassin, Josh spun, reached down, ripped off his dress shoe, and hurled it with as much force as he could muster at Zack. The black Perry Ellis loafer whistled past Zack's head, just missing his ear, and crashed to the floor.

Zack froze.

Josh looked right at his former friend, looked him dead in the eye, and spoke three words barely above a whisper: "Go to hell." He turned once more, mounted the stairs, and disappeared up into the darkness.

The library door banged.

Zack was so horrorstruck that he stood paralyzed halfway up the stairs. So, this was the way the world ended: via a size-eleven shoe.

He didn't seem to be able to catch his breath, as though he'd been punched in the solar plexus, and his vision was blurred. He reached out and grabbed the banister for support; otherwise, he might have fallen again.

A hand touched his back. Jamie was next to

him, her voice quiet and urgent. He grabbed onto her words as though they were a lifeline in a stormy sea: "It's as much my fault as yours. I'll go talk to him." Through the roaring in his head, Zack dimly realized that he'd never heard her sound so gentle before.

But then Brian shoehorned past them, said curtly, "No—I'm going," and strode up the staircase, cape flapping behind him. He had something in his hand.

There was a long pause, and Zack felt another hand on his back: Chantel. His eyes were still close to filling; he wouldn't let them overflow, but it was a battle. He staggered back to a bench and more or less fell onto it, as the girls settled on either side of him.

No one knew what to say as they contemplated the empty staircase. Then: "Film at eleven," Jamie said weakly, trying for a joke to lighten the mood. At that moment, she had no idea what else to do.

Zack turned to her, and something like gratitude filled his heart. But what he said—smiling through the near-tears—was, "Lady, you are some piece of work."

And Jamie knew exactly what he meant; he

meant, "Thank you." But rather than embarrass him by letting him know that, she just chucked him under the chin and murmured, "You say the sweetest things."

Chantel was vastly amused, but didn't say anything.

The three sat together, waiting.

CHAPTER 47

The interior of the library was dark; only one little wall light illuminated the room. Moonlight came through the windows and reflected on the furniture. There was a distant *thud thud thud* of bass audible through the floor from the dance. Brian entered cautiously, looking around; Josh was seated at a table, his back to the door. The door accidentally slammed shut, causing Brian to jump a bit, but Josh didn't even turn to look at him.

"I can't do it anymore, Zack," he said, his voice sounding like shattered glass.

Brian opened his mouth to say something, to

identify himself, but before he could say anything Josh went on.

"I can't be the good boy anymore. I know I blamed you, but I should've known this would end badly." He began snuffling, and his breathing was ragged. "I just—I didn't realize how much I really loved him until I saw his face yesterday morning. And now ... I can't go on with one foot in one world and one foot—I don't even know where." His voice broke again, and he was openly sobbing; the sound pierced Brian like the volley of arrows that pierced St. Sebastian. "I don't know what to do."

Then he laid his head on his arms and cried, cried as though his heart had been taken from him, as though he'd lost not one but two of the greatest loves of his life.

Brian stood awkwardly in the dimness, not knowing what to do or say first. Suddenly, he looked down at his hand, and a half-smile illuminated his face. He felt almost giddy with joy, but he kept it quiet, oh so quiet.

He moved around in front of Josh, whose sobs were finally abating. When Brian spoke, it was as gently as Josh had spoken to him the night before as he'd been tucked into bed, and his voice was as soft as flannel sheets.

"Josh ...?"

Josh raised his tear-streaked face, and looked, really looked, at the handsome prince standing in front of him.

Brian knelt, reached for Josh's black-stockinged heel, and with the greatest of delicacy, slipped the black Perry Ellis shoe onto Josh's foot, the tiniest of smiles playing on his lips as he did.

Josh was stunned beyond words. Brian extended his hand, and Josh slid his own into it, letting his fingers wrap around Brian's. Brian had strong hands, capable hands—hands that caught footballs and wrote papers and gently, very gently, ran a finger lightly over your knuckles, as if ascertaining that you were, in fact, real.

Brian pulled Josh to his feet. They stood for a long moment, memorizing each other's faces, knowing that the rest of their lives would spin off from this moment.

Then Brian gently said, "Well. We'd better ..." and indicated downstairs with a tilt of his head.

Josh nodded, smiled tentatively as he wiped his face, and followed him out, still holding tightly to Brian's hand.

CHAPTER 48

At the base of the stairs, Chantel, Jamie, and Zack were all huddled in a little knot, whispering together in hushed tones. They heard the library door creak, then the sound of footsteps descending. Zack rose, heart pounding, the girls hanging onto his arms.

Brian and Josh came into view, then descended and reached the bottom of the stairs. There was a moment as everyone stared at each other in various configurations and costumes—the escape artist, the dame, the queen, the prince, and whatever Josh was—and then something astonishing happened: Brian started laughing—a great, booming, roar of laughter that he hadn't unleashed in years.

It echoed and echoed, and suddenly everyone was laughing—Josh a low chuckle, Zack a whoop of mirth, Jamie a hysterical cackle, Chantel a fit of giggles. They all laughed for a minute or two, though none of them could say why exactly they were laughing. They laughed for sheer joy.

Zack was just turning to Josh, about to ask him a question, but the levity was broken by a familiar voice, like a coat hanger on a chalkboard. "Well, well ... Queers 'R Us."

They turned, and there was Hank, wearing a battered football jersey, several of his goons in tow. They stood in a row in the dim hallway, as implacable and immovable as headstones, looking with menace and nausea at Brian and Josh holding hands. There were four of the football players, Zack calculated quickly, and five including Zack and his ... friends. True, that included two girls, but one of them was Jamie. At least it'd be more or less an even match.

As if reading Zack's mind, Chantel turned to the group and murmured, "Amazing ... they've developed an asshole that walks, talks, and does everything but think."

"Listen, Hank, lay off, huh?" Zack stepped forward and tried to take the high ground; it was his fault that he'd dragged Hank into things that morning—God! *That morning?!*—and he wanted to defuse the situation as painlessly as possible.

"Hey Standish, what's your problem? You just did Missy, why're you hanging out with these AIDS traps?" Hank looked at Jamie through squinty eyes, as though she were some sort of rare STD he'd just discovered spotting his genitals. "Especially that muff-diver."

Jamie smiled one of her best blood-freezing smiles. She coiled an arm around Chantel like an octopus' tentacle, and remarked to the air, "Darrrling, do you smell rotten flesh and maggots? Or is it just me?"

Brian now took a step forward, every inch the medieval hero; he even had a fake sword at his hilt. "Gaston, I'm warning you, get away from me and my friends, and fast." Zack was trying to make peace, Brian was ready to start a war; they were well and truly through the looking glass now.

Since Brian had started forward, the others pressed behind him, pushing Hank and his goons back toward the dance. Several kids stepped into the hallway to see what the raised voices were all about.

Brian's boots made a slow *clack … clack … clack* sound, like a weapon being sharpened as he moved forward. Brian repeated, "Get back, or—"

"Or *what*? Or *what*, you homo?" Hank openly yelled.

The guy next to him, a toadying type, punctuated Hank's idiocy. "Yeah, you homo?"

The music had reached a pause, and others were becoming aware of the conflict—except the chaperones, who were on the other side of the dance busting a freshman for having herbal cigarettes with her. Several more kids stepped into the hallway, having heard Hank's epithet. Missy was on the edge of the crowd, watching them, an expression of pain contorting her features. She looked as if she wanted to say or do something, but was unsure what.

And it was at that moment, as approximately fifty kids stood facing the five of them during an ugly pause, that Zack knew what he had to do. He reached out, cool as Kelvin, put his arm around Josh, and pulled his best friend close. Then he leaned in and put a very slow, very deliberate, and very public kiss, like the end of *Snow White*, just below Josh's mouth.

Josh, flummoxed, gaped at Zack in terror; he knew kids in L.A. who'd been gay-bashed for less. But Zack didn't even seem to care. He turned back to Hank, whose eyes looked like eggs over easy, and drawled, "Sorry Hank … if being your friend means being like you, I'd rather stand with the homos."

Hank was immobilized with shock. A ripple of shock went through the crowd, then a couple of kids whooped, a couple of others applauded, and a smattering of epithets littered the air.

Brian turned, looked at his sister and his friends, and said just two words. "Let's go."

He turned to stride forward and break through the line of his former teammates, but Hank suddenly thawed. He stuck out one beefy arm and shoved Brian as hard as he could, knocking both Brian and Josh over in a heap. A cry of dismay and anticipation went up among the students watching.

The air crackled with energy.

Jamie sighed and pulled off her hat, handing it to Chantel. Her voice was regretful. "And this was a new outfit, too."

She pulled her fist back, but Brian was suddenly up and hit Hank squarely in the jaw. Hank fell, knocking over one of his followers. Josh, on his feet next, plunged in to help Zack take out another of the football goons, and Jamie took the last one. The fracas spilled back into the dance, and some students got shoved or knocked over.

In a matter of minutes, complete and utter hell had broken loose.

Streamers were ripped down, tables were overturned, screams and grunts and cries filled the air as costumes were bent, broken, or shredded. Week-long resentments that had been festering between various kids and groups suddenly exploded, and another wave of chaos and violence kicked in. The DJ put on "Zoot Suit Riot," and then ducked as a tray of cookies came flying at his head. Hysterical chaperones, including the slug-like math teacher, ran in all directions trying to contain pockets of mayhem, only to have fresh outbreaks occur right next to them. Jerry Springer couldn't have asked for more.

Missy sat on a folding chair with a cup of punch, calmly sipping it and looking around her casually as the dance was destroyed. Couples were fleeing for the exits, abandoning ripped or destroyed costumes as they went.

Brian and Hank threw themselves onto the refreshment table, still fighting as it overturned, as months of mutual hatred exploded out of them through their fists. In between their grunts, Missy could just make out the growls of *you piece of shit son of a bitch* ... The sound of breaking glassware punctuated their oaths.

Chantel was now under another table, sheltered by the Yearbook Kid's protective embrace. Jamie had somehow acquired someone's flail, and though it was only plastic and foam, she was still nimble and fierce enough with it to have sent several people running for the hills. Josh was swinging a chair as a weapon, and Zack had jumped on someone's back and was beating on their head as they attempted to shake him off. They'd officially crossed the line from "self-defense" by this point.

Brian rose out of the stewing cauldron of teenagers; his face was bruised again. His voice thundered above the din. "Guys, come *on!* Let's move!" He took one more punch at Hank, who collapsed in a heap next to the coat check, then grabbed his sister, who nearly clocked him with the flail before she realized who he was. In short order, they grabbed Josh and Zack respectively, waved frantically to Chantel, and bolted for the front doors. Wailing from the various parties remaining followed them.

Down the main path the five raced, avoiding other kids now in full riot mode. Brian gestured Josh to his car, Zack pulled Jamie to his. Chantel was piling into someone's Jeep, along with several other refugees including Kat, now apparently rocking the global-hippie/refugee-from a-riot look. As they squealed out, Josh had Brian throw the car in reverse just long enough to pull up in between the Jeep and the Beetle and yelp, "My place later! Whenever you can get there!" Brian threw the car into gear and burned rubber so fast that his crown blew off, Zack shortly behind him. At the corner, they turned in opposite directions.

"Where are you going? He said his house!" Jamie yelled over the wind and the engine. Zack was clocking seventy in a thirty-mile-an-hour zone.

"Don't worry, I know a shortcut!" Zack hollered over the din. And then he was laughing again, and Jamie was laughing too, because now he really looked like an escapee, and not only was

Jamie sporting several cuts and scrapes, but her makeup was also a mess, and her hair looked like she'd stuck a nail in a light socket. Both of them felt completely exhilarated and ready for anything, as long as they had each other and a full tank of gas.

Away they drove, into the wild beauty of the night.

CHAPTER 49

In Josh's house, the lights were low. While Brian used the restroom, Josh emptied a kitchen drawer of every half-burned candle he could lay his hands on, including a half-melted baby birthday candle, lit them, and placed them around the dining room, kitchen, living room, and foyer. Josh then poured himself a ginger ale chaser to help ease the journey back to sobriety while Brian kept an ice pack on his temple.

There was a slight pause, but not an awkward one; both smiled at each other. The candlelight made Brian's hair glow golden.

Josh rattled the ice cubes in his glass, held it up. "Want a drink?"

"No thanks, I try never to drink while I'm bleeding."

"Not even a Bloody Mary?" Josh put on a mock-offended expression, then grinned as Brian winced at the joke. "Sorry."

"So …" Brian said, letting the word linger in the air like cologne. "Here we are. What do you want to do?"

Josh knew exactly what he wanted to do. He'd wanted to do it for a long time, but he'd never thought he'd have a chance—certainly not with Brian. But now here they were, and he leaned in close, even though there was no one else in the house, because what he wanted to whisper was so intimate, he could barely stand to have even the air hear it.

He leaned close to Brian, so close his lips nearly touched the edge of Brian's ear, and whispered what he wanted to do. Brian's eyes widened. Josh pulled back and studied his face, to make sure he was okay.

Brian nodded; his throat was parched. Somehow, his words came out in a husky whisper: "Go ahead."

Josh moved to his father's Wurlitzer jukebox, Nick's greatest pride and joy. He nonchalantly punched two buttons; three chords, then Brian Setzer's "Sleepwalk" began to ooze from the speakers.

He raised an eyebrow at Josh, and Josh grinned his assent. Slowly, ever so slowly, they moved into each other's arms and began to dance in the semi-darkened hallway. Their shadows from the candles merged in and out of each other as they rotated to the music, letting the song fill their ears and hearts.

CHAPTER 50

"Well, that was interesting." Jamie's voice was as dry as Death Valley.

"There did *not* use to be a pond there."

Zack's car sat squarely in the middle of a children's wading pond just off the main drag of the park. Zack and Jamie were lying on the merry-go-round, which spun lazily and made the stars rotate high above them.

"Mmmmmm," Jamie said noncommittally. "Speaking of which: I'm glad you and Missy crashed and burned."

"Yeah? Well. I'm glad you recognized that you know Hank is beneath you," Zack said, almost slyly, to see how she'd react.

"*Beneath* me? We're not even on the same evolutionary ladder," Jamie snorted. Zack did the half-smile with one side of his mouth, which he knew made him look cute. Alex wasn't the only one who knew this trick.

Jamie fully smiled in response, so it seemed to work. "It's nice, you and me finally talking."

"It has been several years."

"I enjoy talking to you—or at least, sparring with you. *You* never wanted to talk to me."

"You punched my lights out," Zack said, a little defensively.

Jamie looked nonplussed for a moment. "I did?" She scrunched up her forehead as she tried to remember, which only made *her* more adorable. Light, followed swiftly by embarrassment, flooded her face. "Oh, yeah … I did. Sorry."

Long pause, crickets chirping in the dark.

"You still hate me for a slight overreaction all those years ago?"

Overreaction was putting it mildly, but Zack wasn't in the mood to split hairs.

"Hey. If Josh can still be in love with Brian, I can still be in … dislike with you." It felt odd to say that out loud: *Josh in love with Brian.* Was Josh feeling ladybugs and dragonflies in his stomach, and getting slight chilly-willies on the back of his neck being close to Brian? Odd how, in contrast, Zack was feeling so relaxed at this moment, unlike the previous night's rollercoaster with Missy when he'd first felt like a bolt of pure nervous energy on the patio, then like something heavy and waterlogged on the ocean floor once they'd made it to the bedroom. Instead, right now, he felt … comfortable. A warm glow was kindling inside of him, and it didn't have anything to do with a glass of champagne, a cup of punch, or a flask of God-knows-what. This felt strangely, miraculously right. It felt … well, like home.

"You know, I always liked you." Jamie laughed. The park lights shining on her made her look close to beaming like some sort of retro '40s angel. "You really tick me off sometimes, but … you're really fun. You make me laugh."

"Yeah, well …" Zack wasn't sure this was the compliment he'd been hoping for.

"Hey—don't knock it." Jamie sat up and nudged him, her hair spilling down one side of her face. With the play of shadows and light, her bruises were hardly visible; they could've even passed for heavy makeup. "You're different. How many people out there have the balls to be different, even if that's who they really are?"

"Maybe they're scared," Zack said, almost honestly. He knew something about being lonely, being an outsider, being scared. "Doesn't anything scare you?"

"Just mediocrity. Chances not taken, stones unturned, the works." *And locusts, and clog dancers.* "You know. There's so much to see, to know, to do—I don't know if I'll ever get to it all."

She breathed this with a hint of wonder, as if inhaling the stardust of all her potential. Then a shadow seemed to fall across her face. "But lately … I've started to wonder if I'll be doing it alone forever."

She looked over in the distance at the Beetle, still soaking in the pond, then back at Zack. "What are you afraid of?"

Zack rolled over on his side, ran a finger down a crack in the metal stripe on the merry-go-round. He'd already seen his worst fear realized in the past twenty-four hours; now, hopefully, things were on their way to being set right. He made his voice light and jokey. "That our breakup would be really ugly, if it ever happens."

"*Breakup?* We're not even together."

"Oh yeah ..."

He drew closer.

"...I forgot."

Closer ...

"I foresee us as being an incredibly intense, strange pair," Jamie breathed. Her breath smelled like vanilla.

Zack had been leaning in, but he stopped about three inches from her face. He said, in a normal tone of voice, "Good. We won't get bored easily."

"I really loathe cocky boys," Jamie murmured. Zack's neck smelled like Tom Ford aftershave. She decided that she adored Tom Ford.

"Too bad," Zack whispered. "I really love smart girls."

And then they were kissing, and not talking at all.

After more than a few minutes, Jamie finally came up for air: "Standish, you're one hell of a sexy man."

"Thanks, you're not bad yourself," Zack returned breathlessly. Then: "Sexy girl, I mean." The thought of kissing Brian suddenly shot through his brain in a nanosecond and was gone. Thankfully.

There was a long pause, then Jamie said, a little uncomfortably, "So, do you, uh … want to do something about it?"

The night had been full of surprises thus far, and the words that came from Zack's lips were possibly the most surprising of all. "Actually … no."

He leaned his head over the edge of the merry-go-round and began to laugh. He laughed at the sheer impossibility of this moment happening. He laughed that he'd changed his pants from yesterday, and the condom from last night was still in his pocket and hanging on his bedroom doorknob. He laughed because sex, the most important thing on his mind all this week, suddenly seemed a lot less important than he'd thought.

Jamie, fortunately, after staring at him while he was laughing like a loon, started laughing too. In fact, she laughed even harder, and when she lay back, faced him, and said "Me neither" in a choked voice, both of them laughed until they were almost hysterical. *We must make a hell of a picture, the two of us, lying on a merry-go-round, laughing ourselves nuts in the middle of the night next to a waterlogged Volkswagen.* The thought made

Jamie laugh so hard that her eyes started to tear.

After a few minutes, they finally controlled themselves, but by then Jamie had rolled into Zack's arms, and was snuggled in tight. Their breathing settled down to that hiccupy, shaky breathing you get after laughing too much. Zack nuzzled her forehead and kissed it gently. His voice was as soft as goose down. "Well, maybe some time, yeah. Definitely. But for tonight ..."

"What say we just be friends?"

"Well," Zack said, a little quickly, *more* than friends."

"Friends with ... possibilities?" Jamie rubbed his nose with her own, Eskimo style. She had no idea who she was or what she was doing. Most remarkably, she didn't care.

"I like possibilities," Zack sighed happily.

She was on top of him, her hair covering his face like golden lace. He drank from her lips, became dizzy, became drunk. Or maybe it was just the spinning from the merry-go-round. Either way, he never wanted it to stop.

CHAPTER 51

In a restaurant across town, Chantel was recapping an abbreviated version of the story for Yoshi, Robin the Yearbook Kid, the ubiquitous Kat, and others over plates of Rooty-Tooty-Fresh-and-Fruity crepes. The booth was crammed with people, the table was loaded with food, and Chantel had a brief flash of her future, wishing she could look back on this night and somehow freeze it in time, when everyone seemed young and happy and golden and perfect.

Chantel speared a strawberry, dragged it through some whipped cream, and forked it to her lips, her perfect white teeth biting into its red succulence. It was oh-so, oh-so sweet.

CHAPTER 52

Missy drove home in a daze. Her mother was already in bed. She shucked off her robe and heels, revealing the sweatpants and T-shirt underneath, and tossed them over the arm of the couch. She made a cup of tea and, as if in a dream, wandered into the darkened living room. She turned on the TV; Jack Nicholson was yelling at Tom Cruise, "You can't handle the truth!" *Who can?*

She changed the channel and found *The Lion In Winter* on Turner Classic Movies. Peter O'Toole was yelling at Katharine Hepburn on the balcony of a medieval castle: "Good God, woman, face facts!"

"Which ones? We have so *many*," Hepburn parried, unfazed and unbowed.

Missy stared at her, entranced. For the first time in—well, possibly ever—she suddenly had a flash into how Jamie's mind worked.

And she liked it.

CHAPTER 53

Brian was completely outside of his body, outside of his head, outside of time. The jukebox had stopped playing music a while ago, yet he and Josh clung to each other in the flickering candlelight and the Wurlitzer's glow, unsure of what to do or say next. That is, they knew what they *wanted* to do, but neither of them was sure how to exactly begin.

Something had been bothering Brian for several hours now, and he hoped asking it wouldn't break the mood. He pulled back from Josh just far enough to see his face, and asked, "So, you've never told me ... what's your costume supposed to be?" He knew Josh didn't wear glasses, so they must be part of the ensemble. But what was it?

Josh held his gaze for a moment, then a slightly sheepish look came over his face, and he rolled his eyes upward, as if he were a little embarrassed. He pulled back and stepped away from Brian and began unbuttoning his white dress shirt.

Time slowed to a crawl. Stopped.

Josh's fingers kept going down, down, undoing the buttons of the shirt under the dark suit, until he reached his waist, then paused. Then with one hand he pulled the shirt open, and simultaneously with the other he removed his glasses. He had a T-shirt on underneath the dress shirt.

Then Brian's heart was on the verge of exploding, and his eyes filled with tears; then they were running down his cheeks in streams, and he didn't care. He just stood there in Josh's hallway, pressing his lips tightly together to keep the sobs from bursting out of him, staring at Josh's chest.

At the blue T-shirt.

At the gold-and-red logo: *S*.

Josh was Superman.

Josh was smiling apologetically, then he

looked startled, and wondered why Brian was crying. Then he didn't have any thoughts at all, didn't wonder anything, because Brian took two steps forward, gently took Josh's face in his hands, pulled him close, and kissed him and kissed him and kissed him. Like a handsome prince in a story too wonderful to come true, but it did, oh it did.

And Brian kept on kissing Josh, kept kissing him all the way up the stairs, into Josh's bedroom, kissed him as costumes were discarded, as fantasies became reality, as every dream he'd ever had or wished for came true. If he'd been able to speak, if he'd settled for something as ordinary as words, Brian would've said it was like flying.

CHAPTER 54

Just like the day before, Brian woke up early. The sunlight was streaming through the windows like ribbons of honey, and unlike yesterday, he felt like ten million dollars, taxes paid. He rolled over and checked to make sure he wasn't still dreaming.

Josh lay next to him, still asleep. All this week, Josh's hair had been meticulously combed and styled each day. Now, in the early morning light, it was falling over his eyebrows in shaggy bangs. For some reason, Brian was enormously touched by this.

He smoothed the other boy's hair, touched his head, ran two fingers down his neck, touched the back of his knuckles to the other boy's chest, grazed the dusting of chest hair. Josh stirred a bit but didn't wake up.

This is my boyfriend, Brian thought. My *boyfriend*. He didn't know if his heart or another organ felt more ready to burst at thinking those words.

He eased himself out of bed and found a pair of shorts lying on the floor. They were a little roomy, but not bad. He tiptoed out of the room, closing the door gently behind him.

Brian strode through the house, feeling strangely powerful and reckless. He looked at the light caressing the hallway pictures, mostly black-and-white photographs of mountains and lakes. He passed an antique mirror in the hallway and paused before it, flexing his muscles, shaking his hair back off his face. He made silly faces—a gorilla growling, a clown sticking out his tongue, a gigolo licking his lips. He ran his hands down his bare chest, over his thighs. Someone wanted him. Someone *had* him. He had no idea—not even after years of doing sports—how powerful an instrument his body was, until he used it to give and receive pleasure.

Who *was* he, thinking like this? Who was this

wild, swaggering, giddy, hormonal boy, who normally dragged himself through the mornings but
today felt like he could wrestle a bear, buck-
naked? For the first time in his life, Brian understood why people burst into song in musicals. It
was because they had so much feeling inside
them, mere words weren't enough to convey
it all.

Brian padded downstairs and out the front
door, leaving it unlocked behind him. He ambled
to his car, opened the back door, and pulled out
the T-shirt, socks, and sneakers he'd stashed
there in case he'd wanted to change clothes after
the dance. Well, *that* hadn't exactly panned out,
had it? He grinned sleepily and delightedly as he
remembered the previous night. Then he pulled
out his cell phone—used only for emergencies—
and dialed a number. The voice on the other end
answered, "Hello . . .?" a little groggily.

"Dr. Rivers...? It's me, Brian." He leaned back
against the car, basking in the morning sun, letting his exposed back feel the warm metal. "I just
want you to know ... I feel wonderful." He let the
words taste the air for a moment; he did, in fact,
feel wonderful. He couldn't remember the last
time he'd felt this good. "And I won't be in next

Wednesday. Probably not the one after that either. Thank you."

He hung up amidst the doctor's protestations, tossed the phone back in the car, and began to jog. He jogged down the driveway, out to the street, and down a block. He jogged through a little park, and the sprinklers came on, soaking him. He ran faster and faster, soaking wet, laughing, alive.

AN HOUR LATER, he jogged back to the house, still dripping. By now, Josh should be up, Brian thought. A wicked grin crossed his face as he anticipated their first kiss of the morning, followed by a shower. A *long, hot* shower. The shorts grew a little tighter as he bounded up the steps and pushed the front door open, peeling off his shirt as he entered the front hallway, doing a silent war dance of joyous anticipation.

Then he froze.

Nicholas Bradshaw was entering the front hallway from the garage, the door of which shut with a distant thud. He carried the morning newspaper under one arm, a laptop bag in his hand, and a small travel bag in the other. He tossed his keys on the hallway table, then looked up and registered Brian.

A long pause ensued.

The two surveyed each other, recognition almost simultaneously flooding their faces. Nick spoke first. "If memory serves ... you must be Brian." His voice was polite, with just a hint of curiosity behind it.

Brian stood his ground, but he swallowed before answering. "Uh ... yes sir. I am." He hoped he wasn't dripping on the carpet. He was very glad the shorts were no longer tight.

Nick smiled. He always had a nice smile, Brian remembered. "Mmm. Nice to see you again. It's been a long time." He extended his hand, a hand so similar to Josh's that Brian had to force himself not to stare at it.

"Yeah," he said, in a none-too-swift response.

"That must be your car out there. Did you come over to see Josh?"

"Yeah ..." Brian ventured timidly, feeling the ground beginning to crumble beneath him. A few more words or steps and he'd plunge straight through the Earth toward China.

"I just got in from San Francisco. I was just

about to do up an omelet—I hate airport food. Would you like an omelet? Josh should be up soon ..."

Brian came close to bursting into giggles. "Er —ahh—Mr. Bradshaw, I—that is—I would love an omelet." He would, too. As a matter of fact, Brian realized, he'd barely eaten since Friday night, and he was ravenous.

Nick dropped his bags next to the stairs, and clapped Brian on the shoulder, ushering him toward the kitchen. "Good. Come help me start cracking eggs. I think we'll just let my son sleep a while longer ... Man, you're wet. Did you get in a good workout this morning on your way over here?" It was unclear whether Nick had no idea what was going on or was completely aware and was just trying to spare Brian further embarrassment. Either way, Brian was grateful.

As they started toward the kitchen, Brian managed to turn his head for an instant and look over his shoulder up the stairs. Josh was standing on the landing in his briefs, completely dumbstruck. Nick was still talking: "Was your weekend as exhausting as mine ...? You know, I think Josh has a pair of shorts just like yours."

"No way," Brian said, with a touch of irony.

JOSH DRESSED in what felt like about fifteen seconds—shirt, sweats, sandals. He'd been hoping for a slow wake-up session of lovemaking with his boyfriend, and it had completely slipped his mind that his father had planned on being home Sunday morning. *Curse you, Alaska Airlines, and your stupid 6:30 a.m. flights,* Josh thought through gritted teeth, racing a brush over them and spitting mouthwash into the sink with gusto. His father thought *his* weekend was exhausting? Boy, could Josh compare notes on that one.

He thundered down the stairs as if the hounds of hell were on his heels and skidded into the kitchen. Nick already had eggs mixed up, a pan melting butter, a big frying pan of hash browns going, and was measuring coffee. Brian sat at the kitchen counter, chopping a variety of vegetables. They were laughing and seemed to be enjoying each other's company immensely. Josh slipped into an empty chair at the kitchen table and watched the unfolding conversation between his father and boyfriend with mounting incredulity.

"But Mr. Bradshaw," Brian was saying passionately, "how can you be a Broncos fan? They're deader than dead."

"Oh, ye of little faith!" Nick boomed like an evangelical preacher. "The dead shall rise again. If they don't, I'll start following soccer. Good morning, son. Would you like mushrooms, onions, peppers, or just cheese?"

"Whatever," Josh said absently. Then, "Thanks, Dad." His father smiled at him, then turned back to the food. Brian wiggled his eyebrows at Josh, grinning his head off, and reached over just quickly and unobtrusively enough to rub Josh's foot with his own. The doorbell rang and Nick, frowning a little, excused himself to go answer it.

Josh was up in about half a second, planting a giant kiss on Brian, then grabbed Brian's face in his hands. "If you're trying to give me cardiac arrest, you're doing a hell of a job!"

"It's okay," Brian whispered back, laughing, "don't worry. He seems cool. But he did ask me what my intentions were, and would I make an honest man out of you." He grinned wickedly.

"You told him about *last night*?" Josh squeaked.

"I didn't give him a blow-by-blow description, if that's what you're thinking."

"I don't know what I'm thinking." Josh rested his head in his hands, staring up at Brian with a mixture of adoration and bewilderment. "What am I thinking?"

Nick re-entered the room with—of all people —Chantel. She was wearing what appeared to be a ski vest and a pair of Hawaiian shorts, with not an Egyptian accouterment in sight. She held up her hand as both Josh and Brian's jaws dropped open: "Do not even ask."

"What happened?" Brian ignored her warning.

"I haven't had a chance to get home to change yet. Ooh, are those hash browns?" Chantel pulled up a chair next to Josh. Nick started spooning potatoes into a bowl, then plated the first omelet. He passed everything to Chantel, who set the table. Nick wiggled his eyebrows at the boys.

"Uhh ... Mr. Bradshaw, this is my sister's friend Chantel," Brian offered fumblingly. He felt bad describing her that way, but it was accurate enough for the moment.

"We met," Nick smiled, pouring coffee and passing mugs with various high-tech company logos on the sides of them.

"Charmed," Chantel said brightly, her mouth already full of potatoes.

They munched fixedly for a brief moment, then the doorbell rang again. Josh, shooting the table a disbelieving glance, rose and went to answer it.

"I hope you don't mind," Nick said, poker-faced, "but I'm thinking of taking notes on all this to use someday in a screenplay pitch."

Brian shrugged, undisturbed. Chantel grimaced into her coffee.

In the front entryway, Josh opened the door. The couple on the front porch had their arms wrapped nonchalantly around each other.

"*Good* morning," Jamie beamed. "Have you ever given any thought to the kingdom of heaven?"

Josh's jaw dropped open.

"I think he found it last night," Zack commented, none too subtly, in Jamie's ear.

Josh emitted a tiny squeak of terror and slammed the door shut. It *couldn't* be. He slapped himself across the face, shook his head to clear the cobwebs, and opened the door again.

They were still there, looking as if nothing had happened.

"Sorry, this is not acid or virtual reality," Jamie chirped. "This is indeed your life."

Josh fumblingly gestured them inside. Jamie ran one hand along his jaw in her usual manner and gave him a meaningful look: Josh now held in his hands the hearts of the two young men she loved most in the world. He gestured floridly toward the kitchen, and she, smiling enigmatically, followed the sounds of conversation and the smells of food.

As she left the hallway, Josh turned to Zack, who was grinning sheepishly. *"Well?"* Josh finally stage-whispered.

Zack shrugged and smiled a little moonily. "Life has a very strange way of working out."

Jamie strode into the dining room, tossing her hat onto a corner chair, and took a seat at the end of the table, running her hands along the back of Brian's neck as she passed him. "Hey, Telly. Mr. Bradshaw. Hi, bro'. Any orange juice?"

Chantel passed it to her, rolling her eyes. Brian stared at his sister as she poured a large glass, took a drink, then noticed everyone watching her. Her expression and voice were the pictures of absolute innocence. "What?"

"I'm going to need more eggs," Nick muttered, opening the fridge again.

In the hallway, Zack brought Josh up to speed on the night in the park, both of them giggling like crazy. "So, that's what happened. How's things with you?"

"Good." Josh turned and looked into the kitchen. His dad was busy talking with Jamie and Chantel. Brian turned and looked right at him, giving him a quick, radiant smile. Josh turned back to Zack. "Really, really ... good. Thanks."

"Hey—it happened in spite of me, not because of me," Zack said honestly.

"Who cares?" Josh said. "It happened, and you were there. So ... thanks."

And then Josh was embracing him, really embracing him as he had five long years ago. It was the sort of embrace you give someone when you're saying goodbye to them, or when you finally get to say hello again, and mean it. And Zack didn't stiffen up, didn't pull away; Zack was holding him just as tightly as Josh was holding Zack.

Everything was the same, yet everything was completely different.

Zack's voice was thick against Josh's shoulder, his shirt. "I'm sorry about everything."

"Me too."

As they finally pulled apart, he studied Zack's face for a second. Zack was not Brian; Zack was not his boyfriend. Yet Josh knew instinctively that as much as he loved Brian—and he knew without a doubt that he did—that this face, the face he stared at now, the wild, red-haired, freckled boy who exasperated him beyond measure, would always be one of the greatest loves of his life. He would've sleepwalked his way through life if Zack hadn't woken him up. *Brian is the handsome prince I've always waited for, but Zack was the one who woke me up.*

But he didn't say any of this. What he said was, "So, you want some chow, or what?"

As he put an arm around Zack's neck to lead him into the kitchen, Zack swiped at his eyes, so quickly it was almost unnoticeable.

"You okay?" Josh asked.

"Fine, fine," Zack said, not quite snappishly. "Just got something in my eye, that's all." Nonetheless, he put one hand on Josh's shoulder.

As they went in, Zack added, "Hey ... does this mean you're going to give my Chocolate

Sugar Blasters kaleidoscope to Brian instead of back to me?"

AN HOUR LATER, brunch finished, everyone was sitting around the table reconstructing details from the night before and comparing notes. They all felt full, happy, and loved, and things were about as good as they could be, and as Zack remembered that heartbreaking weekend almost exactly five years prior and how things changed, he couldn't help but grin into his coffee.

That was when the phone rang, and Nick took it in the other room.

He was gone for several minutes, and when he returned, his expression was grim—grimmer than even Josh had ever seen. As he started talking, the rest of the table fell silent.

"That was Professor Falcon's assistant at your school. All of you have a meeting tomorrow morning to discuss your role in what happened last night." Nick looked at each of them, letting the full weight of his words sink in, before his gaze finally rested on his son. Nick's voice was like a birthday balloon with every bit of air and happy wishes squeezed out of it. "There is the strong possibility ... that you all may be expelled."

For a few moments, no one spoke, as the magnitude of this hit everyone at once. Then slowly, one by one, everyone's head turned in the same direction, toward the one person who might seemingly be able to hatch a plan to save them.

Jamie finished chewing her bite, took one last sip of coffee, and blotted her lips with the napkin. She then threw it down onto the plate, pushed back her chair, and rose, her voice and demeanor as crisp as ever.

"Everyone in the living room. Now."

CHAPTER 55

"This is a council of war."

Jamie stood at the front of the living room like General Patton reviewing the troops. The others sat on various couches, chairs, and ottomans, listening to her. Nick, after a serious *sotto voce* conversation with Josh, retired to his office to work, with the understanding that he would be receiving an update by day's end.

Jamie's eyes were tiny slits as her mind clicked along like a stock ticker machine. "Someone wants us out of the way—if they were doing this conventionally, we'd go straight to Falcon's office. Now, what we have to do first is prove that Hank caused all the violence. That's not hard."

Brian exchanged guilty looks with Zack.

"Second, however, they might try to zap us for 'moral degeneracy' or some such crap, and that's harder to escape without bringing in the ACLU or big guns like that." Jamie's gaze lingered on Brian and Josh, and she looked perplexed. "You two can't just say "everyone's doing it," because not everyone is. If we were dealing with the public school system we might have grounds for a legal case here, but a private, Christian institution has a lot more leeway. They may try to rope Zack and me into things as well, on the grounds of—I don't know, sexual manipulation, or blackmail."

"But the school doesn't have any rules for dealing with this," Chantel argued, wanting in on the action.

"That doesn't help—they can do anything if there's no legal precedent to go by," Brian countered glumly. Jamie looked almost startled at her brother contributing to the conversation, and then rather pleased, as though he were a toddler who'd just taken his first steps.

"Besides," Zack added, adding to Brian's argument, "Do you want the publicity of a lawyer? The *expense* of a lawyer?" Silence fell as they all envisioned the fallout from Saturday plastered all over the local news. *Zack's a lot smarter than he comes across*, Brian thought.

Zack, caught off-guard, stammered a bit as he continued: "Look, enough people've been hurt already, most of it my fault. I say I try to patch it up. I'll say it was all my idea. That should get everyone off the hook."

"But if you do that," Jamie warned, "you could lose your scholarship. Also, Josh and Brian are already going to have the free world breathing down their necks for the rest of the year, even if you try to smooth things over. They'd have to meet outside of school, and when they were there, they couldn't even look at each other." She looked concernedly from Josh to her brother on opposite couches. "Could you handle that?"

"No," her brother said, sounding like Samuel L. Jackson in some crime drama. His words were as cool and hard as bullets. "I'll go off the deep end if I go through this garbage again. I'm going to tell the truth and take the risk."

"Me too," Josh concurred, drinking in Brian's steely expression. He looked *hot*.

"Good," Jamie said, pleased by their responses. "That doesn't really *help*, but I'm still glad. We'll go to Plan C."

"Which is?" Zack was almost afraid to ask.

"I find out who the members of the Honor Board are and bribe them."

The room erupted into a chorus of pained groans.

Jamie was nettled. "What? What? You all got a better idea? I'll get Yoshi to uncover it."

"He's not speaking to any of us," Chantel offered gloomily. "His camera got busted last night."

"Well," Josh sighed, "count him out then. So much for accomplices."

The room fell silent again, as everyone tried various mental doors in an attempt to escape the prison in which they found themselves. No rescue seemed forthcoming.

"I think we may be in some very serious shit," Zack ventured at length.

Jamie eyed her brother, and a realization suddenly struck her: her folks, like Nick, would be home early that afternoon. "Brian, are you going to tell Mom and Dad?"

"I'm going to wait and see what happens to-

morrow first. One potential disaster per cus-
tomer, please," Brian said flippantly, but with a
bleak undertone. Josh took this moment to get off
the couch where he had been sitting next to
Chantel, and land next to Brian so he could lay
his head on Brian's shoulder.

"You know," Chantel remarked, breaking
Zack's involuntary staring at Josh and Brian's intimacy, "there's something we've forgotten all
about."

Everyone looked at her. Chantel basked in the
attention for a moment, then dropped the bomb:
"What does Missy think about all this?"

At the mention of her name, Zack winced.
Brian looked grim, Josh looked surprised, and
Jamie looked thoughtful. They were suddenly
confronted with a long-misplaced file that had
been stuck in the wrong drawer and consequently
been forgotten, unnoticed, and uncared about. It
was simply an accident.

MISSY HUNG up the phone and stared into space
for a moment. Then she rose, put on a jacket, and

was on her way to the front door before she started speaking, so she could get out quickly without a lot of questions. "Mama, I'm going out for a bit. I have some things to do before school tomorrow."

LATER, as dusk fell, the five were still at Josh's, sitting around two open boxes of pizza. This alone was like navigating peace in the Middle East, as Zack refused to eat olives, Jamie despised pineapple, Brian wouldn't touch bell peppers or pepperoni, Josh liked extra cheese and light sauce, and Chantel liked extra sauce and light cheese. Still, by ordering two mediums and going half-and-half on each of them, they'd managed to find some common ground.

"Now then," Jamie said around a mouthful of Gamma Nuke (double pepperoni, double linguica, extra cheese, thin crust). "I've managed to track down three people and get some cash "gifts" to them—that's a good reserve if it's a split decision."

"How'd you pull that off?" Zack asked, startled. Geez, the things he could've accomplished if he'd teamed up with this girl long ago.

"I accessed the school's computer and found out who was on last year's honor council that hadn't graduated yet." Jamie smirked, pleased with herself; hacking into the Academy's network and school files was a cakewalk for her. "The problem is, we still have five others and a faculty advisor to reckon with."

"So, what else can we do?" Josh asked uncertainly.

"Nothing," Brian proclaimed with finality, feet on the coffee table. He'd had four pieces of pizza and was feeling extremely sated. "It's out of our hands, so we might as well relax and enjoy ourselves." He took this opportunity to tickle Josh's stomach since Josh happened to be stretching and inadvertently exposing his stomach right then. In short order, sofa cushions and pillows were flying around the room.

A SHORT TIME LATER, Josh timidly knocked on his father's office door, then pushed it open. His father was at his desk working on his laptop, with only a small desk light for illumination. Nick looked up at his son, and the lights glinted off the glass; Josh couldn't read his expression. "Hey, Dad."

"Hey, son." Nick smiled, but Josh sensed tension in the smile, a touch of strain in the voice. "How's it going?"

"Fine …" Josh entered the room, shutting the door behind him. He didn't know what to do with his hands; they were on his hips, then in his pockets, then crossed on his chest. He clutched at his upper torso self-protectively.

"Do we have something to talk about?" Nick was never formal with him, as if he were a client, and Josh felt a quiver of fear in his chest. The past twenty-four hours had been a lot to deal with emotionally, and he didn't know what he was going to do if his father wasn't there for him now.

"You mean me and Brian?"

Nick sighed, rubbed his temples. Josh felt a pang again as he looked at the gray slowly creeping up toward his father's hairline. "I was thinking more along the lines of what happened at the dance. But sure, let's start with you and Brian."

"Um," Josh said hesitantly. "Let's talk about the dance."

His father sighed. "All right. The dance." He leaned back in his desk chair and crossed his arms, waiting.

Silence.

After several seconds, during which it seemed a new Ice Age came and went, Josh finally collected his thoughts, and the words came slowly and carefully, yet without fumbling. "We were at the dance ... and some people Brian knows were harassing him and me ... and Zack came to our defense ... and then someone shoved Brian. And then everyone started fighting and ... we were in the middle of it, trying to defend ourselves. And then we left."

"And *then* you left," his father said, an acidic note coming into his voice. "Do you know what happened *after* you left? Several hundred dollars' worth of clean-up and repairs, apparently, not to mention numerous kids needing medical attention."

He was almost glaring at Josh, and Josh felt tears sting the back of his eyes. He couldn't remember ever having disappointed his father before.

Nick continued, "Fortunately, no one was seriously hurt—just scrapes and bruises and gashes, apparently. But this ... is not what I had in mind when I asked if you could *handle* things while I was gone. Do you remember that conversation?"

Josh nodded mutely. In the kitchen, on Thursday night. It seemed eons ago, in a distant land, like Middle Earth.

Nick's angry look was softening a little, but his expression was still grim. "So, I take it you're going to plead self-defense. Do you think that will be enough?"

"I don't know," Josh said weakly.

"Is this going to be a regular occurrence, now that you're in a relationship that other people aren't always going to react very well to?" His father looked arch. He tapped one finger against the edge of the desk repeatedly, beating out a silent, condemning tattoo.

Josh shrugged, helpless in his vulnerability. He had felt so much stronger in the living room, surrounded by friends in the same boat; here, in the dimness of his father's office, he felt like he was a condemned prisoner first hearing the charges read against him, like Jean Valjean. Only one thing seemed clear and true. "Dad, I ... love him."

Nick seemed to slump a bit, as if he were deflating. He wasn't looking at Josh, and Josh thought for a split second of terror that Nick was ashamed of him and couldn't look him in the eye. Then he realized that Nick was staring at the silver-framed picture on his desk of Josh's mother in her wedding dress. She was standing on a balcony with the late-morning light behind her, holding her bouquet of tuber roses, smiling radiantly. She couldn't have been more than twenty-two.

Nick ran his finger along the edge of the frame, and his voice, when he spoke, was suddenly thick. "Does he love you?"

Josh nodded. When Nick turned to look at him, he finally spoke. "Yes."

"You're sure?" His father's eyes were glistening.

Josh nodded again, more vigorously. His voice was so emphatic that he jumped a bit when he spoke: "Yes."

Nick sighed, leaned forward, and put his face in his hands. Josh thought for a moment that he was crying, but his father only exhaled and said, in a muffled way between his fingers, "Then I need to support you two, don't I." It wasn't a question.

Now Josh's eyes did fill with tears. He moved behind his father, felt his shoulders, felt the muscles all ropy and strained. Overcome, he leaned in from behind, wrapped his arms around Nick, buried his face in his neck. His father reached up and ran his fingers through his hair and mumbled something under his breath that sounded like "My boy." Josh gripped him tighter, and clung to him, as he used to when he was a small boy and his father would carry him during a storm, keeping him close and sheltered till they reached safety. Now his father couldn't carry him anymore.

When they finally pulled apart, Nick said, "I take it that crowd out there is all hanging together on this?"

"Better that than, as Ben Franklin said, 'we'll all hang separately.'"

His father laughed, scattering the last of the room's shadows. "Well ..." He lifted his hands in a kind of helpless gesture as if indicating, what else was there to say? Josh laughed too.

Nick rose and pushed back his desk chair. "Think your friends would like some ice cream?"

THAT NIGHT, Brian entered Josh's room, shutting the door behind him, leaning against it, smiling. Josh came forward, clad in gym shorts and a white T-shirt, which looked just as good to Brian as if he'd been naked. The two boys slid into each other's embrace and held each other for a moment, not even bothering to turn on the overhead lights.

"Did you call and tell your parents you're staying over?" Josh said casually.

Brian nodded. "They're so happy I've made a nice friend. They hope you're a good influence on me." He and Jamie had deleted the phone message to his parents from the Academy, too.

Josh smiled wickedly. "Well, I definitely plan on being *on* you—I'll try to make it extra good."

He did.

IN THE KITCHEN, Chantel, Jamie, Zack, and Nick were perched on barstools, finishing the last bits of breadsticks from the pizza order and scraping ice-cream dishes, listening to Jamie relate junior high school dating horror stories.

"So here I am at the Fun Forest, right?" Jamie took a swig of Green Apple soda, setting the scene. She looked nauseated at the memory. "Thirteen years old, with this supposed dream boy with all the money in the world, nice looks, breeding, and so on and so forth and *blech*. We're on top of the paratrooper ride and he tries to cop a feel; so, I do what any young woman who doesn't want to be felt up does ..."

"Which is?" Nick asked, a half-smile tugging at the corner of his mouth. He'd just met this girl today and had already deduced that Zack had a lot on his plate.

"I pushed him off the ride." Jamie took another drink of soda as Chantel burst into guffaws, Nick chuckled, and Zack's mouth dropped open.

Zack squeaked, "What *happened?*"

"Oh, he broke a souvenir cart, it was a mess. My father had to pay for the crushed pinwheels, the punctured inflatable animals, the works. He was fine. But after being grounded for three months, I decided dating wasn't my thing."

Jamie finished this with a shrug, as if to say, *hasn't this happened to all of us?* She squeezed Zack's hand. Shaking his head, he brought it to his lips for a kiss.

"Well, I'd love to keep shooting the shi-*shinola* with y'all," Chantel remarked, "but I'd better go home and get some rest before Nuremberg. See you in the A.M.?"

"I'll see you out," Nick said. "Zack, Jamie, I'll let you show yourselves out when you're done here, or there's plenty of pillows in the living room as long as you've called your folks so they know where you are. I'll expect a full report tomorrow sometime." He gave Zack a dark look—the same one he'd given Josh earlier in the office—and escorted Chantel out.

He's so nice, Zack thought, a little wistfully. He's always been nice. He's *so* nice, it'd never occur to him to question Josh and Brian retiring to bed early because they were "so tired." He was grateful that Nick's bedroom was at the far end of the upstairs hallway, lest he find out during the night how close Josh and his *friend* really were.

He was unaware that he was staring at the

ceiling until he felt Jamie's eyes on him. "Think they're asleep yet?" he asked, trying to make light of it.

"Nope," Jamie said. "Nuh-uh." An evil little smile curled up the corners of her mouth. She held out her hand again, and Zack took it, swinging her arm a little. They wandered into the living room.

"So ..." Zack began.

"So."

"We have roughly ten hours until we potentially wind up in the streets, our futures trashed forever," Zack cracked. When he thought about the potential consequences for too long, his stomach curdled. It was one thing to dis your school when you still had the privilege of being enrolled in it. Fortunately, Mark had intercepted the call from the Academy and was withholding the information from Beth until he heard from Zack. That didn't mean that Beth still wasn't going to wipe the floor with him once she finally heard about the whole thing.

"Yeah ..." Jamie looked like she was turning something over in her mind—a sure sign, Zack knew by now, that just about anything could happen next. But all she said was, "You know, *The African Queen* is on Channel 3 at ten."

Zack had no idea what this meant, but based on the tone of her voice, it was clearly important to her. "We're there," he said, gallantly.

"I was hoping you'd say that." She linked her arm through his.

They settled on the couch and turned on the TV. Jamie let Zack lay his head in her lap; she ran her fingers through his red spikes. *If someone told me yesterday morning that this was how tonight was going to end, I would never have believed them. How strange life is. Strange and confusing and scary and wonderful.*

"I haven't done hardly *any* homework this week," Zack commented to the underside of Jamie's chest. This was a nice place to be.

"Maybe we won't be thrown out," Jamie commented affably. "Maybe we'll just flunk out."

"Oh, thanks, Jamie."

Zack thought the movie kicked ass. A tough guy, a feisty chick, overcoming all sorts of obstacles, falling in love, and ultimately outwitting the Germans; what could be better? The irony of the whole thing failed to hit him. When it was over, he curled an arm around Jamie, pulled a chenille throw down over them, and drifted off to sleep.

But Jamie stayed up a while longer, her eyes glittering in the moonlight, listening to the rise and fall of Zack's breathing and the feeling of his arm wrapped around her. She was thinking of a song from her childhood, something about wanting to rule the world.

She'd traded the world for a red-haired boy who would love her.

How much might that trade cost her?

CHAPTER 56

The following morning was cool, and the sun hid behind the clouds as though afraid to show its face. Three cars parked in front of the Academy, disgorging five people. Chantel was wearing a knockout three-color blouse and tight skirt. Jamie was wearing an old pair of sweats and one of Josh's Oxfords. Zack also wore an Oxford, plus a tie; he'd also combed his hair neatly. Josh and Brian wore T-shirts and jeans, but Josh had slipped a sport coat on over his. Bells had already rung for first period, so no one was outside when they arrived.

The quiet was unsettling. The five flashed signs of encouragement at each other, then mounted the path to the front door, Chantel taking the lead. Brian and Josh came next, hands clasped tightly, followed by Zack and Jamie.

The building looked unscathed from Saturday night; in retrospect, Zack thought, they probably should've come over yesterday and seen if there was anything they could've done to help tidy up. Too late now.

As they opened the front doors, they understood why it was so quiet outside; *everyone*—seemingly the entire student body—was crammed in the lobby and upper hallway, very deliberately waiting for them even if they were marked "Tardy" or "Absent" for being there. Hundreds of pairs of eyes locked on them—the outsider boy, the new kid, the football star, the school's #1 control queen, and her assistant.

Now, the five of them had new monikers: The Accused.

Jamie could feel their eyes scanning her, like hundreds of little robot sentries in a science-fiction movie. Let them. She'd be damned if she was going to show any sign of weakness at this stage in the game. She inhaled a little too loudly, causing Zack to look briefly at her with concern.

She lifted her chin higher, like the barrel of a tank taking aim.

Brian squeezed Josh's hand a little tighter as they passed three football players, regarding Brian and Josh as impassively as statues of the Greek gods. A wave of whispers passed through the crowd as they surveyed the mighty Jamie Esau, Hitler-as-fashion-plate, now shown to be human—just an ordinary girl with a barely-middle-class boy. All the rules were gone, and all bets were off.

We've been cast adrift, Josh thought. He was used to being an outsider, and Zack, of course, treated the world like it was one big provocation. Even Chantel knew what it was to be an outsider. But Jamie and Brian had leaped off the pedestal and kicked it over behind them—for love. The enormity of it gave him a brief chill, and he shuddered a little.

Brian looked at him, squeezed his hand, and Josh marveled: there was nothing in Brian's face to indicate even the slightest bit of nervousness, aside from some slight tension in his jaw. He was as resolute as a gladiator entering the Roman arena.

The crowd parted like the Red Sea under

Moses's staff; everyone seemed to know where they were headed. They reached the conference room door, and Chantel quickly glanced skyward, then rapped three times.

The voice inside answered. "Come in …"

A look of shock calcified on Jamie's face; no, it *couldn't* be.

Could it?

Silently, they filed into the conference room, like Han Solo and Leia being forced to brunch with Darth Vader. Zack blew kisses to everyone in the hallway as they entered, closing the door behind him.

The room was windowless and painted a sky-blue color. Five chairs were arranged in a row for them. A crowd of some eleven people waited for them at the opposite end, grouped around a ring of tables on which sat a desk phone with a speaker. There was a football player whom Brian didn't know very well and five other random kids from around the school, including—was she *everywhere?*—Kat. The headmaster, Professor Falcon, was glowering in his usual bow-tie ensemble. The Shakespeare teacher, earrings as dangly as ever, was seated in the middle, swathed in yards of Batik. In a corner were Hank, one of his inbred friends, and Callan, the guy Brian beat up in the locker room. Brian swallowed, remembering his fury, remembering his fists smashing into the other boy with a rage he no longer understood. Who was that angry, lost boy from last week? He was so busy trying to remember that he didn't even look at anyone else.

But Jamie, Josh, and Zack were all fixated on another person, sitting to the Shakespeare teacher's left. This girl had pulled her hair back today and wore a plain white blouse and a simple dark skirt. She didn't seem to be wearing any makeup, and her expression was so pallid and gray, she might as well have been invisible. Perhaps she wished she was.

Zack reached for Jamie's hand, and it was like the hand of a corpse. Jamie was regarding the girl with an expression Zack had never seen on Jamie's face before—a look of complete and utter consternation, as a prisoner looks at a waiting guillotine.

"Please take a seat," Missy Hoff said, her voice cold and deadly as an ice pick.

CHAPTER 57

M s. Sullivan rose. "Please make yourselves comfortable. It is the purpose of this Honor Council to act as an intermediary between the students and the powers-that-be as it were— to deal with student affairs and conflicts with as much 'inside' knowledge—from student perspectives as possible. It is all of our hope that a resolution may be achieved with as little animosity and conflict as possible."

Jamie, Brian, Chantel, Zack, and Josh registered this silently, trying to gauge Missy's level of animosity. She was staring at the desk in front of her, as though among the years of continually wiped-off graffiti might be the faint outline of the mysteries of the universe, like something Da Vinci might have drawn.

How had this happened?! Brian vaguely remembered some meetings that Missy had had last week, but she had said nothing to him as to what they were about. Had she never told him, or had it never entered his mind to ask? Maybe he'd never really cared enough to ask. They all cared now, that was for sure.

"Now I'm turning this over to Brad Marker," the English teacher continued smoothly. She sat, earrings swinging like crazed kindergarteners on a playground, and nodded encouragingly to Brad.

Brad rose, clearing his throat. He was also on the football team and was wearing his letterman jacket. He was one of those Paul Bunyan types who'd hit six feet at thirteen, grown a full beard at fourteen, and never looked back. "We've already heard from Hank, Mark, and Callan about some of the incidents last week. Now, we'd like to hear your side of what happened Saturday night. And if there's any other pertinent information you'd like to share with us regarding the rest of the week … it would be greatly appreciated. Everything said in this room is kept in strictest confidence, of course."

Zack snorted ever-so-slightly. When everyone looked at him, he pretended he'd had a tickle on his nose and scratched it accordingly.

The silence was blood-freezing. It enveloped the room, waiting to vaporize the first prey who dared to speak. Nothing happened for a few awful moments, then Professor Falcon spoke. "Well?" His voice sounded like a disposal with a chicken bone in it.

Unexpectedly, Brian stood up. Four heads swiveled to look at him, and Missy's eyes drifted up from the desk's hieroglyphics.

Brian didn't flinch. His voice was as cool and dry as a preserved leaf. He moved as if he were a defense lawyer with an open-and-shut case, beyond question or doubt. "I think I can give you all the answers if you want them."

He moved behind Jamie, resting his hands on her shoulders. "This is my sister, who in the process of trying to help me and reward herself got zapped by her own cleverness."

Jamie blinked a bit at this, but wisely said nothing.

He took a step, and then he was behind Zack, his hands now on Zack's shoulders. "This is Zack, whom I'm now proud to call a friend. He kinda tripped over his libido, but in the end, he caught all of us." He finished this comment with a gentle squeeze, and Zack felt something incomprehensible: a rush of gratitude and appreciation for Brian.

Brian kept moving. "This is Chantel, the innocent-not-quite bystander ... she's mostly here for moral support." Chantel reached up and took his hand for a split second, held it tightly. The gathering at the end of the room was still mostly implacable, though Kat seemed to be smiling at Brian encouragingly.

Finally, Brian was at the end of the row, and his hands were on Josh's shoulders, touching the back of his head, his hair. His voice remained level and conversational, but Josh's heart was beating so loudly that he felt certain that everyone in the room could hear it above Brian's words. "This is Josh ... who just wanted me to be happy, and I was too dumb to figure it out. But he stuck with it ... and I love him for it."

Brian remained standing at the end of the row, keeping one hand on Josh's shoulder, and for the first time, Josh could sense the rigidity in Brian's arm. He'd thought that Brian had been doing what he'd been doing to display affection for each of them; now, he realized that it was Brian's way of keeping himself from collapsing. Yet Brian kept his voice and expression unruffled; only his arm and his hand, fastened to Josh's shoulder like an eagle's claw locking around a tree branch, betrayed his anxiety.

"Now, I don't know what's been said here earlier, but I got a pretty good guess. There are lots of things to say—lots of apologies to make. I think—you guys are expecting some apologies." Brian gulped a little, then plowed onward. "So, here are mine.

"I owe an apology to Hank, for not reacting to him like someone who believes in understanding, even though that's what I ask for. I owe an apology to Callan, whom I took my frustrations out on when I couldn't take them out on myself. I owe an apology to my teammates, whom I've let down." The guys in the corner looked everywhere but his face.

Brian's eyes had been sweeping the room as he spoke, but now they zeroed in on one face, and his voice took on a jagged tone. "But most of all, I owe an apology to Missy—because I lied to her for over a year. For that … more than anything …

I'm sorry." His voice almost caught on the word *sorry*.

Professor Falcon's face looked as dark and threatening as a prairie cyclone, and his voice crackled like a snapped electrical cable. "Are you saying ... *you* are taking full responsibility for everything that's happened?" As Brian nodded, the man added darkly, "What about the rest of these people? How do they fit into the story?"

"They don't, sir. It was all my fault." Brian had switched from defense attorney to perfectly coached witness. He wasn't exactly robotic, but he was clearly sticking with the safest script he knew, and his voice was again smooth and uninflected.

Falcon's voice dropped to the bottom of a coal mine as he growled at the others. "You all. Do you corroborate this ... fantasy?"

There was an ominous pause, and then Zack rose. "Actually, sir, Brian had nothing to do with it. It was all my fault."

Brian's reserve cracked, and his eyes gleamed a little as he looked at Zack.

"And mine." Josh was on his feet, and his hand found Brian's. Their fingers clung to each other, desperately.

"And mine." Chantel, too cool to stand, merely raised her finger, as though signaling a waiter at the Plaza.

"And 'I am Spartacus,'" Jamie commented acidly to the air. As everyone turned and looked at her, she lowered her gaze and shrugged in defeat. "Oh, all right: And mine." She should've worn a hat, or at least a veil. She shook her hair back from her forehead and gave the panel her best Marlene Dietrich in *Witness for The Prosecution* glare. Chantel reached over Zack to squeeze her hand.

Falcon looked like a bomb ready to explode at any moment. The English teacher was as cool and unflappable as the Venus de Milo. Missy's hand was now locked over her mouth, as though she were willing herself to keep from speaking or crying out.

Brad, looking somewhat confused, rose again. "Well then ... I think we've heard enough. If you'd like to give us a few minutes to discuss amongst ourselves ... please wait outside. We'll call you in a few."

In Jamie's ideal movie world, this was where the slow clap would've started; it didn't. They filed out, trying not to look at Missy as they left.

CHAPTER 58

Outside, the hallway was finally empty save for Hank, Callan, and the third boy shooting them occasional dirty looks from where they huddled down by the restrooms. The building seemed completely silent, aside from the distant *click click click* of the office administrators typing on their keyboards like a distant swarm of attacking locusts. It was a forlorn sound, with a haunting finality to it.

Jamie was leaning against the wall in a pose of utter defeat. "I'm going to wind up in vocational school," she muttered. Zack felt a rush of tenderness, but aside from gently stroking her hand, he didn't take her in his arms; something in her facing-the-firing squad posture told him not to.

"What are our chances?" Josh looked grim. Zack thought he resembled his father the night before.

Brian sighed. "One pissed-off ex-girlfriend, one upset teacher, a principal with an ax to grind, ticked off teammates ... do the math. If this was a horror movie, we wouldn't survive the first five minutes." He gave Josh a rueful smile, and Josh silently marveled to himself. He never would've believed Brian even knew how to make a joke, much less do it at a moment as dark as this one.

Chantel checked her watch. They'd been outside for almost fifteen minutes; how long would it take to make the decision? Time seemed to her as elastic as bread dough; it stretched out infinitely, then collapsed in on itself in a dense, sticky heap. Her hands quivered a bit, so she crossed her arms and tapped her long, purple nails against her sleeve.

She caught Zack's concerned face and smiled at him; he abashedly smiled back. They were strangely alike in some ways, she and this freckled, red-haired boy; they both knew what it was like to have so much at stake. Zack, like her, knew what happened if you're not The Right Kind of Kid and you mess up. There wouldn't automatically be someone there to smooth things over, to offer a second chance, a safety net. She remembered the sneering red face of Mr. Trainor, and shivered a little, as though an insect had crawled across her neck. *Oh, you'll get what you deserve, little miss.* If only he knew.

The door clicked, opened, and Brad stuck his head into the hallway, beckoning them back inside. Wordlessly, they filed back in.

As they settled into their seats, Zack looked once more at Jamie. Her head was again held high, her blue eyes blazing with icy defiance. She was so fricking cool; Zack could hardly stand it. How could he not have realized all this time that this proud, scheming, passionate girl was the only one for him?

Almost overcome, he leaned over and whispered, "I know this is a shitty time, but ... I think I love you."

Jamie turned and looked at him, and her smile was like the first ray of spring sunshine after an eternal winter. She reached out and stroked Zack's face gently. Her voice was a caress, filled with loving tenderness. "Yes," she murmured, "this is a shitty time."

Chantel's watch beeped.

Brad rose, shuffling his feet and looking uncomfortably out of his league. His voice came out an over-compensating *boom*, then modulated. "The usual procedure in these cases is for us, the students, to review the charges in the case. We then make our recommendations to the adviser, who offers feedback; the final recommendation is then passed on to Professor Falcon. Having heard from all the parties involved as to what happened at the dance, it is the opinion of this Council—"

Suddenly, the room plunged into blackness.

A chorus of surprise went up from numerous people as the light disappeared, and several phones were immediately grabbed to provide a faint glow of illumination. Amidst the hue and cry, the phone on the table beeped. The voice that issued forth from it was cold and metallic. "Greetings Professor Falcon. Hello Joshua, Brian, Chantel, Zachary, Jamie."

What?!

As they had yesterday, four heads swiveled in Jamie's direction. In the faint glow from the various electronic devices, her expression was as mystified as everyone else's. Someone else was now running the show.

Brad spoke cautiously. "Who is this?"

The voice continued smoothly. "Someone with a vested interest in the futures of those accused at this institution. This is also someone who happens to have a virus at their fingertips and is unafraid to unleash it on the school's computer system with a few quick keystrokes."

Jamie was openly grinning now. She knew from years of chess practice when Checkmate was coming, and this was going to be a corker. But *who* was the other player?

"Now ... what were you about to say?"

"We won't give in to blackmail or threats," Falcon huffed, flipping the useless light switch on and off. He looked as if he was very unhappy with the new lines being added to this drama.

"Hopefully, I won't have to use them," the voice said pleasantly. "The verdict, please?" It sounded like it was asking for more bread for the table.

Brad's keychain had a tiny flashlight. He read off the index card in front of him, struggling to see the words he'd copied down. "It is the opinion of this council, corroborated by Ms. Sullivan and Professor Falcon—"

"—with *extreme* reservations," Falcon interjected in a furious whine.

"—that at this time, expulsion for Mr. Standish, Mr. Bradshaw, Ms. Robinson, and Mr. and Ms. Esau—"

Everyone inhaled.

"—is not necessary."

Score!

Five bodies nearly jumped out of their seats, exhaling, war whooping, hugging each other. Brad's voice sounded above the din like a Klaxon. "*However!*"

The five sank back into their seats.

"It is the opinion of this body that, in addition to repaying the $2,700 in cleaning costs, all parties receive one month's detention, as well as each of you writing a five-thousand-word essay on 'What I Can Do to Promote Ethics in School.'"

Jamie nodded, slowly and thoughtfully. Surely, somewhere on the Internet, there was an essay for sale with exactly this title.

Brad continued, "You will also be on probation till winter break. If no further incidents occur, this will be expunged from your records. If all parties agree, we are concluded."

"Agreed," Ms. Sullivan said quietly, smiling to herself.

"Agreed," Falcon almost snarled, "so long as you all find better and more productive things to occupy your time from now on."

All nodded. Some sixteen sets of eyes fixed themselves on the speakerphone.

"How about a nice game of chess?" the voice queried, almost playfully. There was a click, then a dial tone; abruptly, all the lights turned on.

Everyone leaped to their feet and hugged each other. Chantel ran forward and kissed Brad. Several people leaped on the speakerphone and tried to find a "callback" function, to no avail. Hank awkwardly came forward and, with some degree of surliness, shook Jamie's hand, then Brian's, then Zack's. He dragged Callan away before he could make a fuss.

Unobtrusively, Brad approached Jamie, who raised one eyebrow. Alex would be impressed, Zack thought.

"We didn't need any incentives—we were the ones who voted for you anyway," Brad murmured quietly amidst the celebrations and people filing out of the room. "By the way—Missy did too. Did you have anything to do with ...?"

"No," Jamie said, shaking her head, looking somewhat askance at the phone. "It's a smart woman who admits when she's bested. Speaking of which ..."

She noticed Missy packing up her things at the front of the room, and quietly and carefully began to walk toward her, as one might approach an injured but dangerous animal.

Brian took Jamie's place next to Brad, bumping his fist and giving one of those half-hugs teenage boys give each other. Brian was glowing so much that he looked like he'd swallowed Fort Knox. "Thanks for your support, buddy. I'll be back on the team by Friday, hopefully."

"'s okay," Brad rumbled happily. "Don't sweat it. I'm almost as happy as you are." His voice dropped to a stage whisper: "Wait'll I tell Danny."

"Danny ...?" Brian blinked a couple of times, trying to decipher this. "Who's Danny?" True, there was Danny Cruz, the caramel-haired, green-eyed school soccer star, but he didn't ... he couldn't ...

But Brad just smiled, his eyes twinkling at Brian, slapped him on the arm, and walked away, leaving Brian mentally reeling. He'd heard the expression "taking one for the team" before, but this took things to a whole new level.

CHAPTER 59

Just around the corner from the outside hallway was a little alcove with a closet formerly used by the school's Key Club to store soda. Chantel went to it, looked in both directions to make sure no one else saw her, and quietly unlocked the door with a key she had received from the school secretary prior to her retirement two years earlier. She stepped into the dimness, moving aside what most people would have thought looked like a fixed panel.

In the secret room just beyond, the Yearbook Kid sat at a computer, a headset with a voice distorter around their neck and a flip phone in hand. The kid beamed at Chantel and moved the hat to the side so that Chantel could lean in for a kiss properly.

"Nice work, sweetie," Chantel breathed. "Too bad you didn't get to shut the whole place down."

"There's always next time," Robin smirked between kisses. "All we have to do is keep those four busy enough, and they'll have the faculty so hopped up on paranoia, we can control whatever we want. Now it's your world, baby girl."

"Everyone else just lives in it," Chantel purred, kissing Robin again. She had to admit, it had been an interesting and challenging week keeping track of everyone and everything, but that was *nothing* compared to what the rest of the school year was going to be like. A Black girl and her non-binary romantic partner were now covertly running things around here, and the Watson Christian Academy would never know what hit it. The new millennium was barely a year and a half away; things were going to be changing—big time.

And Chantel—generously—had to give Zack some small, unspoken credit; she never could've moved into this power position without his crazy plan disrupting the status quo in the first place.

CHAPTER 60

In the upper hallway, Jamie reached out and touched Missy's sleeve from behind her. Missy turned as though she'd been burned; the two young women shared a long, appraising look.

Finally, Jamie spoke. "You know—well, yeah. I guess you do."

"I think so." Missy still couldn't look her in the eye, but she kept her head up, as she stared just past Jamie's face.

Jamie felt a small swell of admiration for the other girl. "I misjudged you. I'm sorry," she said, almost in a rush, before she could stop herself. It surprised her, but she liked the way the truth sounded when she spoke it aloud.

"I think we all misjudged each other," Missy said quietly, and now she did look at Jamie, looked right into the bright blue eyes so like, yet so unlike, her brother's. Her voice didn't waver, but she did hug her notebook a little tighter to her chest, as if putting a little barrier between them.

"Yeah ..." Jamie let the thought hang in the air for a moment as if it were some sort of dangly Christmas ornament. She spoke in a tone of genuine wonderment. "Relationships are such simple things, why do people always screw them up?"

Missy shrugged. "If we didn't, we wouldn't have anything to put in the soap operas." Jamie had to admit, there was some sort of demented logic to this. Shaking her head in agreement, she followed the other girl as she walked away.

Chantel surreptitiously rejoined the group in the hall, and everyone seemed to be talking at once. Jamie turned to her brother. "Should we call Mom and Dad? Where do we start?"

"Yeah, soon," Brian nodded, one hand securely linked with Josh's. "We have to. But it'll be okay. I've got Dad's alumnus scholarship to college, anyway." Worst case, he could always go stay with Aunt Jan and Uncle Tad for a while until the storm settled. As long as he had Josh's hand in his own, Brian thought blissfully, he didn't need a Superman anymore. He was his own Superman.

"I gotta call my dad, he must be climbing the walls by now," Josh agreed. Nick had asked Josh to let him know as soon as possible what the outcome was, lest he have to come to Watson and plead with the principal. It was a good day, Josh thought happily, feeling Brian's hand tight in his own. It was one hell of a good day.

"Me too," Zack burbled. "And I owe Alex a hot fudge sundae." In fact, he wanted nothing more than to go for ice cream that night with his brother, his mom, Mark, and Jamie, his girlfriend. How did such miracles occur?

"Make it a banana split, he likes those better," Jamie said automatically, momentarily forgetting how little Zack knew about the behind-the-scenes of last week. "Well, peeps, we still have almost forty-five minutes before the end of the period. What say we blow the rest of it off, make our calls, then go get some doughnuts?"

Movement off to the side distracted her; Missy had been quietly listening to the past few exchanges but was now starting to scuttle away.

Jamie's voice rose to grab her attention, yet it also became warmer. "You could come too, you know."

Missy smiled at all of them, as everyone waited for her response. "I think … I'm just going to fly solo for a while. If that's okay. I need some time to myself." She blushed a bit, as if unused to all their attention and respect. "But thanks. Sometime … sometime soon."

"Sure," Jamie said, somehow cramming a simultaneous apology and a benediction into that one little word.

They all stood, watching her go, as Logan eased himself up from a bench where he'd avidly been pretending to read, and walked alongside her toward the Commons area. Her ponytail swung from side to side, as if it were an impudent appendage with a mind of its own.

They all turned, walked down the hallway, and started to descend the stairs.

"So," Chantel ventured dreamily, "today's the first day of the rest of our lives."

"Oh, GOD, what a depressing thought," Brian commented to the ceiling.

"What shall we do?" Josh smiled at Zack. Zack would have some ideas; he always did.

"Go harass the drive-through wench," Zack said, grinning at his friend. "Wreck a dance. Or maybe just enjoy the peace and quiet." He swung Jamie's hand. "Maybe things'll settle down around here."

"Maybe we should all go drive through the pond," Brian commented playfully, ducking as Zack took a swing at him.

"No, he's right," Jamie said in a brisk-yet-loving voice. "Everything's worked out. Here's to a smooth school year, from here on out."

Yoshi burst out of the garbage can, armed with his camera. "Smile!"

Fortunately, the Academy yearbook cover photo eight months later didn't have audio and couldn't capture what the five students in the front picture were saying to him.

EPILOGUE

Zack and Jamie broke up a year later, then reunited, then broke up again, then reunited. At the moment, they are still together and living in Seattle, where Zack is a video game designer and Jamie runs the state film commission.

Brian and Josh live in Santa Fe, where they own a bed and breakfast. Brian also raises horses and Josh is a young adult novelist in the style of his friend Mark.

When Alex turned nineteen, he moved in with his friend Jacob. They are still living together.

Missy got a degree in theology and is now a minister in the Unitarian church.

Beth married Mark. When he died ten years

later from a sudden aneurysm, she mourned him for two years before Nick finally proposed. It was a huge and joyful wedding with Missy presiding, and everyone came except Vice-President Chantel Robinson, who sent a beautiful floral bouquet from the White House.

ACKNOWLEDGMENTS

This story has passed through many, many hands over the years, and these are just a few of the readers and listeners who gave me encouragement and feedback along the way and earned my eternal thanks: Marcus Boddington, Mari Coates, Christian DeLay, Nathan Dwyer, Reggie Gage, Todd Gerber, Shawn Hall, Alan Nott, the Orange Door writing group, Lloyd Perez, James D. Phillips, CiCi Polson, David Sambrano, J.D. Schramm, Christine Sellai, Joel Viney, Hon Walker, Naomi J. Williams, and Bruce Yunker.

Extra-special thanks and acknowledgments to June Russell, John Munn, and Kraig Blackwelder, who helped with some of the toughest editing choices but still believed in it.

More special thank-you's to Betty Turnbull and Jori Hanna, my editor at Torchflame; my publicist Amy Storey; and Katlyn Slocum, my web designer. Thank you as well to Nancy Canning and Vinnie Kinsella for the business insight.

And to anyone else I've left out who nonetheless helped this book become a reality: thank you a thousand times over.

ABOUT THE AUTHOR

Dean Backus is the solo author or co-author of over eleven plays, one of which *Thus With A Kiss* was a runner-up for Best Play at the 1993 Seattle New Playwright's festival, and another of which won Best Play at the 1996 San Francisco Fringe Festival *Is This Seat Taken?*.

Other play titles produced in Seattle, Tacoma, Berkeley and San Francisco include *Him, Jumping the Broom* (co-scr., BATA winner), *Alec in Wonderland, The Vampers, The P.A. Cooley Show* (co-scr.), *You, You & You* (co-scr.), *Sexy Shorts* (co-scr.), *The Duboce Triangle: A Gay Soap Opera (But Isn't That Redundant?)* (co-scr.), and *Pure*.

His work in San Francisco has been staged at the Alcazar, the Exit, the Shelton, Theater Rhinoceros, the New Conservatory, and Josie's

Cabaret. He has completed three screenplays currently in various stages of development in Hollywood: *Darts and Flowers, Unaccompanied,* and *Big Pimpin'*. He is the author of numerous award-winning short stories, one of which appeared in Alyson's 1998 anthology *Wilma Loves Betty,* and was featured in the book *Gay Marriage Real Life* (2006) by Michelle Bates Deakin.

He has also worked as an award-winning essayist (*Frontiers* magazine), freelance journalist (*The Oregonian,* The Backlot.com), poet (*Just Like Matthew,* a tribute to Matthew Shepard), lyricist, and filmmaker.

Dean resides outside of Portland, Oregon with his partner, Jonathan.

Follow Dean at:
www.deanbackusauthor.com

THANK YOU!

Thank you for reading! The team at Torchflame Books hopes you've enjoyed this book and might consider leaving a review on Amazon, Goodreads, BookBub, The Story Graph, or anywhere else you like to track your recent reads. Alternatively, you could post online or tell a friend about it. This helps our authors more than you may know.

Additional Large Print books are available for purchase at torchflamebooks.com/large-print or may be requested through your local library.

- The Team at Torchflame Books

www.ingramcontent.com/pod-product-compliance
Lightning Source LLC
Chambersburg PA
CBHW030745030726
47497CB00001B/134